Praise for Lucy Monroe's
Annabelle's Courtship

"Monroe brings a fresh voice to historical romance."

~ Stef Ann Holm

"Lucy Monroe captures the very heart of the genre. She pulls the reader into the story from the first to the last page."

~ Debbie Macomber

"Lucy Monroe writes smart, sensual, emotional books for intelligent women."

~ JoAnn Ross

"Lucy Monroe is a wonderful addition to the romance industry. If you enjoy stories by Linda Howard, Diana Palmer, Elizabeth Lowell, then I think you'd really love Lucy's work."

~ Lori Foster

"Lucy Monroe is one of my favorite writers. Witty, passionate, and filled with romantic suspense. I have yet to pick up one of her books that I could put down without reading it from first page to last."

~ Lora Leigh

"Monroe is a masterful story teller who has the knack of weaving in delicious details to her stories. Whether contemporary, historical, or sizzling erotica Monroe consistently hits the right note. Historical romance fans will be delighted with this offering."

~ Marilyn Rondau, Kwips & Kritiques

Rating: 4.5 Stars "I could barely turn the pages quickly enough to find out! With superior characters, a clever plot, and more than enough intrigue to keep things interesting, ANNABELLE'S COURTSHIP kept me entertained from beginning to end."

~ Blue Ribbon Reviews

"I was pulled in to the book and cheered for some characters and mentally boo'd others. I thoroughly enjoyed how she wove the fact that appearances are not everything into the story, as we find Annabelle is anything but plain and ordinary. I am a huge fan of both this genre and Ms. Monroe's writing and Annabelle's Courtship only helps to further cement this feeling."

~ Joyfully Reviewed

Rating: 4 Cups "Lucy Monroe's newest novel is a delight to historical romance lovers. She pairs a classic hero with a not-so-classic heroine and sparks fly. ... Beautifully written to illustrate the characters and opinions of the people of this era, Annabelle's Courtship is true Regency at its best."

~ CoffeeTime Romance

Rating: 5 Stars "Ms. Monroe keeps the readers hooked with her unique and memorable characters and uncanny twists as the story flows."

~ LibraryThing

Rating: Four Angels "In the end, Annabelle's Courtship is all about trust, and the wondrous events which come to pass when it is combined with love."

~ FAR

Look for these titles by
Lucy Monroe

Now Available:

Meagan's Chance (writing as L.C. Monroe)
Miss Fixit (writing as L.C. Monroe with Nicolette Derens)

Annabelle's Courtship

Lucy Monroe

A Samhain Publishing, Ltd. publication.

Samhain Publishing, Ltd.
577 Mulberry Street, Suite 1520
Macon, GA 31201
www.samhainpublishing.com

Editing by Angela James
Cover by Scott Carpenter

First Samhain Publishing, Ltd. electronic publication: August 2007
First Samhain Publishing, Ltd. print publication: September 2008

Prologue

Graenfrae, Scotland 1818

Laird Ian MacKay, Earl of Graenfrae, wanted to slam his fist into the gray stone wall of his study. "Ye're telling me that my stepfather left me a fortune, but I canna get it unless I marry?"

Ian impatiently watched the elderly solicitor, Eggleton, as he removed his spectacles and carefully cleaned them with a cloth. Replacing the eyeglasses on his face, the solicitor shuffled the papers before him. He cleared his throat. "Precisely speaking, milord, if you marry within the year."

A year. Ian clenched his hands and pivoted away from the other man. *Bloody hell.*

The tenants on Graenfrae's farms needed seed and farming implements. Many of their homes would not last another winter without new thatch on their roofs. Ian needed blunt. Money that was only available if he wed within a year.

The urge to slam his fist into something grew stronger. Ian's chest constricted with anger and another emotion. Betrothal and marriage would make him vulnerable to betrayal.

Again.

He had a difficult time believing that the late Earl of Lansing would take such drastic measures to see his wishes fulfilled. "Did my stepfather tell you why he placed this restriction in his will?"

Again the white head bent as the solicitor went through the ritual of cleaning his spectacles. Ian wanted to tear the wire frames from Eggleton's hands. Were na the man's eyeglasses clean enough?

"Lord Lansing believed that after the unfortunate incident with your broken betrothal you might hesitate to marry. He wanted you to secure your line, so to speak."

"Then why did he no just add another rider requiring I set up my nursery?" Ian asked with disgust, ignoring the issue of his ended engagement.

Eggleton appeared to take his sarcastic question seriously. "He did in fact wish to do so. I convinced the earl that these matters are uncertain. It would be difficult to predict, ah hem..." Eggleton coughed delicately. "When your wife might begin increasing."

Things were not as bleak as they could be. Without the requirement for an heir, nothing would stop him from finding an obliging woman and entering a paper marriage. An annulment could be secured in due time. Feeling better than he had since the solicitor had begun reading the will, Ian sat down.

A look of relief passed across Eggleton's face. "There is one final matter regarding the inheritance."

What could be worse than marriage? Ian raised his brow in question and Eggleton continued. "Your wife must be English."

"*Bloody hell.*" Ian shot from his chair. "You canna be serious."

Eggleton looked offended. "I assure you, I would never make light of the last wishes of one of my clients."

An English wife.

"How am I supposed to find an English wife and marry her in the next year?"

Were he looking for a proper wife, he knew it would be easy. He could think of several ladies who would be thrilled at the opportunity to be Lady MacKay. He could not envision any of them going without new dresses and fripperies while he made necessary improvements on his tenants' properties, however. Finding a wife would not be hard. Finding a woman who would sacrifice for the good of Graenfrae might be impossible. Far better to plan a paper marriage.

"The London Season opens in less than a month, milord."

Of course his English stepfather's lawyer would think in terms of London. It was a fair distance away, but the Season attracted many ladies. One of them would surely be practical enough to fit his purpose. He needed a plan of action.

Ian moved toward the desk, amused when the lawyer hastily retreated toward the window. Grabbing paper and a quill pen, Ian dipped it in the inkwell. He started writing. Several minutes later he blotted the paper. Blowing on it, Ian read again the words he had written.

Requirements for a wife:

Plain.

Modestly dowered.

Older.

Eggleton cleared his throat once again. Ian looked up from his paper. The solicitor said, "The late earl instructed me to give you a message when I told you the details of the will."

Ian felt a premonition of disaster on the horizon. "Aye?"

The solicitor shifted from one foot to the other and repeated the process of cleaning his glasses, this time taking an inordinate amount of time to wipe the lenses. "He wanted me to remind you..." The man let his words trail off.

Ian prompted him, "Aye?"

Eggleton coughed. "He said to tell you that when a man takes the holy vows of matrimony, he is giving his word to the woman he takes to wife. The earl wanted you to remember that honor demands the gentleman in question keep that word for a lifetime."

Ian could no more deny the honor demanded by his stepfather than he could deny the responsibility to his tenants he had learned at his da's knee. Feeling like a man facing the gaol, Ian accepted that there would be no paper marriage.

After the solicitor had left, Ian settled against the dark leather of his favorite chair and studied his surroundings with a critical eye. A man's room, his study fit his need for stark simplicity. Bookcases on either side of the massive fireplace relieved the unending gray of the circular stone walls.

Multiple windows high in the walls of the turret's chamber bathed the room in the fading light of evening. A scarred oak table served as his desk. Only two other items of furniture had made it into his sanctuary, another chair and small round table.

Soon a woman, an English woman, would be living in his home. A wife. He did not have time to cater to the needs of a woman, especially the romantic ideals so many ladies seemed plagued with. Taking a sip from his brandy, he thought of another requirement to add to his list for a wife.

Practicality.

The list would do him well in selecting a woman to wed for a lifetime. He would not make the same mistake he had with Jenna. He would find a woman as unlike her as possible, a woman who would be faithful.

Chapter One

Perfection wore a simple gray gown and unadorned poke bonnet.

Ian turned in his saddle toward his companion. "Who is the lady in the gray carriage yonder?"

Finchley, a longtime friend, was one of the few boys Ian had been able to stand at the English school his stepfather insisted he attend. Ian had no doubt the other man, an unrepentant gossip, would know the identity of the vision of plain perfection sitting with an elderly woman in the gray carriage.

Finchley rotated his entire body so that he could look where Ian indicated, the points on his collar too tall to allow him to turn his head. "That's Lady Annabelle. Known each other this age, don't you know? Her father, the late Earl of Hamilton, had estates that bordered ours."

Ian felt his first surge of satisfaction since arriving in London the previous day. This lady was exactly what he needed. Her plain appearance spoke for itself and Ian had to assume that if she were of more than moderate means her clothing would be more elaborate. Ladies liked that sort of thing. Even from a distance, he could tell that she was past the blushing age of most debutantes. Not that she looked old, but her composed expression as she spoke to other members of the *ton* clearly indicated a woman beyond her first comeout.

Nightsong tried to prance sideways. Ian reined in the huge black stallion, not without some regret. Neither he nor his horse enjoyed the slow pace maintained during the social hour on Rotten Row in Hyde

Park.

Finchley asked, "Shall I introduce you?"

Ian's eyes locked with those of his lady of perfection and he could not look away from their hazel depths. His insides tightened in an unexpected way. "Aye. Introduce us."

Without breaking eye contact with her, Ian guided his mount toward the carriage. He enjoyed the way she gave no indication that she found his interest unusual other than her eyes growing wide. She did not blush, or look away. In fact, her shoulders stiffened and he had the sense that she was challenging him to do so first. Unusual behavior for a gentle lady, some might even think it forward. Ian reveled in the strong will that emboldened the plain spinster to meet him look for look. He did not want a mouse for a wife.

Was she married? Ian's mind rebelled at the possibility. Then he remembered that Finchley had called her Lady Annabelle. That indicated an unmarried daughter of the upper nobility, not a woman leg-shackled. He and Finchley drew abreast of the carriage.

She finally broke eye contact to acknowledge Finchley. "Ceddy, this is a pleasant surprise." Her smile sparkled with mischief. "I thought you would be staying in the country helping your family prepare for your sister's wedding this Season."

The dandy visibly shuddered. "Not my cup of tea, eh what?"

She laughed and Ian had an amazing and potentially embarrassing reaction to the melodic sound. He shifted in his saddle, uncomfortably aware of the tight fit of his riding breeches.

The older woman seated next to his lady spoke. "Cederic, I would expect you to show more family support than that, though I will admit a young gentleman underfoot is the last thing a mother needs when preparing for a wedding." Sighing, she looked sideways at Annabelle, her expression speaking volumes. "Not that I would be averse to any manner of annoyance were I given the opportunity to plan one myself in the near future."

The older woman gave Ian a pointed look before turning back to Finchley. Ian's friend might be a dandy, but he was far from stupid. He introduced them. "Lady Beauford, Lady Annabelle, may I present to you, the Earl of Graenfrae, Mister Ian MacKay?"

Turning his head toward Ian as far as his high shirt points would allow, Finchley said, "MacKay, this is Lady Beauford and her niece, Lady Annabelle."

The older woman smiled and Ian found that he liked her frank regard. "It is a pleasure to meet you, my lord."

Annabelle said nothing, merely inclining her head. The coolness of the action amused, rather than irritated him. Was she embarrassed by her companion's thinly veiled hint at her unmarried state? If so, she gave no indication. Still, her aunt's words implied the courtship should be an easy one.

Finchley asked a question of Lady Beauford and soon the two were engrossed in Town gossip.

Annabelle smiled at Ian, her hazel eyes lit with warmth and genuine interest. "Are you new to Town, my lord?"

He once again had to rein in Nightsong. "Aye. 'Tis no my intention of staying any longer than necessary either." His irritation at having to control his mount in the park came out in his voice.

A small smile twitched the corner of her lips, making them look very kissable. Demme. Had he been so long without a woman that he could not hold a conversation with a lady and not think of kissing her? Other images had popped into his head as well, images that would undoubtedly shock the plain spinster to her dainty toes.

"I see," she said. "I assume you are not in Town to enjoy the Season, then."

"I'm here to find a wife," he said, agreeing silently that his task was not an enjoyable one and then added honestly, "Though I look forward to discussing the new theories in sheep breeding and crop management with members of the local natural sciences club."

He could have sworn she stifled a laugh. "You have a great deal in common with my brother, the Earl of Hamilton."

"Really? Which plan for land management does he follow?" As he spoke the words, Ian realized how foolish they were. A lady of the *ton* would not interest herself in her brother's estate management.

"He has read several essays by the American, Edward Elliot, and

13

the former president, George Washington. Robert leans toward their view on land management rather than the popular thinking currently held among English estate owners."

Interesting. "I dinna ken if I have heard of this Edward Elliot you speak of."

"You'll have to discuss the matter with my brother. He is also experimenting with a fertilizer combining fish heads and marl to improve his crop yield." She spoke in a tone that implied she knew he would find that bit of information interesting.

She was right.

"Fascinating." He had not heard of fish heads. Marl, on the other hand, was quite common. "Please go on."

This time she did not stifle her laughter and once again his body reacted in a very physical manner. Even the knowledge that she was laughing at him did not diminish it. What was it about the clear, honest sound that affected him so strongly?

Cℨ

Ian reclined in a comfortable chair in Finchley's library. He sipped at brandy he had brought from his cellars at Graenfrae. His grandfather had let the tenants starve, but he had kept the wine cellars stocked.

"Thank you for inviting me to stay with you. My trip to London was no expected," Ian said to Finchley.

"Not at all. Glad to be of service." Finchley cleared his throat. "The earl was a good man. He'll be sorely missed."

Ian nodded his agreement. Despite his current anger at his stepfather, the earl's absence would leave a permanent hole in Ian's life. The Englishman had taken on the role of father seriously and treated Ian as a natural son until his death. He could even accept that his stepfather had intended the codicil to his will as a way of helping Ian, regardless of how much he disliked the notion of taking on a wife.

Finchley took a sip of his brandy. "You may live like a Puritan, but you certainly know how to stock your cellars."

Ian grimaced at the other man's implication that Graenfrae was too austere. "Do you think a lady would find the surroundings too simple?"

Finchley gave him a startled look. "You're planning on getting leg-shackled?"

"Aye."

"Who's the lucky gel?"

"I dinna ken."

The other man's eyes opened wider. "You don't know?"

Ian laughed mirthlessly. "No." He told his friend the details of his stepfather's will.

"You don't say. That's infamous."

"Aye, 'tis infamous indeed, but true nonetheless."

Finchley shook his head. "What are you going to do?"

"I dinna ken."

"But you *are* going to marry?"

"Aye. My tenants' needs are great."

"And you say you must marry an Englishwoman?"

"Aye."

"Your mother or brother could recommend someone."

Ian grew cold at the thought of going to his brother for help. Innate loyalty toward his family had prevented Ian from even telling his closest friend about his brother's betrayal. "I can find my own bride."

"Do you have any possibilities?"

Ian shuddered when he thought of the few English ladies he knew. They lived near his brother and would expect to keep the family connection with someone as important as Lansing. "Nay. 'Tis why I have come to London for the Season."

Finchley nodded. "Plenty of gels eager to marry, eh what?"

"Perhaps you wouldna mind giving me some advice."

"Whatever you need," Finchley replied.

"I've made a list of requirements for a wife. You can help me determine if ladies are suitable. I dinna have time to waste with them if they are not."

"Of course, of course. What are you looking for?"

Ian retrieved the folded foolscap from his waistcoat pocket and handed it to Finchley. "I have one more to add. The lass needs to be practical."

Beginning to read, Finchley took a sip from his brandy. Suddenly he started coughing and choking. Ian jumped up to pat his friend's back. "Are you all right, man?"

Eyes watering, Finchley gained control of his paroxysms. "Yes." He coughed again lightly. "Quite all right. Brandy went down wrong. That's all."

Ian nodded. "What do you think? Will it be difficult to find a lady with those attributes?"

"Attributes? Oh, eh, no, of course not. Matter of fact, I can think of one right off. Lady Annabelle. You met her today. Good sort, but she's got some funny ideas."

He had been right. Annabelle was all that she seemed. And his body reacted to her in an unexpected, but wholly pleasant way. "What kind of funny ideas?"

"She's a bluestocking." Finchley said it as if he was confessing that Lady Annabelle was not all that she should be.

To Ian's way of thinking, Annabelle's intelligence was not a shortcoming. "I dinna think her mind is filled with a bunch of silly romantic nonsense."

Finchley shook his head violently, or as violently as his high pointed collar would allow. "She's not romantical at all, don't you know."

Ian smiled. Perhaps this trip to Town would not be so bad after all. He would get to know Annabelle better and if she met his requirements, they could be married and return before the spring lambing.

CB

Annabelle watched the glittering crowd at Almack's and tried to ignore the leap of her heart every time a new arrival entered. She must stop acting like a silly schoolgirl. The Scottish laird most likely would not come. For the past two weeks, he had singled her out for attention whenever they attended the same affair and on one such occasion, he had told her that he no more cared for this bastion of the *ton*'s doings than she did. Since her first Season when she had been labeled *the Ordinary*, Annabelle had detested the midweek soirees.

The unimposing building and less than stellar décor served as a backdrop to the *ton*'s most initiated hunt—that for the advantageous marriage. Her aunt insisted they come each week. Although the rest of the *ton* considered Annabelle, at the age of four and twenty, to be firmly on the shelf, Lady Beauford would not give up hope of seeing her niece wed. Annabelle could have refused to attend the Season at all, but that would have curbed her own plans.

Stifling an unladylike urge to yawn, she tried to pay attention to her current companion's meandering. A young buck enjoying his first Season, Mr. Green still had the spotty complexion of youth. Experience had taught her that dancing with him required vigilance on her part to protect her tender toes. Safer to sit, sipping tepid lemonade and listening to his monologue. Unfortunately, it was not more enjoyable.

Annabelle's mind drifted. So did her eyes, back to the entrance. Her heart skipped a beat. Laird MacKay stood in the doorway, surveying the room as if he was looking for someone. She could not tamp down hope that the person he sought was herself.

His gaze locked on her and their eyes met. His firm lips, lips that she had spent entirely too much time daydreaming about, tipped at the corners. It took all her self-discipline not to return his smile across the crowded room in a most unladylike manner. He began moving toward her. He ignored bids for attention by lovely young debutantes and their fond mammas.

Unbelievable as it seemed, Ian found her company more fascinating than the loveliest creatures of the *ton*.

It was extraordinary, but then so was Ian. He towered above his peers and walked with an air of authority that would have done Wellington proud. Annabelle no longer even made a pretense of listening to Mr. Green. She simply waited for Ian to arrive and stop the boredom threatening to overwhelm her.

Would he ask her to dance? She experienced the most extraordinary feeling whenever he touched her, as if her corsets were laced too tight. Although she lectured herself severely on being a modern woman of the nineteenth century who did not need a gentleman in her life, he invaded her dreams and the thoughts of her waking hours.

However, Ian never called on her. He did not send her posies and notes. He did none of the things a gentleman falling in love was supposed to do. She chastised herself for being a ninny and wanting him to. She had given up finding a love like her late parents had enjoyed. Hadn't she?

Mr. Green's monologue stopped abruptly. "I say. Do you know this gentleman?"

Annabelle forced herself back to the present. Ian stood in front of her, a sardonic smile on his face. "Yes, indeed, Mr. Green. Lord Graenfrae and I have been introduced. Do you know him?"

"We have not had the pleasure." Ian's voice filled her being and Annabelle wanted nothing more than to find a secluded spot and continue their latest debate on Greek antiquities.

Mr. Green looked pained. Ian had that effect on people. He could be quite overwhelming. Annabelle smiled at Mr. Green reassuringly and introduced the two gentlemen.

Mr. Green stood and bowed toward Ian. "Pleasure."

Ian inclined his head. "Same."

Annabelle offered her hand to Ian and he bowed over it. "'Tis a pleasure to see you again, Lady Annabelle."

Without releasing her hand, he turned to Mr. Green. "I believe the music for this set has ended." Under Ian's gimlet stare, Mr. Green hastily made his excuses to depart. Ian turned back to Annabelle as she vainly attempted to remove her hand from his powerful grip.

"My lord, if you will permit me." The breathless sound of her voice shocked her.

He looked down at their joined hands and let hers go. "Sorry, lass."

Annabelle opened her fan and brushed it gently before her face. "You seem a bit preoccupied."

He nodded absently. "Finchley was right. You are perfect. 'Tis an advantage so early in my hunt, don't you see?"

No, she didn't see. Her cheeks heated. She fanned herself more vigorously. His hunt for a wife? Feeling lightheaded, she watched the whirl of dancers forming the next set. Ladies in high-waisted silk gowns danced with gentlemen in breeches and black coats. The lights reflected garishly off the jewels adorning the *beau monde*.

Annabelle's attention shifted back to Ian. Eyes the color of chocolate sauce bore into hers and she could not form a thought in her head. She had an inexplicable urge to touch the silky blackness of Ian's hair. Grateful that he could not read her mind, she dropped her eyes to his waistcoat. Something about this man filled her with desires that had not plagued her before.

"May I have the pleasure?" Ian's voice intruded on her thoughts.

She nodded her assent before she realized that the orchestra had begun a waltz. Dancing with Ian never failed to set her pulse racing. Waltzing with his hard, muscled body so close to her own devastated her senses.

She had to swallow a sigh of pleasure as he pulled her into his arms. She tilted her head to maintain eye contact.

He asked, "This isn't your first Season then?"

Disappointment coursed through her. Annabelle had grown addicted to the stimulating conversation she usually shared with Ian. Discussing banalities like this were a far cry from it. "No. It's my fifth, but it should be my sixth."

"Why is that, lass?" The thick Scottish burr of his voice caressed her.

"My parents died of the flu the year I planned to attend my first Season."

19

His eyes filled with understanding and he nodded. "I'm sorry." He whirled her around the room, his dancing as pleasing as the rest of him. "I suppose your first Season would have been when you were seventeen?"

Understanding dawned. "If you are fishing to find out my age, I will gladly tell you. I am four and twenty." Well past her first blush of youth as her aunt would have told him.

"'Tis just as I thought."

"Surely you could have asked Ceddy my age. We've known each other since we were in leading strings."

"Aye. I wanted to hear your answer, though." He winked at her and she winked back, surprised by her own audacity.

"Did you think I might lie about my age?"

"Nay."

She almost asked him to explain, but there was something else she wanted to know more. "It's your turn to answer a question from me."

Her knees went weak at his smile and she felt gratitude that his arms held her so firmly as he led her in the seductive steps of the waltz.

He said, "'Tis only fair, that."

"What did you mean when you said I was perfect earlier?"

The brown velvet depths of his eyes took on a deeper intensity. "'Tis quite simple. I am in need of a wife and you are perfect."

Chapter Two

She must have misunderstood. "Did you just say I would make a perfect wife?" Her voice squeaked on the word *wife*.

"Aye."

Air whooshed from her lungs. "Why, please?"

He smiled. "You fit my requirements."

"Requirements?" She must stop squeaking.

"Your looks are not too grand and you are well past the age for marrying. You do not wear expensive jewels or gowns, which bodes well for future demands on my purse."

Annabelle's elation vanished. She stared at him, her cheeks growing hotter with each sentence he uttered. He listed her particulars as if he were buying a horse at Tattersall's. Although the Marriage Mart was in many ways mercenary, she had never known any gentleman to be quite so blunt about it.

Her eyes smarted and she blinked at the tears, unwilling to make a spectacle of herself. She had finally met a man who stirred passion in her and he looked at her as nothing more than a dowdy spinster conveniently on hand when he decided to find a wife.

Ian gently squeezed her, the troubled concern in his eyes small comfort in the face of his words. "Dinna be distressed. You have all the qualities I'm looking for in a wife."

"You already said that and it's not a compliment."

Thoughts kaleidoscoped in her brain like bits of glass crushed and tossed in the air, left to fall where they may. Just like the rest of the *ton,* Ian saw only her plain looks. He did not see the heart that beat beneath her breast, the mind that longed to share thoughts and ideas with a kindred spirit.

"I'm not looking for a long engagement. Would you be ready to take up residence in Scotland in a month or so?"

The words stung her bruised heart like a thousand embroidery needles pricking the message that he did not love her, would never love her. He found her so unremarkable that Ian had no doubt of his success. Resolve beat against her bleeding heart. Ian would soon learn that not all things were as they seemed. Not all bluestocking spinsters longed for wedlock, especially those who had read Wollstonecraft.

She straightened, pulling as far away as his restraining arms would allow. "I am not interested in marriage. If I were, it would not be to an arrogant Scotsman who believes my lack of face and fortune make me willing to marry on such short acquaintance."

"I dinna need a long acquaintance to determine that you are all that I could wish for in a wife. I will make you a proper husband." He gave her an engaging smile. "We will deal well together."

So angry she could not speak, she glared at him.

"Surely you can see the benefits of marriage to me," he cajoled her.

She felt an unladylike urge to box his ears. "On the contrary. I am a modern woman and I do not see the benefits of marriage at all, particularly to you."

Ian's grasp on her waist tightened. His eyes darkened. "'Tis no my intention to upset you."

She felt the tension in his body and it was matched by an unwelcome sensation in her own. She wanted to melt into his embrace. The feeling infuriated her. She struggled to be released from his hold, not caring now if she caused a scene. "Let me go."

"Nay, the music has not ended." His reasonable tone enraged her all the more.

She was desperate to break his hold on her before her body betrayed itself. How unfair to experience her first taste of desire with a man who believed her too ordinary to court. "Do you really think I wish to dance with you after your insult?"

"'Twas no an insult, lass. 'Twas a proposal."

"My name is not 'lass'. It is Lady Annabelle, as Ceddy told you these many days past. Are you hard of hearing? Perhaps you need an ear trumpet."

"Nay, 'tis no an ear trumpet I need, but a wife. You're neither too beautiful, too rich, nor too young to pass on the proposal I'm giving you."

She almost choked on her anger. "Must I be subjected to your list of slurs again? You may need a wife, but *I do not need a husband.*"

Ian danced toward an unoccupied corner and pulled her into it. "Do not be so foolish as to label virtues insults."

"They are only virtues because you believe that by possessing these traits, or rather lack of traits, a woman would willingly marry you without even rudimentary courtship." She tried to step around Ian. He blocked her path like a marble column. She glared at him. "That, my lord, is not a list of virtues, but an insulting recipe concocted by you to gain a wife without the customary work or effort."

At Ian's look of consternation, she was convinced that she had guessed correctly. "I'm right. You are too indolent to properly court a woman. I can only assume some catastrophe has generated the need for you to take a wife."

"'Tis no indolence that causes me to avoid the playacting of courtship, but aversion to the games ladies play."

The genuine emotion she heard in his voice confused her. He stood so close she could feel the heat of his body. It did strange things to her insides. Drat. Now was not the time to become a simpering twit. He would not win this argument.

"I may not be a beauty, but I do expect to be courted and I will only marry the man who convinces me I cannot live without him." Her voice vibrated with emotion she wanted to suppress.

She had to leave before she turned into a watering pot and completely disgraced herself. She could not stand the strain much longer. When she tried to sidestep him again, he placed his hand on her arm. He squeezed gently. Against her will, she found comfort in the gesture.

Her breath started to come in short gasps as the nearness of his body continued to affect her equilibrium. He looked into her eyes as if searching them for the answer to some question.

Finally he sighed. "If it's courting you want, lass, it's courting you shall get. I'll give you until the end of the Season to reconcile yourself to the idea of our marriage."

The man was mad. "Courtship is wooing, not giving me a set time to reconcile myself to your arrogant plans."

"If it 'tis wooing you need, then wooing you will have. I'll call on you tomorrow."

She couldn't believe his denseness. "You may call on me until I'm old and gray, but I will never marry a man I do not love and respect."

It would have been a wonderful last word had he still not blocked her path. "Please, let me by. The set has ended." She could not prevent her voice from trembling.

Thankfully, she was promised for the next set. She watched her partner approach with relief. "I must go."

"We are no finished with our discussion."

"Please." She hated that she begged him, but she needed to get away before her devastated emotions slipped her control.

Mr. Green's voice came as welcome relief. "Lady Annabelle, I believe our set is forming."

Ian turned and gave the younger gentleman an arrogant glance. "'Tis our dance, I believe."

Fury overcame Annabelle's pain. "It most certainly is not." She wanted to throttle the man.

Ian just stared at Mr. Green who mumbled an excuse and retreated. He had deserted her. The coward.

Yanking her arm from Ian's, she said, "Regardless, I did not promise this dance to you." She turned to hurry away.

"'Twas an oversight, I'm sure."

In her haste to get away from Ian, she bumped into another gentleman. "Pray excuse me. I did not realize you were there."

The gentleman placed a monocle in his eye and gave her a condescending stare. "It was nothing, I'm sure."

Annabelle's skin grew unbearably warm. Twisting her head, she hissed at Ian, "Do you see what you made me do?"

His rich laughter stoked her fury. "Dinna let that popinjay upset you, lass. 'Tis of no account." He took her hand and placed it in the crook of his arm.

"Release me."

He sighed. "Would it no be easier to finish our talk?"

"It is finished."

He shrugged.

"Your arrogance is only exceeded by your stubbornness." Conceding defeat, but only for the moment, she said, "Fine."

She would convince him to leave off this ridiculous courtship. "Wouldn't you do better to search among ladies more amenable to marriage for the sake of marriage than myself?"

Rather than answer her question, he posed one of his own. "Marriage for the sake of marriage? What do you mean, lass?"

She twisted her fan with her free hand. "There are many ladies of the *ton* whose greatest desire in life is to be wed."

"Yours isn't?" The words held a hint of mockery.

"No, it is not." She spoke forcefully, willing him to believe her.

"Why come to the Season if you dinna wish to be married?"

If only he knew. She was tempted to tell him and see how quickly he would go looking elsewhere for a wife. She would not betray her secret in a fit of temper, however.

"I would gladly marry if I knew I would share a union like that of my parents." The emotion she felt when she thought of her parents' love spilled over into her words.

"And what was so grand about your parents' marriage?"

"They loved each other."

"You canna expect a love match?" Ian sounded horrified.

"Yes, that is exactly what I do expect." For the first time,

Annabelle felt she had succeeded in piercing Ian's complacent assumption that she would marry him. Giving him a full-blown smile, she nodded her head for emphasis.

"Ye'll get over that soon enough. Love is no basis for a marriage." In his agitation, Ian's burr was more pronounced.

Her smile died on her lips as indignation filled her. "I will not *get over it.* Marriage for me will have a great deal to do with love or I will not get married at all."

"Finchley said your head was no filled with romantic drivel."

Incensed, she frowned at him. "Love is not drivel."

He put his finger under her chin and forced her to look into his eyes. "You will marry me."

"Never."

He shrugged and stepped aside. "I'll call on you tomorrow." Catching Annabelle's hand, he bowed over it, never taking his eyes from hers. When he let go, she felt she had been branded by his touch.

She stood dazed for several moments after Ian left. She noticed that he left after speaking to her without dancing with anyone else. Why should he? He had found what he was looking for, an aging spinster to marry.

CB

The rest of the evening was a trial. When she was not dancing, Annabelle fielded questions from young ladies and their mothers regarding the handsome laird. This had become a normal pastime since Ian had singled her out. Never before had it been such a chore. By the time she and her aunt retired to their carriage to travel home, Annabelle had a pounding headache. Removing her gloves, she massaged her aching temples.

"Annabelle, are you quite all right?" Lady Beauford's voice registered concern.

"I am simply tired."

The other woman's smile alerted Annabelle to the fact that she should not have been so quick to dissuade her aunt's concern. "Ah, then you won't mind telling me what you and the Lord Graenfrae discussed quite privately in the corner?"

Annabelle groaned. The inquisition had arrived. "I'd rather not."

"Really, Annabelle, you cannot make a public display of yourself in that way. Do not tell me that you risked your reputation to argue political reform." The horror in her aunt's tone made Annabelle want to laugh hysterically. She would much rather have been discussing political reform.

"I'm sure the content of our conversation would entirely meet with your approval. He proposed."

Lady Beauford's eyes grew large in the light from the carriage's inner lamp. "You cannot be serious."

Annabelle sighed wearily. "Never more so."

"But that is wonderful. Of course, I could wish that he had sought out your brother's approval first." Annabelle did not reply. "It is not technically necessary. You are of age and in control of your own fortune. You'll want to get the solicitor working on marriage settlements."

"I'm not going to marry him."

"Of course you are. Now, what about your fortune? I don't suppose you have told him about it? Money is such an indecorous thing to discuss. I'm sure we can leave the particulars up to your brother and his lordship."

Annabelle sat up straight on the cushions of the coach. "If I were going to marry him, which I am not, I would be perfectly capable of discussing the particulars of my fortune with Ian, I mean Lord Graenfrae."

Lady Beauford made an impatient sound. "That Wollstonecraft woman has a lot to answer for, if you want my opinion. Although, the young fry never do want to listen to the wise counsel of their elders."

Annabelle cringed. Not another lecture on the vagaries of youth. She certainly didn't consider herself "young fry" as her aunt called it.

"Another thing, my dear, you may not be willing to marry that handsome gentleman, but I can think of several ladies who would be. I asked Lady Markham about him when he first sought your acquaintance. He has land, a title and stands to inherit a fortune from his late stepfather when he marries."

Annabelle digested her aunt's words. "What do you mean he will inherit a fortune when he marries?"

She sat in stunned silence as Lady Beauford related the details of the late earl's will. Apparently, she fulfilled another one of Ian's "requirements". She was English. His proposal made an awful kind of sense now. Ian had no choice but to wed. Being a logical man, he had gone about choosing a wife the same way he would have chosen a horse. Drat the man. He had misjudged his quarry though. Marriage for the sake of convenience had no place in her plans.

"Where did you hear this, Aunt Griselda?"

"Cederic. The dear boy was most forthcoming."

Annabelle could well imagine. Ceddy's love of tittle-tattle was legendary. "I can certainly understand the laird's need to marry. However, he will have to find a different bride."

Lady Beauford snorted. "I should have known you wouldn't show any sense about this."

Annabelle looked at her aunt with speculation. Could it be true that a bevy of ladies would leap at the chance to marry that crude man? Well, actually she herself could think of almost an entire dozen.

Smiling for the first time in hours, she said, "Perfect."

"Yes, he is. I'm glad you are finally showing some sense."

Annabelle ignored her aunt's words. When Ian came to call, she would have her own list comprised of possible candidates for him to marry.

⋈

William walked into the solicitor's office feeling like he entered purgatory. Didn't the old fusspot realize that he had better things to do than listen to another lecture on those foolish tradesmen trying to collect their debts? William was a landholder, an important man. He smoothed his graying hair against his temples and tugged at his waistcoat. Who was going to pay a tailor that made one's clothes too tight anyway?

Marks, his solicitor, waved him to a chair. The man looked like an undertaker. What was a gentleman to do with an undertaker for a man of business? "It's not a funeral, man, don't look so mournful."

His attempt at humor fell flat. The solicitor sniffed with disapproval. Marks never could take a joke. Hang him anyway.

"It may not be a matter of death, but it is certainly a matter of import. You are once again extended well beyond your means."

William shifted impatiently, the constriction of his tight waistcoat making him uncomfortable. "We've been through this before. I can't be expected to concern myself with petty things like tradesmen's bills. What do you think I pay you for?"

Marks cleared his throat. "I cannot pay your bills when there are no funds in your accounts. I am afraid that things have come to a dangerous pass."

It was just a matter of a few tailors' bills after all. "What's dangerous about a few outstanding accounts?"

"There are many more than a few and your tradesmen are threatening to sue. You do realize what that means, don't you?"

William glared at Marks. "Of course I know what that means. I would be humiliated in front of all the polite world."

Marks gave a humorless chuckle. "That would be the least of your troubles. If the court finds in their favor, and I cannot see them doing otherwise, you would be facing debtor's prison until your debts could be satisfied."

Debtor's prison? Marks must be mad. William could not be thrown in prison. He was too important.

"I'm afraid the time has come for drastic measures."

"What measures? You told me there was nothing else I could sell. Are you saying you have found a way to bypass my father's will and sell a parcel of land?" William demanded.

The other man sifted through the papers on his desk. "No. The

29

land is held in perpetuity for the heir. I was thinking about your horses."

William leapt from his chair. "There is a hunt in Sussex in six weeks time. You cannot expect me to sell my prime horseflesh with something so important in the offing. It's impossible."

"Perhaps, if you had paid more of your tradesmen's debts and less gaming debts—"

He didn't let Marks finish. "A gentleman pays his gaming debts. There must be an alternative to selling my hunters."

Marks passed a hand across his eyes. "You could always marry an heiress."

William stared at the solicitor. Marry again? It had been a relief when he had finally been rid of his first wife. She had nagged him constantly about his gaming and horses. The silly woman had not understood what was important. Just the thought of getting leg-shackled again made him shudder.

"I suppose I can retire to my estate briefly like you have suggested time and again." Come to think of it, Marks was a great deal like his dead wife. They both nagged a man.

"I'm afraid it's past time where that might help. If we act quickly, before the *ton* learns of your financial ills, we can still get a top price for your horses."

Sell his horses? It was not to be born. William turned and walked toward the door of the office. There must be another way. "I'll contact you later."

He stumbled out the door and almost bumped into Marks' clerk.

"I couldn't help overhearing your discussion, governor."

Something in the clerk's voice made him glance up. There was an unmistakable look of avarice on the other man's face. The door had appeared closed, but William did not quibble. He recognized opportunity when it came knocking.

"Oh?"

"Aye. Spinks is me name. Perhaps you and me could take a little walk."

William drew himself up and spoke with a haughtiness he knew impressed the lower classes. "Why would I do that?"

"You're looking for an heiress, I heard."

His interest was pricked, but it didn't do well to appear too eager. He had learned that buying and selling horseflesh. "I might be."

"Come now. You're in dun territory and you need a fat goose to get you out."

Flicking a nonexistent piece of lint from his sleeve, William looked down at the clerk. "I assume this conversation has a purpose?"

"Aye, it has a purpose all right. I like me position, see? I see lots of interesting things. For instance, you could have knocked me over with a feather when I found a certain statement of a lady's groat sticking out of a file."

More likely the man had done a search when Marks was not in the office. "Whose assets might those be?"

"Well, now, governor, I wouldn't want to be too free with my client's information, see?"

He did see, very well. "How much?"

"Now, that's what I like about you toffs. In dun territory, and you still got the blunt to buy an interesting bit of information."

"How much?"

The clerk named a sum that made William swallow. "How do I know it's worth it?"

When the clerk listed the lady in question's assets, William's eyes bulged.

Several hours later Spinks took William's money. It hadn't been easy to raise the funds, but William had done it. Gad, it had been worth it too. His golden goose was a bluestocking spinster who hadn't had a real suitor in three Seasons. She would be easy prey. The courting wouldn't come too expensive either. He had no competition, not for Lady Annabelle.

Chapter Three

Ian felt a deep sense of anticipation as he drove his curricle toward Lady Beauford's townhouse. Why had he waited to call until now? He had liked Annabelle from the moment Finchley introduced them. Her quick wit and strong intellect intrigued him. He should have called sooner. The lass clearly expected more courting before she would agree to marry him.

He could tell she was attracted to him. When they danced, her body reacted to his—even when she was angry. She enjoyed their discussions as much as he did. So, why had she been so affronted at his proposal? Surely a woman of her intellectual leaning was not expecting moonlight and roses.

Love. She said she wanted love. He could more easily give her moonlight and roses. He wondered if she liked the blooms he had sent over earlier that morning. He would give her the trappings of courtship, but he could not give her love.

Drawing up in front of Lady Beauford's townhouse, he handed the reins to his tiger. He waited in the doorway of the drawing room for the butler to announce him. Lady Beauford and Finchley conversed on a sofa that looked too delicate to hold them. Annabelle stood near tall windows. The sun filtered through and outlined her body against the bright yellow muslin of her gown. Ian's body tightened painfully at the sight.

The thin fabric clung to her small, high breasts and fell gracefully over her hips. He pictured those hips writhing below his and wondered at this unbridled passion. The more time he spent in her company, the stronger this inexplicable reaction to her became. During their discussion the previous evening, it had taken all of his self-control not to pull her trim little body flush with his and kiss the glare right off her face.

She played with a single rose bud from the arrangement he had sent. She sniffed it as she read the card he had sent with his flowers. Her delicate brows drew together in a frown and he wondered what she had found to offend in his compliment.

The butler announced, "The Earl of Graenfrae."

Annabelle whirled to face him. The bud she had been holding slipped from her hand. He moved forward to pick it up from the brightly colored carpet. He handed it back to her. "Good morning, lass."

She gave him a piercing frown. "Your presumption will not convince me of your suit."

"'Tis no insolent to compliment a lady."

She came toward him until her nose nearly met his cravat. Giving a significant look to the other occupants of the drawing room, she spoke in a low tone. "It's not your empty words of praise that I find fault with. It's the way in which you chose to sign the card. I am not your future wife."

The intensity of her denial filled him with unanticipated anger. She belonged with him. Why could she not she see it? His course was mapped. She wanted to be courted. He would court her. More importantly, he would marry her. After which he would receive the money necessary to improve Graenfrae. The stubborn look of determination on Annabelle's face gave him slight pause. She definitely needed more persuasion.

"My lord, how nice to see you again. Won't you come and sit down?" Lady Beauford asked from across the room.

Ian turned toward her and bowed, but declined her invitation to sit. "Your servant, Lady Beauford." He nodded to his friend. "Finchley."

"I say," Finchley quizzed him, "I did not know you intended to call. You could have ridden in my carriage."

Riding with his friend would have included following the other man on his morning calls, something Ian had no desire to do. "I'm hoping to take Lady Annabelle on a wee drive."

Finchley nodded in understanding.

Annabelle let out a small gasp. Turning back toward her, Ian saw that she had pricked her finger on a thorn. He withdrew his handkerchief and gently tugged at her arm. She resisted. He tugged harder until he could see the drop of blood on the end of her forefinger. He wrapped it in the square of white linen.

"Really this is not necessary." Her chest rose and fell in agitation and her hand trembled in his. "It's just a prick."

He refused to release her hand, welcoming any excuse to touch her. "I dinna want you to spoil your lovely frock."

She pulled her hand from his grasp. "Do not think to turn me up sweet with empty flattery, my lord."

She looked like a daffodil, but she pricked him like the rose she held. "I'm sorry the flowers caused you injury. In future I will make sure they have no thorns."

She broke her gaze from his and looked at the pink rosebuds. "They are beautiful. A prick does not signify."

Aye, not in a spirited lady either. "So you like them?"

She turned and placed the bud back among the other blossoms. "The roses are more palatable than their sender."

He nodded gravely. "I shall send them often then."

"It will do you no good."

He smiled at the challenge. "We'll see."

She walked past him, a swirl of yellow muslin. "Yes, we will."

He reached out and stayed her with a hand on her arm. "Will you go driving with me?"

She didn't answer at first. She began to pace back and forth in front of him. Her brisk movements caused soft brown curls to escape their pins. Short breaths forced her bosom to strain against her bodice. The tightness in his lower body intensified. Soon, it would be obvious to those around him. He shifted to ease the tightness of his buff pantaloons.

"Enough of this farce, Laird MacKay." She stopped moving and offered him a piece of paper with several names written on it. "I have taken the liberty of preparing a list of possible candidates for you."

He ignored the paper. "Candidates?"

"Yes, ladies that would make you a respectable wife." She looked at him quizzically, as if waiting for his response.

He made no move to take the paper from her. She sighed. "After speaking to my aunt last evening, I understand your need to marry quickly. I believe the ladies on this list would suit your needs better than I."

He stalled for time to consider the best way to handle her tactics. "How did you determine their suitability?"

"They are all ladies of good family who have shown marked desire to marry and do not have a number of admirers with which you will have to compete. Some are even marginally pretty and a few have substantial dowries."

Finchley sat with his mouth agape. He turned to Lady Beauford. "I cannot credit this conversation."

"Neither can I. The girl is daft. This is her fifth Season and she's turning down the only man to have offered for her in the last three," replied the older woman.

Ian couldn't help smiling at Lady Beauford's words. Just as he thought, Annabelle should be ready to marry. He did not understand his own certainty that Annabelle must become his, but he knew he would not look elsewhere for a wife. He wanted the stubborn woman standing before him looking so bloody pleased with herself. "I have already found a lady who meets my every requirement."

Annabelle did not appreciate the comment. Her hazel eyes narrowed. A rapid pulse beat in her neck. He fought the urge to pull her to him and place his lips over the fluttering pulse.

"Ian, I mean Lord Graenfrae, you are being absurd." She waved the list before him. "The other ladies on this list have the same combination of insulting attributes you require."

He was tempted to smile, but it would only infuriate her.

"In addition, these ladies have something I do not. They have a desire to be married regardless of finer feelings."

35

More wisps of her silky hair flew loose as she shook her head in agitation. Her militant stance and triumphant look convinced him that she believed her argument ironclad. He would not waste time debating it with her.

"Come for a drive."

When she looked ready to argue further, he added, "You may go over your list. Mayhap we will see some of the ladies on it. You can make them known to me."

Annabelle appeared undecided so he inclined his head to indicate Finchley's gaping mouth. The look must have decided her. "With your permission, Aunt, I'll accompany Laird MacKay on a drive through Hyde Park."

The older woman gave an approving smile. "Yes, of course."

Annabelle had a distinctly hunted look when she left the room to don her pelisse and bonnet.

C3

William watched his prey and smiled. She came out of the townhouse on the arm of a new arrival to Town. It was Finchley's friend, Laird MacKay. Satisfied malice swept through William. A Scotsman would be no competition for the hand of a gently bred English lady.

Lady Annabelle might be as ordinary as London fog, but she was definitely gently bred. Who would have thought the plain spinster was an heiress? She wore the dowdiest of frocks and never any jewels. Amazing. Not that he minded. Once they were married, she could continue her dowdy ways and molder in the country studying Roman history for all he cared. His only interest was in her fortune. A fortune that she and her family had successfully kept secret from the *ton*.

He could not understand why. Surely she would have nabbed a husband by now if the truth had been made known. The lady's family were all fools, but he would not complain. Her secret fortune was the answer to his current tribulations.

The Scottish laird took Lady Annabelle by the waist and swung her into his curricle. Uncouth barbarian. William frowned. Why would even a barbaric Scotsman court the unimpressive spinster? Had William been betrayed? Had Spinks sold the information of her fortune to other gentlemen of the *ton*? If Spinks had been foolish enough to do so, he would pay for his folly. Cursing, William stepped back into the shadows as the carriage came near.

He tossed the small posy he held onto the cobblestone. He would not be thwarted now that his luck had turned. He would marry Lady Annabelle and save his hunters. He stepped on the flowers, crushing their fragile petals into the cobblestone. No one would stand in his way. No one.

CB

Ian could not help smiling at Annabelle's hurried breaths, pleased by the evidence that she was not immune to his touch. Sitting with her back ramrod straight and her gaze fixed in front of her, she admonished him, "That was not necessary, my lord. A simple hand up was all I required."

He shrugged, unwilling to admit that he could not help touching her. "I'll remember that in the future."

"See that you do."

When he did not take the turn toward Hyde Park, she squirmed in the seat beside him. He continued past two more roads that would have led him to the park. He could feel her tension mounting.

She said, "Perhaps you are not aware, but you must turn up one of these streets to the left in order to go to the park."

He smiled at her condescending tone. "Lass, what good would going to Hyde Park do my courting?"

She turned her head so quickly, her bonnet nearly went sailing. Putting up a hasty hand to right it, she stared at him. "But you told my aunt we were going to the park."

"Nay, 'twas you who told your aunt that."

"What of meeting the ladies on my list?" she asked, her voice heavy with accusation.

"If you see any of these ladies, you're welcome to point them out to me." He could not be more reasonable than that.

"How convenient, however it is highly unlikely that we will see any ladies of the *ton* while driving aimlessly about."

Although he enjoyed the angry sparkle in her eyes, his intention was not to incite further hostility. "If your heart is set on going to a park, I'll oblige you."

She sighed heavily. "It is not that I wish to go to the park. What I wish is to present my list to you and convince you that you have better prospects elsewhere for a wife."

He did not reply. He was busy trying to avoid an urchin who had run in front of his horses to retrieve a ball. Deftly handling the reins, he missed the boy by inches. The youngster looked up and saluted Ian with a cocky wave of his hand before running back to a tree-lined park.

"Here is a park. Will it do?"

"Frankly, you could take me for a drive through Cheapside. All I want is for you to listen to me about my list."

He would listen to her list and then he would explain that he had already made his choice.

The commons looked pleasant and empty of the crush of people they would be subjected to at Hyde Park. The few people present appeared to be children with their nursemaids or mothers. Their dress indicated that although it was near fashionable residences, the park was not frequented by the *ton*. In the middle of the park a small pond glistened in the sunlight. Waterfowl swam near its shores.

Ian offered Annabelle his arm. She ignored it. He sighed. The stubborn set of her jaw did not bode well for courting this day. He took her hand and led her to the water.

She surprised him by asking about his list rather than trying to tell him about her own. "How did you come up with your requirements for a wife?" She looked at him sideways, her eyes lit with curiosity. "In general, I've noticed that men are looking for beauty, money and youth. Yet, you spurn all three."

How much should he tell? "I dinna trust beautiful women."

"Why not?"

He struggled with the answer. He had never told anyone about Jenna and wasn't sure where to start. "I was engaged to a beautiful woman. In truth, she was the most beautiful lady of my acquaintance. When she discovered better prospects elsewhere, she set her sights on him instead."

Annabelle laid her hand on his arm. "I'm sorry. That must have been terrible. Did you love her very much?"

"Nay."

"How sad."

Sad? Not likely. If he had loved Jenna, her betrayal would have been even more devastating. He did love his brother and the thought of Edward's disloyalty still had the power to make his gut churn.

"'Twas for the best."

"Surely, you don't think all beautiful women cannot be trusted because of one incident." She sounded incredulous.

"A plain woman is not going to tempt other men."

Annabelle stiffened beside him. "That's a terrible thing to say. I cannot believe that you would exile yourself to life with an ugly wife just to avoid the possibility that another man might find her attractive."

He had offended her, again. "I dinna say ugly. I said plain. 'Tis no an exile," he added.

"What else could it be? If you don't believe other men will be tempted by your wife, I assume you won't be either."

Tears sparkled in her eyes. They brought back the feeling of helplessness he had experienced the night before in the face of her hurt. He stopped walking and pulled Annabelle around to face him. She looked away. He put his hand under her chin and gently guided her face until her eyes met his. "I didna say I wasn't tempted, lass."

"But—"

"I would show you just how very tempted I am if we were no in a public park."

"You said—"

"I wasna talking about you."

"I'm plain. You want to marry me so other men won't be tempted."

He didn't like hearing it come out of her mouth. It sounded brutal and cruel on her lips. "You are no plain."

She shook her head. "I'm not beautiful."

"You tempt me."

"I don't understand."

Releasing her face, he began walking again, pulling her beside him. "'Tis no difficult to understand. You are tempted as well. 'Tis another way we will deal well together."

"I am not tempted. You should not say such a thing."

He did not reply. If she wanted to hide from the truth, he would let her. For now.

"What of your other requirements? Why do you want a woman of modest means? What could be wrong with getting a substantial dowry with your wife?" Her questions came out in a rush.

He felt on firmer ground with this answer. He couldn't possibly provoke her. She was plainly not a lady of great means. In the two weeks he had been in Town, he had never seen Annabelle wear expensive jewels or ornate gowns. "A woman with a large dowry naturally comes from a wealthy home. She is accustomed to every desire being met. I have an estate full of tenants with many needs. I dinna want to indulge a wife who would have new ball gowns while her tenants starve."

"Surely you do not think that all ladies of means would be so cold-hearted." Annabelle frowned.

What had he said now? "Perhaps not, but a modest dowry still recommends a wife to my way of thinking."

Her hands clenched at his coat. "Being an heiress certainly would not indicate that a lady was spoiled, or willing to see her tenants starve while she bought more new gowns. Your attitude is ignorant in the extreme."

Retreat seemed the wisest course of action. "Perhaps."

She harrumphed. "Might I ask why you prefer a woman of advanced years such as myself to the more congenial and, I am told, more easily molded young debutantes?"

"There are two reasons for that, lass. I found the young ladies just out, in Edinburgh, to be mindless widgeons."

"And the second reason?"

He may as well be honest, but Ian expected an eruption after his words. "I thought an older lady would be easier to persuade to marry quickly as her prospects were dwindling."

Her glare was hot enough to singe him.

"In essence then, you want a wife who will not tempt your neighbors, requires no consideration on your part and is willing to live without luxury in order to see your estates prosper?" Annabelle's voice began in a deadly quiet but rose with every word until she was almost shouting.

"'Tis no exactly that." Although she was close enough to the truth that he did not contradict her.

"My lord, you are insufferable." She stopped walking, forcing him to stop as well. "Do you not realize that no lady, however desperate and advanced in years, would wish to marry a gentleman so unwilling to expend any effort to see her happy?"

Why could she not understand? He was looking for a mate, not a spoiled beauty whose every whim must be catered to. His experience with Jenna had shown him that no amount of physical beauty was worth the consternation it brought. However, he did want a content wife. What man did not?

"'Tis no that I dinna want a happy wife, 'tis simply that I dinna want to spend all of my time making her that way."

"I know of no lady, no matter how old, ugly and poor, who would not desire some regard from her husband."

"I dinna wish to marry a woman for whom I have no regard. I want to marry you and I hold you in great esteem."

Annabelle laughed mirthlessly. "How very kind of you. You have known me but two short weeks. All that you esteem is my supposed desperation to marry, which I promise is not the case."

"I ken you well, lass."

"What exactly do you think you know, besides the erroneous conclusion that I am desperate to marry?" She met his stare with unflinching regard.

He said, "You are an intelligent and practical lady of good humor, with a compassionate nature and fine breeding."

Her eyes softened momentarily, then hardened again. "I am not nearly so practical as you believe. I have no desire to marry without love."

All women wanted to marry. 'Twas their lot in life. Someone had forgotten to tell Annabelle this truth.

She turned and faced the pond. "Do you know that according to the Common Law of England, when a woman marries she loses all of her rights?"

From the tense set of her shoulders and the fervent tone of voice, Ian knew her words were important. He strained to understand what she tried to say. "I dinna ken your meaning."

"If I were to marry you, even the clothes on my back would become your property. I would have nothing of my own, no recourse if you mistreated me. If we had children, you would have sole control over them."

The image of Annabelle big with his child sent pleasure coursing through him. "I willna mistreat you. We can protect your dowry with a marriage settlement."

Annabelle shook her head. "Without love, I have no guarantee."

"Love is no a guarantee either."

She sighed. "I know, but without it, marriage is a bleak prospect for a lady."

"I canna promise love, but you will be happy." He wanted her to believe him. "I will never betray you and I will protect you and your property. You will no be forced to sell your things to finance my whims."

He would not make the same mistake his grandfather had made. His wife and children would never pay for his beliefs.

"It won't work. I must have some security. Marriage has little enough as it is. I will have love."

Ian frowned. Love was the one thing he could not give her.

Chapter Four

The ball was an absolute crush. The Markham townhouse, already crowded with heavy, ornate furniture, reverberated with a cacophony of voices and movement. Lady Markham and her husband had a penchant for Gothic furnishings and entertaining. No one turned down an invitation issued by the elderly couple.

Perfect conditions for slipping away to a clandestine meeting, thought Annabelle. Except that Ian stuck to her side like paste. Just as he had at every social occasion for the past week. Although she took some small satisfaction in introducing him to women on her list, his persistence had an adverse effect on her equilibrium. In addition, if she didn't dislodge him and her aunt soon, Annabelle would never be able to make her meeting.

"Lady Beauford, what a pleasure to see you."

Annabelle turned and saw Miss Caruthers, the current toast of the *ton*, greet her aunt. Although Ian had made his view of beautiful women clear, Annabelle thought he would be unlikely to stand against Miss Caruthers' charm. A diamond of the first water with her blonde ringlets and peaches and cream complexion, Miss Caruthers could be just the diversion Annabelle needed.

"Miss Caruthers. I believe you know my niece, Lady Annabelle." Lady Beauford then turned as if to go.

Miss Caruthers smiled. "Indeed I do. Lady Annabelle, how very nice to see you again. I so enjoyed our discussion of music at Lady Diddisham's."

44

Annabelle arrested her aunt's progress with a hand on her arm. She had no intention of giving up this opportunity to break away. "Miss Caruthers, you played charmingly at the last musicale."

"Thank you, Lady Annabelle."

Annabelle returned the girl's smile before introducing her to Ian. "Lord Graenfrae, may I present Miss Caruthers?" She leaned toward Ian, speaking in an undertone. "She is not on the list, but perhaps she should be."

Ian raised his brow mockingly at Annabelle before bowing politely over Miss Caruthers' hand. The debutante fluttered her eyelashes at Ian as Ceddy arrived to claim her for the current dance. Ceddy greeted Annabelle and her party before offering to lead the beauty out on the floor.

"Oh, Lord Finchley, I'm certain I could not dance another step without a bit of refreshment. It is that hot in here." Miss Caruthers fanned herself, managing to draw attention to both her grace and her bosom at the same time.

Annabelle had to admire the other girl's obvious skill in campaigning while unaccustomed feelings of jealousy beset her. Her plan to slip away from Ian lost merit by the second.

Ceddy replied, "Must get you some lemonade then, eh what? Perhaps you could sit with Lady Beauford while you wait."

Miss Caruthers gave Ceddy a dazzling smile, but it dimmed when Ian spoke. "How kind of you to escort her ladyship to a seat, Finchley. Lady Annabelle and I will take advantage of the forming set. 'Tis a dance with some Scottish flair."

He placed his hand to the small of Annabelle's back and led her into a set shy one couple. She bristled at Ian's cavalier treatment. As they faced each other to begin the dance, she admonished him. "Do you not think you could have asked me?"

Though, her wayward heart insisted on thrilling that Ian had indeed been immune to the beauty's charms and had made his preference for Annabelle's company known.

The steps of the dance separated them and Ian did not answer. However, when they came together again, he said, "Las—Lady

45

Annabelle. Your eyes sparkle like the stars above my home when you are angry."

Nonplussed, she stared at him. He had not apologized, but he had given her what she considered a very nice compliment. "That is not the point."

"Dinna argue with me now. I'm enjoying the Scottish music and dancing with such a fine partner," he coaxed.

Annabelle gave an exaggerated sigh. "Very well."

When the music ended, Ian escorted Annabelle to her aunt. As they approached, Annabelle could hear Miss Caruthers' voice. "Does he spend a great deal of time in Scotland?"

"Should say so. Don't think he likes the Season much. Just here to find a wife, eh what?"

"But surely he wouldn't expect his wife to live in the wilds of Scotland all year," she exclaimed.

"On the contrary, Miss Caruthers. I canna imagine living in England and would expect my wife to reside with me in Scotland. My estate requires a great deal of attention," Ian said as he escorted Annabelle to her aunt.

Miss Caruthers blushed becomingly.

Ceddy came gallantly to the rescue. "MacKay, I've just been telling how we met. Don't you know?"

Annabelle thought she could guess who had raised the subject and she was sure it was not Ceddy. Interested to see how Ian responded to Miss Caruthers, she said nothing. He had appeared immune to her charm earlier, she wondered if that would hold in the duration of their acquaintance.

Ian turned to his friend. "Finchley, you've been my boon companion."

Ceddy puffed up under the praise. Annabelle noticed and liked Ian better for his kindness to her old playmate.

Miss Caruthers looked pointedly at the dance floor. "Ah, I do believe the next set is about to begin." She managed a convincing look of distress. "I have no partner and I'm weary of sitting."

Annabelle's Courtship

Annabelle did not like the speculative gleam she saw in Miss Caruthers' eyes when she looked at Ian. The girl acted like she had been sitting for hours, rather than for one dance.

Ian fell for the bait. "May I have the pleasure?"

As they walked away toward the dance floor a young swain who had been making his way to Miss Caruthers' side stopped abruptly and cursed as he watched her take the floor with Ian.

As Ian took the younger woman into his arms, Annabelle said to no one in particular, "That certainly didn't take long."

Ceddy asked, "What was that you said?"

"Oh, nothing, Ceddy."

His eyes searched hers. She tried to appear unaffected. Ceddy asked gently, "Won't you do me the honor?"

She nodded. Trust her old friend to come to the rescue of her pride. They joined the set with Miss Caruthers and Ian. Annabelle smiled brightly at Ceddy, determined to show Ian that he held no particular place in her affections.

"Capital orchestra, don't you think?" Ceddy's words forced her to focus on him and she agreed.

"Oh yes, I think they are just wonderful. Lady Markham never stints on her entertainment."

"That is true. Her midnight suppers are legendary," Ceddy said, exposing his favorite part of the evening.

Annabelle laughed. "Ceddy, you should look like a roly-poly baker, liking food as much as you do."

"I take after my grandfather. He was a true food connoisseur."

Annabelle agreed as the pattern of the dance separated them. She found herself facing Ian, who looked daggers at her.

"Have you a fondness for Finchley, then, Lady Annabelle?"

Annabelle was so startled by his accusation that she laughed out loud. "You're far off the mark. He is my dear friend, just as he is your boon companion."

His glare lessened infinitesimally. "Aye, friendship is a good and sometimes rare thing."

47

Annabelle nodded. "Yes, friends are a blessing, especially in the life of the *ton* where appearance is so important and often deceiving."

Would Ian ever understand how deceived he was about her? He insisted on seeing her as the rest of the *ton* did, an aged spinster desperate to marry. She turned again to face Ceddy.

"MacKay looks like thunder. Is all as it should be?"

"Yes, but, Ceddy, he thought I had a *tendre* for you and that would have disarranged his well-laid plans of being married to a paragon of plainness within the month."

"Don't say such things. You have much to recommend you, Annabelle."

A trill of laughter from the other couple in their set caused Annabelle's head to turn. "Lord Graenfrae may say he has no use for beautiful women, but it would seem that he and Miss Caruthers are getting along splendidly."

"I'm sure that if MacKay said beauty doesn't interest him, then it doesn't, eh what?"

Annabelle admired Ceddy's loyalty and did not wish to test it any further. She knew that in times past, the dandy had similarly held up her cause. When the dance ended, Ian approached Annabelle to claim her for a turn around the room. She knew if she didn't break away now, she might not have the chance later. Faking a tear to her hem, she pretended to make her way to the ladies' retiring room.

William's temper was beginning to fray when he saw Lady Annabelle leave the annoying Scotsman's side. He could tell even from a distance that she was telling the big brute that she had a tear in her hem. William would follow her to the ladies' retiring room and wait for her outside, where he would bump into her and start up a conversation. No doubt, after an evening spent predominantly in the barbarian's company, she would welcome the opportunity to converse with an *English* peer of the realm.

As soon as she made it to the other floor, Annabelle scooted down a dimly lit hall. A hand reached out from the shadows.

Annabelle stifled a gasp. "There you are. I wasn't sure I would get away to meet you."

Vivian Graves nodded. "I wasn't sure either. George didn't make for the card room immediately like usual and I lived in fear that he would never go."

Annabelle understood her friend's concern. George Graves, Vivian's brother, had a tendency to play too deeply on occasion and then swear off cards for weeks at a time. This of course seriously hindered Vivian's freedom in working for their common cause, women's rights. "Did you speak to our new recruit?"

Vivian shook her head. "She was surrounded by admirers like usual. I'm not certain that she's a good prospect, no matter what others may say."

Remembering the scene in the ballroom, Annabelle concurred. "You may be right. Do you have the pamphlets for me?"

The other woman nodded. Pulling Annabelle by the sleeve, she slipped into a nearby room. Light filtered in through the partially cracked door and Annabelle could make out the shadowy shapes of a four-poster and wardrobe. Vivian bent and removed a thin stack of pamphlets from a pocket sewn into her petticoat. Annabelle took the papers from Vivian and stored them in her own petticoat. "I'll see that these are passed on to our contact in the House of Lords. He will see them distributed to the parliamentary members."

"Will you be at the lecture in Cheapside?"

Annabelle grimaced. "I don't know. There are new complications. It's not just a matter of escaping Aunt Griselda for the day. I now have a rather persistent suitor as well."

"A suitor?"

Annabelle smiled at the surprise in her friend's voice. "Yes, a suitor. I'll tell you all about him at the lecture."

Vivian pulled on Annabelle's arm. "Tell me now in case you don't make it to the lecture."

Annabelle sighed at the other woman's curiosity. She went over the bare bones of her circumstances with Ian, mindful of the time she had been away from the ballroom.

Vivian made shocked noises as Annabelle described Ian's requirements for a wife. "That is unconscionable. I cannot believe his effrontery."

"It's not that bad. He truly is in a tight situation with his stepfather's will."

Vivian gave her a searching glance in the dim light of the bedchamber. "You must find him more appealing than you admit to defend him."

Annabelle wished she could deny Vivian's insightful words, but knew that she could not.

CB

Ian stood at the bottom of the wide staircase and waited impatiently for Annabelle to reappear. He toyed with the idea of looking for her, but could not very well barge into the ladies' retiring room. If that were indeed where she was to be found. His mind whirled with unwelcome thoughts. Had she gone to meet a lover? Pain at the memory of another night, another ball sliced through him.

It had been the ball to announce his betrothal to Jenna. His brother, Edward, had returned from school for the event. A young man, barely twenty, Edward had been overwhelmed with Jenna's beauty. Ian could see that now. Then he had been fool enough to believe that loyalty between brothers would prevent Edward from forming an attachment to Jenna.

Ian could still remember the smell of heather and the unnaturally warm air in the garden that evening. He had lost sight of both Jenna and Edward. Assuming his betrothed had gone to attend to some feminine necessity, Ian had gone in search of his brother. Although several years separated their ages, they had always been close. Until that night.

Ian had found Edward in the garden. He had also found Jenna. Together. Their lips touching lightly, Jenna clinging to Ian's brother as if he were a lifeline.

"What will we do?" she had asked.

Ian had not been moved by the tears he heard in her voice, but the look of agony on his brother's face had swayed him. His brother loved Jenna. Ian would never love a woman and risk the vulnerability of her betrayal. Nor would he ever be weakened by an emotion that could cause an honorable man like his brother to behave without integrity.

"Tell my father I have decided we will not suit."

Edward and Jenna had jumped apart at his voice. They turned, their faces confirming their guilt. Edward had demanded Ian let him explain. Unwilling to listen to lies on top of the betrayal, Ian had refused.

"I hope you will both be happy," were the last words he had spoken to his brother. He had left for Graenfrae that night. He had not even gone home for his stepfather's funeral. He had mourned the earl's passing alone, just as he had lived the two years since his brother's betrayal. Alone.

Unable to stand the suspense and remembered pain any longer, Ian determined to go looking for Annabelle. He would know the truth, whatever the cost.

Ian waited for her at the bottom of the stairs. He looked prepared to come up, his expression thunderous. Her heart sank. So much for secrecy.

"Where have you been?" His question came out like an accusation.

Startled by his vehemence, she couldn't think at first. She met his gaze. "I...I was in the ladies' retiring room. Why?"

"You weren't in the retiring room all this time." He looked intently into her eyes. "I canna see you meeting a lover either." He sounded perplexed.

Offended, she glared at him. "Why not? Let me guess. I am too ordinary to attract a lover."

His smile fueled her anger. Placing his hand on her back, he steered her toward the doors leading to the garden. "Dinna be ridiculous."

She tugged at her arm. He could take some more appealing female into the garden. Someone who could attract a lover. He refused to let her go, however.

They passed another couple and Ian nodded his head in greeting. Annabelle seethed silently until they were out of earshot. "Where are you taking me?"

"The garden."

She had guessed that much. She renewed her efforts to get free. "I must return to my aunt."

"You look breathless. Do you want Lady Beauford to wonder as I do what you have been up to?"

She gave him a mutinous frown, but stopped trying to get away. Explaining herself to Aunt Griselda did not appeal, nor did having others overhear her arguing with the stubborn Scotsman. For she had no doubt they were about to have another argument. A man could not accuse a lady of being too unappealing to attract a lover and get away with it.

Walking into the night air, the fragrance of spring blossoms assailed her. The perfect night for lovers. The thought did nothing to soothe her irritation. Ian led her to a stone bench and pulled her down to sit beside him. He forced her to meet his eyes. "What is it, lass?"

"Lady Annabelle."

"Very well. What ails you, *Lady Annabelle*?"

She didn't speak for a moment, but toyed with her fan. Finally words came out in a rush. "You don't believe I could have a lover. In the park you said you were interested in me, but now you make it clear that you think I'm as boring as a biscuit made without sugar."

He tipped her chin up. "I didna say that."

"You said I wouldn't have been meeting with a lover. It's the same thing." He would not get out of apologizing for this insult by pretending not to have said it.

"Nay, 'tis not the same thing at all."

Ha. "Yes, it is."

"If you had met a lover, it would have been obvious."

Her attention was caught. "It would?"

"Yes. You would have returned to the ballroom mussed."

She flipped her hand, dismissing his statement. "I could have straightened my appearance."

"Your lips did not look kissed."

What an interesting thought. "They didn't?"

"Nay, they did not." He sounded so certain.

"What do kissed lips look like?"

"Fuller, ripe."

What did he mean? "Your lips become fuller when you kiss? This is most interesting." She folded her hands in her lap, letting her fan dangle from her wrist. "Pray continue. What do you mean by ripe?"

He made a strangled sound, but answered her. "Like a peach that is ripe. Soft and juicy, ready to eat." His eyes glittered with intensity as they fixed on her unkissed lips.

She sat silent for a moment, thinking about what he had said. It did not seem possible. Ready to eat? "Are you quite sure, my lord? I have never seen anyone's lips look like ripe peaches before."

He laughed softly. "'Tis no surprising if you have never been kissed."

She drew herself up, indignant that he could believe such a thing. "I am four and twenty. Of course I have been kissed."

"No doubt your experience is broad."

His sardonic tone annoyed her. "I am quite serious. However, I find it odd that I have never experienced the kind of kissing you speak of."

"'Tis no surprise. 'Tis the kiss of a lover."

She expelled a tiny puff of air. "Oh." She thought for a moment. "So you meant it when you said you would be able to tell if I had met a lover." She was still uncertain, but perhaps he had not insulted her attributes again.

"Yes."

She sighed. "I feel much better."

He raised his brow in question.

"Yes. I do. I believe we can return inside. I'm sure my aunt will have no cause to cross-question me now."

"Not yet." He spoke quietly, barely above a whisper.

"Why not?"

"Because lessons are best learned through experience." She would have asked what he meant, but his mouth covered hers. His lips caressed hers softly over and over again. The few fumbling kisses she had received in the past paled in comparison to this gentle onslaught to her senses.

Annabelle felt bewildered by the sensations shooting through her. She had never felt this desire to get closer to a gentleman. She wanted to press her body against his and curl her arms around his neck. The thought was so shocking that it broke the numbing effect his kiss had on her limbs. She pushed against him and pulled her mouth from his.

He would not let her go. She could not catch her breath. "You shouldn't have done that." She tried to sound firm, but knew she failed miserably.

"Nay, I should have done it sooner." His first kiss had been gentle and probing, this one was full of passion. His lips demanded a response from her, but she did not know what. All thought of resistance had faded and she sought to experience more of the wonderful sensations brought on by his caress.

Putting his arms around her, he pulled her across his thighs, settling her on his lap. He must have removed his gloves because she could feel the warmth of his fingers against the nape of her neck. She shivered with longing.

The fragrance of the garden mixed with his masculine scent, sending her further into the maelstrom of passion. His tongue roved over her lower lip. He wanted something, but she couldn't tell what. Her mind felt fractured like light splintering off the crystal of a chandelier.

"Open your mouth for me," he whispered against her lips.

It seemed natural to obey. He tenderly swept her mouth with his tongue. It felt so incredibly wonderful. It must be sinful. She linked her hands behind his neck and closed her eyes, melting against him.

Laughter broke through the passionate haze surrounding them. He groaned and pulled back slightly. "Belle, we must stop." She did not react to his words, but remained melted against him with her face nuzzled against his shoulder. She could not get enough air and her mind was fuzzy. Gently disentangling her arms from him, he set her back on the bench. She slowly opened her eyes.

His were dark with desire. She thrilled at the knowledge his desire was for her. He smiled. The moonlight illuminated his expression. Satisfaction shimmered in his gaze.

"Now you look kissed, Belle."

Chapter Five

William considered the practicality of ridding himself of the Scotsman's presence...permanently. If he had the funds, he could hire it done, but he was unsure of soiling his own hands in that way. Perhaps it would be unnecessary.

He could not believe that even the uncouth man continued to pursue the unremarkable Lady Annabelle without knowing of her secret fortune. However, pursue her he did. The laird had waited for the chit to return from fixing her hem, just as William had done, forcing William to do so in the shadows.

And then, when she had not shown, the Scotsman had found her first. William had only spied her returning from a walk in the garden with the other man.

Looking quite flushed. If he did not know better, he would believe the couple had been engaging in a passionate tryst. But he could not believe that of a proper English lady, even a dowd like Annabelle.

Annabelle shivered and yawned as she made her way to Aunt Griselda's room. She had slept very little the night before, restless with thoughts of Ian's kisses. Those of a lover, he had said. Whatever the term, they had left her breathless and wanting more.

She fervently wished that Diana and Robert were already in Town. Her brother and his wife had promised to arrive sometime this week. She prayed it would be soon. She desperately needed to talk to someone about her relationship with Ian. Aunt Griselda would not do. She would likely faint if Annabelle admitted kissing Ian in Lady

Markham's garden. Either that or insist on posting the banns. Neither reaction appealed.

Ian stirred her passion, but passion was not love. He did not believe in love. Annabelle was almost convinced that she was having her first encounter with the emotion. What a muddle!

Stopping at her aunt's door, she peeked in.

"Don't stand there peeping around the door like some child caught sneaking treats from the tea tray. Come in and tell me what had you woolgathering on the journey home last evening."

Annabelle moved into the room. Lady Beauford sat up in bed, the heavy damask draperies pulled aside. A tray with chocolate and the remnants of breakfast reposed beside her on the ice blue coverlet. Beneath her attractive lace cap, the dowager's face was wan.

"Aunt Griselda, are you feeling quite the thing? You look a bit peaked."

Taking an imperious inventory of Annabelle's appearance, Lady Beauford harrumphed. "This from a gel who doesn't know any better than to dress like a governess when she's expecting gentleman callers?"

Annabelle quelled under her aunt's scrutiny. Her choice of dress had made sense in her chilly room. Knowing that it was unlikely to be warmer anywhere else in the house because the dowager had a tiny idiosyncrasy about saving money on coal, Annabelle had opted to don a fawn-colored wool dress. Its only claim to fashion the suitably high waist and long sleeves puffed at the top. She lifted her shoulders in a shrug. This particular argument with her aunt was long standing.

"It is uncommonly cold this morning. Had you noticed?"

"It must be. You are wearing a perfect fright of a dress. You look like someone's housekeeper."

First a governess and now a housekeeper. It could only get worse. It would not do to give in too easily, though. "Never say so. This is a perfectly reasonable dress especially for a day like today with no fires lit."

The argument had at least brought the color back to Lady Beauford's cheeks. "In my day, gels were not so worried about comfort as looking their best when callers arrived."

Going forward to adjust the shawl around her aunt's shoulders, Annabelle said, "Undoubtedly it would be better were I made of sterner stuff."

Lady Beauford allowed the ministrations. "Humph. I'll order a fire lit in the drawing room and you can change your dress to one of your new lawn gowns."

Annabelle smiled at the concession. "Aunt Griselda, that is very kind of you, but I like this dress. I'm sure we won't have any callers as it is not typically our at-home day."

"You do not expect me to take you calling in that?" Lady Beauford looked properly horrified.

"Of course not, Aunt Griselda. I had thought to take care of some correspondence today. Now, you can see that my dress is hardly significant."

Lady Beauford sighed and rested against the pillows. "Very well. Dress as you like, but if the laird comes calling today, do not pretend I did not warn you."

Poor Aunt Griselda. "I'll change my dress after breakfast. All right?" Annabelle asked.

The other woman nodded. "Now, be off with you."

As Annabelle approached the breakfast room, she heard Ian's deep burr and the deferential tones of the butler in the hall. Annoyed that her aunt had indeed been right and that she would be caught dressed like a governess, Annabelle moved forward to greet him.

She could have waited and Cresswell would undoubtedly have told Ian that they were not yet receiving. The irresistible pull of Ian's presence overcame her frustration at being caught dressed so practically, however.

He stood with his back to her, still wearing his many caped great coat. A large basket of red roses dangled from his hand.

"Good morning, my lord."

His head came around at the sound of her voice. Her knees went weak at the potent masculinity in his smile. "Good morning, Belle.

Although it's near enough to afternoon."

"I suppose that is your excuse for calling so early?"

His brows raised in question. "You are not yet ready to receive callers?"

She wanted to throttle him. Of course she wasn't ready yet. She hadn't even had her breakfast. Her aunt was still abed and it must be obvious she was not dressed to receive visitors. She decided to fall back on the excuse of her aunt. She had to stifle a sigh of disappointment, however, at the thought of sending Ian on his way.

"My aunt is still indisposed so I cannot receive callers."

He inclined his head in understanding. "I had hoped to be granted your company for a trip to the museum today."

"I adore the museum," she replied.

In truth, it was one of her favorite places. She could wander for hours room to room getting lost in the paintings, sculpture and even the Kings Library. Embarrassingly, her stomach chose that moment to make its empty state known.

"You havena eaten yet this morning?" Ian frowned at her. "You have no call to be standing in this drafty hall conversing with me."

She bristled at his tone. One minute he was kissing her like a...a lover and the next he was scolding her as if she were a child. "I'm sure my eating habits are my own concern."

He did not react to the frosty tone of her voice. "They should be someone else's as well if you are no going to take proper care of yourself."

He looked at her like an angry parent.

She could not help laughing at the absurdity of being upbraided for not eating her breakfast. "My lord, I have not been chastised for like misbehavior since my old nurse was retired to a country cottage." She smiled at his set features. "You don't look a bit like her, but you do sound like her."

His face registered disbelief. "I canna believe that Lady Beauford would not take it into her head to scold you on occasion as well."

He had read her aunt very well. Aunt Griselda did like to scold.

"True, but she reserves her reprimands for my clothing."

"What is the matter with the way you dress?"

Laughter bubbled up yet again at the sincere confusion in his voice. "My lord, you may like the fact that I dress like a dowd, thus making me more suitable in your eyes, but I can assure you that it does quite the opposite for my aunt."

"Belle, there is nothing the matter with your choice of attire."

Her insides warmed at the approval she heard in his voice. "Really, my lord, you must stop addressing me as Belle."

He shook his head as if her complaint were a pesky fly trying to land on him. "Dinna try to change the subject."

"Fine." She lifted the unfashionable wool skirt of her gown slightly. "Take for instance my dress today. Aunt Griselda would have heart palpitations if she realized that you had caught me wearing this."

He stared at her as if he could not believe what he was hearing. "What is the matter with that dress? It looks warm enough for the day. Your aunt's house is no warm, I have noticed."

Annabelle smiled at Ian's understatement. When the fog moved in, her aunt's townhouse became downright chilly. "My aunt can sometimes be parsimonious. She prefers to save money rather than have fires lit in all the grates."

"Your aunt would do well with my housekeeper. The woman is cheeseparing, no doubt about it."

Annabelle warmed under their shared smile.

The front door knocker sounded. "Are you expecting other callers this morning, Belle?"

The suspicion she heard in Ian's voice was laughable. Of course she wasn't expecting callers. Hadn't she made that clear enough? There was a flurry of activity at the door. She found herself enveloped in masculine arms and quickly released.

"Annabelle, I have missed you."

She looked into her brother's eyes and hers became misty. They had always been close. She impulsively leaned forward and gave him another hug. "Nothing like I have missed you, Robert."

She looked around him for Diana and came face to face with a fire-breathing Ian.

"Belle, I dinna know this gentleman. Won't you introduce me to your caller?" The question came out as a command.

She took her brother's arm and beamed up at him before acknowledging Ian's demand. "Robert, this is the Earl of Graenfrae, Mister Ian MacKay. My lord, my brother, Robert Courtney, Earl of Hamilton."

It was her brother's turn to stiffen. "Lord Graenfrae."

His words came out in the pompous tone he sometimes used, a tone Annabelle had come to despise. She could not deny that where she had shared in her parent's cavalier attitude toward society's rules, her brother kowtowed to them. Sickeningly so.

Ian's shoulders relaxed and his hand that had been fisted at his side unclenched. He inclined his head to her brother, more arrogant than even Robert in his acknowledgement. "Lord Hamilton, it is a pleasure."

A delicately cleared throat and Annabelle knew her brother was in deep trouble. He had been so busy matching Ian arrogant look for arrogant look that he had neglected to introduce his wife. Spinning away from Robert, Annabelle threw her arms around her beautiful sister-in-law.

"Diana, I was about to ask Robert where he had hidden you."

Momentarily ignoring her husband and the laird, Diana returned Annabelle's embrace. "Darling Annabelle, how I've missed you. Your letters have been all that has kept me sane these months with just your brother for company." Leaning closer to Annabelle, she whispered, "So who is this gorgeous man and do tell me the roses are for you?"

Annabelle laughed at her incorrigible friend. "Surely you heard me introduce him to Robert."

Diana gave her a disgusted frown. "Of course, how could I miss it and my husband's subsequent posturing? But *who is he*?"

Robert interrupted. "Annabelle, if you are finished greeting Lady Hamilton, perhaps you will allow me to introduce her to his lordship."

"Of course, Robert. By all means. I wouldn't want *Lady Hamilton* to think you had forgotten her," Annabelle mocked.

Diana winked at Annabelle before turning a perfectly composed face to her husband.

When the introductions were finished, Ian offered the roses to Annabelle. "I'll return another time for our excursion. No doubt you want to visit with your family and eat something."

Diana and Robert turned startled eyes to her at Ian's injunction that she eat.

"Ian is under the delusion that I still need a nursemaid."

She took the basket of flowers from him and couldn't resist leaning forward to inhale their fragrance. "They are lovely. Thank you, my lord."

"'Tis my pleasure, Belle." Bowing to her brother and Diana, he took his leave.

Annabelle stared after him until Robert's words interrupted her thoughts. "Where is Aunt Griselda and why were you entertaining a gentleman unchaperoned in the hall?"

"Aunt is still abed." The butler came forward and relieved her of her flowers. "Please put them in my room, Cresswell."

He nodded before leaving.

Ignoring Robert's censure about entertaining Ian without a chaperone, Annabelle took Diana's arm and headed toward the breakfast room. She *was* hungry. "So, he calls our aunt by her given name, but calls his wife Lady Hamilton. Have my brother's brains gone to let?"

Diana looked over her shoulder and smiled indulgently at her husband. "He calls me Diana in private, but believes it lends me countenance for him to address me more formally before those who are not our intimates."

"How interesting."

"Yes, isn't it?" Diana caught Annabelle's eyes and they went off into peals of laughter.

Annabelle hugged her friend's arm. "I'm glad you're here."

Remembering her first two Seasons, Annabelle grimaced. She had not wanted to come out of mourning for her parents, but Robert and Aunt Griselda had been adamant. Robert told her that he was worried she would never get over their parents' death if she did not start living again. So, he insisted that she attend the Season.

No amount of persuasion on her aunt's part, however, would convince Annabelle to wear gowns adorned with flounces and furbelows. The ornamentation seemed obscene to her grieving mind. With average looks and no interest in the social games of the *ton*, she had soon been labeled *The Ordinary.*

She had not cared.

Then she met Diana. They had been sitting near one another at a ball. Diana, resting because she had danced too much, and Annabelle because she rarely danced at all. Someone had raised the issue of women's rights. Annabelle shocked both herself and those around her when she made an impassioned declaration about the plight of women in England. Diana had stared at her with wide eyes and avowed that she was not ordinary at all.

They had been fast friends ever since.

Robert followed them into the breakfast room and took a seat next to his wife at the table. "I'm quite serious, impending engagement or no, it is highly improper for you to be entertaining the laird alone."

"What on earth are you talking about?" Honest bafflement overrode any other reaction to her brother's words. There was no way that Robert could have heard of Ian's plans at his country estate so far north. "What impending engagement?"

Robert said, "It's hardly a secret. You needn't play ignorant with me."

Annabelle turned to Diana in desperation. "Has Aunt Griselda been communicating with you?" She didn't see how it could be the case, unless her aunt had envisioned her current circumstance with the laird on their first meeting.

Diana picked up the paper and opened it to the society page. "Here, read this."

Annabelle scanned the column and all vestiges of hunger drained from her.

"*A certain Lady A. has been seen often in the company of Lord G. of Scotland since his arrival to Town. Could Lady A. be making a match at last?*" queried the impertinent writer.

Annabelle put a hand to her head. What had she expected with Ian making his suit so obvious? Looking at the speculative gleam in her brother's eyes, she groaned. Robert was almost as fixated with getting her married as their aunt.

"It's not what it seems."

"He is not courting you?" Outrage vibrated through her brother's words.

Visions of dawn appointments swam before Annabelle's eyes. Sometimes her brother went over the top on the issue of family honor. "Well, yes, he is courting me."

Her brother's anger turned to a look of complacence and he smiled. "Well done, Annabelle."

"I'm not going to marry him."

Hoping to change the subject, she turned to Diana. "I've been waiting impatiently for your arrival. I'm so glad you are finally here. We have much to discuss."

"How could that be? You two corresponded more than I did with my estate managers."

Giving her husband a condescending smile, Diana said, "Naturally." She faced Annabelle and grinned. "You couldn't keep me away a day longer."

"Diana, you know quite well I was content to molder away on my country estate to keep your lovely person all to myself."

Diana gave her husband a look full of warmth and secrets. A timeless moment passed in which Annabelle was overcome with longing. For all their banter, her brother and Diana's was a love match.

"You certainly don't look like someone who has been moldering away, Diana. You are positively blooming with happiness," Annabelle said with fondness.

"You will be having your own dish of happiness soon," quizzed

Robert.

Annabelle frowned at her brother. "I told you, I am not going to marry Laird MacKay. Besides, even were I to agree to such a ridiculous notion, it would be quite different than the union of minds and hearts you and Diana enjoy."

"Surely it is too early to make such an emphatic pronouncement," declared Diana.

There was nothing for it, but to explain the matter in its entirety. Well perhaps not the entirety, her brother need not know of Ian's passionate kisses in the garden. Annabelle felt Ian's proposal did her no credit, but it would be the only way of explaining her aversion to his marked attention.

As she spoke, her brother looked hard-pressed not to laugh. The mirth in his eyes did nothing for her sense of injured dignity. She scowled at him.

"It is not amusing." She waved the newspaper before him. "Now this. How would you like to be painted in such unflattering terms and the latest *on-dit* on the tip of everyone's tongue?"

His mirth vanished. Robert had a horror of being the center of gossip or scandal.

Diana's reaction aligned itself immediately with Annabelle. "How dare he. The brute. You are a perfectly lovely creature and if he's so blind he can't see that, he doesn't deserve you. As for this rag," she said, indicating the paper with a condescending sweep of her hands, "they simply do not understand a lady taking her time to the altar."

Her friend's staunch support went a long way toward restoring Annabelle's good mood.

Cresswell entered the room. "There is a fire lit in the drawing room per Lady Beauford's orders." When no one moved, he spoke again. "It is quite comfortable in there."

Diana took the situation in hand. "Robert, go pay your respects to your aunt. She's undoubtedly ready to receive company by now." When he hesitated, she shooed him with her hand. "Go. I will be up momentarily."

Robert left the room and Diana tugged on Annabelle's arm.

"Come, let us retire to the drawing room. Cresswell seems quite put out that no one is in there to appreciate Lady Beauford's generosity in ordering the fire lit."

Annabelle followed Diana to the other room. They sat on matching tapestry chairs near the brazier. She regretted her choice of dress for the second time that morning. The heat of the fire made the wool prickle against her skin.

"Tell me all," Diana said firmly.

Annabelle grimaced. "The proposal was truly awful."

"Yes, yes, so you've said. What about the rest?"

"The rest?" Now that the opportunity had come for Annabelle to unburden herself, she wasn't entirely sure she wanted to. Would Diana understand her quandary? Happily married to the man she loved, could she understand all the riotous emotions coursing through Annabelle?

"Yes, the rest. You would not be so beside yourself if Lord Graenfrae had simply made a proposal of no consequence."

"You cannot believe an impertinent marriage proposal of no consequence," Annabelle exclaimed.

Diana patted her arm. "Of course not. Haven't I already said so? But your sense of humor has served you well in other circumstances that could have been equally devastating."

Annabelle stood and moved away from the heat of the fire. She spoke with her back to Diana. "Nothing has ever been this provoking."

Diana laughed. "That is hard to believe. Remember when Freddy Jenkins was on the verge of proposing and then he fell for that empty-headed Mary Potts? When he came to explain his change of heart to you, you laughed him out of the room. You were not affected at all."

Recalling Freddy's ignominious exit, Annabelle could not help smiling just a little. Picking up one of the trinkets on a lacquer table she idly played with it before setting it down with a thump.

"This is entirely different. Freddy's idea of our relationship was amusing in the extreme, but Ian is an infuriating man with no concept of the tender emotions, much less the meaning of denial."

Diana shifted in her chair to face Annabelle. "My dear, you are putting too much importance on this matter. The Scotsman will eventually give up when you continue to deny his proposal."

Annabelle whirled around to face her friend, nearly knocking the entire grouping of knick-knacks off the shiny black table. "I would think that if he has the effrontery to say he is going to court me, then he is honor bound to do so."

"Yes of course, I'm sure he'll continue to court you if that is what you want," Diana said, obviously trying to soothe, but failing.

"It's not a matter of what I want. The man is stubborn as they come and will not give up easily," Annabelle insisted.

ଓ

Annabelle fingered a piece of silver trim and thought morosely that she had been quite wrong about Ian's stubbornness. Moving away from where Diana discussed the merits of some dyed muslin with the modiste, Annabelle tried to find something of interest among the bolts of colorful fabric. Her mind persisted in dwelling on Ian's easy defeat.

Although he continued to claim the customary two dances when they attended the same fête, he had not offered his escort for the evening since the Markham ball. He had not called at Lady Beauford's townhouse either, nor had the promised trip to the museum materialized.

He had sent her a Kashmir shawl with a note saying it was to ward off the chill of London's fog without putting undue constraints on her aunt's coal supply. The jest had made her smile. Her smile had come rather sparsely of late when the gift was not followed up with a visit.

The final bit of evidence that convinced Annabelle that Ian no longer sought to court her was the fact that although Robert had been in Town for nearly a week, Ian had not approached him for permission to pay his addresses to her.

Diana would have told Annabelle, even if Robert did not. To hear Diana tell it, the two gentlemen found a great deal else to discuss.

Lucy Monroe

Annabelle had been right. They shared a mutual interest in crop rotation and fertilizers. In fact, the last time Annabelle had seen Ian had been in her brother's drawing room. She had been visiting with Diana. Ian politely inquired about her aunt's health and then went off to find Robert.

Diana's voice interrupted her thoughts. "Oh, look at this one. It is so lovely."

Annabelle peered at the fashion plate Diana waved before her. It showed a split gown with a surprisingly low décolletage over an underskirt of contrasting color, both skirts ending in a double flounce. It was just the other woman's style. "It would be scrumptious on you, I'm sure, Diana."

"I was thinking of you."

"I don't carry off flounces well and the bodice is a bit low for my figure."

Diana frowned. "You are too hard on yourself by half. If you would give some of these fashions a chance, I'm sure you would be surprised at how well they look on you."

"You know what I think—" Annabelle began, but was interrupted by a raised hand from her friend.

"I know, I know, you can't make a peacock out of a peahen with tacked on feathers. Really, Annabelle, I can't imagine why anyone would want to make a peacock out of a peahen anyway."

Annabelle smiled at Diana's assertion. "Come, show me something more my style."

"This is your style if you would but try it." When Annabelle moved away, Diana abandoned the fashion plate. "At least you wear some interesting colors now, but you still have a lamentable tendency to dress plainly."

Annabelle grinned. "Now you are starting to sound like Aunt Griselda. If you begin comparing my dress to that of the domestic help, I shall not be responsible for my actions."

"Perish the thought," declared Diana.

The modiste caught Diana's attention and soon she was busy looking through another set of fashion plates.

68

As Annabelle picked up bits of lace and rubbed fabric swatches between her fingers, she wondered why she was not a great deal happier that Ian had finally accepted her refusal of his marriage of convenience. She should be elated, but instead an awful sense of desolation pervaded her.

The interest of other suitors did nothing to dispel it. It had come as something of a shock when more gentlemen began sending her flowers and calling on her. Lady Beauford was convinced that Ian's suit had sparked interest in other gentlemen.

Annabelle smiled cynically to herself. Undoubtedly, her aunt had the right of it. Several had become quite marked in their attention. Mr. Green had called at her aunt's townhouse twice and sent her a small posy of violets. Ceddy had also become a frequent guest in her aunt's drawing room.

At first, Annabelle had believed that to be because he was looking after his friend's interests. Now she wasn't so sure, considering the fact that Ian no longer showed any particular desire to be with her. Two widowers had also taken it into their heads that she would make the ideal wife.

She wanted to laugh, but felt more like crying. The constant callers and attention took precious time away from her causes. Ian had no right to set such a course in motion and then abandon her.

A masculine hand reached out and plucked the mustard lace from her fingers, catching her gloved hand. "I dinna think this color suits you."

Annabelle's head shot up and her eyes clashed with dark brown ones. "Ian." His name came out in a disbelieving whisper.

"Good day, Belle."

"How did you come to be here?"

"Hamilton and I have just attended a very informative talk on sheep breeding."

"Sheep breeding?"

"Aye, 'tis something I wouldna mind improving at Graenfrae. My father kept good diaries. He wanted to follow in Sir John Sinclair's footsteps and bring the latest farming techniques to Graenfrae." A

69

brooding look settled on Ian's face. "I have taken his dreams as my own."

"I see." She did too. Ian needed the money his stepfather had left him to keep his father's dreams alive. Realizing that he still had hold of her hand, she pulled it free.

She noted her brother and Diana looking through the pattern books. Diana had confided that Robert believed she wore her necklines too low. From the mutinous look on her friend's face, Annabelle surmised that to be the topic of their current debate.

"I did not realize that Robert intended to join us on our shopping expedition today."

Ian raised his brow. "I believe your brother seeks his wife's company as often as possible."

Annabelle bridled at Ian's amused tone. "My brother *loves* Diana. It should come as no surprise he enjoys being with her."

"Dinna bite my head off, Belle. I dinna mean insult."

She inclined her head, in no mood to extend him forgiveness. The man had promised to court her and then promptly lost interest. Righteous indignation coursed through her. He should be ashamed of himself. "As you say."

She turned back to the display of lace and pretended absorption. "This lace is not up to Madame's usual standards."

"I dinna know about that."

"No, I do not suppose you do."

His eyes narrowed. "What is wrong, Belle?"

"Whatever do you mean?"

"Come, are you two ready?" Robert's voice penetrated the silent battle of wills between Ian and Annabelle.

"Ready for what?" Annabelle asked.

Robert faced Ian. "Didn't you ask her?"

"I didna have the chance."

Annabelle crossed her arms under her chest and tapped her foot. "Ask me what?"

"Whether you and Diana would like to take a small break from your shopping and visit Gunther's with us."

Usually, Annabelle would like nothing better. Shopping was not her favorite pastime. Ian's unsettling presence caused her to consider declining, but she could think of no way to gracefully abandon the foursome. "Very well."

Robert raised his brows. "I thought you would be relieved to get a reprieve from Diana's zealous shopping."

"Your sister is not so weakhearted," Diana said. Robert led Diana out of the modiste's and Ian offered his arm to Annabelle. She acted as if she did not see it and followed the other couple on her own. As she came into the street, she nearly bumped into a woman passing out penny pamphlets. "A pence to help war widows, milady?"

Annabelle dug in her reticule and extracted some pence. The woman smiled brightly. "Thank you, milady." She handed Annabelle a pamphlet before moving on.

Annabelle seized the pamphlet without looking at it and made her way to Robert's carriage. He was already seated inside with Diana, so Annabelle had no choice but to accept Ian's help in ascending. As he grasped her firmly by the waist and lifted her up, Ian gave her a mocking smile. She gasped and glared at him. "You forget yourself."

Ian ignored her rebuke and leaped into the carriage beside her. She scooted as far away from him on the seat as she could get. His eyes filled with sardonic amusement, but he said nothing.

"What is that you have in your hand?" Robert asked.

Annabelle looked down at the paper. "Oh, it's just a penny pamphlet." She handed it to Robert.

He scanned the pamphlet and then slapped his leg with it in disgust. "Do not tell me you paid someone a pence for this?"

Already annoyed with Ian, Annabelle had no patience for a remonstrance from her brother. "No. I paid several pence."

"Annabelle, you must stop and look before giving your money to this riff-raff on the street."

Sitting up perfectly stiff, she matched her brother glare for glare. "The woman was a war widow, not riff-raff."

"You expect me to believe a respectable war widow would be peddling this?" He waved the paper in the air between them.

She snatched it from him and read the first paragraph. It was a statement deploring the state of laws regarding women in England. Annabelle's temper ignited. "Yes. As a matter of fact I'm certain the woman selling these is indeed respectable. What is wrong with making the shocking plight of women known?"

"This is not about the plight of destitute women. It is an indefensible attack on English Common Law and should not be tolerated." Robert's voice had taken on the pompous edge that Annabelle despised.

"It is narrow thinking like yours that has kept women under the tyranny of men for centuries."

At the look of shock on Diana's face and the fury on Robert's, Annabelle knew she had gone too far.

"Is that what reading that *Rights of Women* book has done to you? You think I tyrannize my wife?" Robert's angry words slashed at her like a knife.

"I didn't say anything about Diana. I was talking in general and for your information, Wollstonecraft is not the only voice in the debate about women's rights."

Robert made a sound of disgust. "I know. They are having some lecture in Cheapside tomorrow on this very issue. My solicitor's wife has insisted on attending. He is beside himself what to do with her. And I have the unenviable task of deciding whether or not to get another solicitor."

Annabelle grew cold. She almost blurted out that she planned on attending as well. Would he then consider getting another sister? Sanity intervened, though. It was no use. She and Robert simply came from two different viewpoints.

Diana's soothing voice entered the fray. "Come, Robert. Do not argue so vehemently with Annabelle. You and she do not have to agree on this issue."

Annabelle felt unexpected tears prick her eyes. If only her parents had lived. They would have understood her need to do something. Even

Diana did not comprehend how important this issue had become in Annabelle's life.

Ian had sat silent during the argument. He now reached out and squeezed Annabelle's hand. "'Tis all right, Belle."

She swept her gaze to his and read nothing but sympathy in his eyes. No condemnation, just compassion. She felt comforted. She turned her hand under his and returned the pressure, feeling an immeasurable peace at the contact.

Ian met Robert's still angry gaze. "Dinna raise your voice to your sister. 'Tis no gentlemanly."

Pleasure rippled through Annabelle at Ian's support. He knew exactly what to say to her brother as well. Robert prided himself on being the perfect gentleman.

Her brother laughed and her eyes flew to his. "I'm sorry, Annabelle. I don't know what came over me. I know how you feel about your causes. Call pax?"

Unwilling to remain angry with him, she nodded. She smiled at her brother's use of their childhood term. "Pax."

She did not let go of Ian's hand.

Chapter Six

The chatter of women's voices washed over Annabelle as she stood near the back wall of the public room. She did not see Vivian anywhere. Perhaps George had foiled the other girl's plans to join Annabelle at the lecture in Cheapside. A woman walked up to Annabelle and shoved a paper in her hand. It depicted a woman behind bars and each bar was labeled with a law that restricted the rights of women. Clever.

A hand gripped her shoulder. "Lady Annabelle, I must admit I am surprised to find you here."

Annabelle turned swiftly to place the country accents of the man speaking. "Squire Renton, I did not realize you had an interest in the Rights of Women."

In fact, astounded would be a better word. Like many Englishmen, Squire Renton's chief interests seemed to be hunting and his club.

The squire extended his neck, turtle-like, to see the crowd around them. "Can't say that I am. Came to find out what she has to say. A gentleman should not get too set in his ways."

She smiled at him. "Why, Squire, that's very forward thinking." Considering her brother's blatant rejection of the efforts women were making for improved laws, she was all the more impressed with the squire's apparent interest in the cause.

"Not at all, my dear. A wise man knows when to adjust his thinking. That's all." She was taken aback by the fact that the squire managed to make a humble speech sound quite superior.

Spying Vivian on the other side of the room, she said, "I believe I see my friend. If you will excuse me, sir."

Squire Renton nodded. "Of course. Perhaps I will see you both after the lecture."

Her attention more on her friend than the man at her side, Annabelle agreed absently. "Perhaps."

She made her way through the crowd of milling women, noting that the squire was one of less than half a dozen men in the room. It surprised her, but she recognized one of the other gentlemen. He had asked her to dance at the last few soirees she had attended. Perhaps men in the *ton* were starting to see how serious an issue reform was.

Annabelle gave Vivian a smile of welcome. "Miss Graves, you made it. I had almost given up hope of you doing so."

"I was not sure I would."

"I thought perhaps your brother had gotten wind of your plans and scotched them."

Vivian grimaced. "Very nearly. He took it into his head to stay home today. I could not believe it. The last time my brother stayed home from his clubs he had a head cold."

"What did you do?"

Vivian leaned forward and whispered, "I told him I was going to the lending library." She blushed after her admission.

"Well done." Annabelle believed in honesty, but some things required subterfuge. Her and Vivian's activities on behalf of the rights of women was one of those things.

Annabelle had become involved with women's rights after the flu epidemic that took both of her parents in one devastating blow. She stumbled upon a meeting quite by accident. The speaker at the meeting had been so very passionate. Afterward Annabelle had waited to speak to the lecturer and soon found herself involved in the dissemination of pamphlets and attending lectures both in London and in the country. However, she accomplished most of her work in London.

A hush fell over the crowd. Annabelle and Vivian craned their necks to see the speaker. Annabelle thought it would have surprised those who passed her on the street to discover that Mrs. Burnaby, a short woman of matronly appearance, was one of the great orators for Reform.

She began speaking and all talking ceased. Not even the occasional rustle of clothing could be heard as the charismatic woman mesmerized her speakers with tales of efforts to gain advances on behalf of women in England and abroad. She quoted Wollstonecraft and other voices of their movement.

Annabelle was entranced and did not at first notice the men filing in through the doors. They came in silently, but eventually her head and others began to turn. Several men now filled the small spaces that had been open in the aisles. The lecturer ignored them and continued her speech.

One of the men near Annabelle raised his voice to speak. Burly, he stood a head taller than most of the men crowded into the room. "What you tryin' to do, duck? Talk our women into acting like men?"

Several men guffawed. Another man spoke from the opposite side of the room. "Next thing you know you'll be wanting to wear trousers and share a pint down at the pub." The men broke out in raucous laughter.

The speaker did not flinch. She caught the eye of the man and spoke coolly. "You may keep your pubs and your pints. We seek equality in rights and property."

Annabelle nodded her head in agreement. She noticed many other women doing the same thing.

The big man glared at the speaker. "Ye wants us to give up our manhood is what ye wants."

At that the men cheered.

Annabelle had endured all that she was going to. First her brother, now this ruffian. Could the men not see that she and the others sought equality, not emasculation of their men? She started forward, ignoring Vivian's pleas not to get involved.

Annabelle poked the huge man on the back. He turned around and she spoke to him. "Sir, you may hold your own public forum, but right now Mrs. Burnaby is speaking and I and the rest of the audience would like to hear what *she* has to say."

"I'm not so sure about that." Raising his voice, the man asked, "Do we wants to hear this Burnaby woman speak, lads?"

A resounding chorus of "no's" went up.

Annabelle was incensed. How dare this man make light of Mrs. Burnaby in this way? She raised her own voice, glad that Aunt Griselda was not there to hear her unladylike bellow. "That will be quite enough, sir. No one invited you and your uncouth friends to join us. I think you should leave."

The man advanced on Annabelle, forcing her to back away. "Who's going to make us, ducks? You?"

Annabelle raised her parasol and pointed at the man. "I should not have to make you leave. Good manners should be enough to make you realize that you're not wanted here." She punctuated each word with a poke from her parasol to the man's chest. Now he was backing up and her voice had risen to unladylike proportions once again.

Vivian hissed at her. "Lady Annabelle, stop that. Come back here."

Annabelle ignored her friend's pleas and continued to berate the intruder. "We are doing nothing to warrant your foolish interference."

The man's face mottled with rage. Perhaps she should not have called him uncouth. He roared an expletive and snatched her parasol from her, wrenching her hand in the process. Annabelle pulled her stinging hand back in shock.

One of the women near them lifted her reticule and slapped the offending man on the side of the head. "Give 'er back 'er property, you filthy blighter!"

The man turned and shoved Annabelle's champion back into her seat. "Stay outta this if you knows what's good for you."

The woman stood back up. "I will not."

"You will too." Another man stepped forward and picked her up and slung her over his shoulder like a sack of potatoes. "Bessie, time you were home cooking supper."

Pandemonium broke out. Annabelle and several women nearby tried to pull Bessie from her captor's arms. Other men decided to

Lucy Monroe

follow the man's lead. They were bodily picking up the women and carrying them out the doors, while women from the crowd attempted to stop them. One man shoved an old woman out of his way as he tried to carry someone out of the building. Another man took exception to the action and belted him. Within moments it was a full-fledged riot.

Annabelle could not believe what was happening. She was headed to give aid to a young woman when Vivian tugged on her sleeve.

"Lady Annabelle, we've got to get out of here." The terror in her friend's voice arrested her.

Annabelle turned to look at Vivian and could not miss the other woman's white face and eyes rounded in shock. She had to protect her friend.

"Come."

Annabelle grasped Vivian's arm and dragged her toward the door. They dodged flailing arms and legs, trying desperately to find a way out of the room without joining the melee in the aisles. When their progress was blocked again and again, Annabelle began to despair escaping the room unscathed. She and Vivian were backed into a corner when the man Annabelle had confronted started toward them. He looked drunk with fury.

Annabelle started to pray.

Cold chills coursed down Ian's spine when he caught sight of Belle in the riot. He uttered quick instructions to Finchley. Then Ian headed for Belle, ignoring the scuffle around him. When he reached the man who threatened her, Ian latched onto the marauder's shirt and waistband. He picked the blackguard up and sent him flying toward the wall.

He then grabbed Belle by the arm and pulled her against his body, tucking her head under his arm to protect her from waving fists. He led her through the fray to the door, dodging flying chairs and swinging arms. When they gained the outside, he did not let up his fast pace. They reached his carriage and he swung her up, jumping in after her. Finchley neatly tossed the other lady up and Ian helped her settle while his friend leaped into the already moving carriage.

78

Ian bellowed at his coachman, "Move, man. Move."

His coachman listened and before long they were headed at a fast clip toward west London.

"Neatly done, my lord. For a moment I was certain Miss Graves and I faced imminent danger." Belle nodded her head for emphasis.

"Yes, my lords, this is most fortuitous. Thank you for rescuing us." Miss Graves gazed at Finchley with awe.

Finchley's cheeks turned crimson as he attempted to restore the perfection of his cravat. "Think nothing of it."

"Oh, but it was wonderful. The way you handled those ruffians was superb." Unmistakable hero worship shone from Miss Graves's eyes.

"Yes, wonderful, but how did you happen to be there, my lord?" asked Belle.

"I stopped by Lady Beauford's townhouse and was told you had gone out. I decided to follow you."

She gave him a perplexed frown. "How did you find me? My aunt was unaware of my plans to attend the lecture."

Ian felt his hands fisting in his lap. Aye, Lady Beauford had thought her niece was busy shopping. He had known better. The feeling of unease that had settled on him during Belle's discussion with her brother the day before had intensified.

"I had a feeling and searched out Finchley for the particulars. I have noticed that he knows everything that is going on in Town."

"That was well done of you, but why did you come? Are you interested in reform issues as well?"

"Nay. I am interested in you and your safety."

"Oh." She seemed nonplussed. "I don't know how you could have known that I would be facing any sort of danger. I can tell you that for me it was completely unexpected."

Belle's naïve assessment sent his temper spiraling. Turning to her, he gripped her arms. "What were ye thinking of, Belle? You could have been hurt."

A rapid pulse beat at the base of her neck and she trembled

79

slightly under his touch. It reminded him of her body's response to his kiss. For a moment, he forgot about his anger and her near miss. All he could think about was taking her into his arms and pressing his lips to hers. She had responded so sweetly, with innocent passion, in the Markham garden. He silently vowed to further her education in this area at the closest possible opportunity.

She trembled again. Belle might not want to show it, but the fracas had upset her. She took a deep breath before answering him. "It was just a lecture. The men that came turned it into a riot."

He shook his head. She could not be that blind. "After the reaction you got from your brother over that penny print, how could you doubt it?"

She jerked her arms away from him and looked fiercely at him through narrowed eyes. "My brother, or even the reactions of those men, will not stop me from listening to my sisters in the cause speak out."

He felt his insides churn. The words were so like those of his grandfather. The man who had fought England's rule at any cost, including that of his family and the people on his estates. "At what price, Belle, your life or another's?"

She stared at him and the innocent confusion in her eyes added fuel to his rage. She had no idea what risk she took or who might pay the price.

"That's not it at all." Her words came out in a shocked whisper.

He had hurt her. He swore under his breath.

The other woman spoke up from her seat next to Finchley. "Lady Annabelle has done nothing to put her family at risk."

Ian glared at her. "No, it's her own person she's put in danger."

Miss Graves blushed at the rebuke, but did not give up. "When she went to the lecture, she had no way of knowing some unruly men would arrive and cause a scene."

"Was more than a scene, eh what? That chap looked ready to do you and Annabelle some harm." Finchley's voice carried conviction for all of his dandyish ways.

Miss Graves turned to him and smiled tremulously. "Yes, I do believe he was, but you and Laird MacKay appeared at just the right time."

Finchley patted the chit's hand. "Forget about it."

"Bloody hell." Ian wasn't going to be able to forget it. The sight of Annabelle trapped in the corner, trying to shield her friend, would haunt him for the rest of his days.

"My lord, your language," Annabelle chided him.

"My language? What about you? Belle, you shouted like a fishwife and started a riot."

"It is unkind of you to remind me of my behavior. I had great provocation."

"And I dinna?"

She pursed her lips. "I will not debate it with you."

He laughed. He couldn't help it. She was so prim and proper when minutes before she had been abusing a man with her parasol.

Belle frowned at him. "It is hardly gentlemanly to laugh at me, Lord Graenfrae."

"Ian."

She started to shake her head and opened her mouth to speak. He wouldn't let her. "After what we just went through, you can bloody well call me Ian."

She closed her mouth with a pop.

He crossed his arms over his chest and stared at her in silence. She gave him a mutinous frown.

"Well?" he demanded.

"Very well, *Ian.* I can see that it is important to you, although I cannot imagine why."

Satisfied on at least that point, he nodded. "As to why, you ken well enough that I'll no have my wife addressing me by my title."

Her eyes grew wide. "I thought... I mean you haven't... It's impossible." She opened and closed her mouth several times. She closed her eyes for a few moments. When she opened them again, her expression had cleared. "Never mind. If you are finished ringing a peal over me, I will introduce my friend."

He shrugged.

She looked like she wanted to throttle him. He understood the feeling.

"This is Vivian Graves. Miss Graves, I would like you to meet Laird MacKay and Lord Finchley."

"It's a pleasure to make your acquaintance, my lords."

Finchley took her hand and bowed his head over it. "The pleasure is all mine, Miss Graves."

Miss Graves blushed and smiled.

Ian grunted. "Miss Graves, I willna lie. I would rather we had met under other circumstances."

Belle shifted impatiently next to him. "Really, must you continue harping on the unfortunate occurrence? Your resemblance to my old nurse is most regrettable."

Miss Graves gasped. "*Lady Annabelle.*"

Belle tugged her spencer to smooth it. "It's true. Laird MacKay has a lamentable tendency to nag at me like a nursemaid."

He didn't know if he would rather pull her into his lap and kiss her or turn her over his knee. The second image was so ludicrous in the face of her independent nature that he almost laughed aloud. Belle would never tolerate that form of husbandly discipline.

"This inclination you have to laugh at me is most unpleasant, Ian."

"I wasna laughing at you, Belle. 'Twas something I was contemplating."

"Oh." Her shoulders relaxed. They rode in silence until they reached Miss Graves's home. Belle said good-bye to the other woman and Finchley escorted her to the door.

As the coachman drew away from Miss Graves's home, Belle turned to Ian. "Do not speak of me as your future wife in front of others, Ian. It is unseemly."

"What is unseemly about the truth?"

She twisted the strings to her reticule. "I am not your future wife and I do not like being the brunt of gossip because of you." Tears sparkled in her eyes.

Pulling her near, he pressed her face into his coat and massaged her back. "Dinna cry, Belle."

"I'm n-not crying. It's just that you keep saying that I'm going to marry you, but you don't mean it and there was an article about us in the society pages in most unflattering terms, and my...my hand hurts."

He latched on to the last thing she said. Nothing else made sense to him. Of course he meant to marry her. Hadn't he said so? As for the article, he had read it too and been satisfied that the *ton* recognized his claim on Belle. Robert had told Ian that it upset Belle to be the center of gossip. So, Ian had made an effort not to single her out or call on her too frequently.

Pulling away from her, he lifted her hand to examine it. "Let me see, Belle."

When she didn't resist, he drew her glove off, being careful not to squeeze her hand in the process. An ugly purple bruise marked her palm. He wished that he'd taken the time to leave a few bruises of his own on the man who had done this.

"We'll have the doctor look at it."

She stiffened, blinking away the remnants of her tears. "I'm sure that's not necessary. It's just a bruise."

"We must make sure nothing is broken."

"Better safe than sorry, eh what," Finchley said.

"If you are both going to badger me, I suppose that I have no choice."

Ian smiled at her cranky tone. "Aye, Belle, you have no choice." And she had no choice about marrying him either. She would be his. She needed him to watch over her.

CZ

The Scotsman was becoming annoying again. William had thought the laird had moved on to greener pastures. For the past two weeks, he had found the field wide open. William had danced with

Annabelle at soirees and even managed several bouts of uninterrupted conversation. The laird had been conspicuous in his absence and William was certain his suit was progressing nicely.

Now this. Following Annabelle to the lecture had been easy. He hadn't even had to pretend any real interest in the misguided woman speaking.

Property rights for women. Ludicrous. Where would William be now if his dead wife had had control of her own property? She had whined enough about the sad state of her wardrobe and the house. Would she have let him sell her small properties to buy his hunters? Of course not. No one had the right to tell a gentleman how to spend his money. Especially not his wife.

When Lady Annabelle had instigated a riot, William had been incensed. She was weak-minded like the rest of her sex. He had barely escaped the room with his skin intact. His coat had been ripped. A new one was unthinkable right now. His tailor was not receiving him. Him! It was infamous. Did the man not know what a favor William did in giving the tailor his business?

Money. Money was definitely becoming a problem. He needed to marry Lady Annabelle soon or he would lose his hunters and maybe even his freedom to debtor's prison. Maybe he should speak to Spinks again. The man was full of information. Perhaps there was something else William could use to his benefit. He needed stakes for a night of gaming. One good night at the gaming tables would set him up nicely until he could convince the spinster to marry him.

Chapter Seven

Annabelle twirled the pencil lead in her hand and stared at the blank foolscap on her escritoire. She had come to her room for some needed peace and quiet. The soft lavender walls and white bed hangings offered refuge from her tumbling thoughts. She smiled at the posy of violets her maid had placed on the white gilded table at which she sat. Purdy liked to remind her mistress that for all her modern ways, she was still a lady.

She couldn't focus on writing her treatise on women's issues. Her mind insisted on dwelling on the previous day's events. Had she truly cried all over Ian's shirtfront?

He had indeed insisted on calling for the doctor. Aunt Griselda had been beside herself and all over a little bruise. Okay, not so little. Her hand had throbbed well into the night, although the doctor had treated it with a topical salve. Surely that was why she had such trouble sleeping. It was merely coincidence that she spent the dark hours tossing and turning as images of furious brown eyes flashed through her mind.

Ian had been so angry. It made no sense. The day before he had defended her to Robert, but when he rescued her from the riot he had been livid. And then he had held her when she cried. His hands had been so gentle against the back of her spencer. She still tingled when she thought of him rubbing circles on her back.

She scratched a few lines on the foolscap. Looking down at the paper she couldn't even remember what she had written. Restless, she stood up and moved to gaze out the window. The brown air of Town put a pall over the beautiful garden behind her aunt's townhouse. She did not want to go back downstairs and listen to further lectures on her behavior. Lady Beauford had not exhausted her ire and continued to chastise Annabelle with very little provocation. To hear her aunt or Ian, one would think that she had deliberately put her very life at risk.

Ridiculous. The man who had called her *ducks* had indeed been angry, but not murderously so. It would be worse tonight. Undoubtedly Aunt Griselda would inform Robert of Annabelle's mishap when they met at the theater later that evening. Her one consolation was that Ian had declined her aunt's invitation to join them. She would at least avoid his disappointment.

She did not understand his refusal. For a man who must marry within the year, he was taking quite a cavalier attitude toward courtship. She paced to her wardrobe and looked through the simple gowns inside. A few were actually quite lovely. She had found some vibrant color combinations that she liked. Her aunt had approved. Being on the shelf had its advantages.

Mr. Green had complimented her attire on more than one occasion. Ian should take some lessons from the young gentleman. Perhaps she would tell him so.

☙

Ceddy joined Annabelle and her family in Lady Beauford's box. She couldn't quite summon a smile of welcome for her old friend. His and Ian's interference had led to a rather ugly bear-jawing by her brother earlier. Aunt Griselda had not waited until they met at the theater to tell him about Annabelle's mishap.

"This seat taken?" Ceddy asked with obvious deference.

She inclined her head. "You may sit there if you wish."

He cleared his throat twice before speaking. "Lady Beauford still angry with you?"

She knew what he was asking. He wanted to know if *she* was still angry with *him*. "A little."

His face fell. "Sorry to hear that, don't you know?"

Yes, she did know, but she could not help it. Annabelle still smarted from some of the things Robert had said earlier. He had accused her of not caring about him or the family name. His final words of thankfulness that she was all right had done little to assuage the pain in her heart at his allegations. She sighed heavily.

Ceddy looked at her with alarm. "Feeling quite the thing?"

"I'm fine." Her hand still pained her, but she wasn't about to admit it. "Ceddy, I do appreciate you and Ian showing up when you did yesterday."

He leaned his head to one side. "Thought you weren't too happy when MacKay went for the doctor."

Annabelle grimaced. "No. I was left with a great deal of explaining to do to Aunt Griselda. She was terribly upset to discover I had attended the lecture. That was nothing compared to Robert's reaction when he found out."

"Regret that, don't you know?"

She nodded. It was no use staying angry with Ceddy. "Apology accepted." He had not been the one to insist on telling her aunt anyway. "Where is Ian tonight?" She hadn't meant to ask that.

Ceddy tugged on his ear and harrumphed a couple of times. "He's about, I'm sure." His gaze slid to a box opposite theirs.

Annabelle's eyes followed his and her heart constricted. Ian, the blackguard, was sitting for the entire polite world to see, next to Miss Caruthers. Annabelle wanted to say something pithy, but could not speak past the lump in her throat. So, he was not interested in beautiful women? She wanted to look away, but could not make herself.

Ian chose that moment to look her way. He inclined his head in acknowledgement. She ignored him and finally managed to turn away. She stared toward the stage, her eyes unfocused while her heart cracked into a million little pieces.

It was Freddy Jenkins all over again. Only this time it hurt, bone deep. Freddy had courted her for an entire Season before discovering that his heart belonged to the beautiful Miss Potts. The only thing injured that Season had been Annabelle's pride. As Diana had reminded her, she had been able to laugh. She didn't feel like laughing now.

"I say, Annabelle, are you all right?" Ceddy's worried tones penetrated the fog of pain surrounding her.

"Yes, of course." She flicked the moisture from her eyes with her gloved fingertip. "I'm just impatient for the play to start. Do you suppose it is as funny as everyone says it is?"

Ceddy didn't look as if he believed her, but mercifully the curtain went up on the first act of *As You Like It*. Annabelle forced herself to laugh when those around her laughed. By the time intermission came, she had better control of her emotions.

Diana touched Annabelle's arm. "My hem caught on the carriage when we arrived. Won't you come to the ladies' retiring room with me to fix it?"

Annabelle latched on to the excuse to leave the box. Ian might come during intermission to chat with Robert. If he could pull himself away from Miss Caruthers, that is. "Certainly."

When Robert made noises about escorting them, Annabelle looked imploringly at Ceddy. Her friend understood immediately.

"I'm hankering for a cup of punch, myself. I'll escort them."

Annabelle stifled a sigh of relief when Robert agreed. She and Diana followed Ceddy out of the box.

"Is anything the matter, Annabelle? Was not the first act exceedingly amusing?" asked Diana.

Annabelle forced a smile. "It was too funny by half."

"Annabelle, I know that Robert rang a peal over you earlier, but you must realize that he did not mean to injure your feelings. He was scared for you and when your brother gets frightened he can act like a fool."

Diana's fervent words brought a genuine smile to Annabelle's lips. "A fool, Diana?"

"Yes, a fool. And you may tell him I said so. Though I doubt it will do any good. I've already told him myself."

Annabelle said, "You are a true friend."

Diana squeezed Annabelle's arm. "Now and forever."

Annabelle returned the gesture of affection. "Thank you. You may set your mind at rest. Robert has not done any lasting damage to my feelings." If only the same could be said for Ian.

Diana searched Annabelle's face. "If you say so."

"I do. Now, let us take care of your hem."

Ceddy agreed to wait for them in the lobby. They made quick work of Diana's hem. Annabelle discovered that she needed to use the necessary.

"I'll wait in the lobby with Ceddy. It's much too warm in here," declared Diana, fanning herself vigorously with a silk fan dyed blue to match her overdress.

Ceddy must have gone for refreshments because he was not waiting when Diana came into the lobby. She decided to stand just beyond the door of the powder room, so that she could easily see Annabelle emerging or Ceddy returning. Robert would be furious to know that she was by herself in the lobby. She could not face the heat of the room filled with women. It made her nauseous.

Taking a deep breath to dispel the sensation, she scanned the crowd for any sign of Ceddy. A man approached her. He did not look as if he had shaved in a week and his clothing was a rude parody of the clothing her husband wore to perfection. She shivered. Perhaps she should return to Annabelle.

He did not give her the chance before boldly greeting her.

"You'd be Lady Hamilton?" His voice held an insolent edge.

She turned to go back to the overheated room without acknowledging him. His next words startled her into immobility.

"You and I would be related, we would."

Diana stared. Her mouth opened but nothing came out.

"You look as if you don't believe me. Well, our grandfather had taste for other women besides his wife and I'm the living proof," said the offensive man.

Suddenly, Diana's power of speech returned. "I don't know to what you are referring and if you do not cease speaking to me, I will be forced to call for help."

"Oh, high and mighty, aren't we? Just how uppity are you going to be when I make our family attachment public?"

She could not believe what the man was saying. She, related to this ruffian? It could not be true. "You must be mad."

His smile made her shiver. "Do you think I would make such claims without proof? Not Chester P. Thorn." He patted his breast. "I've got letters written by our grandfather to my grandmother, an uncommon pretty bit of fluff in her day."

Diana felt faint. Five minutes before she had been much too hot. Now she felt like ice ran through her veins. The very thought of Thorn claiming a familial relationship sent all the air flying from her lungs. Robert would be appalled to have his wife the center of such an ugly scandal.

Thorn chuckled nastily. "You are beginning to see things my way, I think."

"What do you want?" She forced the words from lips barely able to move.

"Nothing too much. It's time your side of the family shared a little of the goods with my side, meanin' me. I thought you might want the letters as mementos of our grandfather. I could not give them to you for nothing, naturally. They should be worth a few hundred pounds to you for sentimental reasons."

She wanted to slap Thorn's greedy grin right off his face. She had never been so angry in all her life. Nor so helpless. She tried to rally. "How do I know you really have these letters? I'm sure your family would have tried to sell them before if you did."

"My grandmother had her own code of conduct, for all the good it did her. I didn't find them until the old bird passed away a month ago. She had 'em hidden in her room." He pulled a piece of folded stationary from the pocket of his rumpled coat. "Brought one along for you to see."

He wouldn't let her hold it, but even from a distance she recognized her grandfather's bold scrawl. The ink swam on the page before her. Her grandfather wrote in such a way that there could be no doubt that he was on intimate terms with the recipient of the letter. She blinked away useless tears. Crying would do no good. This disgusting little man had her in his power and he knew it.

"Now, don't try to weasel out of sharing the goods. You could come up with plenty o' loot selling those pretty baubles around your neck."

Diana's hand flew to her neck and grasped the flawless pearls Robert had presented her with on the day of their wedding. What he suggested was impossible.

"You'll be hearing from me. Be ready when you do." With those final words, Thorn melted away in the crowd.

Within moments Ceddy had returned. "Should have waited with Annabelle, eh what? Don't know who might accost you in a public place like this." Diana almost laughed hysterically at Ceddy's chastisement. She wished with all her heart she had stayed in the stifling powder room.

Ian brushed the curtain aside to enter Lady Beauford's box. He searched for Belle and swore under his breath when he realized she was not there.

Hamilton greeted him. "Annabelle has gone to help my wife with her hem."

Ian's brows rose in question. "You didna go with them?"

Hamilton cleared his throat and tugged the sleeves of his already impeccable coat. "Finchley accompanied them."

Ian stared at Belle's brother and tried to fathom the message in the other man's eyes. "Why?"

With another man he would not be surprised, but Hamilton let his wife out of his sight only under duress.

"I am not in either of their good graces right now."

Ian nodded in understanding. "Lady Beauford told you about Belle's adventure yesterday."

"Adventure? She could have been seriously injured."

Ian felt a rush of sympathy for the other man. It could not be easy being the brother of a woman as independent as Belle. He knew being her husband was going to be a challenge.

Once he got her to agree.

At least Hamilton's words explained Belle's refusal to acknowledge him. She was angry with him for telling her aunt about the riot. He had no intention of letting her get away with sulking. "I'll see about finding her in the lobby then."

Hamilton's shoulders stiffened. "I believe I would care for some refreshments. I will come with you."

"Do not let us detain you then." Belle spoke from the entryway. She moved forward to take her seat, giving her brother a cursory nod and ignoring Ian altogether.

Lady Hamilton sat down next to Belle, giving the impression that she had not seen either man. Hamilton frowned. Finchley came in. He offered Lady Beauford, who had been dozing in her chair, some punch.

"What, oh thank you, Cederic." Belle's aunt patted Finchley's arm. "You are a very thoughtful boy."

Ian took the chair next to Annabelle. "Good evening, Belle. Enjoying the play?"

"My lord. I thought you and Robert were leaving." She did not look at him as she spoke.

"I was coming to look for you. I dinna need to leave now."

She opened her fan and began waving it before her, still keeping her eyes focused away from him. She looked regal as a queen in her gown of silver net over a pale green underskirt. Her hair had been piled on top of her head. Curling tendrils escaped and tempted him to touch them.

Finchley offered her some punch.

She turned to greet him with a smile and Ian felt jealousy flash through him. "Thank you, Ceddy, you are always kind." She finally turned to face Ian. "My lord, I believe you have taken Ceddy's chair."

He glared at Finchley and his friend shook his head in denial. "Not at all. I believe I will go try my charms on your aunt, don't you know?" He was gone before Belle could protest.

"Finchley was there yesterday, too, Belle. Surely, I dinna deserve all your wrath."

Her shoulders lifted in a movement of disdain. "He did not insist on going for the doctor or alerting my aunt to the afternoon's events."

He was right. Her anger from the day before was still fresh. "Belle, you canna continue in this independent fashion."

"What I can or cannot do is of no concern to you."

"You are mistaken if you think that, lass. I'll no have my wife putting her life at risk."

She went back to gazing out at the audience. "Then I suggest you save your breath for Miss Caruthers."

How had Miss Caruthers gotten into their discussion? The beauty could do as she pleased. Ian had concern only for the stubborn woman sitting next to him.

Insight came slowly. "You're jealous."

Her fan closed with a snap. "Don't be ridiculous. I merely think you should save these little lectures for the lady who holds your true interest."

He did not like the unhappy timbre of her voice. "I'm no interested in Miss Caruthers."

She turned blazing eyes to him. "You have exhibited many faults since I met you, my lord. You are arrogant and make erroneous assumptions. Until now I had always at least believed you to be a man of honesty."

"*I havena lied to you.*" Several heads turned at his roar.

"You are causing a scene."

He stood up. "Finchley, please make my excuses to Miss Caruthers." Ian turned to Belle's aunt. "Lady Beauford, your niece is a trifle overset. I will see her home."

He extended his hand to Belle. "Come."

She glared at him for a full minute before giving a miniscule shrug and standing. "The evening is ruined already. I may as well go home, but I would rather Ceddy escorted me."

"Finchley has other business to attend to."

When she looked like she would argue, he grasped her hand and turned to leave the theater.

Belle did not say another word until he had placed her in his carriage. "I hope you are satisfied with this night's work, my lord. Dragging me from my aunt's box is bound to make us the latest *on-dit* for many a day."

The carriage lamps illuminated her mutinous expression.

"I didna drag you and my name is Ian." Her eyes widened at his enraged tone. Good. "Say it."

"There is no reason to shout."

"Say it."

She winced. "Ian." She crossed her arms over her chest and frowned at him. "I've said it. Now you can stop shouting."

He nodded and spoke in a more reasonable tone. "Explain to me again why you think I lied."

"Do not order me about."

"'Twas a reasonable request."

"It was not a request."

She was going to make him daft before he finished courting her. He asked with overstressed courtesy, "Would you please explain to me why you think I have lied?"

"You said that you didn't want to marry a beautiful woman."

That was all? "I didna lie, Belle. How was I to ken ye'd change from one meeting to the next?"

"What are you talking about?"

This conversation was getting more bizarre by the minute. "I swear, Belle, I dinna understand the way your mind works."

"You said you would not marry a beautiful woman and you have given up courting me to pursue Miss Caruthers. Either you lied or changed your mind. Neither speaks well of your honor."

Pain lanced through him at her accusation. Just as his family had done, Belle assumed that the only excuse for his actions precluded integrity. His parents had believed that he had acted dishonorably when he cried off from his engagement to Jenna. He had not told them about the incident in the garden, but it should not have mattered. His stepfather and his mother should have believed in him.

As should Belle. "Ye believe I am without honor?"

Belle's expression changed. He watched as first confusion, then uncertainty clouded her eyes. She sighed heavily. "No."

A band that had been constricting Ian's heart loosened.

"The only woman of beauty I would willingly marry is you."

Her eyes widened. "You think I'm beautiful?"

"Aye, Belle."

Her expression said that she did not believe him. He waited for her to call him a liar again. When she did not, he began to relax.

She uncrossed her arms and stared at the reticule in her lap, playing with its strings. "I was not talking about me."

"But you are the lady I want to marry."

"Then why did you escort Miss Caruthers to the theater and refuse Robert's invitation?" When he did not answer fast enough, she gasped. "I will not believe it."

Now what had her fertile imagination conjured up? "I probably willna either."

She ignored him. "You will not marry me and take another lady as your paramour."

His temper exploded. "Ye will no question my honor in this way." She huffed in outrage when he pulled her into his arms. "I dinna want a paramour. I want a wife." He ground the words out past the anger in his chest, his lips almost touching hers.

She trembled at the intimate touch. She twisted her body in his lap. "Let me go."

Her squirming rapidly turned his fury to another, stronger, emotion. Passion. He tightened his hold on her, reveling in the torture of having her body so close. "Nay, Belle. I'll no let you go."

Her struggles ceased the moment his lips covered hers. It was as if she was too shocked to move. Ian took advantage of her confusion

95

and deepened the kiss. He let go of her waist and buried his hands in her hair, untying the ribbon that held the silken mass atop her head. It tumbled over his hands. He felt all control desert him. He barely had enough sanity to reach out and close the curtains on the carriage windows. This is what he had wanted since the night of the Markham ball.

She renewed her struggles to get free. She pulled her mouth from his and he concentrated on kissing her shell-pink ear. She shivered. "Ian, you must stop."

"Nay."

"We were having an important discussion."

He kissed her throat and she groaned. His lips moved back to cover hers. "We will finish our argument later."

She sighed against his lips. "Very well, but it was not an argument." He would have disagreed with her. 'Twas definitely an argument, but she tugged his mouth close for a deeper kiss. He obliged her willingly, sliding his tongue into her mouth and exploring its warmth.

She moved restlessly in his lap and he grew hard in response. It felt so good. She was like sunshine on the heather-strewn hills of home. His hand dipped to caress her soft flesh through her bodice. She whimpered.

Her head tilted back. The look of utter abandon on her face pushed him over the edge. He was desperate to see her. Slipping the tiny cap sleeves of her gown down her arm, he freed her breasts. Pulling back, he took a moment just to feast on the sight of her bare skin. The flawless shape of each creamy white mound peaked in a pink succulent nipple.

"Perfect."

She expelled the breath she had been holding. He cupped one breast, tenderly playing with the nipple between his thumb and forefinger. She acted as if she had been jolted with an electricity machine.

"*Ian.*"

"Hush, Belle, 'tis all right, lass." He continued his ministrations as she moaned with increasing passion. She mindlessly rubbed her backside against him. Thoughts of embedding himself in her body filled his mind. Breaking his lips away from her mouth, he trailed hot kisses down her neck and to her breast. When he took her already taut nipple in his mouth, she screamed.

He sucked rhythmically, thinking of all that he wanted to do to her sweet body. She was coming apart in his arms and he loved it. He moved his hand under her skirt. Feeling her silk pantalets, he groaned. When his fingers encountered the slit in the fabric between her legs, he growled in satisfaction. She tried to press her legs together and squirm off his lap.

Her movements nearly pushed him past control. He spoke soft words of reassurance in her ear and moved his hand over her breasts. He prayed she would not make him stop. He wanted to give her pleasure. He needed to give her pleasure.

She began to writhe. "*Ian, do something.*"

He smiled at her demand. "I am, Belle, trust me."

He slipped one finger into her tight heat and kissed her, using his tongue to imitate the movement of his finger. She writhed more frantically against him. He placed his thumb on the sweet button above where his finger did its gentle dance.

She tore her mouth from his. "No. Stop. I can't..."

He fondled her breast with his other hand. "Trust me." He kissed her again. Soft tender kisses that turned passionate as she moved against his hand.

"*Ian.*"

"Aye, Belle. That's it, lass."

She went completely rigid and then convulsed around his hand. She cried out and collapsed against him. He kissed her once more. Taking several deep breaths, he tried to get his raging passion under control. He had never wanted another woman like he wanted Belle. He wasn't going to take her for the first time in a carriage in the London fog though.

She hid her face against his chest. "That was amazing."

He smiled at the awe in her voice. "Aye, it was."

Chapter Eight

Annabelle's heart had begun to slow, but she doubted she would ever be the same again. No wonder Diana liked being married so much. She nestled closer to Ian, his distinctly masculine scent surrounding her. The rapid tattoo of his heart against her ear gave her pleasure. He had been as affected as she even though he hadn't...her thoughts trailed off.

"You didn't..." She couldn't go on.

Lifting her chin, he met her eyes. "Not this time."

The tenderness she saw in his gaze washed over her wounded heart. "You wanted to."

"Yes."

She sighed and snuggled against his chest. "Thank you."

He righted her clothes and continued to hold her. "You're welcome."

She played with the button on his waistcoat and enjoyed the feel of his arms around her. "Ian, it seems to be taking an inordinate amount of time to get home. Had you noticed?"

"I told my coachman to drive around until I signaled otherwise."

Her head flew up. "Did you know we were going to...to do this?" The thought that he could be that certain of her when she had been so angry left her insides churning.

He shook his head. "Nay, Belle. I wanted to talk without interruption."

She giggled. "I'd say we were interrupted."

"Aye." She heard the satisfaction in his voice.

"Ian?"

"Hmmm?"

"Why did you go to the theater with Miss Caruthers?"

"Hamilton told me that you were upset when our names were linked in the gossip column." He wrapped her hair around his hand and rubbed the strands with his thumb.

She leaned back to look in his eyes. "You were trying to protect me from gossip?"

He nodded.

"I don't understand."

"I didna mark you for attention and spent time with Miss Caruthers so that it would not be so clear I was courting you."

She stared at him without speaking and then she burst out laughing. She laughed so hard that tears trailed down her cheeks. He commanded her to stop. When she didn't, he shook her lightly. "Stop that, Belle. What is so funny?"

She gasped for air. "Ian, you do not understand the ways of the *ton* very well."

He wasn't happy to hear that if his suddenly rigid body and angry eyes were any indication. She wanted to laugh some more, but controlled herself. "There will still be gossip."

"Why?"

She shook her head at his ignorance. "Our names have already been linked. Those who have noted your lack of interest and your escort of Miss Caruthers will assume you have given up courting me in favor of her."

Like Annabelle had.

"What would I want with her?" Ian asked.

"Do not be dense, my lord. Miss Caruthers is beautiful and most gentlemen would be pleased to gain her interest."

"I am no most gentlemen."

She smiled against his chest. He seemed to be waiting for her agreement. "No, you are not."

Ian's tense muscles relaxed. "You must call me Ian now. A wife should not call her husband 'my lord'."

She sat up straight to look in his eyes. "We have had this discussion many times."

"Aye."

"I do call you Ian sometimes."

"As my wife, you will always use my name."

"But I'm not your wife."

Comprehension emerged at the look of complacency on his face. "Ian, you cannot believe that I am now going to marry you because of what just happened."

"I bloody well do."

"Do not swear at me."

"You are going to marry me, Belle."

She scooted off of his lap to the opposite seat in the carriage. "I am not going to marry you, Ian."

She was thankful for the dim light in the carriage. Ian's glare was intimidating enough and she could barely see him.

"After what happened, do you deny that you love me?"

"Should I now believe that you love me?"

"Men are different."

She did not know if she wanted to cry or box his ears. She ended up shouting instead. "*So, you are saying that any woman could have been in your arms just now?*"

"Dinna be foolish."

"Do not call me a fool."

"I didna call you a fool."

The urge to cry grew stronger.

He grabbed her hand and yanked her back into his lap. He pressed her backside against him. She felt his hardness. "Do you feel that, Belle?"

She squirmed in anger and embarrassment. "Don't." Her voice cracked.

"Do you feel it?" His words were no longer angry, but had grown gentle.

She nodded, refusing to answer.

"Belle, no other woman has ever affected me like you do."

Her eyes flew to his. "No one?"

"No one."

"Not even your ex-fiancée?"

"No."

"But it doesn't mean you love me."

"It means I want you to marry me."

"Ian, passion is not love and I cannot marry you if you do not love me." She wanted to bury her head against his waistcoat and bawl like a baby.

He pressed her face against his chest and soothed her. "We will not discuss this anymore right now."

They would discuss it again soon, though. She was sure of it. The thought left her both dreading the next time and relieved that Ian had not given her up for Miss Caruthers.

ᔆ

Annabelle walked into her aunt's garden unnoticed by Diana and Robert. The smell of freshly tilled earth attested to Aunt Griselda's recent efforts in the flowerbeds. Daffodils fluttered in the soft spring breeze and their bright yellow reflected the warm rays of the midmorning sun.

Her brother was gone on his favorite subject, farming. "Diana, this is really something to take note of. Aunt Griselda has certainly made extensive research into the proper planting patterns for her herbs."

He pointed at a clump of purple and green leaves surrounded by tall stalks of green shoots. "Look at this basil near the garlic. I'm told planted that close together the one picks up the flavor of the other."

"Robert, I'm sure that is all that is interesting, but can we not just enjoy the flowers without discussing the merits of planting one closer to the other?"

"I'm discussing herbs, dear, not flowers. Look at this-"

Annabelle interrupted her brother's discourse. "Robert, I think Diana is trying to tell you that she does not share your interest in horticulture."

Robert and Diana both swung around to face her. "Alas, no, but then I cannot expect my wife to enjoy everything I do." His indulgent tone of voice made Annabelle smile.

Diana rolled her eyes and Annabelle found it difficult not to laugh. She greeted her friend with a hug.

"Hello, Diana. Cresswell informed me you were out here." She turned to her brother. "Hello, Robert."

Diana squeezed her arm. "Annabelle, you look delightful." Honest admiration mixed with ill-concealed surprise in her tone.

Annabelle couldn't hide an amused smile. "Thank you."

She looked down at her dress. The skirt tiered to her ankles in several layers of bottle-green gauze cut like Gypsy scarves. The high-waisted bodice had small cap sleeves that ended in points like the skirt. She liked the gown. It made her think of woodland fairies.

Recalling her previous discussion with Diana about fashion, she said, "I believe I am finally finding my style."

Diana looked at her with a critical eye. "Yes, I do believe you are."

"Annabelle has always had her own style," Robert asserted.

Annabelle smiled at her brother's staunch support. "Thank you, Robert. You're the best of brothers. Aunt Griselda did not tell me you were planning to call today." They must have made their plans after Ian and she left the theater the night before. "It's a glorious day for meandering in the garden."

Diana laughed. "Robert is regaling me with his knowledge of herbs."

Robert drew himself up. "Now that my sister is here, there is no reason for you to bore yourself with my company. I'm sure MacKay will appreciate Aunt's herb beds even if you do not."

Diana patted his arm soothingly. "Calm down, Robert. I have no intention of abandoning you just because Annabelle has joined us. I'm sure she would be delighted to hear your thoughts on gardening."

Annabelle nodded. "Delighted."

Robert laughed. "I'm not in the least bit fooled. You two baggages can go gossip. MacKay will be here soon enough."

Diana reached up and planted a kiss on her husband's cheek. "Very well, dear, but we won't desert you completely. We will go have our coze on that stone bench over there."

Robert smiled at his wife, obviously forgetting that he considered public affection unseemly. Diana indicated that Annabelle should follow her.

"Wait a moment." Annabelle did not move. "Robert, did you say that Ian was coming to call this morning?"

She did not want to face Ian today. Her body still reacted every time she thought of their interlude in the carriage. She had woken twice in the night, hot and aching after dreaming about him. She was not ready to confront him in the flesh.

"We are going to the museum. MacKay told me that you wanted to go."

She did want to go, just not today. Besides, she had plans today. Not that she had any intention of telling Robert. She'd listened to more than she wanted to from him on the subject of her involvement in women's rights already.

"He did not ask me about today." She frowned.

Robert said, "I'm sure it was an oversight."

"Indeed." She moved away from Robert to look at her aunt's prize rosebush. It was not yet in bloom, but buds had formed on several of the branches. "Then he will not be disappointed when you and Diana are his only companions on the excursion."

"Do you have other plans today?" Diana's obvious regret pricked at Annabelle's determination not to go. Now that her friend was married, excursions together were not nearly as common as they once were.

"It's simply that I'm not sure I want to spend the day with Ian." She knew her friend would understand and from the look of compassion on Diana's face, she was right. Robert was not so easily swayed, however.

"Annabelle, it is time you stopped being so intractable about this. MacKay is courting you. How will you know if you wish to marry him if you do not spend time with the man?"

She sighed. "Robert, he wants to marry me because he thinks I'm an aging spinster desperate for marriage."

"He is being practical. I wish you would be a little more so. I want to see you married."

She would be deeply offended if she did not know that her brother was motivated by genuine love and concern for her. He truly believed that she would be happy as a wife and mother.

"Ian's reasons for marrying me don't make any sense."

Robert jumped to defense of his friend. "MacKay's views are logical based on what he wishes to do for his tenants."

"What of his wife?" Diana asked.

Robert turned to her. "Diana, you and I both know that Annabelle is all that is wonderful in a woman and will make an excellent wife. Ian will be the ideal husband for her."

Annabelle had heard enough. Ideal? When the man refused to even discuss love. Even after what they had shared in the carriage. "Will he love me as you love Diana? Will he be unfashionably willing to live in my pocket as you often seek to be with Diana?"

Her heart constricted at the thought of Ian expressing even a fraction of the devotion to her that Robert showed his wife. "Will he cherish me and care only for me and never look at another woman with that look men get when a beautiful woman enters the room? Will he be an ideal lover as well as husband?"

She knew her words were improper, but they were torn from the very depths of her soul.

The skin on Robert's neck turned a rosy shade. He tugged at his cravat. "Annabelle, those are not questions that I could possibly answer and I hope you would not pose them to MacKay."

How unfair of Robert to think that she did not need the very things he gave his wife. "Are these not promises you made to Diana in your courtship?"

The blush spread from his neck to his face and her brother refused to meet Annabelle's eyes. "That is not the point. You should not be discussing these things with me."

"But, Robert, you have just told me I cannot discuss them with the man you think I should consider marrying. Is it because Diana is lovely and I am plain? Do I not deserve the same care and consideration?"

"You are all that is lovely, Annabelle. I won't hear you criticizing yourself this way." He frowned fiercely at her. "It is simply something not done. A lady does not discuss these things," replied Robert, this time sounding quite desperate.

She had shocked her brother enough. It was not his fault that Ian wanted to marry her for all of the wrong reasons.

Diana brushed her husband's coat sleeve to gain his attention. When he turned to face her, she spoke. "Robert, there are many women of the *ton* who would be pleased to accept a gentleman without their affections being engaged."

Robert nodded, obviously pleased at the agreement of his wife. Annabelle, who knew her friend better, waited for Diana to take up her defense. She was not disappointed.

"In fact, that is the norm for a society marriage, but your parents had something different. We have something different and that is all that Annabelle wants."

Robert frowned, looking harassed. "Yes but, Diana, you and Annabelle must see that if the other is the norm it is because love between suitable parties is not."

"Perhaps, but if I could not be married to you, I would rather not be married at all," replied his wife.

Diana's voice had risen in agitation and Annabelle sensed that something lay behind her friends words, something she did not understand.

Robert remained oblivious. "Sweet sentiments, to be sure. However, if all the *ton* felt as you do, many successions would die out."

"Are you saying that you do not share my sweet sentiments?"

Her friend sounded truly distressed. Annabelle felt guilty for starting a quarrel between Robert and Diana.

"That is a foolish question, dearest. I did marry you."

Diana's face blanched. "Yes, but I cannot help thinking you would not have done so if I had not been eminently suitable." She spoke in almost a whisper.

Robert drew her near and kissed her. Annabelle smiled through her surprise. Her brother was human after all.

"You are intent on quarreling over nothing of import." He brushed his wife's cheek. "You were suitable and we are married. Can we not cease this discussion?"

He waited for Diana to answer.

Finally, she nodded. "Yes. I'm sorry. I still think Annabelle is entitled to marry for love if she wishes to."

"No one is going to force her to marry MacKay."

Annabelle almost laughed at Robert's words. Her brother suffered under a delusion if he thought anyone was capable of forcing her to marry. Love was the only thing that could drive her to enter the wedded state.

The skin on the back of her neck prickled. She turned slowly toward the house, knowing what she would find. Ian stood framed in the doorway. He looked much too virile in his coat of blue superfine and buff pantaloons that accentuated his muscled thighs. Memories of how those hard thighs felt under her own made her cheeks grow warm.

Ian walked toward her, ignoring both her brother and sister-in-law, until he stood mere inches away. He caressed her face with his gaze. He took several moments to look at her before speaking. She waited, not even breathing, for him to say something. How would he respond to her after last evening?

He reached out and touched her cheek. "Hello, Belle. I've missed you."

The words, spoken after a separation of less than twenty-four hours, should have seemed absurd. They didn't.

"I missed you too, Ian."

All thought of refusing to accompany him and the others on their outing fled from her mind.

೮෩

Blackmail could be a tidy source of income. Who would have believed that his luck could have changed so completely? First, to have stumbled on the truth about Lady Annabelle's fortune. Now this, a tidy packet of letters that would raise an ugly scandal if they were made public, had fallen into his lap.

To think the letters affected Lady Hamilton, his intended's best friend and sister-in-law. The entire *ton* knew how her husband indulged her. It was too good to be true, for anyone but William. When he was finished plucking Lady Hamilton's plump purse, he would find a way to use the letters to further his advantage with Lady Annabelle. There would be a way. His luck demanded it.

William walked into the seedy pub, tugging his cloak more firmly about his face. His cohort should be waiting at a table near the fireplace. He spied Thorn. The man looked like a proper villain, unlike William. William could never have carried off the blackmail bit. He was too refined.

"How did it go?"

Thorn jumped. "Ah, it's you, guv. Went just like you said it would. She turned white as a bloody sheet on a nobleman's bed. She'll pay alright."

William nodded. He knew it. Lady Hamilton *loved* her husband and her husband had a horror of scandal. Another tidbit the entire *ton* was privy to.

"Send her a message where to meet you with the money."

Thorn shifted in his seat and slid a sidelong glance at William. "I don't write so good, guv."

What was the weasel up to? Stench from the man's unwashed body assailed William's nostrils and he wanted to gag. Soon, he would not need to consort with any but his own class. For now, this degenerate was a necessary part of his plan.

"You will write the note."

The miscreant shrugged. "I'm thinking I might need a little more loot to go on. This is a risky business."

William leaned across the table and curled his fingers around Thorn's throat. The other man's eyes began to bulge.

"You will send the message and you will accept the risk. You have given your word and a gentleman keeps his word."

The dirty man bobbed his head. William let go of the other man's throat, satisfied when his associate choked and wheezed an apology before making a hasty exit from the stew.

Soon, very soon, William would have the money he needed to court his prey properly.

It would not be necessary if that stupid Scotsman had stuck with Caruthers. The beauty had not been subtle at all in her preference for him. None of Lady Annabelle's other suitors worried William. She did not look at them like they mattered, even if they were proper Englishmen.

Not like she looked at Graenfrae.

William had seen her with the Scotsman in her aunt's box the night before. So had everyone else in the theater. The way the barbarian had drug her from the theater had been on everyone's tongue. The oaf did not have a clue how to court a lady properly. William would show the boorish Scot, as he engaged Lady Annabelle's affections for himself.

He laughed and the tavern wench who had come to serve his ale stepped back quickly.

"It's daft, you are."

Her words could not touch him. She would see. Everyone would see.

William's luck had changed.

Chapter Nine

The classic Greek columns of the British Museum struck a discordant note with the bustle of London. Carriages and pedestrians vied for space on the busy thoroughfare in front of the museum's entrance.

Ian longed for the quiet solitude of Graenfrae.

Annabelle must make up her mind to marry him soon. He would not last the Season breathing the brown air of London and listening to the cacophony of sounds that greeted him at every turn. Annabelle certainly didn't mind the bustle. She sat next to him, her eyes darting alertly from one scene to the next.

After their initial greeting she had looked at everyone but him and tried to evade speaking to him at all. The lass was going to drive him daft. One minute she was soft and willing in his arms and the next denying she wanted to marry him. Her eyes had devoured him in her aunt's garden and now she wouldn't look at him if his pantaloons caught fire.

"It won't work, you ken." He spoke near her ear so that Hamilton and his wife would not hear.

She jolted, but she continued to keep her gaze fixed on the approaching museum. "What do you mean?"

He waited patiently for her to meet his eyes.

Finally, she turned her head and repeated her question. "What won't work?"

"Ignoring me, Belle. I'll have my way in the end and pretending I'm not here isn't going to change that." He wanted to smile when her eyes narrowed. He could feel her body tensing next to him.

"I thought we were going to discuss this later," she hissed.

"'Tis later, lass."

He had her full attention now. "I do not wish to discuss things of an intimate nature with an audience." She indicated Hamilton and Lady Hamilton with an inclination of her head.

The couple wouldn't notice if he took Belle in his arms and kissed her. They were too busy looking raptly into one another's eyes and whispering ridiculous nonsense. If Belle wanted this from marriage, she would be disappointed. Ian had no intention of making a fool of himself over his wife.

He would not mind kissing her, though. The thought conjured up the scene in the carriage the night before and he felt himself reacting physically. He could still hear her moans of innocent abandon. Willing his body to be still, he shifted on the seat.

"Very well, when would you like to discuss our future?"

"Not now."

He had already gathered that. "When?" he pressed.

"I don't know. Must we have this discussion yet again? Hasn't everything of import already been said on the subject?"

Her voice had a desperate edge. She must realize that her continuing refusal was futile. The woman came apart in his arms. If she thought he was going to leave her to experience passion with someone else now that he had introduced her to it, she was in for a shock. The very idea filled him with fury.

"You needn't glare at me like that. If you are that set on going over our circumstances again, I will do so." She managed to convey an attitude of long-suffering with her sigh.

He nodded. "I will call on you tomorrow to take you driving." The time had come to settle matters.

"Very well." She sighed again. As the carriage drew near the front door of the museum, she perked up. "I cannot wait to see the antiquity room. It is my favorite place in the museum."

Later in the antiquity room, Belle's rapturous expression did not dim. Ian could not understand what she saw in the jumble of poorly maintained Greek and Roman statuary. The pieces were covered with a gray film, undoubtedly due to the smog-filled air of London. The room was much too small and poorly lit to display them with any effect and yet Belle moved among the figures as if she were in God's own antechamber.

Hamilton and his wife had cried off coming in with them. Lady Hamilton had declared that Belle would take more time in the antiquities room than they would take in the entire museum. Hamilton had suggested they meet in an hour's time. It appeared they would be spending the entire hour in this dusty, close room.

Careful not to touch it, Belle bent close to a bust and intently studied it. "Do you see the nobility of expression on this woman's face? She's really quite lovely."

'Twas not the statue that looked lovely to him. Belle's expression of enchantment lit her face with a beauty all its own. She had looked the same while listening to the Burnaby woman speak.

"Aye 'tis lovely to be sure."

She turned and gave him a smile laced with approval. It faltered when her eyes met his. The temptation to kiss her was overpowering. Her eyes widened as he leaned forward. The sound of voices entering the room brought him to his senses. What was the matter with him? He was not some callow youth who could not keep his libido in check. Yet, he had been near publicly humiliating an unmarried lady. He shook his head with disgust.

Belle beat a hasty retreat to the other side of the room. He smiled at her swiftly moving figure. She could run for now, but eventually he would catch her. She belonged to him, even if she did not realize it. Surprised, Ian realized that marriage to Belle had become every bit as important as inheriting the money left by his stepfather. She was no longer a means to an end, but an end herself. The knowledge did not please him.

When had she become so important?

"I understand your disappointment. It's hardly a top notch display, is it?" The gentleman speaking looked around the room, his lip curled in disgust.

112

"I dinna ken your meaning."

The other man smiled conspiratorially. "I couldn't help noticing your scowl. Don't worry, I'm not about to tell the ladies. My wife is just as enthralled with the room as your companion."

Ian nodded.

"It's hard to comprehend, but there it is. I've learned with my wife not to question her passions. She takes them rather personally."

Ian thought of Belle's passion. He took it personally too. He smiled. "I ken."

The other man winked and nodded. "We have an entire room filled with vases. She collects them you know. Some are truly hideous, but you didn't hear that from me."

Ian laughed. He liked the man. Extending his hand, he introduced himself. The other man turned out to be Sir Percy Stanton.

Lord Stanton asked, "You're Scottish, aren't you?" He nodded answering his own question. "You should see about getting cards to see Wedgewood's Rooms. Truly fantastic. He hails originally from Scotland himself."

Ian thought the name sounded familiar and said so.

"It should, the man's made a name for himself with a home that's no more than a bloody museum. My wife is enamored with his vases of course."

Lord Stanton stiffened and Ian turned to see what had caused the frown to crease his new acquaintance's features. A man stood conversing with Belle and Lady Stanton. Belle's eyes were illuminated with interest as she listened to whatever it was the man was saying. Ian and Lord Stanton moved toward the ladies in one accord.

When he reached Belle, Ian pulled her into his side and held her there with a hand planted firmly around her waist. Lord Stanton took a position between his wife and the newcomer.

The newcomer's eyes narrowed. "Lady Annabelle, won't you introduce me to your escort?" His voice came out in a nasally whine that grated on Ian's temper.

Belle, who had been trying to extricate herself from Ian's grasp, gave up and made the introductions.

The squire bowed formally. "Graenfrae."

Ian frowned at the familiar address and would have ignored the squire, but Belle jabbed him in the ribs. He grunted.

He inclined his head. "Squire."

The squire turned toward Lord Stanton and greeted him. "I was just telling your lovely lady about some vases I saw at an auction on Marle Street."

Lord Stanton gave the squire a less than friendly look. "Thank you."

"We'll have to go directly there," his wife breathed. "I don't want someone else to get to them first."

"Yes, dear, of course."

Ian felt sorry for the harried husband. He doubted very much that Lord Stanton shared his wife's sentiments. Squire Renton was aware of that fact as well if his look of satisfied malice was any indication.

Belle squirmed so she could face him when she spoke. "The squire was giving us a most interesting lecture on this set of carvings. He is truly a man of varied interests and knowledge."

The squire smirked at Ian before bowing toward Belle. "You are too kind, dear lady, too kind."

The approval in Belle's voice for the other man twisted Ian's insides. "'Tis time to meet your brother and Lady Hamilton. Come, Belle."

Her eyes opened wide. "I'm sure you are mistaken. It could not possibly have been an hour."

He didn't bother to answer, but continued to guide her toward the door. She twisted against him. "We should at least invite the squire to join us for tea." Quickening her steps to keep up with him, she panted, "Ian, you are being rude."

"The squire came to look at the display, Belle, not have tea with us."

"Well, yes, I suppose you are right, but we should have asked." They were in the outer corridor now.

Ian stopped and glared down at her. "Why? Do ye wish to sit and discuss the man's varied interests?"

She moved a step away from him. Belle stared up at him. Ian grew uncomfortable under her gaze.

"You're jealous," she accused.

"Dinna be ridiculous."

"I'm not. You are jealous. Surely you cannot believe that I find Squire Renton more interesting than I do you." The disbelief in her voice went a long way toward soothing his raging emotions.

"If you find me so interesting than why are ye refusing to marry me?" The woman was so full of contradictions, he doubted he would ever understand her.

She crossed her arms over her chest. "We agreed to discuss this tomorrow. Besides, one has nothing to do with the other." She turned and headed toward another hallway. "Let's find my brother and Diana."

CB

Annabelle paced her bedroom, waiting for Ian to arrive. He had reminded her in no uncertain terms to be ready for their drive today. He wanted to discuss their future and wasn't going to take no for an answer. Wringing her hands, she sat down on the white coverlet of her bed.

Reminding herself that she was an independent woman of the nineteenth century did nothing to settle the mass of butterflies that had taken up residence inside. Drat the man. Could he not just accept that she would not marry without love?

No, of course, he could not. Did she truly want him to?

No. She wanted him to fall in love with her, just as she had with him.

The truth would not be denied. She loved Ian and doubted she would ever love another. He understood her even when she didn't understand herself. He had proven that in the carriage when he had brought her body such pleasure. She could have felt like a complete wanton. He had made her feel lovely, not cheap.

She twisted her fan, nearly breaking it. What was she going to do? If she refused Ian again, he might give up and pursue someone else. Her heart rebelled at the idea while her mind accepted that it was a possibility. If she accepted his offer and he never came to love her, she feared that her life ahead would be filled with misery. Her heart cried that it would be worse misery to live without him.

She was not altogether certain that her heart was wrong.

The door to her room burst open and she looked up, startled to see her sister-in-law. Diana's face was devoid of color and her eyes flew wildly around the room. Her normally perfect coiffure showed signs of agitated tugging. Wisps of hair floated around her face and her gown was crushed at the sides as if she had been gripping it in her fists.

Annabelle rushed to Diana's side. "What is the matter?"

Tears welled in the other woman's eyes and slid unrestrained down her pale cheeks. "I c-can't bear it, Annabelle. You must help me."

Putting her arms around Diana, Annabelle tugged her toward the window seat. "Certainly. You have only to tell me."

Diana sank onto the window seat. "I-I... This man came and... Your brother..." Unable to finish a complete thought, Diana thrust a crumpled up piece of paper at Annabelle. "Read this."

Annabelle scanned the note.

Lady Hamilton,

Meet me today at Gunther's with one-hundred pounds or I'll be forced to share my grandmother's letters with your "friends" in the ton. Meet me at 3 p.m. with the money, or your husband will learn all.

Most Sincerely,

Your Cousin, Chester P. Thorn.

She would have laughed at its ludicrously overdramatic tone if Diana had not been so upset. "This is obviously the work of a lunatic. There is nothing here to concern you."

Diana shook her head wildly from side to side. "Oh, but there is."

116

Pulling another folded sheet from her reticule, she handed it to Annabelle.

Annabelle unfolded the paper and saw that it was a love letter from Diana's grandfather to a woman clearly of the demi-rep set.

Diana's tears were falling in earnest now. "Isn't it awful? Oh, what shall I do?" She wailed the last question.

Annabelle stood up and rang her maid for some wine. When Purdy brought it, Annabelle dismissed her without letting her into the room to see Diana's overwrought condition. She went back to her friend and forced a glass of wine into Diana's hands. "Drink this."

Diana nodded her head like a child and took a sip of the wine.

"Start at the beginning and tell me all," Annabelle said.

Annabelle's insides churned with anger as her friend told her about meeting a man at the theater who threatened her with exposing the old scandal.

"And he wants me to meet him this afternoon. I don't have a hundred pounds. I've spent most of my allowance on shopping." She let out a long breath. "He even told me to sell my wedding pearls if I couldn't come up with the money on my own."

"The first thing we'll have to do is tell Robert."

Diana grabbed Annabelle's shoulders in a painful grip. "No, we mustn't. It would devastate him. I could not stand it. Please, Annabelle, you must promise me that you won't tell him."

Annabelle gave up on telling Robert for the moment in lieu of getting more information. "Tell me more about the letters."

"My grandfather had a peccadillo with this creature's grandmother and evidently, Mr. Thorn's mother was the result. He claims to have several love letters from my grandfather written to his grandmother," Diana said.

Annabelle patted Diana's arm. "I still think the best course of action would be to tell Robert and he will take care of this odious person. It is not the end of the world. Many gentlemen of the *ton* have had similar peccadilloes. Your grandfather was certainly not alone in his sin."

"You don't understand, Annabelle. Your brother must never find out about this. He is so proper and reputation is so very important to him. He would lose all respect for me." Diana's wooden tone worried Annabelle far more than her tears had done.

"Nonsense, Diana. Robert may take himself a bit too seriously, but he is not about to blame you for your grandfather's indiscretion."

"You are not like Robert. You don't care so much what the *ton* thinks of you, but he is so very particular."

So this was the reason for Diana's questions in the garden the day before. If Chester P. Thorn were within striking distance right now, Annabelle had no doubt she would have boxed his ears without the least remorse. Poor Diana.

It shocked Annabelle that Diana could doubt Robert's true affection. "Robert is as in love with you as any gentleman has ever been with a lady."

"His love is as dependent upon my position in society as upon myself," Diana stubbornly insisted. "If I lost that position or tarnished it, his love for me would be affected and I could not bear it. You must promise me that you won't tell Robert about Mr. Thorn."

Annabelle did not see another option. Diana's fear may be unfounded, but it was real. "Very well. You must not attempt to meet this man alone. We will deal with this together."

Diana nodded vehemently. "That is why I came. I know it isn't fair to involve you, but I shall go mad otherwise."

Annabelle thought furiously. The first thing they had to do was get hold of some money. She doubted the man would hand over the letters for the first payment, but by the time the next demand came she intended to have a plan in place to stop him.

Annabelle stood up and pulled the Kashmir shawl that Ian had given her around her shoulders. Its heavenly warmth lent her strength. They would defeat the miserable Thorn. "We need to go to the bank before we go to meet this odious little man."

Diana smiled tremulously. "I knew I could count on you, Annabelle. You are the best of friends."

Annabelle returned Diana's smile. "The feeling is mutual."

On the way out the door, Annabelle took Creswell aside. "When Lord Graenfrae calls, please tell him that something unavoidable has come up and we will have to postpone our drive." Relief surged through her that their discussion would have to be delayed. "Also, please inform my aunt that I have gone with Lady Hamilton and do not expect to return until late afternoon."

Ian stared at the butler and swore. "Did the lass say where she was going?"

Annabelle had promised and she would bloody well keep that promise, even if he had to track her down and have their discussion in front of Beau Brummell himself.

Creswell stood perfectly straight, looking neither to the right or the left. "No, milord, she did not."

Ian swore again.

The butler bent forward slightly and spoke in a voice barely above a whisper. "However, milord, were you to ask John Footman, he might have heard the direction given by Lady Hamilton to her coachman."

Ian smiled. "Thank you, Creswell."

Creswell unbent a bit more. "You're welcome, milord. The staff is quite pleased with your suit, if I may say so."

Ian only wished that Belle shared her servants' enthusiasm. "That's high praise indeed. I didna realize I had passed muster, but am proud to have done so."

The butler nodded regally.

The footman had indeed heard Belle's direction. What could be so important at the bank that she had broken her word to meet Ian? He gave up trying to figure out what it could be as he came upon Threadneedle Street. Interesting that Belle would do her banking here among the greatest financial institutions in London. Although her family was an old one, he would have expected her to have an account with one of the smaller banks. Fifteen minutes later he was back behind the reins, not one whit closer to Belle. She and Lady Hamilton had come and gone. An indiscreet clerk had let pass that Belle had withdrawn a hundred pounds and then made a remark about going to

Gunther's. This little farce was growing by the minute.

As he drove his team toward the popular treat shop, Ian mulled over things about his intended that didn't add up. She had a reputation among the *ton* for being plain, but in fact she was enchanting. He lost his train of thought more than once when she gave him that particular quizzical glance she had. Her face might not be classical, but when she smiled all he could see was the sparkle in her eyes.

She did not wear expensive gowns or jewelry and from that he had inferred that she had mediocre means. Yet, she showed no interest in nabbing a rich husband. Belle was passionate about the rights of women and reform of England's Common Law in regard to property rights for women. He would think she would be a woman void of romantic notions, but that was far from the truth. Her chief reason for refusing his offer was based on the ridiculous notion that marriage without love was not acceptable.

She was a confusing muddle of ideas and contradictions. He would be better served seeking a more amenable wife among that infernal list she kept. The very thought left him cold. He would bloody well have Belle, or no one at all. The fact that his inheritance was in jeopardy he laid squarely at her door. The foolish lass needed to realize that they belonged together.

The sight that met him when he entered Gunther's did nothing to calm his raging temper. Belle sat at a small table in the corner with Lady Hamilton and a man. Ian could not see the man's face because his back was to Ian. From the back, it did not look like that pasty-faced squire, or Mr. Green. Both of whom seemed to be underfoot whenever Ian wanted to see Belle, not to mention several other irritating hangers on.

The cut of the man's coat was all wrong. If he didn't know better, Ian would think that Belle and her sister-in-law were conversing with a cove from one of the stews near the docks.

Unreasonable fear crawled up his spine. No. Surely not. This could not be one of her new cohorts. He swore under his breath. It made sense. Belle would believe that her precious cause would justify breaking their date. She refused to accept that her involvement in the volatile political issue put her at risk. Now, she appeared to be placing her sister-in-law at risk as well. Hamilton would be livid if he knew.

Ian frowned. His first reaction was to storm over and demand an explanation, but he had learned from past experience that demanding anything with Belle led to more argument than acquiescence. He moved farther into the room, taking up a position where he was partially shielded from view by a large cabinet. He watched Belle speaking passionately to the man in the ill-fitting coat. After shaking his head, the man shrugged. He handed Belle what looked like a letter. She unfolded it and read it. When she looked up again, her eyes were shooting sparks. Lady Hamilton looked ill. Well she should, getting herself involved in one of Belle's schemes.

Belle reached into her reticule and handed a wad of notes across the table to the man. Ian felt his gut clench. She was too bloody trusting. There she was giving this sly-boots her hundred pounds, based on some caper-witted story.

Ian waited until the man rose from the table and followed him. He would seek Belle out later and they would discuss more than their future.

Chapter Ten

That evening, Annabelle looked in consternation at the array of posies resting on her dressing table. She knew which one she wanted to wear. Ian was already infuriatingly arrogant regarding her eventual surrender, however. She *had* stood him up this afternoon. Some attempt at appeasement was called for. Ian's flowers were also the loveliest arrangement of the bunch.

Mr. Green had sent her a fistful of wildflowers. Romantic to be sure, but hardly fitting with her formal gown of silver net over Bordeaux underslip. A posy from a widower with six children did not even tempt her. Although the orchids were exotic, she had no desire to become his brood's newest mother. Word among the *ton* was that not only was he under the hatches, his children had gone through a record nine governesses since their mother's death less than two years ago. She shuddered.

Smiling, she looked at Ceddy's offering. It was a simple arrangement of tiny burgundy flowers and silver ribbon. It would match her dress perfectly, but then so would Ian's.

She lost her smile when her eyes fell on the squire's posy. What had the man been thinking? It was an elaborate concoction of some of the ugliest flowers Annabelle had ever seen. The note that accompanied it explained somewhat. It was a verse comparing her attributes to the flowers. Something about strength of character and mind being like the unattractive blooms. Hardly flattering, but then she was sure the squire had not intended insult. He was just a forward-thinking man, a man who understood women's rights and her interest in antiquities.

He was nothing like Ian, who argued with her at every turn and thought her interests more dangerous than noble.

"Which one will you wear, milady?"

Annabelle sighed and gave up arguing with herself. "I'll wear Lord Graenfrae's flowers in my hair and Lord Finchley's attached to the bosom of my gown." There, that should prevent Ian from believing his offering had been singled out.

When Purdy was finished dressing her hair, Annabelle looked at herself critically in her dressing table mirror. Soft tendrils of hair fell from the pile of curls on top of her head. Purdy had expertly attached Ian's flowers amidst the curls so the effect was something like a fountain of roses and ringlets. Ceddy's flowers enhanced the neckline of her gown.

C3

Later, at the Beauford ball, Annabelle wondered if it had been wise to wear flowers at all. They were bound to wilt in the heat caused by the packed rooms and plethora of candles. Having been deserted by her aunt for the card room, she made her way toward the sound of Diana's laughter.

A hand on her arm stopped her. "Good evening, Belle."

Lifting her eyes, she looked into the fathomless mystery of Ian's gaze. "Hello, Ian."

He seemed to take in her entire appearance with one sweeping glance. He scowled at the flowers on her bodice.

She was quite proud of herself when she was able to smile at him serenely. "Surely you didn't think I would refrain from wearing other gentlemen's favors, Ian. I've made it perfectly plain that I do not consider your suit settled."

His look sent shivers down her spine. "Aye, Belle. 'Tis no that I mind you wearing Finchley's flowers. 'Tis where you have them placed. Is the neckline on your gown not low enough that you need to draw more attention to it?"

She frowned at his words. "I didn't notice you minding the neckline of my gown in the carriage the other evening."

She regretted speaking the moment the words left her mouth. The last thing she wanted to do was remind Ian of her wantonness in his arms after their quarrel.

His eyes darkened with something other than anger. "Nay, and I wouldna mind it now if we were alone either."

She felt her skin heat with more than embarrassment. Ceddy's voice came as welcome relief. "I say, Annabelle, you look all the crack tonight."

Turning to her old friend, she smiled at the compliment. "Thank you, Ceddy. You appear to be the only one who appreciates my appearance."

Ceddy looked properly shocked. "Never say so. A gentleman would have to be blind to not see your loveliness, eh what?"

Ian's gaze swept over her once again, causing the strangest sensation in her innermost places. "Aye, blind indeed."

An unaccustomed feeling robbed Annabelle of breath and she concentrated on not swaying. Ian must have noticed her discomfort because he raised his brow in silent query. She wanted nothing more than to smile coolly and shrug, but could not summon the necessary insouciance. How could she when her entire body felt like it had caught fire? Her eyes were locked with Ian's and no amount of self-will on her part could make them break contact.

"Hello, Lady Annabelle." Vivian Graves's soft voice finally broke Annabelle's paralysis.

She turned gratefully to her friend. "Miss Graves, I have not seen you since our little contretemps. I hope you are completely recovered."

Vivian smiled. "Quite recovered, thank you. Lord Finchley has been most assiduous in his attentions."

Surprised, Annabelle turned to her old friend. "That is wonderfully gallant of you, Ceddy."

His cheeks turned a delightful shade of red and the dandy twisted his neck as if his shirt points had suddenly become too tight. "Was nothing, don't you know?"

Annabelle couldn't help smiling. She again met Ian's gaze and he winked. So the wind was blowing in that direction, was it? She couldn't be happier. Vivian certainly deserved better than her life of uncertain means with her wastrel of a brother.

As they spoke, Annabelle and her companions had been edging their way toward the drawing room. With relief, she realized that they had made it to a relatively uncrowded corner. Diana and Robert stood nearby conversing with an elderly military man. Annabelle waited until he moved on to gain their attention.

Diana fanned herself forcefully. "I declare the crush in here is any hostess's dream."

Ian frowned. "I canna imagine why. 'Tis much too crowded and warm for her guests' comfort."

Annabelle laughed at his naiveté. "That is not the point at all, Ian. A guest's comfort has very little consideration for the successful hostess, but the crush in her drawing room is another thing altogether."

When both Vivian and Diana nodded in unison, Ian shook his head in disbelief. "It makes no sense, that."

"It's all a matter of making the right impression on the polite world," explained Vivian.

"I care not at all for all this folderol. If taking my place in the *ton* requires me to entertain my guests by crushing them to death, I'll forego the pleasure."

"What of your future wife?" asked Annabelle mischievously. "She will certainly expect you to maintain your place in the *ton* and provide her with reflected social glory?"

"You canna be serious. Once we are married, I've no intention of returning to London."

His casual assumption of their impending marriage annoyed Annabelle, but his comment about foregoing the Season caused real consternation.

"Were I to marry, I would not be willing to forego the Season on my husband's whim," she informed him.

"You canna be serious, Belle."

"Oh, but she is." Vivian's voice rang with conviction.

Annabelle smiled at her friend's support. She and Vivian attended the Season for much the same reason, to further the cause of women's rights. In addition, it gave Annabelle an opportunity to stay connected with her friends and family who were scattered across the breadth of England.

When she said as much Ian shrugged. "If ye wish to visit your family and friends, then invite them to stay at Graenfrae."

Not wanting to argue in such a public forum, Annabelle sought to change the subject. "Did you notice Miss Caruthers practically cut you, Ian?"

He looked unconcerned. "I canna say that I did."

Ceddy looked up from his conversation with Vivian. "It's to be expected after the theater, don't you know?"

Diana nodded sagely. "Yes, I imagine the beauty was not pleased to be deserted by her escort."

Ceddy agreed. "She was furious. She refused to allow me to conduct her home in MacKay's stead."

Vivian inclined her head. "You must have been terribly disappointed to have been deprived of her company. She is an acknowledged Diamond of the First Water."

Ceddy frowned. "Never say so. I prefer the company of truly gentle women to spoiled beauties."

He spoke so earnestly that none of the ladies present demurred. Ceddy was well and truly caught. Annabelle hoped Vivian returned his feelings. If her look of pleased confusion was any indication, she did.

"'Tis a sight too warm in here." Ian's complaint brought another smile to Annabelle's lips. He sounded cranky.

"Perhaps the garden would be cooler," Robert suggested.

It wasn't easy, but their entire party managed to make it to the open doors leading to the garden. Once they were outside, Ian maneuvered them so that he and Annabelle were separated from the rest of the group. She slid a curious glance toward him and sucked in her breath at the expression on his face. He looked angry.

She tried to edge away from him, back toward the others but his grip on her arm prevented it. "I believe it is time you explained yourself."

She did not like the peremptory tone of his voice. "I'm not sure what you mean."

He pulled her behind a large shrubbery. "What were you doing today that made you break your promise to meet with me?"

She had been mistaken. Ian wasn't just angry, he was furious. She could hardly tell him the truth. She had been too busy meeting with a blackmailer. She would not lie to him. She stalled. "Didn't Creswell tell you? Something came up."

If anything, Ian looked more incensed. "Aye, your butler told me. What came up?"

She sought desperately for something to say that would not give Diana away, but was not a lie. "I was helping a friend."

Ian's frown grew fiercer. "I followed you."

Fear that Diana's secret had been discovered gave an edge to her voice. "You followed me?"

"Dinna sound so offended. I was not about to let you get away with avoiding our talk this afternoon."

He thought she had been avoiding their discussion? "What kind of caper-witted fool do you take me for? I will admit that I did not relish the thought of rehashing the same ground, but I am not such a ninny that I would have left just to avoid it."

"Nay, you are merely foolish enough to meet with some sharp and give him money."

Annabelle went cold inside. Ian knew about the money. Then he must know about the blackmail. A niggling sense of satisfaction edged her conscience. At least now she could share Diana's problem with someone who wouldn't go into hysterics.

"Belle, you canna continue pursuing your cause with such disregard for your own safety."

"What?"

"How do you even know that the money you gave that blackguard

127

went toward your cause? You are too bloody trusting." Rather than sounding angry, Ian's voice now had a resigned edge to it.

"Too trusting? My cause?" Annabelle's brain scrambled to make sense of Ian's words. "You think I met with that man and gave him money to support my efforts on behalf of women's rights?"

"Aye. 'Tis no secret you have no common sense where your cause is concerned."

"I am not lacking in common sense."

Suddenly Ian was furious again. "Not lacking in common sense?" He fairly roared the question. She involuntarily clapped her gloved hand over his mouth.

"Hush. Do you wish to bring attention to our private discussion, Ian?"

He pulled her hand from his mouth, but not before kissing it. The sensations that shot through her palm and up her arm made it difficult to make sense of his next words.

"I followed that blighter down to the stews before I lost him. Have you gone to meet him there? I have been tormented with images of your broken body floating in the Thames ever since this afternoon. How can you bloody well say that you have common sense?"

It struck her that Ian's fury was fueled by concern and that gave her hope. Perhaps he would come to care for her as she cared for him. "I have not met him anywhere but Gunther's"

Ian did not look as if he believed her.

"I give you my word."

He nodded. "You will not meet him again."

She bristled at the dictatorial statement. "I cannot promise that."

"Aye. You will promise, or I will be forced to bring the matter to your brother's attention."

She gripped Ian's arms and tried to shake him. The man was immovable. "You will not tell Robert anything. Promise me."

"Promise me you will not meet the blighter again."

"I can't, Ian. You must believe me. If I could, I would." Remembering Diana's stricken face, she knew that she could not cease

128

helping her friend. "Did you say you followed him?"

Ian nodded.

"But you lost him near the stews?"

"Aye."

She chewed on her lower lip, lost in thought. Someone from the stews must know Thorn. There had to be a way of tracking him. Then perhaps they could find his lodging and search it for the remaining letters. The wicked man had only brought one to their meeting. He insisted on selling them one at a time. Poor Diana had grown nearly hysterical at the implication of a long and drawn out ordeal. She was terrified that Thorn would decide to make the letters public out of spite. Annabelle had tried to convince Diana that Thorn wanted money too much to risk losing his golden goose through any foolish action like making the letters or their contents public.

Ian had reversed the position of their arms and now he rubbed hers up and down in a soothing motion. "What is it, Belle? I am beginning to think there is more to this business than you throwing your money away on some sharp's scheme."

She looked up into his face and was nearly undone by the concern she saw there. If only she could tell him, but she had promised Diana. She could not break her word. Besides, her plan to find Thorn's lodging was a sound one and soon the whole business would be over. She lifted her hand and caressed her finger along Ian's jaw. "Everything will be fine."

In a bold move that surprised herself as much as him, she stepped forward and softly kissed his lips. When she would have backed away, he reached out and caught her to him. His mouth moved over hers in a sensual dance. The feelings she had experienced in the carriage came flooding back. Her knees turned to jelly.

He continued to kiss her with hungry passion. She sighed and parted her lips. His tongue swept her mouth. She felt as if her body was on fire. Of their own volition, her hands sought his broad back and the column of his neck. She restlessly rubbed her body against his, needing more of this incredible feeling. He groaned and ran his hands down her back, cupping her bottom and pulling her against his male hardness. Feelings exploded inside of Annabelle like firecrackers on Boxing Day. She moaned, pressing her body against his.

She felt him shift and realized that he had moved them farther into the shrubbery. The feeling of his hands caressing her breast through the thin silk of her gown took her breath away.

The knowledge that his kiss could affect her so easily terrified her. The fact that they were in a public place did not seem to affect her desire, or her body's response to Ian's touch. She tried to pull away.

"We must stop." He ignored her and continued to kiss her down the side of her throat. "Please, Ian, someone will see."

His instant withdrawal left her feeling bereft and confused. Her cheeks heated and she tried to cool them by touching her gloved hands to them. Ian's mouth was set in a grim line. If only he would smile at her, she wouldn't feel like such a wanton hussy. Had her forwardness disgusted him? Her heart beat a rapid rhythm, both from passion and from shame. She had no control.

"I'm sorry, Ian. I don't know what came over me." She realized that she had whispered the words, but it was hard to speak past the obstruction in her throat.

He reached his hand out and gently brushed her forehead. "'Tis nothing to be sorry for."

"You're angry with me." She hated the weakness in her voice.

He groaned and pulled her toward him until her face rested against his waistcoat. "I'm not angry, Belle."

"You're glowering at me."

His harsh laugh surprised her. He thought this was amusing? She tried to pull away from him, but his arms had become like steel bands around her. He rubbed her back with one of his hands. "Hush."

His caress was soothing and she relaxed against him. It felt so good to be held by him. She wished they could stay this way forever.

"It is not an easy thing for a gentleman to stop such a pleasurable pastime."

She heard the strain in his voice. He was a gentleman. He had not taken advantage of her in the carriage and he had been willing to stop now. Admiration for his strength and character welled up in Annabelle.

"I'm truly sorry, Ian." At her words, he stiffened.

Pulling away from her, he spoke. "Why are you sorry, lass? You canna tell me you didna like it."

She felt herself blushing again. "Yes, I liked it, but I shouldn't have kissed you. It wasn't ladylike."

His laughter caught her unawares.

"I don't know what you find amusing about this situation. No lady wishes to be caught behaving like a Cyprian." She did not think it necessary to mention that she had been far more wanton in his carriage.

"Dinna worry, Belle. A Cyprian has a lot more experience and would have offered me more than her mouth."

His words caught her on the raw. She would have struck him, but for the amusement still lurking in his eyes. "Ian, do you think to tease me?"

"Aye, Belle, I do." He laughed aloud when she said a word that ladies never say.

Thinking a little of his own medicine wouldn't be amiss, she said, "I see that I'll need to gain more experience before I can truly shame myself with brazenness. One illicit evening in your carriage is not nearly enough."

His laughter died and his face took on a chilling quality. "Dinna try it, Belle. I'm not known for my even temper."

She should be frightened by his intensity, but she wasn't. His possessive tone exhilarated her. Still, he needn't think she was so easily cowed. She did not agree with his demand.

"Oh there you two are. Annabelle, your aunt is looking for you. She is ready to go home." Annabelle jumped away from Ian at the sound of Ceddy's voice.

She turned to follow Ceddy to her aunt, but Ian pulled her back. "This conversation is not over, Belle."

She did not reply. There was nothing to say.

The others joined them and she bid Ceddy and Vivian farewell before following her aunt to the carriage. Ian insisted on escorting her outside. He held her back in the shadows while Lady Beauford, Robert and Diana made haste to get in the carriage. A chilly wind had begun to blow and the fog clung damply to Annabelle's dress.

"I must go." She tried to disengage her arm from Ian's grip.

"In a moment."

He could not mean to finish their conversation now. The man was stubborn, but this was ridiculous. She turned her head to tell him so. Ian claimed Annabelle's lips in a short, passionate kiss that totally took her breath away. This was no tentative and gentle exploration, but the staking of a claim.

She sighed. "Good night, Ian."

"Good night, Belle. I meant what I said. Your passion belongs to me now." His voice did not encourage disagreement. She merely smiled. He pulled her forward and gave her another kiss that left her breathless. "Remember what I said."

When Ian was finished he led her to the carriage. He made short work of helping her in. Grasping her waist as he held her hand firmly, he lifted her until she had ducked her head into the interior and her satin-clad feet were firmly planted on the floor of the carriage.

Leaning in through the open carriage door, he met her eyes. "We will have our drive tomorrow."

She nodded.

He left.

"Could you believe those draperies in the drawing room? And fires in every grate. Unbelievable," remarked Lady Beauford once the carriage was on its way. "You wouldn't have seen anything like that when I was in residence."

"Of course not." Annabelle absently agreed with her aunt.

Across from her, Diana tried to smother a yawn.

"You need your sleep now, Diana. I do hope you plan to go directly to bed when you reach home," said Lady Beauford, laying stress on the word *now*. Annabelle wondered at the significance, but her mind was too full of blackmail schemes and an intriguing laird to pay close attention.

She realized her aunt had asked her a question when the other occupants of the carriage stopped talking to stare at her. Even Diana looked curious. "What? Did you ask me something, Aunt Griselda?"

"No, my dear. I made the observation that although your engagement is imminent, it is not seemly to be seen carrying on a private discussion in a dark garden with your suitor."

Annabelle's head snapped up and all of her vagueness dissipated like fog in the noonday sun. "For the last time, my engagement is not imminent."

Lady Beauford turned to Robert. "I cannot imagine what is the matter with the gel. She is acting all over strange about Lord Graenfrae. It is not as if this were her first Season and she had suitors filling the drawing room of an at home day."

Annabelle might as well not even be there, for all the attention her aunt paid to what she said.

"Frankly, Aunt Griselda, I believe that Annabelle has finally met her match and she's fighting it tooth and nail." Robert's words grated her conscience. If only he knew. She had met the one man who could inspire love. It was fate's cruel joke that Ian thought love mere romantic drivel.

"Really, Robert. The expressions you use. You have spent far too much time in the wilds of the north. However, if I understand your meaning, I believe I concur. Perhaps Annabelle's heart has finally been engaged."

Aunt Griselda stopped talking to give Annabelle a quizzical look.

Annabelle remained mute. Let them continue their conversation without her input. She definitely had no plans to admit to her feelings for Ian. It would only strengthen her brother's arguments in favor of the marriage. He would not understand that far from reconciling her to the idea of marrying Ian, her love for him made it impossible until she was certain he returned the emotion.

"At any rate, I hope she is wise enough to realize that men like Ian do not come along every day in a woman's life."

She would have to be a fool not to realize that Ian was unique among men. Annabelle was not a fool.

cs

Throwing the glass of inexpensive port against the wall, William growled curses he had learned playing cards in the seedy hells his fortunes had forced him to. The sound of glass shattering did not abate his fury. The nerve of the chit! Once he was married to her, she would learn the folly of ignoring him for another man. How dare she wear some other man's flowers when he had spent his precious blunt on a posy for her?

She had also allowed the laird to monopolize her time. William had struggled in vain to get near Lady Annabelle in the drawing room and join her party. When he had finally come within speaking distance, the upstart Scotsman had spirited her out to the garden. The ignorant gel didn't have the sense to stay out of dark gardens with gentlemen. If William was not careful, his prey would end up in a compromising position with Lord Graenfrae and all would be lost.

The almost empty port bottle joined his glass in a splintering explosion across the room. The smell of cheap wine mixed with his own sweat as he threw himself into his favorite chair. The only piece of furniture not covered with soiled garments. His disloyal valet had left. Could William help it if he was a little behind in the man's wages? Surely a loyal servant would have stayed, but William had returned to his rooms to find his valet gone the day before.

Toying with the money he had left over from the Lady Hamilton's first payment, William considered his options. He had over ninety pounds still left after buying the posy, a few bottles of port and dinner at his club. Ninety pounds wasn't a bad stake in the games of chance to be found in the lower east side of London.

Mulling the idea over, he pulled off his sweat-stained shirt and dressed in garments more suitable to the stews. He headed out the door and hailed a passing hackney. If his luck continued, he would be a good deal richer in the morning.

Then he would rehire his valet. He discarded the idea. He would hire a new man. Why reward the disloyalty of his old servant? William's mood improved by the prospect of a night spent in his favorite pursuit. He smiled to himself.

Lady Annabelle would be his, and soon.

Chapter Eleven

Ian walked toward Rundell, Bridge and Rundell, surprised that such an unimposing building housed one of London's most prestigious jewelers. Finchley had been insistent. This jeweler serviced the needs of most of the polite world.

Ian's grandfather's resistance to England had not only cost his estates and his people, all of the family baubles had long since been sold off as well. His mother's wedding ring had been a simple band of gold. He wanted to give Belle a ring to seal their betrothal. Something that would declare to the world that she belonged to him.

He just had to convince her of that fact.

It would also do his nerves a world of good to convince her to leave off pursuing her causes. He grew cold at the thought of Annabelle in the clutches of a man like the one she had met with at Gunther's.

Thinking back over his conversation with her in the garden, Ian was convinced that she was hiding something from him. He couldn't begin to guess what. All he knew for certain was that the lass was in over her head with a man like that.

The door to the jeweler swung open and a lady came out. Her head was bent, so Ian did not at first recognize her. As she passed him, however, he noticed something familiar about the set of her shoulders and shape of her head.

It was Lady Hamilton.

"Good morning, Lady Hamilton."

She walked past him as if he had not spoken and it was then that he noticed tears sliding down her cheeks. She rushed to her waiting carriage and stepped inside before Ian could form a question in his surprised brain.

Deciding he might find some answers for the lady's strange behavior within, he stepped into the jeweler's shop. It was empty save a wizened-looking man who stood behind the farthest display case appraising a strand of pearls. They looked remarkably like the ones Ian had seen on several occasions gracing Lady Hamilton's neck.

Stepping forward, he decided to test the theory that had formed in his mind. He could not credit that Belle would countenance her friend selling her wedding pearls, even for Belle's cause. "A lovely strand of pearls, that."

The jeweler looked up. "They are. They are. Just as lovely as the day I strung them."

Ian put his hand out to examine the necklace. "I might be in the market for something like this."

The jeweler shook his head sadly. "Can't sell them to you yet. Promised the lady to keep them for at least two weeks. To tell the truth, once her lord finds out she's sold 'em, I'm betting he'll be here post haste to buy them back."

"Did the lass who was just in here sell those to you?"

"Right you are. Gambling debts or some such thing, I'm bound. Thinks she'll keep it from her husband, but things like this have a way of becoming known."

Ian nodded. They did indeed. "You promised to keep them at least two weeks?"

"Yes, but if you're that interested in some pearls, I've got a nice set here in my display case."

The jeweler leaned down and pulled out a beautiful strand of beads. They made a soft clicking noise as they rubbed together. When the jeweler named a price, Ian winced. Several cottage roofs could be thatched for the money. When he pictured how the glistening pearls would look nestled around Belle's slender throat, Ian was tempted to buy them anyway.

He shook his head, not without regret. "I'm looking for a betrothal ring."

The jeweler laid his finger alongside his nose and tugged on his ear. "Ah. It's that way, is it?" He nodded again. "I think I have just the thing."

He pulled a display case from the cabinet and laid it before Ian. Pulling back the protective velvet, he exposed several rings of various stones and settings. Ian's eye was drawn to a ring that resembled a rose. It held no gems like the others, but the artistry of the delicate rose could not be denied. Lifting the ring from the tray, Ian announced, "I'll take this one."

The jeweler offered him a keepsake box carved in the same rose motif to carry it in. Ian agreed to buy that also. Belle, with her fondness for roses, would love it.

Now he just had to convince her to accept the gift.

CƷ

Annabelle paced the drawing room. Ian had not said what time he would call today, but she knew in her heart he was coming. What would she say? He had told her she had until the end of the Season to accustom herself to the notion of their marriage, but she felt as if time had run out. She knew that she could not go on rejecting a proud man like her Scottish suitor and expect him to continue calling.

"Annabelle, sit down. Your pacing is going to wear a hole in my carpet." Aunt Griselda sat near the empty fireplace working on garments for a soon to arrive grandchild.

Annabelle smiled at her aunt's irritable tone. The dear woman hated fancy work, but forced herself to complete a perfectly gorgeous christening gown for each of her grandchildren.

"I'm sorry, Aunt." Annabelle sat down at the spinet and trailed her fingers across the keys aimlessly.

The older woman harrumphed. "If you are going to make noise at least make it pleasant."

Poor Aunt Griselda. She must be tatting lace to be this cranky.

"Very well." Annabelle began to play a soft Scottish ballad.

"That's nice, dear." Her aunt worked in silence, letting Annabelle play first one, then another song from the North. "Have you discovered that Laird MacKay is the best you are likely to do for a husband, yet?"

A discordant note sounded as Annabelle's fingers slipped on the ivories.

Aunt Griselda lifted her gaze from her tatting and frowned. "He *is* a good man. If you let him go looking elsewhere, I'll wash my hands of trying to find you a proper mate once and for all." The deep concern in her tone belied the severity of her speech.

"He is a good man." Annabelle spoke the truth quietly and let her fingers still above the keys of the spinet.

Ian *was* a good man. He was also a stubborn man, an arrogant man and a man who affected her equilibrium by walking into the room. There was nothing simple or straightforward about her feelings toward the maddening Scottish laird.

Aunt Griselda set the fold of snowy white fabric in her lap. "I only knew your uncle a week when I decided he was the one for me. However, it took another month to bring him to the same conclusion. Men can sometimes be dense."

Annabelle felt a faint stirring of hope. "Yes, it took Robert two Seasons to discover he couldn't live without Diana."

Returning to her work, Aunt Griselda nodded. "Just so."

Annabelle remained silent. Could Ian live without her? Or, was she just a means to an end? She was certain of only one thing. *She was approaching the condition when she could not live without Ian.*

He was all that she wanted in a husband. He turned her insides to butter when he kissed her. He listened when she talked. He did not criticize her views or her cause. He might criticize his perception of her putting herself in danger, but even that was a nice change from being ignored. He lacked only one thing, the proper view of love. Oh, she knew he cared, but did he care enough?

How could she marry a man who did not love her, and yet how could she not when she loved him so much she ached with the strength of it?

"You'll work it out in your mind, my dear. Just do not take too long in doing so. I would hate to see that dear boy go looking elsewhere."

The thought of Ian as a dear boy brought a small smile to Annabelle's lips, but her aunt's other words filled her heart with dread. Would he go looking for another wife, a more tractable woman?

She read similar concern in her aunt's eyes and knew the source was not Annabelle's status as a spinster. Aunt Griselda loved her and wanted her to be happy.

A rush of warm feeling toward the older woman spread over Annabelle and she got up from the music bench to give Aunt Griselda's shoulders a squeeze. "You have been a rock since Mama and Papa died. I don't know what I would have done without you."

Her aunt's eyes were suspiciously misty, but she said, "Enough of this maudlin talk. Just see that you don't ruin your chances at happiness, gel."

That was exactly what Annabelle did not wish to do, but what way would lie happiness? Marriage to a man who did not love her or the desolate years stretched out ahead of her without the man she loved?

She was no nearer a solution to her dilemma when Creswell announced Ian's arrival an hour later. Ian gave her aunt a perfunctory greeting and then turned to Annabelle.

"Belle, do you still have the list you made for me when we first met?"

Annabelle felt a lead ball forming in the pit of her stomach. *He wanted the list? Now?* Surely, not. She took a fortifying breath to steady her voice before speaking. "Yes."

"I would like you to fetch it for me."

Her heart contracted painfully. He had given up. He was ready to move on to more easily wooed ladies. She could not help herself. She asked, "Do you need it *now*, Ian?"

"Aye, Belle, now."

She felt her world constrict around her until she was conscious of only the overpowering man before her and the shattered sensation in her own heart. She inwardly cursed her own stubbornness. She had started this by making the now hated list for Ian. She had even been proud of herself when she had successfully introduced several of the ladies on it to him, but then she had fallen in love.

None of the women whose names were on the list would make Ian a proper wife. How could they? They did not love him as she did. They would not ache to help him rebuild his lands and improve the lives of his tenants.

She felt like cursing and crying at once. She didn't want him to give up. She wanted him to love her, to care enough to demand marriage to her and her alone. Tears burned her eyes, but she blinked them away. She could cry later. She would not lose her composure now and become an object of his pity.

He waited silently, his face expressionless, for her to do as he bid. She could think of no alternative, but to get the list.

Turning to her aunt, she excused herself. The look of disappointment in Lady Beauford's eyes sliced through Annabelle like a blade.

Having retrieved the list and gotten a measure of control over her emotions, she returned to the drawing room.

In a final effort to stave off the inevitable, she babbled, "I made the list before I knew you well, Ian. I'm not sure any of the names would be that helpful to you now. It's probably not at all what you are looking for."

Ian wordlessly put his hand out for the list. She handed it to him, trying to control the fine tremor in her hand as she did so. Ian took the paper and began to methodically rip it into shreds. She watched stupidly while he reduced the heavy stationary to nothing more than a pile of bits. He then threw it into the dustbin near her aunt's chair.

"I told her it was no use making it. When a gentleman of character makes his plans, he does not change them." Her aunt's words were complacent, but she had not been able to mask the relief in her voice.

"Aye." He nodded toward Aunt Griselda and then turned to face Annabelle. "Are ye ready to leave now?"

She nodded wordlessly. After the past horrifying moments when she thought she had lost him, she was more than ready to discuss their future.

She met him in the hall. He did not say anything, but led the way to his carriage without a word. Hardly the day for a drive, gray clouds filled the overcast skies and an unseasonable chill filled the air. She shivered in her light muslin clothing and wished she had thought to bring her Kashmir shawl.

Ian pulled a soft carriage blanket from the seat of the carriage and wrapped it around Annabelle so that it not only covered her shoulders like a cloak, but it also draped across her legs. She smiled her thanks.

He nodded, then climbed to the seat beside her and flicked the reins. The horses started forward. The intensity of the silence between them added to her already somewhat overwrought state.

"Are we going back to the park with the pond?" she asked in an attempt to break it.

Ian shook his head.

"Are we going to Hyde Park?" She did not think he would do so willingly, but she couldn't think of where else he might be taking her.

He again shook his head without uttering a word.

Her nerves, stretched taut from the events of the past two days, felt ready to explode in the face of Ian's silence. "Is it too much to expect you to tell me where we are going, then?" Her voice sounded harsh even to her own ears.

"Aye."

If he expected her to plead for the information, then he would be disappointed. She sat back against the squabs and tried to relax, focusing on the sights and sounds that met her as Ian drove through London. The traffic around them thinned and she realized that Ian was taking her out of the city. He drew the carriage into an inn yard and she expelled her breath. As improper as it might be for an unmarried lady to meet with a gentleman at an inn, she trusted Ian and was not worried.

A boy ran into the yard to help with the horses. Ian swung down and lifted her out of the carriage. The carriage blanket slipped off from around her shoulders and he tucked it more securely against her.

He led the way into the inn and when they entered the private parlor, she realized that Ian had planned their meeting to the smallest detail. Two worn but comfortable-looking chairs sat before a cheerful fire blazing in the grate. She moved nearer the fire and unwound the blanket from her shoulders. She folded it neatly and placed it over the back of one of the chairs before noticing a cold collation on the table between the two chairs.

"How long do you think this discussion is going to take? It looks as if you have prepared for a siege."

Ian did not laugh at her attempt at humor. "As long as necessary, Belle."

His answer had not reassured her. Ian could tell from the look of worry in her eyes. He sighed. Evidently, she had not reconciled herself to their future yet. He removed his greatcoat, taking the keepsake box with her ring out of the pocket before laying the coat across the other chair.

Turning away from her, he put the small box down and poured himself a glass of port from the bottle on the table. "Belle, I asked you once to be my wife and live your life with me in my Scottish home." He turned back to face her and took a sip from his glass of wine. "At the time, you made it clear that you expected to be courted."

He waited for her to acknowledge his words.

She nodded.

"I have courted you."

"Ian, the courting is but a small part of the picture." The earnest expression on her face told him she believed what she was saying. "I want an abiding love in my marriage."

Love. He cursed and her eyes widened. "I have proven to you that you are not immune to me, Belle. It should be obvious that I am not immune to you either."

Her gaze flew to his and seemed to ask a question.

"I want you more than I thought possible to want a woman."

Heat stole into her cheeks, but at the look of warmth in her eyes, he knew his words had pleased her. He put his wine down and picked up the ring box. Pulling her into a chair, he knelt on the floor in front of her. "Will you be my wife and share my life with me, making my days bright with your quick wit and my nights warm with your generous heart?"

She didn't answer him immediately. He wanted to press her, but knew the time for that was done. He placed the box on her lap and waited for her to answer.

She opened it and gasped when she saw the ring inside. She touched the filigree rose with the tip of her finger. "Do you love me, Ian?" The words sounded torn from her.

He stiffened, but resisted the urge to jump to his feet and put distance between them. "I care for you and want to be with you. The passion between us is too strong to deny, Belle. Say you will marry me, lass."

Would it be enough? He did not know. Looking into her face and seeing the sadness there, he wished he could give her the words she wanted to hear. He could not be weakened by love.

She was convinced that love would guarantee happiness; he was living proof that it did not. Jenna had vowed her love for him, but it meant nothing. She married his younger half brother when he ascended to his father's title. His brother loved him, but that had not stopped him from betraying Ian.

"Will you be faithful?"

The words were barely more than a whisper, but had the effect of a bucket of water from the lochs back home being tossed in his face. His head snapped back as if she had struck him. Did she not ken him better than that?

"Aye. I'll be faithful."

She searched his eyes, seeking an answer beyond his words. "You will never take a mistress? Not even for one night?"

Her words conjured up a fury so intense he had to get control before he answered. The idea of taking any woman to his bed besides

Belle was obscene to him now. She questioned his honor by asking again. Did she not understand that?

"You have my word." He spoke through gritted teeth.

She bit her lower lip. Her gaze dropped to the ring in her lap. "It is beautiful." Her eyes came back to his face. "The thought of settling for marriage without love frightens me."

A cold wind blew through his soul. His father had taught him about his duty to the land and its people. His stepfather had taught him about many things, honor the most important among them. Neither man had taught him about love. The only experience he had with the emotion had left him bitter. Love had caused his own brother to betray him.

He laid his hands over hers. She was trembling. "I canna promise you love, Belle, but I can promise you devotion. I will never take another woman to my bed."

"But will you want to?"

Words were not going to convince her. Only one thing would show Belle that her fears were unfounded. Passion.

Leaning forward, he pressed his lips to hers. She remained stiff against him. He coaxed her lips with his own, tenderly kissing her until he felt her body relax. With a soft moan of surrender, her trembling hands stole around his neck. He rejoiced in her response to him. His lips moved more purposely over hers and he slid his tongue across the seam of her mouth, silently demanding that she part her lips for him. She complied and his heart filled with joy as his tongue slipped into the sweet recesses of her mouth.

Her fingers tunneled through his hair and he groaned. She made him forget his motive in kissing her. All he could think about was how much he enjoyed the feel of her tender lips under his and the sensation of her hands in his hair. He leaned completely into her, forcing her back against the chair. His hands moved to cup the sides of her breasts. She squirmed against him, making erotic noises in the back of her throat.

She broke her lips away from his. "Ian."

His name was a demand. He smiled. Love was a mystery to him, but this was not. He knew what she wanted and he was more than willing to give it to her. He deftly unbuttoned her pelisse and removed it. The thin muslin of her gown did nothing to hide the points of her erect nipples. Taking one between his thumb and forefinger, he squeezed. At the same time, he covered her mouth with his, swallowing the scream that his touch evoked.

Her legs spread and he pulled her body flush against his own. She moved restlessly against him and he felt his body heat with desire. He wanted her so much he would die of it. His hands locked behind her, holding her body prisoner against him. Breaking the kiss, he panted. "Do you truly believe that as long as I have you in my arms, I will ever want another woman?"

"I don't know. I don't understand this, Ian." She sounded like a bewildered child.

"Ah, but I do." Once again he sealed her lips with his own. He kissed her until she writhed against him with abandon.

"Ian, you must do something. I cannot stand this."

Carefully, wanting only to prove to her that they did indeed have a physical bond strong enough for marriage, he drew the cap sleeves of her dress down over her shoulders. She groaned. With shaking fingers, he caressed her soft skin. She moaned, her head falling back against the back of the chair.

"Please, Ian. This is too much." Her broken words only fueled his passion.

"Nay, 'tis not enough, Belle." He stood up and she protested when he pulled away from her.

"Ian."

Spreading his greatcoat on the floor before the fire, he said, "Just a minute, lass."

She stared at him, her eyes clouded with passion. He took off his cravat and waistcoat before pulling her to her feet. His hands shook with desire as he undid the tapes on her gown. She made no protest as he slipped it off of her. She stood before him in a chemise of fine lawn. The dusky points of her breasts tantalized him through the nearly transparent fabric. He almost exploded then and there at the sight of her feminine body exposed to his view.

Reaching out to her, he drew her to the floor beside him.

"Are we going to make love, Ian?"

He couldn't help smiling. She sounded both curious and passionate. "Nay, but I am going to prove to you that with you in my arms, I will need no other."

She stilled against him. "Truly?"

"Aye, lass, truly." He went about proving it. Within minutes, he had her so hot she was tearing at his shirt seeking his bare skin.

He didn't mind at all. He caressed her thighs, teasing her with little circles that drew ever closer to her feminine center. When he finally touched her there, her entire body came off the floor. She would have brought the innkeeper running with her shout if he had not covered her mouth with a passionate kiss. He gently massaged her with his fingers until she convulsed around him.

His breathing was ragged and he wanted to bury himself in her softness so badly that he almost gave in to the temptation. He could not do that however. She would be his in name as well when he joined his body with hers in the complete act of making love. Holding her tightly, he willed his body to relax. "Ian?"

"Hmm?" How she could talk now was a mystery to him.

"You didn't experience what I did again, did you?" She sounded worried.

"I experienced it with you, Belle. Your pleasure is like taking my own."

"So, you don't particularly want me to do this?" He was unprepared for the rush of almost painful pleasure when she rubbed his hardness through his pantaloons.

It felt so good he thought he could die of it. When she started unbuttoning his pants, Ian nearly came undone. "You mustna do that, Belle."

She smiled into his eyes, her face a mask of feminine mystery. "Why not, Ian? You said you needed me and I must assume your need is at least equal to my own. Therefore you cannot convince me that you would be horrified by my bold behavior." She ruined her confident statement by ending it with a worried frown and stilling her hands in their struggle with his buttons. "Are you?"

He growled. "The only thing I don't like is how long you are taking to touch me, Belle. You're teasing me to near death with your hesitancy."

Her smile was like the sun breaking through the gray skies of London. It warmed him and filled his heart with peace. She finished the task of opening his pantaloons. He muffled a shout as she grasped his hard member in her hand. "You are much bigger than I expected. Is this quite normal, Ian?"

Her words and touch sent his senses scattering. He could not form a response to her question. She curled her fingers around him and squeezed. Ian arched away from the floor. "Show me what to do," she demanded.

He did. When he came, she gave a husky laugh. He kissed her until every last bit of pleasure had been wrung from him. He collapsed on the floor.

Now she would understand that her fears were foundless.

"Will it always be like this?"

He sat up and began buttoning his shirt. "Like what?"

"So...so combustible between us?"

"God willing it will only get better."

"You mean it can be better?" She sounded doubtful.

"Aye. We have not yet made love, Belle. Our bodies have not joined." He resumed dressing.

She pulled her dress over her head and turned for him to fasten the tapes. Pulling a small comb from her reticule, she began to straighten her hair.

"Why didn't we make love, Ian?"

Her question took him by surprise. "I will not dishonor you before we are wed."

She thought about this for awhile. He could see her mind wrestling with his words. "What we did just now. You don't think that was the same thing?"

He shook his head. "What we did was share pleasure, but when we make love we will join our bodies. We will become one. It is not the same. It is more and it is for marriage."

She stared at him. "I want to become one with you."

He felt something inside of him expand. Pulling her back into his arms, he asked, "Does that mean you will marry me?"

"Yes." She buried her face in his neck and he felt tears against his heated skin.

Pulling away from her gently, he looked into her face.

She smiled tremulously. "It seems I have no choice."

He didn't like hearing that. He wanted her to choose to marry him, but realized that if she felt trapped by her passion he should be glad. "You will be happy, Belle."

She did not answer.

"Shall we go and let your family wish us happy?" He wanted to kiss her again, but feared he wouldn't be able to stop with a kiss if he did.

"Now?" She sounded surprised.

"Did you think to wait?" Was she trying to stall him?

"No, it's just that I can't see wasting all this food. Besides, I'm a little hungry."

He smiled. "Your passion has made you hungry. Remind me to make sure we have a repast set aside on our wedding night."

She blushed, but laughed.

The ring box had fallen on the carpet at her feet. He leaned down and retrieved it. "Come here, lass."

She did. He lifted her hand and placed the ring on her finger. "Now you belong to me."

She cocked her head to one side and gazed at him through her lashes. "I see. Does this mean you belong to me as well?"

He did not smile. "Can you doubt it?"

She shook her head. "Ian?"

"What?"

"Will you kiss me again?"

The smile that would not come earlier split his face. His hands cupped her cheeks and he lowered his lips to hers slowly, inch by inch. Her eyes fluttered closed and he touched her lips gently with his own. He felt the tension drain from her. When he did not repeat the kiss, she opened her eyes to look into his. She smiled and he lowered his lips to hers again.

He started this kiss with the same gentle caress, but soon deepened it to a passionate melding of their mouths. She parted her lips for him and tentatively touched his tongue with her own. He groaned and pulled her close. He slid his hands possessively down her spine, holding her tightly against him.

When she responded with moans of desire, he slid his hands down to cup her bottom. He kneaded her flesh and she squirmed against him, rubbing the juncture of her thighs against his. He felt like his loins were on fire and hardened against her again.

Breaking off the kiss, he pushed her face into his waistcoat. "If we don't stop now, we'll no make it back to your aunt's house before dark."

She responded with a shaky laugh. "We can't have that. Perhaps we should not stay to eat. Shall we return to my aunt? Her relief that I am finally to be married will be profound."

They had some other things to discuss first. "Tell me about the man in Gunther's."

The look of fear that flitted across her features was enough to convince Ian that there was more to the story than she had first told him. She opened her mouth to speak, but he put his finger over her lips. "Wait. Dinna bother trying to dissemble, lass. I want the whole story and I'll settle for nothing less."

Chapter Twelve

Annabelle turned from Ian's probing gaze. Her heart was at war within her. She wanted nothing more than to spill the burden of Diana's blackmailer. She could not betray her friend however. "I cannot tell you about the man, Ian."

Instead of erupting with an angry outburst and demanding she comply, like she expected, Ian nodded. He motioned for her to take a seat and served her a plate full of thin slices of bread and meats with cheese. "Eat."

Grateful that he wasn't going to push her to answer, she said a quick prayer of thanksgiving. The food was delicious and she had eaten everything on her plate before she realized it. She looked up to find Ian watching her. His expression was brooding and he had barely touched the food before him.

"We really should head back. Aunt Griselda is bound to be concerned. We have been gone quite a long time," she said.

Ian's expression did not change. "I'm waiting, Belle."

She grimaced. "Has no one ever told you that you are too stubborn by half?"

"You will tell me about the man."

She could not stay seated any longer. Jumping up, she moved restlessly around the room. The windows were too high to see anything going on outside. She stopped in front of a painted garden scene.

"This is really well done, don't you think? I would not have expected something of this quality at a public inn."

"The painting is no of interest to me. Your safety canna be ignored," Ian replied.

"You are like a dog with a bone," she exclaimed with exasperation. "Would you please just accept the fact that I cannot tell you what you wish to know? It would mean breaking a confidence and I cannot do that."

He moved so quickly that one moment he sat in his chair, glaring at her and the next his hands were gripping her upper arms as he turned her to face him squarely.

"You willna keep another man's confidence, Belle. You are to be my wife. I willna have it."

Outrage at his arrogance bolstered her courage. "What exactly are you saying? Do you think now that I am to marry you that you own me, Ian?"

"I am not unreasonable." His eyes registered confusion. "'Tis no more than any man would expect from his wife."

Twisting from his arms, she backed away until she could look him in the eye without craning her neck. "Of course not, but I thought you understood that I expect something different from marriage than to become some man's glorified bond slave."

Ian's eyes glittered darkly in his anger. "I am no going to make you a slave."

"No. You are not." She crossed her arms over her chest. "Ian, I am aware that in marrying most women abdicate their rights, but I am not willing to do so. The Common Law of England may dictate that I am little more than a possession, but I demand that you give me your word as a gentleman that you will allow me to be my own person."

"You want me to agree to have no say in your life at all? You are to be my wife, Belle. I canna agree to that."

Why couldn't he understand? "That is not what I am saying. I merely want an assurance from you that I will have the freedom to pursue my own interests without interference."

He stared at her like she had gone mad. "I'll no agree to anything so ridiculous."

Her spirits sank. She could not marry him. She withdrew the ring from her finger and held it out to him. "Then I regret to say that I cannot marry you."

He refused to take the ring from her. "You asked if I would be faithful."

She nodded. It had been difficult to voice her doubts, but it was important to her.

"If I were to take a mistress, would that not be pursuing my own interests without interference?"

She let the hand holding the ring drop to her side. "It is not the same thing at all. It would hurt me terribly if you were to share yourself intimately with another woman."

"Ah so, 'tis only your own feelings that concern you then?"

She frowned. How could he believe that? "Of course not."

"You expect me to let you do what you like, even pursue a clandestine relationship with another man. 'Twill not work."

Appalled that he could believe such a thing, she said, "I am not having a relationship with Mr. Thorn. How could you believe that after what we just shared?"

His eyes lit with interest. "If you are no having a relationship with him, then why are you keeping his secrets?"

How could he have gotten everything so muddled? "I'm not keeping his confidences. I'm keeping Diana's."

Gasping, she put her hand over her mouth. She had said far too much. From the look of satisfaction on Ian's face, he was not surprised. "You tricked me."

He shrugged at her accusation.

"Ian, this is unacceptable. You cannot go about tricking me into telling you things."

He reached down and grasped her hand. He opened her fist one finger at a time. Pulling the ring from the palm of her hand, he slid it back on her finger. "Dinna take it off again."

"I cannot promise to agree with you on everything."

"I dinna ask you to. But you will keep your pledge to marry me."

"I won't be a bond-slave."

153

"I dinna want a bond-slave. I want a wife."

"You will not dictate my every move."

"There isna a man alive who could."

She could not help smiling. He sounded so resigned.

"Very well."

"Are ye sure, lass?"

She looked into his eyes. The uncertainty she saw there settled her heart. Ian might not realize it, but he needed her. That was a fair step toward love, she hoped.

"Aye, I'm sure," she said, copying his brogue.

He leaned down and placed a quick, possessive kiss on her lips. Taking her arm, he pulled her toward the chairs near the fire where he sat and pulled her into his lap. She adjusted to the strange sensation of sitting so intimately with a man.

"Now, tell me about Thorn."

He was not going to let up. She sighed and started her account of the letters and Diana's quandary.

He remarked, "That explains it, then."

"Explains what?" she asked.

Her heart broke for Diana when Ian told her about discovering that the other woman had sold her wedding pearls. She also accepted that with all that Ian had seen, she would never have been able to keep the blackmail a secret from him.

"I told her not to concern herself with the money. Why did she sell her wedding gift from Robert?"

"I dinna ken."

"Ian, we've got to do something. Diana is up in the boughs as it is. I cannot imagine what she is feeling now."

"Dinna worry, I'll think of something."

The chilling look in his eyes made her almost pity Mr. Thorn. Almost. She snuggled into Ian's lap and tucked her head under his chin. "As to that, I've already come up with a sound plan."

He caressed her back. "Aye?"

She explained her idea to go to the east side and inquire among her acquaintances there about Mr. Thorn. Ian's arms tightened around her like a vice. He cursed long and loudly.

"You are not going anywhere near there. If anyone is going to search for Thorn, it will be me."

She struggled in his arms until he loosened them enough for her to lean back and see into his face. The anger she saw there made no sense. It was a sound plan. However, she had no objection if he chose to take over the investigation.

"That's a wonderful idea. I had thought that the women I knew might not be acquainted with a man of Mr. Thorn's ilk. You, on the other hand, can disguise yourself as a common gamester or something and ferret out the information." Her easy acquiescence to him taking over this part of the investigation should soothe him.

It did not. "I'm not a bloody ferret."

"I understand." Ian's inconsistency annoyed her, but she did not argue with him. "Well, if you don't think you can find Mr. Thorn, then we will have to revert to the original plan."

Ian caught her chin between his thumb and forefinger. "Let us get one matter straight, Belle. You are no going anywhere near the stews."

The furious set of his jaw did not suggest she disagree with him. She ignored it. "If I don't, then how are we to find him? You cannot be thinking of hiring a Bow Street Runner. There could be a scandal and that is exactly what Diana is trying to avoid."

"Promise me, Belle."

She stared into his implacable eyes. It occurred to her that even a modern woman of the nineteenth century could have difficulty asserting herself with a man like Ian.

"Very well." She sighed to let him know what she thought of his demand. "I promise."

He smiled. "I will find Thorn."

She ground her teeth. Isn't that exactly what she had suggested? Men could be so stubborn. "What a wonderful idea."

"Ye needna take that sarcastic tone with me, lass."

She disagreed. It was much preferable to shooting him.

He kissed her gently and eased back. "We had best be headed back. I dinna want your aunt sending out a search party."

On the way home, once again ensconced in the blanket, Annabelle's heart beat with a mixture of delight and dread. She was going to marry the man she loved. She was also going to marry a man who believed in passion, but thought love a romantic illusion.

She and Ian returned from their trip to the Inn to discover not only Lady Beauford waiting impatiently for their return, but Robert, Diana and Ceddy as well. Robert had opened his mouth to ring a peal over Annabelle, only to be checked by Ian with an announcement of the engagement.

Her earlier prediction of her aunt's reaction proved to be correct. Lady Beauford gave Annabelle and Ian a satisfied smile. "So, you have finally come to your senses."

Annabelle grimaced at her aunt's words. She truly hoped what she was doing was sensible. She had the terrible feeling that she had made a huge wager and had no clue of the outcome. It felt like someone had her marker and would come to collect when she least expected.

"I say, that's capital news." Ceddy patted Ian on the back. "When's the nuptials going to take place, eh what?"

Annabelle answered. "Not for a while."

"We'll post the banns this Sunday." Ian contradicted her.

"That would put the wedding at less than a month away." Diana's scandalized tones echoed Annabelle's shocked thoughts. She needed more time. She hoped that over their engagement, Ian would come to love her. Three and a half weeks was not nearly enough time.

Lady Beauford started up from her chair at Ian's words. "Impossible. We cannot prepare a society wedding in that amount of time. Annabelle will need six months at least."

"I will be taking Annabelle to Graenfrae in a month. We can be wed here or wait until we reach my home."

Annabelle glared at him. "Do I not get any say in this?"

Ian turned to her, his face an imperturbable mask. "You already agreed to become my wife. You gave me your word."

"Yes, but—"

Ian did not let her finish.

"When we marry should be of little import to you."

"That's ludicrous. Naturally it matters when we marry. I will not be rushed into a hasty wedding." She nodded her head for emphasis.

Ian's impassive face broke into a smile. "I'm not proposing a runaway trip to Gretna Green, lass. A month is sufficient time to plan a wedding."

Lady Beauford snorted. "Spoken like a gentleman. Much they know about it."

Robert asked, "Will that give your family enough time to make the trip?"

"They won't be coming." Ian's words brooked no argument.

Annabelle did not understand. "Why not?"

"They are still in mourning, don't you know," Ceddy answered.

Robert agreed. "Of course. The earl's will forced Ian not to observe the year of mourning, but it would be highly improper for his family to attend a society wedding in London before the year is up."

"Propriety is undoubtedly all that matters. Showing family support and loyalty comes in a poor second." Diana's outburst shocked everyone into speechlessness.

"It's hardly that dire, m'dear. Annabelle will have sufficient opportunity to meet her in-laws in due course."

Diana's eyes glistened. "Without doubt."

Annabelle wished she could strangle her brother. He didn't know about Mr. Thorn, but he needn't be so bloody correct all of the time either.

Robert looked completely baffled. Lady Beauford drew Diana to sit on the settee next to her. "There, there, dear. One must expect to be a bit emotional during this time. Take a deep breath and calm yourself, my gel." She patted Diana's hand. "That's right. Much better."

Not wishing to cause Diana any more distress, Annabelle decided to bow to the inevitable. "You may post the banns this Sunday, Ian."

"I say, famous. Where's Creswell? This calls for champagne." Ceddy rang for the butler and Robert requested champagne. Creswell left the room beaming.

C7

Sunlight filtered through Annabelle's conscious. She opened one eye and confirmed that her maid had opened the drapes and the bright sun bounced off her white coverlet nearly blinding her. She quickly closed her eyes again and snuggled deeper into the covers. It must be late indeed if Purdy had opted to wake her. Unsurprised, she rolled over and tried to ignore the sunlight beating on her eyelids. She had lain awake almost the entire night reflecting on her decision to marry Ian.

The smell of chocolate wafted to Annabelle, tempting her to open her eyes once again. The maid had placed a tray with chocolate and toast on the table beside her bed. The melting butter on the thick slices of toast made Annabelle's mouth water. Groaning, she sat up. Purdy was nowhere to be seen. Relief filled Annabelle. She wasn't up to another bout of congratulations by her ecstatic maid.

The thought of marrying Ian terrified her. Yet, she knew that no other course would do. She could not imagine life without him. When he had kissed her and touched her the day before, she had finally realized that she had no choice. If she didn't marry Ian, she would always wish she had. She found him too appealing for her peace of mind. He said that he wanted her too and if the previous afternoon had been any indication, he did.

It didn't make any sense to her, however. The man thought one of her chief attractions was her ordinary appearance. How could he be so attracted to her? She was still frightened that one day he would wake up and realize that he wanted someone more exciting than *The Ordinary*. Would he break his word and take a mistress? The thought sent her stomach churning.

She took a hasty bite of toast and chastised herself. No matter what Ian felt in the future, he would never betray his word to her. The thought that he might desire to do so continued to haunt her. She had to believe that she truly was all that he wanted. If that were true, then he must care for her. If he could care for her and desire her, he could love her. She was sure of it.

Hurried footsteps sounded outside her door. What could Purdy be in such haste over? Perhaps Ian had called and here she was, not even in her wrapper. The thought galvanized her into action. Throwing back the covers, she leapt from the bed. She took another quick bite of toast before beginning her morning routine.

The door flew open, but it was not Purdy's happy face that greeted her. It was the chalk-white countenance of Diana. She looked about ready to collapse.

"What is the matter? You look as if you have seen a ghost," Annabelle said.

"It's Mr. Thorn. He sent a messenger telling me to meet him again today with another hundred pounds. He threatened to sell the letters to a scandal sheet if I did not do so." Diana's words came out in a near-hysterical rush.

Annabelle pulled her friend to the window seat and forced her to sit. "Then we shall have to meet him. Now, you must calm yourself."

Diana turned wild eyes to Annabelle. "How can I be calm? You heard Robert yesterday. Everything must be proper. He would hate me if I brought scandal to his name." She broke down and began sobbing. "I could not stand it if he hated me."

Annabelle rubbed Diana's back, trying to soothe her. "Hush. Robert is not going to hate you."

Diana began sobbing in earnest. "He already does. I'm sure of it."

Exasperated, Annabelle, admonished her, "Don't be a goose. Robert loves you dearly. Anyone can see that."

"Not anymore." The tears did not abate. "Not after what I've done."

Robert must know about the pearls. "Even if he is angry, he will get over it."

"He won't. He looked so hurt. I've never refused him my bed

159

before. Not in all the months we have been married."

Annabelle began to feel as if she was at the theater and did not know her part. "Your bed? What are you talking about?"

"Last night. I was afraid he would realize that something was wrong and so I told him that I was too tired." Diana wrung her hands. "He offered to just hold me and I told him I would rather not. He'll never forgive me."

Annabelle felt on very shaky ground. What did she know about marriage? Still, Robert loved his wife and wasn't going to hate her for something so trifling. When she said as much to Diana, the other woman's eyes flickered with hope.

"Do you think so?" Then she collapsed in tears again. "It doesn't matter. I can't sleep with him tonight either. I must avoid him or he will discover something is wrong and then he'll find out about Mr. Thorn. Then he'll hate me."

Annabelle wasn't about to point out to Diana that Robert was bloody well going to figure out something was wrong when his adoring wife started avoiding him. Ian would have to find Mr. Thorn and soon.

"Really, Diana, stop crying like this." Annabelle handed Diana a handkerchief. "Mr. Thorn has played into our hands quite nicely."

Diana mopped up her eyes. "What do you mean?"

"When he comes to meet you at Gunther's today, Ian will follow him." And this time, he won't lose him, she mentally added. "He will discover where Mr. Thorn lives and retrieve the letters for us."

Diana stared at Annabelle as if she had suggested dancing naked down St. James Street. "You cannot think of telling Ian. He would tell Robert and all would be lost."

There was nothing for it. Annabelle explained about Ian discovering the sold pearls and following Mr. Thorn once already. "He already knows? This is a disaster."

Annabelle grew impatient with her friend. "On the contrary. This is a blessing and I suggest you see it as one. Mr. Thorn is no match for Ian in any way."

Diana gave her a watery smile. "I see that you think very highly of your fiancé."

160

Annabelle felt herself blushing and turned away. "That is neither here nor there. The fact is, we can trust Ian and he will take care of finding Mr. Thorn's lodgings."

Diana grudgingly agreed.

"What time are you to meet Mr. Thorn?"

When Diana named the time, Annabelle sucked in her breath. It was less than an hour away. "Quickly, I must dress and send a note to Ian."

While Diana pulled out clothes for Annabelle to wear, Annabelle wrote a note for Ian telling him about the events of the morning and instructing him to find them at Gunther's and follow Mr. Thorn to his lodgings. She sealed it and rang for Purdy. When the maid came, Annabelle handed her the missive. "See that this is delivered immediately to my fiancé at Lord Finchley's home."

"Yes, milady."

A short time later, Annabelle and Diana entered Gunther's with trepidation. They had not seen Ian. Annabelle feared that he might have been out when the message was delivered. She and Diana ordered ices and took a table in the corner, partially shaded from view by a Chinese screen.

Annabelle steamed with fury. Every nervous gesture detected in her friend just served to increase her rage at the callous monster who could so spitefully use Diana this way. She wished for the hundredth time that she had not given Diana that horrid promise not to tell Robert about the blackmail.

She had a great deal of confidence in her brother, regardless of his sometimes sanctimonious ways. She believed he would have thoroughly dealt with the menace of Chester P. Thorn. When she said so to Diana, the latter became almost hysterical in her pleading for Annabelle to keep her secret.

"Calm yourself, Diana. I gave you my word and I intend to keep it. Robert will not hear of your secret from me."

"I'm glad to hear that, yer ladyship," said Thorn as he pulled a chair from a nearby table to join the ladies.

"You can't sit here. Are you mad? Someone will see and it will be remarked upon," said Diana anxiously.

"What, I can't sit with my own cousin?" asked the oily man.

Some of Annabelle's fury spilled over. "You may have these spurious letters you have threatened Lady Hamilton with, but there is absolutely no proof that you and she are in any way related. You will not address her as such either."

"High and mighty, aren't we? Well, your friend here," he pointed at Diana with his thumb, "knows I mean what I say. If you don't want my company, then the easiest way to rid yourself of it is to pay me the money that you owe me."

Annabelle saw no sign of Ian. She needed to prolong the meeting with Thorn for as long as possible. "First, you will show us the letters."

"You know I only bring one at a time like." He pulled a creased piece of paper from his wrinkled coat and placed it on the table in front of Diana. She took it and slid it immediately into her reticule.

"I'll take my money now." He put out a hand, dirt encrusted under his fingernails.

"When can I have the rest of the letters?" Diana asked desperately.

"I told you. One at a time." Thorn was starting to sound agitated.

"What guarantee does Lady Hamilton have that you won't publish the remaining letters?" inquired Annabelle coldly.

"You'll just have to trust me, now won't you?"

Annabelle wanted to take a horse brush and wipe the malicious grin right off the evil man's face. She would sooner trust a snake. Diana opened her reticule and Annabelle sent a silent signal for her to wait. Diana looked at her questioningly, but redid the drawstring on her bag.

"I am afraid that we need a little more assurance." Annabelle fought to keep the contempt she felt for Thorn from her voice.

He glared at her. "You ain't gettin' it. Now, where's my blunt?"

Diana again opened her bag and withdrew the money. "Here is the hundred pounds." She handed Thorn a pile of banknotes. "When can I expect delivery of the other letters?"

"I'm thinking I need two hundred pounds for this letter."

Diana's eyes took on a desperate quality. "I only received two hundred pounds all together for my wedding pearls. How am I to pay for the next letter if I give it all to you now?"

"That's not my worry, cousin."

When Thorn emphasized the word 'cousin', Annabelle had to take a deep breath and let it out slowly or she would have put her parasol to good use over the man's head.

Annabelle laid a calming hand on her sister-in-law's clutched fingers. She gave her a reassuring squeeze before turning to confront Thorn. "If you want to see one more pound out of Lady Hamilton then you will keep to the original agreement. If you do not, I will tell my brother about the letters and let him deal with you."

Thorn squirmed in his seat. "Here now, you wouldn't do that. It would upset your friend here and your brother wouldn't thank you none either."

Annabelle let all the disdain she felt for the odious man show in her face. "I have only refrained from telling my brother because of a promise I made to Lady Hamilton. If, however, you change the terms of your agreement, I will consider my promise null and void."

"There's no reason to get hasty now. I was just trying to get a little for meself." Thorn's voice took on a whining quality.

His words didn't make any sense. "Don't try to convince me that you are giving the proceeds of your little scheme to an ailing mother, or any such thing. Every guinea is going into your greedy pockets."

A look of fear suffused Thorns features. "Just give me the hundred and be done with it. I'm in this alone, I am."

Diana did as he asked and Thorn jumped from the table. He headed toward the door like all the demons of hell were after him. What had gotten into the man?

"I don't see Ian. Do you think he is waiting outside?" Diana asked.

Annabelle stood up. "I don't know. We'll have to go outside and see."

When they came out of Gunther's, they saw nothing of Ian. Thorn got into a hansom cab.

"We'll lose him if we don't do something quickly," Annabelle exclaimed.

Diana twisted her hands together. "I don't know what we could do. He'll recognize us if we try to follow him and it might make him angry enough to publish the letters."

A gentleman alighted from a hansom cab in front of the ladies, almost blocking their view of Thorn. Annabelle jumped into the cab.

"Annabelle, what are you doing?"

"I'm going to follow Thorn. Find Ian and tell him that I will meet him at Aunt Griselda's." She tapped on the roof of the cab. "Follow the cab that has just pulled into the street. There's an extra guinea for you if you don't lose him."

The cabbie took her at her word and lurched into the horse and carriage traffic on the street. Annabelle waved at Diana from the window before turning her attention to the direction they were going. She had to brace her feet against the bench opposite to stop herself from ending up a heap on the floor as the cab lurched from side to side.

After what seemed like an interminable time in the swaying conveyance, Annabelle perceived a change in the sounds and sights around her. She could hear the loud calls of street vendors selling meat pies amidst the piercing call of gulls. Strong odors wafted in through the cab window. They must be near the docks.

The carriage came to an abrupt halt. Annabelle peeked her head out the window in time to see Thorn walking up the street. She recognized the area as one she had been to once to meet with some women concerning her cause. Jumping down from the carriage, she paid the driver and offered to double his wages to wait for her.

Following Thorn up the busy street, she thought the area looked rougher than she remembered. Women stood leaning against the buildings and called to the passing men, offering things that made Annabelle's ears burn.

Thorn turned up an alley and Annabelle followed. The buildings on her right and left blocked the light, casting things into sinister shadows. She wondered at the wisdom of following Thorn on foot. In his hurry, he did not notice Annabelle or anyone else for that matter. Annabelle heaved a sigh of relief when he led her out of the alley and she once again was bathed in daylight.

Oh no. Thorn was meeting someone. He went to a closed carriage and climbed inside. The curtains were drawn so Annabelle could not see if it was occupied. Intuition told her that it was. It was not the sort of conveyance that Thorn would be using. Knowing that she could not possibly follow the carriage on foot, she headed back toward her waiting cab. When she came to the alley, she had to force herself to go inside.

The relief she felt when she came out on the side where she had left her cab was short lived.

Two rogues blocked her way almost immediately.

"Olly, looks like we've got ourselves a new bird. What do you say, ducks, you want to play wiv' me and Olly?"

The man speaking was short and so thick with muscle that he looked fat. Olly, a tall man with more than one day's stubble on his unwashed face, greeted the suggestion with a leer. The sight of his thin lips open over brown and decaying teeth sickened Annabelle.

Her stomach lurched at the thought of "playing with" the pockmarked and greasy-haired man. Her knees grew weak with fear. She darted a glance to where her cab was waiting and felt her first tremors of terror. It was gone. She turned to run back the way she had come, but got no more than a step before Olly's friend grabbed her from behind.

Chapter Thirteen

Ian heard Belle's scream before he saw her. His insides, already tight as the spring on a wrist-clock, went cold with fear. He kneed his horse to a gallop and sped toward her defiant cries. Whoever had her didn't know what they were getting into, he thought with grim satisfaction as the sound of scuffling and men's curses reached his ear.

The scene he came upon turned his insides to water.

Belle was caught between two men. The first had her arms in his mangy grip and the other, a short powerfully built man, was fighting to control her legs. The fury that had been eating Ian since he found Diana outside Gunther's and she had told him about Annabelle following Thorn raged out of control now.

The tall, ugly man yanked on Belle's arms and Ian vowed that was the last thing the ugly rotter was going to do. He swung off his horse and commanded the animal to stay. Knowing Nightsong would not move until he gave the signal again, Ian stormed over to the bastards with their hands all over Belle.

He took great satisfaction at the sound of bone crunching as he planted his fist in the jaw of the man holding Belle's arms. The miscreant howled in anguish and dropped his hold on Belle. Gripping Annabelle's torso with his left hand, Ian let his right elbow fly back and connect with the face of the shorter man.

The bastard didn't fall, but did grunt and let go of Belle. Ian scooped her up and headed back to his horse. Belle clutched at his shoulders, her face pressed against his neck. The trembling in her body infuriated him. Ian swung her up onto his horse and made sure she had a firm hold on the saddle before turning to finish the work with the two bastards who had dared to touch his fiancée.

The ugly one was standing again, but he swayed on his feet. Ian ignored him. One good blow and he would be history. The short man was smiling at Ian, clearly every bit as stupid as he looked. Ian moved forward with sure deliberation. The short man bellowed as Ian picked him up and tossed him against the wall of the building. A demi-rep who had been watching the entire exchange with interest screeched as the man rolled off the wall and landed on her feet. He did not move again.

Ian turned his attention to the one with a broken jaw. He must have been smarter than he looked because he was already running down the street. Two short whistles brought Nightsong near. Swinging up behind Belle, Ian kneed the horse into a gallop. They had to get out of there before more of the blackguards' friends showed up.

"You know, if you had gotten here just a few minutes before, I would not have lost Mr. Thorn. What took you so long? Did you not get my note?"

Ian thought he had been angry before, but that was nothing compared to how he felt when Belle took him to task for his lack of timeliness. "And if I had come five minutes later, you would be lying on some bug-infested cot with one of those bastards buried between your legs."

She flinched and he felt guilty for putting the fear back in her eyes. She opened her mouth to speak.

His arms tightened around her of their own volition. "Dinna say another word, Belle."

She opened her mouth to protest and he put his hand over it. "Not one word. Agreed?"

She nodded her head. He removed his hand.

And then she proceeded to do exactly what he'd warned her not to. She spoke. "I'm sorry, Ian."

When he did not respond, she clung more tightly to him. "The world can be a frightening place, especially for a woman. I sometimes fight the fears that beset me with conviction that I can face any circumstance as well as a man, but…" She paused and shuddered. "I cannot deny that there are times my limitations are as frightening as my circumstances."

He recalled that day in the park, when she had explained her reasons for not wanting to marry without some certainty her husband would cherish rather than harm her. The law was not a good enough protection, neither was common decency, as she had learned today.

"I knew you would come for me, but I should not have said what I did about your timing. It was uncalled for."

But true, which was where some of his fury came from. The sense that if he had not arrived precisely when he did, she would have been irreparably harmed. And that if he had come a few moments earlier, he would have caught the blackguard.

"Shh…it is all right, lass."

They rode in silence until they reached the edge of West London. Ian hailed a hansom cab.

Belle chewed her lower lip. "What are you doing, Ian?"

"Did ye want to arrive at your aunt's doorstep in my lap?"

She seemed to consider it for a moment. "Well there is that, but I'm not exactly in your lap. I mean, I'm actually in front of you."

The cab stopped and Ian swung down off of his horse. He reached up and pulled Belle down.

She stared up at him, her eyes wide. "Are you going to send me in the carriage alone?"

That was exactly what he had intended, but the continued fear in her eyes changed his mind. "Nay. I'll tie Nightsong to the back of the carriage and ride with you."

Her shoulders relaxed. "That is an excellent idea." She bit her bottom lip. "Thank you."

She was too independent by half, but he had to admit that he did not like seeing his feisty bluestocking so subdued.

"It will be my pleasure, lass."

He secured his horse and gave the driver his direction before swinging up into the carriage behind Belle. She sat on the cushion, her hands clasped tightly in her lap. He ignored the empty seat opposite and sat down beside her. Then, he lifted and settled her snugly in his lap. He began to rhythmically rub her back.

She shuddered again and buried her face against his chest. Her tears started almost immediately.

"They were going to hurt me, Ian. They wanted to play with me." She clung tightly to him. "If you had not come..." Her words trailed into a sob.

"Ye would have found a way to free yourself, lass. You have resources they know nothing about." He couldn't stand the brokenness he heard in her voice.

She hiccupped against him. "Do you really think so? What resources?"

"Intelligence. They wouldna know what to do with your brains, lass, considering they have none of their own."

He felt like a rich man indeed when she let out a small laugh.

Sighing, she snuggled closer. "I was terrified."

"Aye. But you were no helpless. You were giving them more trouble than they knew what to do with."

"I was foolish to get out of the cab."

He didn't say anything. She hadn't been just foolish, she had been a bloody idiot, but he wasn't going to tell her so and start her tears all over again.

"Dinna ever do that again," he said.

"I won't."

Her fervent promise soothed his nerves until he remembered the sight of her stretched out between the two men, battling for her freedom. It was not a sight he would ever forget.

Needing the reassurance that she was indeed all right, he tipped her head up and pressed a soft kiss on her lips.

She smiled. "That was nice. Thank you, Ian."

"You dinna have to thank me for kissing you. I enjoy it."

She blushed. "That's not what I meant, you daft man. I was

169

thanking you for saving me."

He grew serious. "You promised me that you would let me search for Thorn. You broke your word to me, Belle."

"We waited for you, but you never came. I was certain that we would lose our chance to catch Mr. Thorn if I didn't follow him."

He could not believe her reasoning. "Do you think that matters one bloody bit if you end up hurt, or worse?"

She jumped at his roar. "Do not shout at me. I have had enough of bad-mannered men to last me a long while."

"You dare to compare me to those two bastards?"

He wanted to toss her off his lap. He was furious that she would accuse him of being like the two men who would have done unspeakable things to her. Ian cared about her, damn it.

"That is not what I meant."

He was having none of it. He pulled her arms from around his neck where they had come to rest and began to set her on the cushion opposite.

She clung to him. "What are you doing?"

He glared at her. She had managed to lock her hands behind his neck again. "I wouldna want you to force you to endure my mannerless touch."

He again tried to put her away from him.

She wouldn't budge. "No."

"Nay?"

She scooted even closer to him, until her body was molded against his thighs and chest. Even in his fury, he reacted to the feel of her sweet bottom against his thighs.

Annabelle appeared oblivious. "I'm not going anywhere. I have had a terrible experience and I need comfort." She burrowed against him. "You are my fiancé and it is your job to comfort me."

He stared at her. "'Tis my job, lass?"

She nodded. "Yes." Then two lone tears trickled down her cheeks. "I need you to hold me. I told you I know I was foolish and that I am sorry. I certainly did not mean to compare you to those awful men. You

170

are not usually so easily offended," she said with a small sniffle.

She was right, but he was still angry with himself and despite her apology, frustrated with her actions. Regardless, she deserved his tender care, not anger. He would finish yelling at her later, when she was feeling better. For now, she needed his comfort. She had said so. It was his job. He smiled.

He wasn't sure what to do. She said she wanted him to hold her. So he did. Putting his arms back around her securely, he held her as if he never wanted to let her go. He didn't.

It must have been what she needed because she gave a satisfied sigh and relaxed against him. By the time they arrived at her aunt's home, Belle had calmed down considerably. Her hands no longer trembled and there was not a tear in sight. He expelled a sigh of relief. He did not like seeing his spirited lady terrified and weepy. As the carriage drew to a halt, she laughed softly.

"What is amusing you, Belle?"

"I am now in your lap, Ian. Is this more proper than us arriving together on your horse?"

He smiled at her humor. "Aye, lass, no one can see us."

She agreed. "In the *ton* appearance is all."

Perhaps that is what he needed so desperately in Belle. Everything about her went bone deep. She did not use a flirtatious manner and tantalizing cleavage to hide a cold heart. Her passionate nature was as much a part of her as breathing. She was passionate in his arms. She was passionately loyal. She was passionate about her cause. Although, he wished she were not.

Her character and courage influenced everything she did. The knowledge that Belle was everything he could ever want in a wife humbled him. He vowed that she would never regret her decision to marry him.

C3

William stared in stupefaction at *The London Times*. There must be some mistake. His plans could not be destroyed like this. It all started when he lost the ninety pounds gaming. Who would have thought those fools down at the dock would be so lucky? He picked up the paper and reread the announcement, hoping he had misread the parties mentioned. He had not. Lady Annabelle Courtney, sister to Earl of Hamilton, announced her engagement to the Earl of Graenfrae. Impossible.

William played with the hundred pounds in his pocket. Thorn had tried to tell him that Lady Hamilton had balked at the price and only paid fifty pounds.

The marks William had left on Thorn's throat would be a constant reminder not to try something so foolish as to cheat his employer again. Flexing his fingers, he saw Thorn's grimy countenance in his mind's eye. It wouldn't be long before the fool would be of no use to him. Then he would see about getting rid of him permanently, just as he had his wife when her nagging became too much to bear. A man like William could not be expected to suffer the presence of fools in his life.

He stared out the window of his room with unseeing eyes. He had to do something immediately. Not only was his personal situation getting risky, he had actually had to promise the full hundred pounds to his man of business to keep his creditors from taking him to debtors' court. They were going to try to sell his hunters, but he would not let them. The wedding was set for less than a month away. Desperation seized him.

He must think of something to force Lady Annabelle to wed him. Only one thing would break a formal engagement. Scandal. If he compromised Lady Annabelle, surely even a Scottish laird would look elsewhere for a bride. William put the paper aside and turned his mind to ways of compromising the spinster heiress.

ഗ

If she had not agreed to meet Vivian, Annabelle would never have accepted the invitation to Lady Markham's musicale. She would have pretended a head cold or a severe headache. Just like the one plaguing her now. Lady Markham had a fond grandmama's view of her descendant's musical ability. A view that the rest of the Polite World did not share. The debutante attempting to sing right now could make an owl wince with her screeching, Annabelle decided.

"Does the lass not ken she sounds like a barn owl then?"

Ian's whispered question so perfectly matched her own thoughts that Annabelle had to bite her lips together to keep from laughing.

"Hush, Ian. She is doing her best."

He shrugged his powerful shoulders. "Aye."

Since the debacle when she followed Mr. Thorn, Annabelle had determined that she appreciated Ian's size. He made her feel safe. He also knew how to ring a peal that put both her aunt and Robert to shame. His furious demand that she never, ever do anything so foolish again still echoed in her mind.

He had waited until the following day when she was feeling much more the thing. Then he had taken her for a drive and by the time they reached the park with the duck pond, her ears had been ringing. She didn't complain, though. She had been foolish and Ian had not shared her misfortune with Aunt Griselda or Robert. Besides, his fury was spurred by caring.

The music finally came to an end and she stood with Ian. She introduced him to an acquaintance that she knew was as batty about new farming techniques as Ian and Robert. That should keep him occupied while she found Vivian and exchanged information. After his fury over her following Mr. Thorn, she wasn't about to risk another confrontation by telling him about her clandestine activities on behalf of women's rights.

She excused herself from the discussion of fertilizers on the pretext of speaking to a friend. Which was indeed the truth, she consoled herself. She *was* going to speak to a friend. Hurrying up the stairs, she headed for the vacant sleeping chamber she and Vivian had agreed upon. Squeezing through the cracked door, she found Vivian already waiting.

"I wasn't sure you would get away from your fiancé. Since you announced your engagement, he is never far from your side." Vivian's voice held a teasing quality.

Her words were nothing less than the truth. Ian had informed Annabelle that he no longer saw the need to pretend he wasn't singling her out. It should be obvious, even to the densest members of the *ton,* that a gentleman would spend time with the lady he planned to marry.

"I introduced him to someone who shares his interest in horticulture." Annabelle used the small candle Vivian had brought to light one of the wall sconces. "Did you bring the pamphlets?"

Vivian nodded and carefully rolled up her skirt to access the pocket in her chemise. She pulled out some papers and gave a sigh of relief. "You have no idea how nervous I have been all evening. For some reason every time I moved, I could hear them crinkling." She handed the crisp stack of folded leaflets to Annabelle. "I was terrified Ceddy would hear."

"*Ceddy?*"

Vivian's cheeks grew pink. "He told me to call him that. I could hardly refuse after all he has done."

Annabelle smiled. "I do believe that you have developed a *tendre* for my old friend."

Nodding shyly, Vivian sighed. "Do you think it is possible that he shares my feelings?"

Remembering her impression of the other evening, Annabelle nodded. "I would say there is an excellent chance." Then, impulsively, she leaned forward and gave Vivian a hug. "I am very happy for you. You must let me know the minute he comes up to scratch."

Vivian hugged her back. "Oh, thank you." She pulled away and straightened her gown. "I must go. I'm sure Ceddy will be looking for me."

Annabelle waved her off. Then she turned away from the door and lifted her skirt, intent on getting the pamphlets secured so she could return to Ian. Her skirt got caught on the one of the flyers sticking out of the pocket and she tried to dislodge it without ruining the paper or creasing her gown.

"Annabelle. My dear." The sound of a man's voice from behind her shocked Annabelle into immobility. Then she whipped her head around and the unbelievable was true. Squire Renton stood not two feet behind her and was staring at her exposed legs as if they were a lobster patty and he was a starving man in search of food.

So great was her shock that she did not immediately react when he pounced on her and attempted to plant a kiss on her astonished lips. Regaining her senses at the last moment she turned her head and felt a wet smack planted firmly on her cheek. His hands roved down to meet hers, where they were desperately trying to get her skirt down. He caressed her bare thigh and groaned as if in pain.

"My dear, you are such a temptation."

Taking a deep breath, she shoved against him with all her might, but his hold was much stronger than it appeared. She twisted violently, trying to get away from him.

"Let me go."

He ignored her half-shouted plea. In her struggle, she tripped. The squire took advantage of her unbalance to tip her onto the bed, falling heavily on top of her.

"My dear, I have worshipped you from afar." He placed wet kisses on her neck and face that made her want to gag. "You cannot be thinking of marrying that Scottish ruffian. He does not share your interests like I do."

"Get the hell off my fiancée."

Ian's roar was loud enough to wake the dead. She was sure of it. When the squire, who had gone suddenly still, did not move fast enough, Ian grabbed him and tossed him away from her. Then Ian grabbed the hem of her dress, which had ridden up to expose most of her legs, and yanked it down.

The cold fury in his eyes terrified her. He would believe that she had betrayed him like his first betrothed. She could not let that happen.

"Ian, it is not what you think," she said.

"I dinna walk into a sleeping chamber and find ye practically naked with a man on top of ye, doing his best to seduce you?" A tick in his cheek belied the conversational tone of voice Ian used.

175

"Well, I suppose it did look like that, but—" She wasn't allowed to finish.

Squire Renton had picked himself up from the floor and spoke. "You must not blame the dear girl. She is merely a victim of her passion. Just as am I."

She stared at the squire. Had the man lost his mind? "I am not a victim of my passion."

"My dear, you must not try to hide it. It is better for Graenfrae to discover our mutual affection and interests now than later."

Fury tempered by pity coursed through Annabelle. Obviously the ridiculous man had developed tender feelings for her and in his besotted state, he had convinced himself that she returned them. It was not something she was familiar with. The hysterical urge to laugh almost overwhelmed her. Prior to this Season, gentlemen of the *ton* had left her alone.

"There is no mutual affection." Turning to Ian, she grasped his coat. "You must believe me."

Ian looked down at her, his expression unreadable. "We will discuss this later."

She felt the cold weight of fear settle in her stomach. If only she had told Ian of her real reason for coming. An idea struck. She would show him the pamphlets. But she had to do it now, so he would believe her that she had just gotten them.

"No, Ian, we must discuss this now."

She turned back to the squire. "Please go. I will explain everything to Ian."

The stupid man shook his head. "I cannot leave you to the mercies of this Scottish savage."

Finally fury overcame pity and Annabelle stood. She stormed over to the squire. "He is not a savage, he is the man I love and you will do well to remember that. If you do not leave this very minute, I will not be responsible for my actions."

The man was more stupid than she thought. He actually took a step toward her. "Do not worry. You do not have to pretend. I will marry you. Your reputation is safe."

Annabelle wanted to scream. Instead, she took action. Pulling her arm back, she swung forward with all her might and punched the stupid man in the stomach. He doubled over.

"I do not wish to marry anyone but Ian." She emphasized each word slowly, so the ridiculous man would understand.

Then, while he was still debilitated from her blow, she pushed him out the door and shut it. After turning the key in the lock, she faced Ian.

"Now, I will explain."

She began rolling up her skirt again.

"Dinna think to sidetrack me with your body, Belle."

She stopped rolling and stared at him. She cocked her head to one side. "Why? Would it work?"

He shrugged. "Perhaps."

She resumed her task of lifting her skirt. She then withdrew the pamphlets. "I came in here to get these."

Ian took the pamphlets from her and when he saw what they said, his grim countenance returned.

"I was in the process of hiding them in my chemise, when the squire leaped on me. He must have followed me in here and when he saw my bare legs it was too much for him."

The very idea was ludicrous to her, but what else could explain the squire's inexplicable behavior?

Ian must not have thought it was such a strange explanation because he did not laugh. "What was all that business about your mutual affection?"

"I don't know. It is true that we share some interests, but nothing more than that. I have never given him any reason to believe I encourage his suit." She forced Ian to meet her gaze. "You must believe me."

"Lower your gown, Belle, 'tis much too distracting."

She wondered how long it would take him to notice. "No."

He glared at her. "Nay?"

"Uh-uh." She shook her head. "I don't want to."

He moved toward her. "Why not?"

"I had hoped that if the sight of my bare legs would inflame the squire's passion, it would do no less for you. Does it?" She couldn't keep a niggling worry from her voice. What if it didn't? What if Ian had only used passion to convince her to marry him and now his true feelings would come out?

He closed the rest of the distance between them and pulled her into his arms. As he lowered his lips to hers he said, "The mere sight of you inflames my senses, Belle. You could be covered from head to toe with only the sparkle in your eyes visible and I would want to bed you."

His lips swallowed her response. She released her gown to fall about her ankles and twined her fingers in his hair. His kiss said that he trusted her, that his passion for her was real and that she belonged to him. She melted against his length, content to be held by the one man she could give her heart.

Several minutes later, Ian pulled away. "We must stop, Belle. Your aunt will wonder where we have gone."

She nodded. "You are right."

Taking the pamphlets from where Ian had dropped them on the bed, she lifted her skirt for the third time that night. After securing them she turned to Ian. His brooding expression made her nervous.

"Ye canna keep exposing yourself to risk for your cause."

Her heart sank. "I cannot stop. It is too important."

He sighed and ran his fingers through his hair. "'Tis just what my gran-da thought. He gave up everything for his cause."

"What do you mean, Ian?" Finally, she would understand his mixed messages regarding her cause. He didn't seem offended by the nature of the cause, but by the risks she took for it.

He turned away from her and moved toward the window that looked out into the black night. "My grandfather did not believe in English rule and he sacrificed everything to fight against it, his family, his estates, his life." He swung back around to face her and the intensity in his eyes frightened her. "The price was too high, lass."

"This is not the same thing, Ian. The fight for the Rights of Women does not require that sort of sacrifice." He had to believe her. He had to

178

understand. She could not give up the one thing that had saved her from despair after her parents' deaths.

"No sacrifice? If you had been killed at the riot, would ye call that no sacrifice?"

She shook her head. "But I wasn't killed, or even in danger of dying." Remembering the look on the angry man's face when Ian tossed him away, she wasn't absolutely sure on that point, but saw no reason to fuel Ian's fear.

"And tonight? If our engagement had ended because of Renton's actions when he caught you half-naked, would it have been worth it? No one would blame me for breaking our betrothal after what I witnessed." He took her shoulders in a powerful grip. "Is it worth it, Belle? Is it?"

Her throat constricted. She willed herself to stay calm. He did not mean it. He would not break off their association over something so trivial.

"Don't make me answer that. Do not make me choose between you and my beliefs." She couldn't help it, her voice cracked.

He glared at her. "Dinna cry, lass."

She brushed at the moisture under her eyes. "I'm not."

He sighed. "Aye, you are." He opened his arms and after a brief hesitation, she ran into them.

"You won't break the engagement, will you?" She spoke against his waistcoat.

He rubbed his chin on the top of her head. "Nay, lass. I fought too hard to get you. I'm never letting you go."

Her relief was so profound that her tears spilled over and slipped silently down her cheeks. "It will be all right, Ian. You must trust me."

He pulled away from her and met her gaze with tender eyes. "Aye. But you must compromise with me, Belle."

Compromise sounded better than choosing between him and her beliefs. "What do you have in mind?"

"I want to know all of your plans before you do them and you will not attend any more lectures without me." The tenderness in his eyes had given way to implacability.

She did not mind. "You would go to the lectures with me?"

"Aye. If it is safe to attend."

She nodded. He would take some convincing at times, but she trusted him. If he promised her now, he would not renege later. He would not use estate business or a full schedule to get out of taking her. She sensed that Ian would always fulfill his promises to her to his utmost ability.

"I agree to your compromise." She thought for a minute. She owed him complete honesty. "But there may be times I forget to tell you first. Sometimes, I act on the spur of the moment."

His smile felt like the sun coming out after a bone-chilling fog. "I ken, Belle."

He squeezed her one last time before setting her away from him. "We must go. I have something of import to discuss with your squire."

The look of cold menace was back in Ian's eyes.

"He's not my squire," she protested, offended at Ian's choice of words. He clearly was not completely over his anger at finding her in the arms of another man.

Ian did not respond and moved toward the door.

"Wait. Ian, what do you need to discuss with Squire Renton?"

"'Tis between gentlemen, Belle. You need not concern yourself."

She flew at him. Grasping his arm, she shook it. "Tell me what you are talking about." She had a terrible feeling that she already knew. "Ian, you cannot mean to challenge him."

The idea was too ridiculous. This was the nineteenth century. Gentlemen had far more civilized means of settling their differences.

"I can no let the insult pass, Belle. He had his bloody hands all over you."

Ian had to be joking. The set of his jaw and look in his eyes said otherwise.

"I forbid it." She tried to shake him, but found him as moveable as a mountain. "You will not challenge the squire. It was just a misunderstanding."

"I dinna call finding my fiancée pinned to the bed by a lecherous fiend a misunderstanding." The rigidity in his voice convinced Annabelle that Ian was determined to follow through with his plan.

That did not stop her from trying to convince him otherwise. "You are taking it too much to heart. I'm sure he has already learned his lesson. I did strike him after all."

Amusement gleamed briefly in Ian's eyes. "Aye, lass, you did."

She smiled and sighed with relief. "Then you will give up this plan to challenge him."

Ian unlocked the door before answering. He opened it and stepped into the hall.

"Ye should have realized by now, lass, that I dinna give up my plans once I've set my mind on them."

Chapter Fourteen

"Did you say, *Squire Renton* is here to call?"

The man could not be that foolish. Perhaps he had come to ask her to plead with Ian on his behalf. That would be an intelligent thing to do. Not that it would make any difference of course. Ian had remained impervious to both her threats and her pleas. She would have to explain this to the squire.

"Show him in, Creswell." At the look of disapproval on her butler's face, she sighed. "Please call my aunt down as well."

The servant's demeanor lightened infinitesimally.

Moments later, a shaken-looking squire entered the drawing room. He fell on his knee by Annabelle's chair. "My dear. I am so sorry to have caused you distress."

She frowned at the man on the carpet at her feet. "You may not address me so familiarly, Squire Renton. You have greatly mistaken yourself and caused us both a good deal of trouble."

The squire dropped his graying head, his chin touching his chest. "I know. I am terribly sorry, Lady Annabelle."

"Perhaps if you said that to my fiancé, he would not feel the need to act out this farce."

At her words, the squire's head lifted. Putting his hand to his heart, he sighed. "So, you know about the duel. I suppose it was too much to think it could be kept completely private."

Annabelle could not hide her exasperation. "You are dueling with my fiancé over a perceived insult to me. Naturally, I know about it. Oh, do sit in a chair."

He looked wounded, but did as she bid. "I came to seek your mercy, Lady Annabelle."

She wished she could offer some measure of hope, but knew it was useless. "I have already begged Ian to call off the duel and it is no use."

A spark of anger showed in the squire's eyes, but it was gone immediately and she wondered if she had seen it at all. "I did not come to ask you to plead on my behalf, my dear lady. I had hoped that for the sake of our once great friendship, you would be willing to accompany me to a lecture by Mrs. Burnaby."

The man truly suffered delusions. Great friendship indeed. They had run into each other on occasion and discovered a very few mutual interests. "I am afraid I must decline."

"You would not deny possibly my last request, would you?"

Annabelle was much more moved by the fact that Ian might be hurt than the squire's theatrical fear of his own demise. However, she did feel some responsibility. The man had believed she shared his feelings. "I do not think that would be wise."

"I wanted to fill my now empty life with service to the cause. I hope you would introduce me to others involved in it."

"If you are dead, you won't have a life to fill," she could not help pointing out.

His hand went back over his heart. "I do not believe I have dishonored you. My actions were prompted by the purest of motives. Love." He sighed. "Therefore, it would not be dishonorable to leave Town rather than meet the laird at dawn."

He was willing to leave Town? Ian would not risk hurt or worse. She had promised Ian that she would not attend any lectures without him. He would be angry when he found out, but he would be alive.

"I merely sought something to fill the vast void left in my life by my unrequited love."

At least now he realized she did not return the feelings. Besides, his desire, so like her own when her parents had died, moved Annabelle. She would introduce him to leaders in the cause, who could give him fulfilling assignments in the country. He would leave Town.

Ian would be safe and her guilt over this ridiculous man's *tendre* would be assuaged.

"Very well. When is the lecture?"

He smiled and stood. "In less than an hour. We must hurry if we are to arrive in time."

At that moment, Lady Beauford entered the room. She looked at the squire with mild interest. Thankfully, Ian had told no one about the altercation in the bedchamber. "Squire Renton. How are you?" Her tone implied: *and what are you doing here?*

"I've come to take Lady Annabelle to a lecture."

Annabelle's aunt turned a troubled gaze to her niece. "It isn't one of those lectures in Cheapside again is it?"

Before Annabelle had an opportunity to answer, the squire jumped in. "No, my lady. We will be attending a lecture on the scientific properties of magnetism. Quite the rage."

Lady Beauford's eyes lit up. "I should love to accompany you." Her face fell. "However, I promised the mantua maker I would be in for a fitting this afternoon."

Annabelle breathed a sigh of relief. If the squire was going to lie to her aunt, he could at least have made their excursion sound boring. She gave him a look that she hoped expressed her displeasure. "We must be off then. You did say the lecture was to begin any moment."

"When shall I expect you back?" asked her aunt.

Again the squire spoke. "There is to be a reception afterward, it could be quite late this afternoon."

Annabelle frowned. "I'm sure we won't stay for it."

Neither her aunt nor the squire said anything and Annabelle followed him out to his waiting carriage, much to Creswell's obvious dismay. The rumor mill among the servants was much more up to date than her aunt's cronies.

As the squire helped her into the carriage, Annabelle glanced briefly at the horses. Not an avid rider, horseflesh usually did not interest her. However, there was something familiar about the squire's steeds and carriage.

The squire didn't seem inclined to speak, so Annabelle held her own counsel. Perhaps accompanying him to the lecture was not a good idea. Could she not have simply sent him with a letter of introduction? Annabelle admitted to herself that she was motivated in no small part by guilt. The squire was giving up his life in London because of his affection for her.

They had been riding in silence for several minutes when she suddenly remembered where she had seen the horses and carriage before. It was very similar, if not identical, to the one Mr. Thorn had disappeared into.

Did Squire Renton know that his friend was a blackmailer and a rogue? An even more unsettling thought surfaced. Was the squire in collusion with Mr. Thorn? Fear curled up her insides. She had to get out of the carriage immediately.

"We must return to my aunt's house. I had forgotten, but my fiancé is coming to call. He will be furious to discover I am gone."

A look very like satisfaction settled on the squire's face. "I am certain he will survive your absence for one afternoon. He will have your company every day for the years to come."

"I really must insist that you return me to my aunt's house immediately."

All pretense of the grieving, rejected suitor vanished. The squire stared disdainfully at her. "Frankly, your preference is of little moment to me. Do you truly believe that I would let you marry that Scottish buffoon and waste your treasure on his estates?"

Desperation seized her. "What are you saying?"

"My dear, we are very nearly to the North Road and from there, it is but a few days to Gretna Green. I'm sure if you think hard, you can imagine my plans." The sneer in his voice frightened her more than the words.

"If you love me as you say, you cannot consider forcing me to wed you."

He laughed and the sound brought forth feelings far from joy in her chest. "Love? You're no more than a whey-faced, bluestocking spinster. The only thing I love about you is your fortune, which I will have complete control of once we are married."

The dishonest poser. "What fortune? My dowry is no more than moderate."

His evil laugh issued forth again. "Do not attempt to deceive me as you have the rest of the *ton.* You are an heiress and your money is going to bring my life back to rights. Now be quiet. I am not a man with patience for foolish chatter."

Annabelle had no intention of sitting back and calmly allowing the blackguard to kidnap her to Gretna Green. If she did not get out of the carriage now, they would be on the North Road and going too fast for her to make the jump. She could not wait any longer.

Moving as quickly as possible, she dove for the door handle. Shoving the door open, she tried to leap out of the moving vehicle.

The squire cursed. He grabbed her gown. Hauling her back into the carriage, he slammed her against the upholstery. He pulled a pistol from his waistcoat and pointed it at her.

"I do not have to kill you to stop you. A bullet through your shoulder or leg would be enough to prevent any more attempts to escape."

Her mouth went dry at the threat. Forcing herself to remain calm, she sat up straight against the cushions and averted her face.

"You may ignore me for now. You'll learn soon enough how to treat your lord and master after we are married."

She turned back to glare at him. "I will not have a lord and master. I do not believe in that drivel."

"Drivel. It's the Common Law of England. Once we are married, I'll as good as own you. Drivel is what that old biddy spoke before the riot. What I put myself through to woo you." He gave her a disgusted look. "I tried to give you a proper courtship, but you would have none of it. You insisted on engaging yourself to that barbarian."

With each word spewed forth from his mouth, her apprehension grew. The man was totally wicked. She had no doubt now that he was connected to Mr. Thorn and the blackmail scheme. Well, she wasn't going to marry him, no matter what he believed. She would find a way to escape. She averted her face again and set her mind to the task of outwitting the evil man.

ᢙ

"She's with *who*?" Ian's voice rose in fury as the words Creswell had spoken registered.

"Just so, milord. They left not an hour ago. I took the liberty of listening at the door while waiting for Her Ladyship to arrive for propriety's sake."

"Where did they go?" Ian would kill her when he caught up with her. What did she think she was doing going driving with that fiend Renton? The man could not be trusted.

"The squire told Lady Beauford that they were attending a lecture on magnetism."

Something in the butler's voice made Ian look closer at the man. "And?"

"I heard him ask Lady Annabelle to attend a lecture by Mrs. Burnaby. It is one of milady's friends with her cause."

She had promised only the night before not to attend a lecture of this type without him. She had also warned him that she sometimes acted precipitously. Instinctively, Ian knew that Annabelle would have what she considered a very good reason for going with the squire. He had no doubt that his unpredictable fiancée would never betray him. She was nothing like Jenna.

Creswell cleared his throat. "I doubt that was his intention, milord, and that is why I took the liberty of sending you a message."

Ian felt foreboding creep along his skin. "Where do you think he took her?"

"His carriage was set for traveling, milord, and I noticed luggage stowed in the luggage box." He said no more, leaving Ian to draw his own conclusions.

"Lady Annabelle, did she take anything with her?" He nearly choked on the question, but he needed to hear the butler tell him no.

"No, milord, she believed he was taking her to a lecture. He promised her that he would leave Town afterward. If I may be so bold, I believe she is trying to circumvent the duel."

Ian cursed. Belle was unlike any other lady of his acquaintance. Why had he believed she would sit idly by and allow him to participate in a duel she strongly opposed? The thought of his Belle in the clutches of the lecherous squire sent his stomach plummeting to his toes. He had to find her.

"There is one more thing, milord. Whilst engaged in conversation over a cup of ale with John Footman, the coachman made a comment about the weather in the north. One might assume from this comment that he expected to head that direction."

Creswell's words brought the first smile to Ian's face since he had read the butler's note requesting his immediate attendance at Lady Beauford's townhouse. After asking detailed questions regarding the squire's equipage and the livery of his coachman, Ian stormed outside. Instructing Creswell not to alarm the dowager, Ian gained his horse and was off.

His first stop was Finchley's home. He needed a pistol. It would be foolish to face a man of Renton's ilk unarmed. He updated Finchley on the latest development and asked his friend to go directly to Hamilton and apprise him of recent events.

"Send a note, eh what? Can't go tearing after the blackguard alone."

Ian didn't want to take precious time arguing. "I'll write the note while your mount is brought around."

Finchley raced upstairs to don a pair of riding breeches. When he came back down, Ian was ready. "I told Hamilton to follow in his carriage with Lady Hamilton. I will not allow the cur to tarnish Belle's reputation."

Hours of hard riding later, Ian spied the coach ahead of him on the highway. The horses and coachman's livery matched Creswell's description. Ian considered his options. The most important thing was to get Belle from the man's clutches. He could deal with the squire later.

"Is that the coach?" Finchley rode close, so his voice would not carry and alarm the coachman.

"Aye."

The fury that had abated on the long ride returned full force. Indicating with an inclination of his head that Finchley should go to the right of the carriage, Ian rode up on the left. He waited until the coachman turned nervously at the sound of the thundering hoof beats behind before firing the pistol.

"Stop the coach or I'll put a hole through your heart." Ian roared the command.

The coachman didn't take time to think about it, he immediately sawed on the reins and within minutes, the coach came to a standstill. Finchley rode to the front and trained his weapon on the coachman.

Ian heard Belle scream from the inside and he was off his horse in a moment. He reached the coach just as the door flew open. The squire held Belle around the neck and pointed a cocked pistol at her head. Ian froze in his tracks.

Renton's gaze swept past Ian to where Finchley sat atop his horse, his gun aimed and ready. Gripping Belle more tightly, he smiled. "It would appear that we are at a standoff."

Ian ignored the remark. "Let her go."

"I'm afraid I can't do that. Tell your friend to move away from the coach and drop his weapon."

When Ian didn't comply immediately, Renton yanked his forearm against Belle's throat until she could not breathe. She twisted wildly in his arms, but could not gain a foothold. Her face turned a dangerous shade of red.

"Finchley, do as the man says," Ian commanded.

When his friend had obeyed, the squire loosened his hold and Belle took several choked gasps of air.

"Well done. I do believe you realize the precarious position of Lady Annabelle," the squire said.

Ian's fury was barely in check. He focused on keeping it under control as the squire instructed Finchley further.

"Now, dismount from your horse and send both your horse and

Graenfrae's off."

Finchley looked to Ian for direction. Ian gave a short nod. Finchley did as he had been told. The stupid squire was looking quite pleased with himself. He then demanded that Ian throw away his gun.

"Nay."

The squire's polished veneer dropped. "No? Do you want me to shoot Lady Annabelle?" he screeched. "If you do not drop your weapon she does not have a prayer."

"If I do, she has less of one." Ian started toward the carriage.

"Stay back." The squire sounded desperate.

Ian ignored him and kept going. The squire threw Belle away from him and gave his coachman orders to go. Ian caught Belle as she tumbled toward the ground. By the time he set her on her feet the coach was already out of pistol distance.

Ian cursed.

Belle shuddered against him. Giving a piercing whistle, he hugged her close. Within seconds Nightsong stood before him. Turning to Finchley, he instructed him, "Take my horse and find your mount. He will not have wandered far."

Ian swept Belle into his arms and carried her off the road. He found a likely boulder and sat on it with Belle in his lap.

"He wanted to take me to Gretna Green. He's mad, Ian. He thought I would marry him."

"Dinna fret, Belle. You are safe now."

She pushed away from his chest and glared at him. "I'm not fretting. The man could have shot you. Do you realize that?"

The squire had held a gun to her head and she was worried that he might have shot Ian? Ian could not fathom the working of her mind. "'Twas not likely. I am sorry I could not throw down my pistol. I dinna wish to risk you, but the risk of letting him leave with you seemed greater."

She nodded. "You are quite right. He wanted to marry me, not kill me. I'm no good to him dead."

"The man must be mad."

"Or desperate. There have been rumors that he was in deep water financially. Perhaps he sought to repair his fortunes."

Ian caressed Belle's back and pulled her close into his embrace. "I dinna think your modest dowry would tempt a man to kidnapping, Belle."

She went stiff in his arms. "Ian, there is something I must tell you."

What was she going to say? For an insane moment, he feared she would confess involvement with the squire. He rejected the thought the minute it entered his mind. She had said she loved him. True, she had been under emotional strain when she had said the words, but that did not negate their commitment. He would hold her to them.

"What is it?"

"It's about my fortune."

"Here you are." Finchley rode up leading Ian's horse. "You were right, Buttercup had not gone far at all."

Ian wished the horse had ridden into the next county. He wanted to find out what Belle meant when she spoke of a fortune.

Finchley said, "We'll want to make for that inn several miles back, eh what?"

"Aye." Their horses would not stand the ride back to London without rest, water and food. Ian stood and set Belle on her feet. "Are you ready to ride?"

She nodded. "I am completely unhurt, except of course my pride. I do not know if I will tell you the terrible things that odious man said."

She was wrong about that. She was going to tell him everything, including what she meant about a bloody fortune. He helped her onto Nightsong and then swung himself up behind her.

They did not try to talk on the way to the inn. Ian wanted all of his senses on the ready. Travel was never safe, but the thought that the squire might turn around and chase after them was a real possibility. The man had given up much too easily after going to the trouble to kidnap Belle.

They reached the inn and Ian dismounted, pulling Belle down

after him. She stumbled a bit. He put his arm around her to steady her. Finchley stayed outside to see to the horses. A round woman in a mobcap came forward to greet them.

Ian said, "We need a private parlor."

Remembering what had happened the last time he and Belle had shared a private parlor, he looked down at her. She remembered too, if the blush on her cheeks was any indication. She met his gaze, her eyes pools of passionate mystery.

Giving them no more than a mildly curious glance, the woman led them to a chamber. "I'll get Polly in here to lay a fire right away, milord."

Ian nodded. "We are expecting another gentleman and lady. See that they are brought to our parlor when they arrive."

"Very good, milord." Bobbing her head, the woman then left the room.

Belle shivered and Ian immediately began unbuttoning his coat. He slipped it off and placed it around her shoulders. Holding the lapels of the coat, he looked into her eyes.

"You promised not to attend a lecture of that sort without me, Belle."

Her eyes filled with regret. "I know. I am so sorry, Ian." She took a long breath and let it out. "I was trying to prevent the duel. Instead, I managed to get myself kidnapped and you had to rescue me."

She sounded so pitiful that he could not be angry with her. "You did tell me that on occasion you would act without thinking."

Relief filled him when her eyes shot angry sparks. "I did not say without thinking. I never act without thinking."

He lowered his head and brushed his lips lightly across hers. "If you say so."

At the sound of Finchley clearing his throat, Ian released Belle. Within a half an hour a fire blazed in the small fireplace and Polly had brought three cups of steaming wine and supper.

Belle played with the food on her plate. Ian frowned at her. "Ye must eat, lass."

She laughed. The spontaneous sound loosened something inside of him.

"Yes, Nurse."

He smiled in return, remembering her accusation that he had acted like her nursery governess. She took up a small bite and began chewing. He stood up and moved around the room. He wanted answers, but they would have to wait. He could not cross-question her in front of Finchley. Belle had finished her meal and sat with her feet propped up before the fire. Her eyelids were drooping when Hamilton and his wife arrived.

Diana rushed to Belle. "Are you all right? What happened? I don't understand. Ian's note implied you were being kidnapped. I cannot believe such a thing."

"I couldn't either, until the foul man started spouting off about my fortune," Annabelle replied.

Robert turned to Ian, his face full of fury. "What is going on here, MacKay?"

Ian shrugged. "I think Belle could explain that better than I."

Everyone turned toward Belle. She pulled Ian's coat around her although the room was now warm. "It's a long story."

Robert took command. "Then it will have to be told in the coach on the way home. If we are to avoid a scandal-broth and Aunt Griselda collapsing from shock, we must return to Town."

Diana looked up from Belle. "Must we leave right now, Robert? I do not know if I can stand the carriage ride back just yet. I'm not feeling quite the thing."

"You told me that you were quite recovered. I would not have allowed you to accompany me otherwise."

Robert scowled at his wife and she promptly burst into tears. He looked helplessly at Ian. Ian shrugged. What did he know of teary-eyed females? Belle should be in hysterics after her ordeal, but she was busy comforting Diana and trying to glare some sense into her brother.

"Robert, you needn't be so unkind." Belle turned concerned eyes on Diana. "What did Robert mean? Are you ailing?"

"I'm just a little queasy. I am sure it is all of the turmoil lately."

Belle patted Diana's shoulder. "Undoubtedly. It would make the heartiest lady ill."

"I have been having terrible nightmares and I feel ill all of the time." Diana collapsed into another spate of tears.

Hamilton stared at his wife. His face was that of a man facing the scaffold. "I did not realize."

Ian hated the torment he heard in the other man's voice. This is what love did to a man. Annabelle had told him that Diana was deceiving her husband because she loved him. Love. Ian would not become so vulnerable.

Diana looked up. Hamilton's eyes bored into hers and Ian had the impression that no one else in the room existed for the unhappy man. "I will not press you again. I did not realize that my affection had become such a burden."

Diana tore herself from Annabelle's grasp and flew to her husband. "Robert, you cannot believe that. It has nothing to do with you." She threw her arms around him.

After a moment of staring in stunned disbelief at the top of his wife's head, Hamilton closed his arms tightly around her. "I do not understand, my love."

Ian could not stand the pain he saw in his friend's face. He fixed his eyes on Lady Hamilton. "It is time you told your husband. If you are making yourself ill with worry, you canna keep it a secret any longer."

Diana's shoulders sagged. "You are right." She pulled out of her husband's embrace and wandered over to the fire. Warmth emanated from the flames, but the poor lady shivered anyway. "Living like this is terrible."

Robert's scowl encompassed Ian as well as his wife. "What have you been hiding from me?"

Diana shuddered. "I cannot bear the thought of you hating me, Robert."

Hamilton stormed over to his wife and spun her away from the fire. "I will never stop loving you."

194

The fierceness of his voice and expression did not seem to frighten his wife. In fact, Diana smiled softly.

Pulling her to a chair, Hamilton forced her to sit. "Tell me." This time his voice came out in gentle command.

Diana responded immediately. "It began at the theater."

Chapter Fifteen

Throughout the ordeal, Annabelle had felt that Diana needed to tell Robert about Mr. Thorn. Now that the time had come, she prayed that her faith in her brother's love for his wife would not be disappointed. Ian walked over to stand behind Annabelle. He placed his hand on her shoulder.

Gratitude for being with Ian after her near disaster poured over Annabelle. If Ian had not stopped Squire Renton, she might very well be in another inn somewhere fighting for her innocence and her life. The man was a monster. She shuddered and Ian put his other hand on her shoulder. The soothing caress of his thumbs against her neck soothed her.

Diana's broken voice faded as Annabelle's attention focused on Ian's soft caresses. She wanted nothing more than to curl up in his lap as she had after her ordeal following Mr. Thorn. The presence of the others in the room prevented such forward action on her part. She sighed.

Ian pulled her until her body rested against his. "Dinna fret, Belle."

Would he be as understanding when he learned the truth about her inheritance? Would he still want her when he learned she did not fit his requirements? She pushed the thought from her mind and drew strength from his hard body supporting hers.

Anger shimmered in Robert's eyes. He did not utter a word or ask any questions. The more Diana said, the fiercer the look in Robert's eyes became. Annabelle hoped his anger was directed at the absent Mr.

Thorn.

Finally, Diana stopped speaking. She took a deep breath and let it out slowly. "That is all, my lord."

Robert's face relaxed momentarily from his grim expression. "Do not cry, Diana. All will be well."

Rather than comforting her, his words sent Diana over the edge of control. Tears spilled over her eyelids and down her cheeks in a cascade.

Robert dropped on to his knees by his wife. Putting his arms around her, he closed her in his embrace. "Diana, m'dear, please don't take on so."

Diana covered her face and shook with quiet weeping. Her voice came out muffled through her fingers. "How can all be well? You will be hurt when Mr. Thorn publishes the letters." She spoke between sobs. "I have sold my wedding pearls. Nothing can possibly be well." She hiccupped as another bout of crying overtook her.

Robert stiffened. Above Diana's head, Annabelle could see a look of cold rage settle on her brother's face. "How could you sell my wedding gift to you?"

"I needed the money and I was terrified of you finding out why," whispered Diana.

Far from assuaging her husband's anger, this only increased it. "Diana, do you not trust me to take care of you? How could you bring yourself to deal with vermin like that? Why did you not come to me?" The questions came out like angry gunshots.

Annabelle interrupted before Diana could answer. "Why not, Robert? You prose on so incessantly about propriety and tonnish behavior. It is no surprise your wife believes you care more for her reputation than you do for her."

Ian did not appreciate her blunt declaration. His hands stopped their gentle massage. His fingers tightened on her shoulder in warning. "Hush, Belle. 'Tis Lady Hamilton's place to speak."

She wanted to argue, but deep down Annabelle knew that he was right. Diana had to fight this battle on her own.

"Is this true, Diana?" Robert made the question sound like an accusation.

Diana raised her head and dried her tears. She pulled from Robert's arms and stood up. "I have always felt that you would not have married me if I was not so perfectly suitable with a reputation above reproach."

Robert stared at his wife. "Is that wrong? To desire a suitable wife?"

"No, of course not, but your requirements for suitability are so high. Lord Graenfrae desires many things in his future wife, but is willing to accept a flawed specimen. Annabelle is not a patterncard of propriety and that does not matter to him."

Annabelle did not take insult at her friend's words. Diana spoke the truth. Annabelle did test the limits of acceptable behavior on occasion and Ian did not seem to mind, except for the fact that sometimes it put her in danger, which was quite understandable really. She had come to realize that Ian was far more concerned with loyalty than respectability.

The knowledge pleased her considerably.

"Annabelle is highly regarded and comes from very good family," Robert replied defensively.

"There." Diana pointed an accusing finger at her husband. "That is exactly what I mean. Annabelle associates with people who are not accepted in society on behalf of her cause, spends time doing things that some might criticize and yet you refuse to admit it. You require perfection from those you love."

"I do not expect you to be perfect."

Diana's look of disbelief said it all. "You were the only one for me. Had you been the base born son of a rakehell, I would have married you."

Ceddy let out a shocked gasp. Diana smiled. "It's quite true, you know. Love can make one quite shameless. I only hope someday you know what I mean."

She turned back to her husband. "I knew that my greatest attraction to you was my suitability. When Mr. Thorn first told me about the letters, I was terrified. I was certain that if you found out

198

about them, you would stop loving me."

"Do you have so little faith in my love for you?" Robert frowned at his wife. "I assure you, my love is not so shallow as you seem to think."

Diana sighed. "Tell me that when Mr. Thorn publishes the letters."

Robert swore. "Thorn could post the letters in *The Times* for all I care. I will never stop loving you." Taking his wife's face between his two hands, he said, "Diana, you are more precious to me than my own life."

Diana's eyes burned with hope. "Truly?"

"Truly."

Ian pulled Annabelle to other side of the small room. She smiled. From the silence that followed them, she assumed that her brother was giving Diana proof of his devotion. Ceddy accompanied them.

"Have to find this chap Thorn and deal with him, don't you know?" he said.

Ceddy had Annabelle's complete agreement. Thorn deserved to be horsewhipped for what he had put Diana through. Now, there was a man that she would not mind Ian facing with a pistol. She gasped. "There is something I forgot to tell you."

"What is it, lass?"

"I think Mr. Thorn and Squire Renton are in league."

"They are both blackguards to be sure, but 'tis no reason to believe that they are in league."

"I know." She told him about the coach she had seen when following Thorn and then about recognizing the horses on the squire's carriage. "They are quite magnificent beasts. I am not mistaken."

Ceddy nodded. "Squire Renton's been accused of thinking more of his horseflesh than he thought of his first wife."

Annabelle shuddered. "I can believe it."

Ian slipped his arm around her waist and pulled her close. It suddenly occurred to her that Ian was being entirely too familiar in front of Ceddy. She felt heat steal into her cheeks. She squirmed. Ian would not let her go. She protested. "Ian."

He ignored her. "When Hamilton is finished making up with his

199

wife, we will make our plans."

A soft laugh alerted them that Diana had heard Ian's words. "He is quite finished and we thank you for sitting through our little melodrama."

They joined the reunited couple.

Diana's face was radiant and around her neck, over her pelisse and traveling gown, a magnificent strand of pearls glistened.

Annabelle turned to her brother. "How did you manage it?"

Diana did not let him answer. "He went to the jeweler to pick up a gift he had commissioned for me and saw them in the display case. Recognizing them immediately, he repurchased them and had every intention of taxing me with how they came to be there when the message arrived about Annabelle." Diana smiled softly at her husband. "I have promised never to sell them again."

She then lifted her wrist and Annabelle saw a matching bracelet made up of four strands of pearls with a diamond-studded clasp. "This is the gift he had commissioned." Diana hugged her husband's arm. "However, the most magnificent gift he has given me is assurance of his never-ending love."

Robert smiled down at his wife and gently caressed her cheek. "I could do no less for a woman made so eminently worthy of my love by her kind and generous heart."

Annabelle smiled. "From the look on your face, I must assume you are now ready to make the return journey to Town."

Ceddy went to order the carriage and horses readied. He kindly offered to ride his horse, so the carriage would not be crowded, but Ian would not hear of it.

"'Tis a long ride we've both had and I'm thankful for your company. I'll no have you riding back."

They all crowded into Robert's carriage. Robert and Diana sat on one side of the carriage. Diana scooted over to make room for Annabelle. When Annabelle went to sit next to her, Ian pulled her by the waist toward him.

He settled her into the tiny spot left open between him and the wall. He and Ceddy took up the rest of the carriage cushion. He tucked his coat around her and settled his arm over her shoulders. Although it was anything but proper, Annabelle felt cared for and safe.

She was too tired to give Robert the accounting of her adventure that she promised. Her eyes slid shut almost immediately. She heard Ian's voice telling what he knew through a sleepy haze.

Belle did not wake up until Ian nudged her gently when they arrived at her aunt's townhouse. In the dark carriage, he could not see her face, but he could feel the way she clutched at his arm while orienting herself. She was not completely recovered from her ordeal.

Ceddy and the others had already alighted from the carriage. Diana, ill again, insisted on going into Lady Beauford's home for a cup of tea before making the journey home.

"Are we home already?" Belle's voice, groggy from sleep, melted Ian's insides. She sounded exactly like an innocent child. His anger burned at the thought of what Renton had tried to do to his pure Belle.

He swung her down and kept his arm around her as he guided her past a satisfied-looking Creswell. "I knew you would take care of the matter, if you don't mind my saying so."

The butler's voice, rife with approval, brought a smile to Ian's lips. He'd have a talk with the man later about allowing his mistress to embark on such journeys again.

Belle gave a huge yawn and stumbled over the doorstep. Ian righted her and tightened his hold. "Be careful, lass."

"Oh, excuse me. I am just so weary." She sighed. "It has been a trying day."

He would let her sleep, just as soon as she told him what had happened with Renton. He led Belle into a scene of chaos in the drawing room. Lady Hamilton bent over a chamber pot and retched. Hamilton demanded that a doctor be called immediately. Lady Beauford demanded an accounting of the recent events.

Belle came erect at his side. "I thought she was over this sickness now that she told Robert all."

Lady Beauford's head turned toward them and she gave Ian an eagle-like stare. He felt like he was in leading strings again and had been caught sneaking a biscuit from the tea tray.

"Would you care to explain why my niece is wearing an article of your clothing and you have kept her out well past the dinner hour?" she asked austerely.

Belle gasped. She would have taken off his coat, but when she shivered he forced her to put it back on. She fought silently with him for several seconds. Giving him a frown, she finally conceded and kept the coat around her shoulders. She faced her aunt.

"Ian did not keep me out, Aunt Griselda. Surely, you remember that I went for a drive with Squire Renton."

The dowager gave a stately nod. "That was hours ago. You are not going to try to convince me that you have been in that milksop's company all this time. Laird MacKay would not stand for it. Anyone can see that he is a terribly possessive gentleman."

"No, of course I wasn't in the squire's company all this time. I have been with Ian the past several hours."

The eagle-like stare returned to him. "What do you have to say for yourself, young man? Do you realize the terrible damage you may have done to my niece's reputation?"

"For Heaven's sake, Aunt Griselda, now is not the time to be concerned about Annabelle's consequence. My wife is ill. Have a doctor sent for," Hamilton demanded.

Lady Beauford dismissed her nephew's words with a wave of her hand. "A few biscuits and a rest on the settee should set her. It worked with all four of my children."

Hamilton called loudly for some biscuits and carried his wife to the settee. He laid her on it. "Then you know what is wrong with her?"

His aunt stared at him. "Don't you?" Turning to the pale woman lying against the cushions, she admonished, "You should not keep such news from your husband, my dear."

Lady Hamilton's wan face took on a puzzled expression. "What am I keeping from him?"

"Why, that you are increasing, of course. Nausea's quite normal in the first few months. What Robert was thinking about dragging you out at night, when you should surely be resting in your bed, is beyond me.

The younger generation is nothing like what it was in my day. Your uncle knew just how to pamper an expectant mother." The older woman went silent, clearly enjoying fond remembrances of her considerate spouse.

Lord and Lady Hamilton looked as if they had been turned to stone. Lady Hamilton spoke finally. "What do you mean, Aunt Griselda?"

Ian smiled at the look of disgust on Lady Beauford's face. "Why, gel, it's perfectly obvious that you will be in confinement by the winter."

Hamilton looked down at his wife and asked, "Is it true?"

She chewed on her lower lip. "I don't know."

The dowager snorted. "Education certainly isn't what it was in my day. If I had married without knowing how to count my monthly flux..." She let her voice trail off.

Lady Hamilton's pale face turned pink. "I well, I... Yes, actually, Robert, it is quite possible."

Hamilton had the look of a man who had taken a punch to his midsection from Gentleman Jackson. "You. I. We. I cannot believe it. We must get you home to bed as soon as possible."

Lady Hamilton laughed. Belle broke away from Ian and rushed across the room to throw her arms around her friend.

"This is wonderful news. I am to be an aunt."

Ian sighed with contentment at the sound of Belle's delighted voice and happy laughter. The news of Lady Hamilton's pregnancy had dispelled the remaining shadows from her eyes.

"I'm not going anywhere until I hear what happened to Annabelle and that terrible Squire Renton," Lady Hamilton said.

The time had come for Belle to explain herself. She looked at Ian. He saw the uncertainty in her eyes. He didn't care what caused it. He did not like it.

Putting out his hand, he silently bid her come to him. After the briefest hesitation, she did. He pulled her down onto another small sofa next to him. The rest of the occupants of the room took their seats, except for Finchley.

He cleared his throat, "Perhaps I should wait in the hall, eh what? Family business and all."

Belle said, "Do not be ridiculous. You are practically family and it is twice now that you have aided Ian in rescuing me. Sit down."

Ian squeezed Belle's shoulder to let her know he approved of her treatment of their friend. Finchley sat down and Ian waited for Belle to begin.

She twisted her hands in her lap. "Actually, it's all connected in some way with that blackmailer, Mr. Thorn."

Lady Beauford demanded an explanation about the blackmailer. Hamilton explained.

"Hmmm, from all that you've said, I would have to say that I'm glad this happened," was Lady Beauford's final comment on the imbroglio.

Ian could feel Belle's body tense next to his. "What? You cannot mean it, Aunt," she exclaimed.

"Yes, dear." The dowager gave her niece a look of complacency. "I know the young are always so outraged. However, Robert has always been just a tad bit too concerned with his place in society." She gave her nephew a smile, implying no insult was intended.

Hamilton nodded and Ian had the impression that Belle's brother wished he had learned the lesson before his wife went through such hardship.

"I'm not propounding your father's views by any stretch, but it did always seem to me that Robert had gone a shade too far in the opposite direction. Now he has settled in his own mind his priorities and both he and Diana will be happier for it in the years to come," Lady Beauford finished.

Belle sighed and cuddled closer to Ian. Did the lass realize how easily she turned to him for comfort?

Lady Hamilton tried to stifle a yawn. "Now tell us about what happened with Squire Renton today before I fall asleep. I still cannot believe that you were abducted."

"You aren't going to credit this, but somehow the squire learned of my inheritance," Belle said.

Ian felt all the tension that had drained away over the past hours come back in rushing force.

Lady Beauford said, "It was just a matter of time, gel. We knew that."

"Yes, well, it happened and he decided that marriage to me would solve his financial problems." Ian felt her looking at him and turned to meet her gaze. "Somewhat like you, my lord."

Fury coursed through him. He was nothing like Renton. He did not want to use Belle. He wanted to wed her. He would be a good husband, better than that lecher. He glared at her to let her know what he thought of her reasoning.

She smiled slightly and went on. "Ian put play to his plans by courting me."

"You wouldna have married him regardless, lass." He couldn't believe she might believe otherwise.

Belle grimaced. "Actually, the squire is quite disbelieving that I chose you over him and thinks that a bluestocking spinster like myself should be most grateful for his interest."

Although she spoke lightly, Ian could tell that the blackguard's words had hurt her.

He caressed her arm. "The daft man doesna ken your value."

She shrugged. "He knows it all right. He knows to the groat how much I am worth and counted on my money to save his hunters from sale at Tattersall's."

Ian looked around the room. Lady Beauford nodded as if it made perfect sense for a crazy Englishman to kidnap her niece. Hamilton tugged at his neckcloth with an expression of extreme discomfort on his face. Lady Hamilton appeared to be dozing for all of her protest about hearing Belle's account. Finchley wore a look of dawning comprehension.

Ian felt close to shouting. It seemed everyone in the room understood Belle's words. He removed his hand from her shoulder, crossed his arms over his chest and frowned.

"Explain."

Belle sighed. "I was afraid you were going to say that."

He wanted to shake her. "Now."

She looked into his face with an expression of earnestness. "When my parents died, we discovered that although Papa had left Robert very well off with two-thirds of his funds and all of his estates, he left me a sizable fortune as well."

"No one in the *ton* knows?" He asked it as a question, but knew it to be fact.

"No. There was concern I would become prey to fortune hunters if the facts became known, so we kept it as a closely guarded secret." Her eyes asked him a question, but he did not have the answer.

Betrayal sliced through him like a sharp rapier. She had lied to him. Did she think he was a fortune hunter like the squire? The very idea that she might compare him to the squire sent Ian's insides churning. "You dinna think to tell me?"

She shook her head. "You made it clear that you were not interested in securing a fortune with your wife, so I did not think it would matter to you."

He saw the lie in her eyes. Something about her explanation did not ring true. He would not find out what it was this evening however. He had spent enough of this day exposed. Finchley had been there when he had rescued Belle and since then he had endured the company of the Hamiltons as well. He would not discuss Belle's betrayal with her in front of others. He longed to shout at her, but even in his pain at her deception, he could not bring himself to humiliate her before her family.

He stood up. "I see." He turned to Finchley. "Are you ready to leave, then?"

"Certainly."

Finchley made a very nice leg to Lady Beauford and said his good-byes to Hamilton and Belle.

Ian turned to go. Everyone in this room had withheld information about Belle's fortune from him. They had let him believe that she was just what she seemed, a moderately dowered spinster. Even as he had the thought, he rejected it. Belle was nothing as she seemed. She presented a façade of ordinariness to the *ton*, but underneath beat a heart of fire and passion. And a heart of deceit.

Her voice made him pause at the doorway. "Will I see you soon?" The worry was there.

He inclined his head. "It is inevitable. We are after all betrothed."

He turned to go and she called after him again. "You have forgotten your coat."

He shrugged without turning. "'Tis of no import."

He left.

Annabelle stared at the door to the drawing room, unbelieving that Ian had just walked out. She met her aunt's gaze and then Robert's. Dazed, she barely registered their looks of concern. Ian had left. She didn't realize that she had spoken the words aloud until her aunt replied.

"Just a bit of gentlemanly ego, Annabelle. He'll get over it in time. I'm sure it was a great shock to discover that he was engaged to an heiress. For a gentleman like MacKay, that could be a difficult obstacle to overcome."

That is exactly what she had feared. She stood up, pulling Ian's coat tightly around herself. "I believe I will go to bed. I am very weary."

She turned to leave. Tears blurred her eyes and she wanted to leave the drawing room before her brother or aunt noticed she was crying. Robert's voice followed her out the door. "Do not worry, Annabelle, MacKay will get over his pique quickly enough. After all your blunt will only make it that much easier for him to make improvements to Graenfrae."

She nodded her agreement, not really agreeing at all, but needing to leave. Ian would not see things that way. He was such a proud man, so independent. It would gall him that his inheritance from his stepfather would pale in comparison to the fortune she would bring to their marriage. She climbed the stairs to her room. Purdy dozed on the window seat, waiting for her return. Annabelle lightly touched her shoulder. "Go on to bed, Purdy. I will do for myself tonight."

Her young maid bobbed a sleepy curtsy and left. Relieved to finally be alone, Annabelle sat in the window seat her maid had just vacated. Had she lost Ian? Another man might ignore her duplicity, but would he? He refused to believe in love because of the betrayal of his first fiancée. He would have no tolerance for her deception.

She admitted to herself now that it had been a deception. She could have told him, but hadn't. Fear had kept her silent. Ian had made it very clear that he did not wish to marry a woman of means. She worried that he would regret his choice to marry her if he found out that she was not the perfect embodiment of his requirements.

He did not love her. She was convinced that the passion they felt together was just a bonus to Ian, not a necessity. If it were the man could not have made his ridiculous list of requirements to begin with.

Slipping off the coat, Annabelle began to undress. She laid her pelisse and dress over the back of a chair. By the time she stripped out of her stockings and chemise, she was shivering.

Her room was chilly. Purdy had not dared to lay a fire without express permission. Annabelle grumbled as she found her nightgown and slipped it over her head. Aunt Griselda's eccentricity regarding coal usage was really out of hand.

Trying to convince herself that it was just because she was cold, Annabelle slipped Ian's coat back on over her nightrail. His smell clung to the blue superfine. She reveled in the heady fragrance of spice and Ian's unique male scent. It reminded her of the wonder she felt in his arms. She longed for those arms now. What would she do if Ian broke their engagement? She would never feel his hard body pressed to hers, never experience the unique blend of pleasure and passion that he gave her.

She punched her pillow and cursed the stupid squire. If not for his machinations, she would have had an opportunity to tell Ian of her fortune. If Squire Renton were within shooting distance, she would go looking for the nearest pistol. He had ruined everything.

She climbed into her bed and curled up with Ian's coat tucked around her. She could have told Ian sooner, but she had been afraid. The squire was a fool and a lecher, but he wasn't the only one at fault in this debacle. Annabelle fell asleep with the concern that Ian would never trust her enough to love her now, much less marry her.

Chapter Sixteen

William gripped the bottle of gin on the grimy table. Thorn's rooms were hardly what he was used to. Boards blocked the meager light that tried to get in through the cracked and soot-encrusted windows. The fireplace smoked more than it burned because of the layers of ash under the fresh coal. William sat on the only chair in the two rooms. It wobbled if he moved, one of its legs shorter than the others. He had commandeered the only bed and left Thorn to sleep on the decaying sofa in the main room. Other than the filthy table his gin rested on, there was no other furniture.

William shuddered when he slept on sheets that had clearly not been washed in a month of Sundays, or more. He had no choice. For now. It had been three days since his botched attempt at kidnapping Lady Annabelle and the failure still rankled. He had acted without enough forethought. The fear that his hasty actions would precipitate a wedding by special license for Lady Annabelle now appeared unfounded. In fact, the street urchin Thorn had hired to watch Lady Beauford's townhouse had reported no sign of the Scotsman at all.

Would he be fool enough to give up Lady Annabelle and all her groat over a botched attempt at abduction? The barbarian had not rejected Lady Annabelle after finding her indecently exposed and in William's arms. Graenfrae would not give her up now. What was his game then?

William poured himself another glass of gin. Thorn had protested buying the gin and hiring the urchin to spy on Lady Annabelle. William smiled at the thought that the man no longer protested anything he did. Not after William had explained what he would do to Thorn before he killed him.

Thorn was a fool. William had the blood of a conqueror in him. He would not be denied. The fortune would be his and his horses would know no other master but him. He might even allow Lady Annabelle to live long enough to give him an heir. She had shown courage in the face of disaster. Frowning, he remembered how she had punched him the night of the musicale. She was not ladylike, but she was intelligent. They were admirable traits in an heir, if not a wife. Besides, he would ensure that she paid for her abuse of him.

He needed to plan for every contingency this time. He had not been prepared for Graenfrae's interference on the road to Gretna Green. It only showed how rattled he had been. His plans never failed. This one had been inferior because the Scottish laird had upset William by responding to him kissing Annabelle as no gentleman should. The Scotsman should have been repulsed by his fiancée, instead he had defended her and challenged William to a duel.

William still was not sure why he had given Lady Annabelle up so easily. All he knew is that when he had looked into Graenfrae's eyes, he had seen his own death foretold in the Scotsman's glare. Fear had engulfed him like it never had before and William had thrown Annabelle from him and ran. He had not stopped running for several hours and had not returned to Town until the next day.

William reminded himself that Graenfrae was just a man, an ordinary man. He was nothing compared to William.

No one knew of William's involvement with Thorn. They would not expect him to strike through that channel. He smiled to himself. He stood up and swayed a bit. Cheap gin. Too potent, by half. He waited until he regained his balance and called for Thorn.

CƷ

"Any news?"

Ian and Finchley looked up at the sound of Hamilton's voice. Ian had still not come to terms with the fact that the man he had begun to call friend had deceived him. He inclined his head in cold welcome and

Lucy Monroe

Hamilton took a vacant chair. The club on St. James was quiet for the afternoon. Few gentlemen graced the well-appointed rooms this time of day.

Ian and Finchley occupied a table in the corner away from the window in which the dandies did their posturing. A light tea tray sat between the two men, for the most part untouched. Finchley offered tea to Hamilton.

Hamilton shook his head. "No thank you. I am more interested in news than tea."

"News about what?" Ian asked.

Hamilton frowned. "Do not try to gammon me. You have my sister convinced you will never come to call again, but I know better. I refer of course to the search you are undoubtedly doing for Renton."

Hamilton knew him well. Above their table hung a painting depicting the hunt. Ian identified with the looks of fierce determination on the hunters' faces. He would find his quarry too. "He has not been seen at his country seat, nor his rooms here in Town."

"So that is where you have been. Annabelle hasn't seen you in three days and she walks around looking like she did after my parents died." Hamilton caught Ian's gaze and would not let him look away. "She even refused to go to a lecture by that Burnaby woman. Miss Graves called to invite her and Annabelle turned her down. I cannot say that I am saddened at the news, but it is most unlike my sister."

Finchley shifted in his chair at the mention of Miss Graves.

Ian felt a stab of guilt, but he squelched it. She had deceived him. "I sent her flowers."

Hamilton set his lips in a straight line. "After the way you left the other night, flowers are not going to comfort my sister. I thought her heart was safe with you."

"I thought I could trust her."

"You can trust her. So, she did not tell you about her fortune. Is that such a crime? Most men would be thrilled to discover the woman they intended to marry possessed such an inheritance."

Finchley intervened. "MacKay ain't most men, don't you know?"

212

Hamilton frowned. "I do know. That is why I encouraged his pursuit of my sister. I don't like finding out that I was wrong." Although he responded to Finchley, his gaze locked on Ian.

"I dinna take to finding out that those I had come to trust had all lied to me." Ian wanted an explanation.

Hamilton did not hesitate. "I did not lie to you. We never discussed Annabelle's finances."

Ian fisted his hands on the arms of his chair. "You knew what I believed, what the rest of the bloody *ton* believes about your sister."

"The *ton* believes my sister is ordinary, a bluestocking spinster of no account. If I thought you believed that, I would shoot you before I let you marry her," Hamilton replied with some heat.

"I am referring to her money," Ian replied, "not her character."

"What does it matter?" Hamilton leaned forward intently. "You are marrying her character, not her money."

Ian sighed. It was no use arguing with Hamilton. The man did not believe that Belle's fortune mattered. Therefore he had not felt the need to enlighten Ian. A small part of the ice around Ian's heart melted. At least the man he called friend had not deliberately misled him. Hamilton waited in silence, as if he expected Ian to confirm his statement.

"Aye, I am marrying your sister."

Hamilton smiled. "Now that is settled, on to other matters. Until we locate Renton and deal with him, Annabelle will not be safe."

"Or until she is married, eh what?"

Ian fixed his gaze on his friend. "What are you suggesting, Finchley?"

"From what I learned while you were gone, Renton is in deep dun territory. Might even be forced to go to court and then prison. The man's got to be desperate, don't you know? He can't afford to give up now that he has discovered Annabelle's secret. No other heiress in Town would have him."

Ian's insides, already tight, constricted further. "Belle willna either."

"Could be he won't give her a choice. If Creswell hadn't sent you a note, he might have succeeded with his attempt to carry her to the border."

Ian would not wager on the possibility. His Belle was both strong and clever. She would not easily have submitted to the blackguard. "What about you, Hamilton? You have not been idle these past days, I ken."

"I have been unable to locate Thorn. I had Annabelle show me where she followed him, but inquiries in the area have turned up nothing." Disgust filled Hamilton's words. "I did not think such a cowardly fool could hide so well."

Ian agreed. "Mayhap he does not live in that area at all. Renton may have instructed Thorn to meet him there to lessen his chances of being followed. The way he ducked through the alley to Renton's waiting carriage is no coincidence."

"What should we do next?" Hamilton glared at Ian. "I will not allow my wife to live under this cloud of impending doom. She is in a delicate condition and must be protected."

Ian did not smile at Hamilton's passionate declaration. He could not. He felt much the same about Belle. He had to protect her, whatever the cost. "The first thing I am going to do is procure a special license."

Hamilton and Finchley nodded. "It is the only way." Ceddy agreed with Hamilton. "Marriage is just the ticket, eh what."

CB

Annabelle hesitated outside of Ceddy's family's townhouse. It was an imposing structure in the best part of Town. Ceddy's family was as old as her own and his father was not only a good manager of his estates, but had developed the reputation for knowing how to play the Exchange.

Standing in front of the huge oak front door, she wondered at the wisdom of her actions. It had all made sense in her bedchamber. She was tired of waiting for Ian to come to his senses and call on her.

After telling an astonished butler that she was there to see Laird MacKay, she waited in the hall for him to receive her. She reminded herself that she was not going to beg.

She wanted to know what her future held. She had a right to know if Ian planned to break their engagement. She knew that in the eyes of the *ton* he had sufficient cause. Not only had he caught her in a compromising situation with the greedy squire, but he had also been forced to follow her the next day and rescue her from the squire's clutches. She sighed. She painted a bleak picture with her thoughts.

Even bleaker was the knowledge that none of this would cause Ian to give up. He believed she had deceived him. She had. He just did not know why. If she told him, maybe he would understand. Maybe he would get over his anger.

Waiting for the butler, she was surprised when Ian himself came storming into the hall. He searched her face and looked behind her, as if seeking someone else.

Her heart constricted in her breast. He wore only a shirt and trousers. He had discarded his cravat, waistcoat and jacket. The muscles of his chest rippled behind the fine lawn of his shirt. Annabelle had an almost overpowering urge to reach out and caress the dark hair peeking out from where the top two buttons were undone. She seemed to have no control over her body's reaction to this man.

"What the bloody hell are you doing here?"

As greetings went, his lacked finesse. She drew herself up to her full height. *I am a modern woman. I am not afraid of this man. I have a right to know what my future holds.* After giving herself this bracing lecture, she met Ian's eyes with as serene an expression as she could manage.

"I am returning your coat." She held out the garment in question.

He could have no idea how difficult she found it to give it up. The coat had become a talisman of sorts over the past three days. She had slept with it each night and spent long hours in her room holding it while considering her future.

Ian stared at her as if her brains had gone to let. "You have risked your reputation to return my coat? Dinna jest with me this way. You could have sent it with a servant."

She shrugged. "Nevertheless, I have returned it."

Ian seized his coat from her extended hand. "You have completed your errand. Now you will retrieve your maid and return to your aunt's townhouse immediately."

"No."

"Aye. I am in no mood for games, Belle." He turned as if to leave, dismissing her.

Furious that he intended to walk away from her again, Annabelle swept by him and headed toward Ceddy's library. It was closer than the drawing room and she had no intention of engaging in conversation with Ian in the hall. The curious butler had heard enough.

"I did not bring my maid and I am not going anywhere until we settle things between us." She spoke over her shoulder while walking away from her arrogant fiancé.

His gasp of outrage could have parted her hair. She sensed rather than saw him turn around and move toward her. "You did not bring a maid? Is it not bad enough, you have come calling at a gentleman's household? Must you compound it by leaving your maid behind? Your reputation is already hanging by a thread. Would you destroy it entirely?"

Annabelle entered the library, pleased that Ceddy was nowhere to be seen. Her friend was not a bookish gentleman, so it had been a safe assumption. However, with the way things had gone lately, she felt justified in her sigh of relief. Not yet ready to face Ian or his outrage over her conduct, she busied herself removing her gloves and pelisse. She laid them on a nearby table along with her reticule. Sending up a brief plea for help, she faced Ian.

"You exaggerate. My reputation is safe for the moment."

If Ian decided to end their betrothal, that would be another story. So far no one knew of her unplanned journey with the squire and Ian was the only one aware of what had transpired the night of the musicale.

"Aye, for the moment. With the foolish way you go on, you are set on a course of destruction."

She was fast losing her temper. "I have survived these four and twenty years without destroying my respectability. I am in no imminent danger of doing so."

Provided the engagement stood.

He laughed, the harsh sound holding no humor. "'Tis a bloody miracle that. You hare off wherever your mood strikes you without benefit of a maid or an escort. I have been called upon to rescue you on more occasions than I care to count."

"Do not be ridiculous. It has been a mere handful of times that you have been called upon to give me aid." She would not say rescue. That would imply that she could not have eventually gotten herself out of trouble.

He did not answer her. She grew nervous in his silence. She twisted her betrothal ring. Would he ask for it back? The wait to know her future was becoming unbearable. "No one forced you to help me, Ian. You needn't act so angry about doing so."

If anything, his expression grew fiercer. "Ye are my bloody betrothed. I wouldna leave ye to your fate, no matter that you brought it on yourself."

Her patience came to an end. Storming across the room to him she stopped less than a foot from where he stood. Pointing her finger at his chest she shouted at him.

"I am not responsible for that stupid squire lusting after my money. Nor am I to be held accountable for some ruffians starting a riot. I will admit that getting out of the hansom cab when I was following Mr. Thorn was not the most intelligent thing I could have done, but I will not take the blame for the sordid actions of others. I have been accosted by miscreants bent on hurting me, by a lascivious squire, been kidnapped and threatened with a pistol."

She gulped in air before going on. "Did I tell you that he threatened to shoot me to gain my cooperation? He wasn't going to kill me, just shoot me. He would have too. I could see it in his eyes. But that isn't the worst of it. Not by a long shot. When I needed you most, you walked away from me and you stayed away."

Tears began to flow and they made her even angrier. He would think she was weak, that she did not mean what she said. "I know you don't love me. But I thought you cared, at least a little bit." She could not go on.

This was foolish. What good was she doing herself or Ian? She would have turned to leave, but Ian closed his hands around her finger and pulled her gently toward him. When their bodies were touching, he let go of her finger and put one arm around her, his hand resting on the small of her back. With the other he pressed a handkerchief into her hand.

"I sent flowers."

She had read the card a hundred times and could not make it any less cold with all the reading. He had simply signed it, "Regards, Ian." She had wanted to burn it, but could not make herself do so. It had been in his own hand.

She sniffled into the handkerchief. "You left without saying goodbye and you have not been back."

He sighed. "I was angry."

"You hurt me."

He tipped her chin up so that she had to look into his eyes. "You lied to me."

"I would have told you."

His eyes burned into hers with an intensity she could not deny. "Why?"

She swallowed. She knew what he was asking. Why had she not already told him? "I was afraid."

His face reflected confusion. "Of what?"

She wanted to move away. To look anywhere, but at him. He would not let go of her chin. "You only want to marry me because I fit your list of requirements."

He did not say anything to that pronouncement.

"I thought that if you discovered that I did not fit the one about a woman of moderate means, you would decide to look elsewhere for a bride."

He tipped his head back and laughed.

She glared at him. "My fear is not amusing."

He let her go and continued to laugh. He laughed so hard that he bent over with the merriment. She wanted to kick him. How dare he respond to her baring her soul in this way? She whirled around, intent on leaving. His laughter stopped immediately and he was at the door of the library before she was. He leaned against it.

What a contrary man. Not a half an hour before, he had been demanding she leave. Now, he appeared set on her staying.

"I want to go home."

"Nay."

She glowered at him. "You hurt me and now you are laughing about it. I am leaving."

His expression turned serious. "I did not laugh because I hurt you, lass."

She didn't believe him. She shook her head.

He moved away from the door. She would have walked around him, but he grabbed her arm. Taking his time, he pulled her close. "I laughed at your belief that I would have given you up because of your inheritance."

She stopped breathing for a moment. "You won't?"

She could not look away from his intent gaze. She wanted him to kiss her so badly that she was weak with it.

"Nay." He leaned his head toward hers. "I will never give you up."

Then he kissed her. It was such a gentle kiss that she almost started weeping again.

He pulled away from her. "I had four requirements on my list, if you will remember, Belle."

She nodded, miserable. She knew that. He had been adamant that the woman he married fit them all.

He began to list them, ticking them off on his fingers as he went. "I wanted to marry a plain woman, older than a debutante, with moderate means and of a practical nature."

"Yes, I know, Ian. You listed them for me in your first proposal at

219

Almack's."

He smiled and she felt her insides melt. "Belle, you meet none of my other requirements either."

She stared at him for long moments, unable to speak. Finally, she asked, "What do you mean? I meet all of your requirements except the one about moderate means. Although, to be fair, you did only stipulate that the dowry had to be of moderate means and mine is. Of moderate means, I mean." She was babbling, but the look of tender amusement in Ian's eyes unsettled her.

"You are not plain."

She laughed then. He had to be jesting. He had said once before that he thought she was beautiful. She did not believe him. "The entire polite world knows that I am plain. You, yourself, said as much when you proposed."

He frowned. "Aye. I did utter that complete falsehood. I canna help it if the gentlemen of the *ton* are blind to your loveliness, but I have never known a lady more beautiful."

The sincerity in his expression told her that he did indeed find her beautiful. Her heart swelled with hope. "Thank you, Ian. That is one of the kindest things anyone has ever said to me."

He frowned. "I wasna being kind."

Her eyes misty, she smiled at the disgruntled sound to his voice. "You cannot pretend that I am not the age you required."

"'Twas not merely an age requirement, if you will remember, Belle. 'Twas my belief that age would make you biddable and accepting of my proposal. No one can accuse you of being biddable and accepting, lass."

She laughed again, joy flowing through her. "No. I suppose not. And the others?"

"You are no practical woman, Belle. 'Tis no merely romantical notions that fill your head, but you see the best in everyone and often act without thought."

She should take umbrage, but she did not. She felt too much relief to know that Ian did not care if she filled his requirements. He must feel *something* for her to abandon them.

"You are wrong."

He gave a long and drawn out sigh. "'Tis nothing new, you believing I am wrong."

She moved closer to him and placed her arms around his waist. His hands came to rest on her shoulders. Hugging him tightly, she did not speak for several minutes. She smiled against his shirtfront. "There is nothing more practical than my love for you."

"Belle." Her name came out like a moan.

He tipped her head up and his lips covered hers in an intense kiss. The passion that was always there between them sprang to the surface. She opened her mouth and demanded his tongue by offering her own. Within seconds, she was so hot, she would have lay down on the floor of Ceddy's library and opened her body to Ian.

He broke off the kiss.

She protested. He picked her up and placed her in a chair then moved away to stand near a wall full of bookcases. "We have much to discuss."

She would much rather be kissing him, but he appeared intent on his course. She let him have his way. She composed herself, placing her hands demurely together in her lap.

"Very well."

He gave a bark of laughter. "Dinna agree so readily, Belle. 'Tis frightening. It makes me wonder what you are planning."

She winked at him. "A woman prefers to keep some mystery."

She could not believe the freedom she felt telling Ian of her love for him. She was still reeling from his reappraisal of her attributes as well.

He did not respond to her teasing. "I am sorry I hurt you. I went to the country to search for Renton, but he did not go to his estate in Kent."

The final band around her heart broke free. He had not been avoiding her. Ian had never meant to break their engagement. He had been trying to find the man who threatened her. She smiled radiantly at him.

"'Tis no good news I'm giving you."

She begged to differ. "What is our plan now?"

"We will be married by special license in three days time."

It was a sound plan. Renton would not attempt to abduct her again once she and her fortune were married to Ian. "All right."

He looked stunned. "You agree?"

She shrugged. "It is the most logical plan of action." She looked at him in wonder. "Did you expect me to disagree?"

"How can you blame me, Belle? You have fought the idea of marrying me with a great deal of energy."

She did not understand. "I already agreed to marry you."

"Aye." He shook his head as if to clear it.

She grew worried at his odd reaction. "You did mean it, didn't you? You do still want to marry me."

He gave her a fierce frown. "Never doubt it."

"Poor Aunt Griselda. She will be heartbroken to give up her wedding plans," she said.

"She can have as fancy of a wedding as she desires." Ian crossed his muscular arms across his chest. "So long as she can have it planned in three days time."

Chapter Seventeen

"Are you all right?" Diana's concerned voice pierced the fog surrounding Annabelle. The closed carriage jolted over the road as the ladies made their way to the Pall Mall to do their last minute shopping before Annabelle's wedding. She wanted to purchase something for Ian as a wedding gift.

Diana wanted to make sure that Annabelle's wedding outfit lacked no accessory. It had taken some subterfuge for the ladies to leave. Ian had insisted that Annabelle stay home and receive no one without her aunt and John Footman present.

Looking at her friend in the shadowy interior of the carriage, Annabelle gave a reassuring smile. "Yes, of course, I'm fine. I'm getting married tomorrow. I should be ecstatic."

"But, you are not?"

Annabelle did not know how to respond to Diana's question. She was thrilled to be marrying Ian. Her love for him grew each day. It was his unwillingness to let himself love her that had her worrying.

"No. Yes. I don't know." She sighed. "I want to marry Ian more than anything I have ever wanted. That frightens me."

Diana put her hand over Annabelle's and squeezed. "You're not the first bride to have wedding nerves. I cried the morning of my wedding, remember?"

Annabelle smiled. "Yes, I remember. You were an absolute watering pot." She lifted the curtain from the carriage window to see how far they were from the Pall Mall. "I just wish I could be sure I was not making a mistake."

Leaning forward, Diana squeezed Annabelle's hand again. "You and Ian were made for each other."

Annabelle agreed, but she wanted Ian to realize his good fortune as well. She wanted more than just his desire to marry her. She wanted his love. "Diana, what if he falls in love with someone else after we are married? I could not bear it."

Diana stared at her as if she had just suggested Ian would murder the Prince Regent. "Do not be ridiculous. Ian has eyes for no one but you. Even a fool could see that."

Then she must be a fool, because she didn't see it. "But he does not love me."

"What do you mean? Of course he loves you." Diana sounded completely disbelieving. Her compassionate eyes searched Annabelle's face.

"No he doesn't," Annabelle argued. "He told me."

Diana's look of concern turned to amusement. "Oh, really, Annabelle. I thought you were wiser than that."

She desperately wanted to believe Diana's views. Ian said she was beautiful and that he wanted her. That he would never let her go. Yet, he was adamant that he did not love her. "I wish I was wise enough to see into Ian's heart."

Diana looked at her pityingly. "Surely you realize that gentlemen would rather lose a bet at White's than admit their tender feelings."

"I don't see Robert having any difficulty where you are concerned."

Diana laughed. "Do you forget so quickly the two years I set my cap for him and he pretended I did not exist? You know he did not even tell me he loved me when he proposed. Had I not been so certain of his love, I would have sent him packing."

Annabelle was shocked. She knew her brother could be stupid, but this was beyond her imagining. So unlike the Robert she witnessed now with his wife. "He's so affectionate."

"Yes, several months of married life and good battle tactics on my part convinced him of the error of his ways." Diana straightened her gloves and gave Annabelle a considering look. "You are the last person I would expect to give up the contest before you have even begun the

224

campaign."

Diana's words had a ring of truth in them. Was Annabelle a weak-willed miss who would concede defeat before she even saw combat? No. She was a modern woman. She did not need to wait for Ian to come to his senses. She would help get him there. She would set siege against each of Ian's defenses and see them fall.

"You are right."

Diana nodded. "Anyone with eyes in their head cannot miss the way Ian looks at you as if he's thirsty and you're the only drink available."

Annabelle grew warm at her friend's words, but they gave her pause. She believed passion did not equal love, but maybe it preceded the deeper emotion. She could not deny that Ian felt a great deal of passion for her. He would have to be a better actor than Keen to have pretended his overwhelming reaction to her body.

Perhaps her battle tactics should begin with a kissing campaign. She chuckled at the thought, but considered that it might well work. It could not hurt and she certainly liked kissing Ian.

They arrived at their first destination, Hatchard's Bookshop. Annabelle wanted to buy a book on the latest farming techniques for Ian. Diana had made a list of those Robert liked the most.

A clerk greeted them upon arrival. "Something I can get for you ladies?"

Annabelle replied, "Yes, I'm looking for a book on farming or sheep. I've got a list here of likely prospects. Do you carry any of these titles?" She handed the list Diana had made to the clerk.

The clerk nodded. "Several. Yes. Several. Perhaps some more beside." Indicating two chairs near the door, he suggested they sit and wait while he collected the books.

Annabelle agreed. She and Diana were busy discussing the changes in Annabelle's favorite magazine, *The Repository of Arts, Literature, Commerce, Manufacturers, Fashions and Politics*, when the door opened.

"I know you like your weightier matters, but I like it better now that it has more fashion and less politics," declared Diana.

Annabelle was about to argue when she recognized Chester P. Thorn. Her insides grew tight. She tried to get Diana's attention, by kicking the toe of her boot. Still in the throes of her argument, Diana ignored Annabelle's tap. Her back to the door, she had not seen Mr. Thorn come into the bookshop.

Mr. Thorn looked haggard with dark bruises under his eyes and his appearance even more rumpled than usual. He smiled at her, showing tobacco-stained teeth.

"Ladies."

Diana sucked in air and seemed to hold it. She whipped her head around. "Mr. Thorn."

Annabelle did not like the look of pallor that came over Diana. She glared at the intruder. "What are you doing here?"

He shrugged. "Perhaps I came to find a book."

Not likely. The vermin was too busy tormenting innocent ladies like Diana to find time to read. More likely he had followed them. The thought rankled. If he had followed them without detection, then that horrible squire could as well. Annabelle wanted to let out an unladylike curse. She had to find a way to turn this situation to their advantage.

"What do you want?"

Mr. Thorn chortled nastily. "You're a right blunt one aren't you? More spirited than your friend here."

Diana looked like she was trying not to be sick.

"Your observations do not concern me. Tell us what you want. Do you have another letter to sell? You must realize that we won't have the money on us to buy it."

Thorn nodded. "Yes, exactly. I want to sell all of the letters. I want five thousand pounds for them and not one penny less."

Diana exclaimed, "I could not possibly come up with five thousand pounds without telling my husband what it was for."

Approval coursed through Annabelle. Diana played her part to perfection. Her friend might be nauseous from her pregnancy, but contrary to what the rat before them believed, she did not lack spirit.

"Ask your friend here for the blunt. In fact, I want her to bring it."

He turned his attention to Annabelle. "Meet me at the North entrance to Hyde Park with the money at six o'clock. Come alone."

Annabelle nearly sighed aloud with relief. That would give her plenty of time to find Ian and make their plans. Renton had to be behind this. It would be his idea to get her to come alone. They would catch both men in their own trap.

"I must at least bring a footman or a maid."

Mr. Thorn lost his smile. "You go where you please without escort. If I see anyone else with you, I will leave and the letters will be published this week."

Although she knew that the foul man would not succeed, the cruelty in his voice sent shivers down her spine. She nodded. "Very well. I will come alone."

Diana protested. "I will not have it."

Mr. Thorn ignored her. He turned to leave as the clerk approached. "Be there." Then, he was gone.

Annabelle hurriedly selected a book about new farming techniques and one about sheep breeding. She and Diana left and headed to the bank.

"Shouldn't we go home and alert Robert and Ian to this development?" Diana asked.

"Mr. Thorn may still be following us. He will expect me to go to the bank," Annabelle replied.

Diana nodded. "I won't feel safe until we are home again, though."

"Neither will I." Annabelle shuddered. "The thought that he has been following me gives me the willies."

"I think we fooled him."

A smile split Annabelle's face. "I am so proud of you, Diana. You did a credible job of looking like a woman in mortal fear of her husband finding out her awful secret."

Diana laughed. "I had a terrible attack of nausea. It helped."

The trip to the bank went without incident. Annabelle was nervous about leaving the bank again. She feared that the plan to meet that evening had all been a ruse and once she came out of the building, supposedly five thousand pounds richer, Mr. Thorn would attack. She breathed a sigh of relief when she and Diana climbed back into the carriage and it started toward home.

☃

"You'll not use yourself as bait."

Belle did not look in the least intimidated by his bellow. She perched on the edge of her chair, excitement radiating from her very being. She thought it a great adventure. He knew better.

"There is no need to shout, Ian. It is a perfectly sound plan." Her certainty did nothing to soothe his temper.

She wasn't going anywhere near Renton. "'Tis a daft plan and that's the truth of it."

Her brows drew together in a frown. "Insults are no more necessary than your bellows, Ian MacKay."

He wanted to kiss her. He wanted to lock her in her room. His fury at discovering her gone when he came to call had only increased upon hearing her plan to catch Thorn and Renton. Did the lass have no concern for her safety?

Hamilton caught Ian's attention. "It is not such a bad idea. We will not allow her out of our sight. She will stay on the bench. When Renton makes his move, we will be there to catch him."

Ian turned the full force of his glare on Hamilton. "Your sister does no ken how to stay out of harm's way. She'll get up and follow Thorn somewhere foolish. 'Tis no to be thought of."

An outraged gasp issued from Belle's lips. "I will not follow Thorn anywhere. Ian, do you think I am so lacking in common sense?"

An honest answer would get her more riled, so Ian said nothing at all.

She would not be deterred. "Do you trust me?"

Aye, he trusted her with his life, but not her own. "Belle, 'tis no a matter of trust. I canna allow you to put yourself in danger in this manner."

He thought he was being perfectly reasonable. She looked ready to throttle him. She stood up and faced him, mere inches from his body. Thoughts totally unrelated to their argument filled his mind. He wanted to pull the pins from her hair and tunnel his fingers into the silken mass. Then he would kiss her until she begged him to do more. His hands would slide down her body to cup her bottom and pull her thighs flush with his own.

She stamped her foot. "Do pay attention." She glared at him. "The least you can do is give me the courtesy of listening when I am yelling at you."

He smiled. Aye, she was yelling all right.

"As I was saying, you do not need to allow me to do anything. I am a grown woman and perfectly capable of making my own decisions."

"Nay."

"Do not be so stubborn. This is important. We must deal with these vermin now. I do not want another heiress caught in Squire Renton's foul grasp."

Ian sympathized. He did not want Belle caught in the squire's lecherous plans either. Not able to stop himself, he pulled her close. Leaning down, he whispered in her ear. "I dinna want you hurt."

She sighed. "I know. I promise not to follow Thorn anywhere. I will stay on the bench as if my skirts had been tacked to it." She played with the buttons on his coat. "Please, Ian."

He knew he was beaten. Taking her chin, he tilted her head up. "If you stand up to stretch, I'll be there by the time you sit down again."

She nodded her head against his hand.

He lowered his head and gave her one, brief, hard kiss to seal their pact.

She blushed. "Ian, we are not alone."

Hamilton cleared his throat. "So, it is settled."

Ian released Belle and faced Hamilton. "Aye." He did not like it, but he had agreed.

Lady Beauford entered the room. No longer green in the face, Lady Hamilton followed close behind.

Hamilton rushed to her side. "All is well?"

She smiled at her husband. "Aunt Griselda took great care of me and I'm feeling much better now."

He nodded. "I will not shout at you again. I did not mean to make you sick."

She laughed. "Robert, my love, I believe the carriage ride and running into Mr. Thorn had more to do with my indisposition than your anger. Although, I would think that you and MacKay would be pleased that Annabelle and I snuck out to do some shopping. Mr. Thorn would never have approached us otherwise."

From the look on Hamilton's face, Ian assumed the other man dinna think any more of his wife's argument than Ian did. It would take him longer than the cold season in the Highlands to get over the fear that had washed over him when he arrived at Lady Beauford's to find Belle missing.

CЗ

Later, dressed in the livery of Lady Beauford's coachman, a muffler over the bottom half of his face, Ian sat in the carriage while Belle perched on the park bench. Her soft hazel eyes darted around, alight with interest. He growled. She looked for all the world like a woman waiting for her lover, not some demented, blackmailing blackguard. Unrecognizable in the guise of servant out for an evening stroll, Hamilton sauntered through the park, not far away.

Ian kept a wary eye on the crowd ebbing and flowing around Belle. Renton could not have chosen a better time for the meeting. With the customary throng in the park, he would be difficult to spot.

His eyes alert for any sign of danger, Ian stiffened at the sight of two heavyset men approaching Belle. They were dressed as typical men about the Town, but something did not ring true. They moved with the swaggering gait more commonly seen down at the docks.

Ian was already jumping down from the carriage when one of them put his hand over Belle's mouth. Her body went limp. Ian bellowed a denial. He would kill the whoreson. The other man swung around to face Ian. The ruffian dropped into a fighter's stance. Ian did not break his stride. He struck out with his fist and the ruffian flew backwards. The other man dropped Belle back on the bench to face Ian.

"I'll teach you to get in me business." He pulled a knife from his boot.

Ian smiled. The man lunged, but Ian was quicker. He kicked the other man's hand and the knife went flying. Belle's attacker snarled. He drove forward. Ian waited until the other man was almost on him before driving his fist into the man's face. He heard bone crack and knew he had broken the man's nose. Shaking his head, the man stood facing Ian. His eyes were lit with bloodlust. Ian did not care. He would kill the whoreson before he touched Belle again.

Hamilton reached them.

"Take Belle to the carriage," Ian ordered.

Hamilton swung Belle up in his arms and headed for the carriage.

Ian did not turn his attention away from her would-be abductor. "Where's Renton?"

The man glared. He took a swing at Ian. Ian was done playing games. He caught the fool's arm and used it as a lever to force the man around and down to the ground.

"Ow, you're gonna break me arm."

Ian moved close to the blackguard. "I'll break your neck if you don't tell me where I can find Renton."

Sweat broke out on the man's brow. "Don't know no Renton. A friend from the stews give me this job. Said it would be a breeze." The tough's voice had taken on a nasal quality from his broken nose.

"Who's your friend?"

When the man did not answer immediately, Ian twisted his arm harder. "Thorn. Chester Thorn."

Ian stood up, dragging the man with him. "Where are you takin' me? I didn't sign on for no fight with a bloody nobleman."

Ian ignored him. He dragged the man past where his friend lay still unconscious in the grass.

"Eh, what about me friend. He'll get his pockets picked if you leave him lying about like that."

It was a far better fate than the thug deserved. When Ian got to the carriage, Belle's eyes fluttered open. Hamilton breathed a sigh of relief.

Ian's fear spilled over in furious accusation. "Ye said it was a sound plan. Ye wouldna move from the bench." Even as he yelled at her, he knew he was angry with himself. He had agreed to the plan against his better judgment.

Hamilton pulled a pistol from his coat and took charge of their prisoner. "Sit there." He pointed to the bench across from him and Belle. "If you so much as sneeze, I'll blow a hole through you."

The scum looked like he believed Hamilton. He climbed into the carriage and sat down, nursing his arm.

Ian wasn't finished glaring at Belle. He had almost lost her, again. 'Twas enough to drive a man mad. He reached out and brushed a curl from her face. Ian recognized the sickly sweet smell of chloroform his brother had used when they were children for his bug collecting.

"Are ye all right, lass?"

Belle nodded. Then shook her head violently. "I'm going to be..." Gagging cut off her speech.

Ian swept her into his arms and deposited her outside the carriage. He held her while she heaved.

He waited until her retching finished and then handed her his handkerchief. She wiped her face. "That is foul stuff."

He soothed her back. "Aye."

She leaned back against him. "I want to go home."

"Are ye well enough to travel?" he asked.

"Yes." She sighed. "You are still upset."

What sane man wouldn't be? "How can you tell?"

"Your Scottish burr gets thicker when you are angry."

'Twas a nonsensical thing to be discussing, but his love was still hazy from the chloroform. He lifted her back into the carriage.

He turned to Hamilton. "If he looks at Belle, shoot him."

232

Hamilton acknowledged the order with an inclination of his head. The tough made a production of turning his head to look out the side of the carriage. Ian jumped into the coachman's seat and set the horses in motion. When they arrived at the townhouse, Ian insisted on carrying Belle inside.

Hamilton locked their prisoner in the pantry. They would see him in the hands of the magistrate later.

After leaving Belle in the capable hands of her aunt and sister-in-law, Ian and Hamilton went in search of Thorn.

CŽ

It had been much too close. If William hadn't insisted on Thorn going with the two fools he had hired to abduct Lady Annabelle, William would have been waiting inside Thorn's lodgings when the angry Scotsman and Lady Annabelle's brother came riding up. Instead he had been sneaking around the back alleyway and had barely taken time to glimpse the two gentlemen on his flight from Thorn's lodgings. They wouldn't find much there. No one knew of his connection to Thorn. No one except Thorn, and dead men could not tell tales.

Lady Hamilton must have told her husband about the blackmail. She had ruined his plan and he would have his revenge. First, though, he would get vengeance on the laird for besting him. *No one* bested Squire William Renton without paying dearly for the privilege.

Chapter Eighteen

Annabelle shivered, but it was not from cold in the cavernous sanctuary of St. George's. Apprehension caused Annabelle's skin to prickle with gooseflesh as she stood at the back of the church clutching Robert's arm. Everything had taken on an unreal quality when he and Ian had returned the evening before with the news that Mr. Thorn was dead.

Annabelle's heart raced with the fear that by marrying Ian, she was exposing him to the dangerous plans of a madman. She had tried to persuade Ian to wait on the wedding until they could track down Renton. Ian refused. The only change he had been willing to make in their course of action, indeed demanded they make, was that they were to leave for Graenfrae directly after the wedding breakfast.

He would have left right after the wedding, but even Ian could not move Aunt Griselda once her mind was set. Annabelle's aunt was determined to give her a proper wedding breakfast, even though she could not have a full-blown society wedding.

At some signal that Annabelle did not see, Robert stiffened beside her. He laid his gloved hand over her own and squeezed her fingers. "You are doing the right thing. Do not fret."

His words did little to tamp down the fear that threatened to spiral out of control. The few guests that Ian had allowed and Aunt Griselda had insisted on watched her formal procession down the aisle. Ian stood next to the priest, Ceddy at his side. His eyes rested on her with an intensity that both calmed and disturbed her. It made no sense, but there it was.

Within moments, the source of Annabelle's fear stood beside her. He turned her insides to jelly. She loved him and this marriage would put him in danger. Certainty about that fact made her knees grow weak as she listened to Ian make his vows.

His voice did not waver as he promised to honor, protect and cherish her. Gazing into his eyes, she almost missed the fact that he had arranged with the priest to leave out the vow of love. Had she thought about it, she would have expected it. Ian would not vow what he could not deliver.

Her fear returned tenfold only now it centered on the knowledge that Ian had just circumvented his wedding promise to love her. It did no good to remind herself of her battle tactics.

Right now all she wanted to do was retreat.

As the priest asked her if she would love, honor and obey, she entertained thoughts of dashing from the church. Ian must have guessed the direction of her thoughts because he put a hand on her arm and squeezed, encouraging her to answer the priest.

"I..." Her voice came out like a croak.

Ian frowned at her.

Looking around wildly, she sought a means of escape from her fear. Her eyes caught those of Diana. Her friend smiled and winked. She mouthed the word, "Remember" and pointed unobtrusively to Robert, who now stood at her side. Annabelle sucked in air, telling herself that Diana was right. Ian took her hand and rubbed the back of it with his thumb. The fear left. She sighed. It was going to be all right. Diana had survived this ordeal, Annabelle would too.

Taking a deep breath she spoke clearly. "I do so promise." And then not being able to help herself she added, "Although, I don't believe I'll be very good at obedience, but I will try."

Why not? Ian had refused to vow to love her. At least she had promised to try. Surely she should not be expected to blindly obey her husband. She would of course obey him when he was right.

Annabelle ignored the sound of her brother choking behind her. Sneaking a peek at her groom, she was relieved to note that rather than glaring his face now wore an amused smile.

"I'll help you, lass," he promised, his voice low enough for only her and the priest to hear.

And I'll help you learn to love me no matter what you promised, she mentally vowed. Annabelle repeated the rest of her vows without hesitation. She spent the remainder of the service kneeling next to Ian, acutely aware of the fact that he was now her husband. The priest gave the benediction.

Taking her arm, Ian led her from the church. His tiger stood ready with the carriage. Lifting Annabelle by the waist, Ian set her inside. The coward in her rejoiced when she saw that her magnificent gown of white silk took up the entire seat around her. Her relief turned to irritation when Ian brushed the folds of fabric aside and took his place next to her.

"You will crush my gown."

He shrugged and lifted her into his lap so that her skirts fell over both their legs. She gasped. "This is not what I meant."

He laughed. "I ken."

Raising her chin, she frowned at him. "You think my irritation is amusing, husband?"

His eyes turned serious. "Say that again."

"You want me to repeat my question?"

"Nay, call me husband again. I like it."

Annabelle could not hold her frown. His admission melted her insides. "Husband, do you find my annoyance amusing?"

"Aye."

"Why?"

"You wanted to sit alone."

She could not deny his charge. She shrugged.

"You are nervous." He made the words sound like an insult.

"This may come as a complete surprise to you, Ian, but many brides are nervous on their wedding day."

The laughter was back. "Aye, but do these same brides consider leaving the church in the middle of their wedding?"

"How did you know?"

"The way you kept looking behind you at the doors gave you away. I wasn't sure you were going to go through with it."

"Neither was I." The admission slipped out.

"What made you?"

"I realized that if other women could survive the ordeal, so could I," she admitted.

Ian didn't like her answer. "You think marriage to me an *ordeal*?"

"You needn't shout. I said my vows."

Her words did not appease him. His scowl grew fierce. "Aye, but I can't help but think you wish you hadn't."

The words shocked her, but the uncertainty in his tone surprised her more. Ian might not love her, but he cared whether or not she *wanted* to be married to him.

"I do not wish any such thing. Do you think I am such a nick ninny that I would have said my marriage vows otherwise? Now, stop your glaring. It's very rude to scowl at your wife on her wedding day."

Ian's face relaxed. "Is this an English dictate?" His teasing tone was like a gentle caress.

"No. It's my dictate."

He smiled into her eyes and moved his mouth closer to hers. "Kiss your husband, lass."

"Is that a Scottish dictate?" she whispered. Annabelle's lips were a mere breath from Ian's as she spoke. She imagined that she could feel her breath caress his lips.

"Nay, 'tis my dictate," he growled before lowering his mouth to hers.

They arrived at Lady Beauford's townhouse moments later. Annabelle scrambled to get off of her husband's lap before the coachman opened the door. He laughed at her attempts to straighten her appearance.

She narrowed her eyes at him. "I'll not have everyone privy to you kissing me."

"Dinna think they will be shocked, we are married."

His words did nothing to settle her mind. Among the *ton,* marriage was hardly license for affection. Annabelle had seen more tolerance shown for the fawning affection of a Cicebo than that of a husband.

As they entered the drawing room to join the wedding guests, Ian leaned down and whispered in her ear. "Wife, your cheeks have the hue of your aunt's roses."

She felt warmth invade her insides at the word "wife". No wonder Ian had made her repeat herself. It felt wonderful to know that from this day forward her life was intrinsically linked with his. She shared a relationship with her arrogant Scotsman that no one else ever would.

Robert approached with a smile. "Hello, Annabelle. I would never have thought it, but you fit the blushing bride to perfection."

Visions of strangling her brother with his cravat floated before her eyes.

Diana came to her rescue in short order. "Robert, you will not annoy your sister or I will be forced to share some well-kept secrets from our wedding day."

At the look of very real chagrin on her brother's face, Annabelle smiled. "Thank you, Diana. You are a paragon."

Diana acknowledged Annabelle's compliment with a quick squeeze to her arm. Then she turned to Ian. "It's too bad that your family could not come for the wedding."

He shrugged. His attitude sparked Annabelle's curiosity. She wondered if Ian even wanted his family to come. He seemed hesitant to speak of them and had been adamant about not waiting for the marriage to take place in order to give them time to travel to London. Was he ashamed of marrying her? The thought did not sit well with Annabelle. He'd best not be. It was too late to regret his choice.

After several exhausting hours celebrating her marriage with family and friends, Annabelle sighed in relief as she leaned against the squabs of Ian's carriage. *Our carriage,* she amended her thoughts.

"Tired, wife?"

"Yes. I never realized how fatiguing it is to receive happy wishes."

This time when Ian pulled her into his arms, she did not yelp. Sighing in contentment, she snuggled up against him.

238

He rubbed her back and it felt heavenly. "Poor lass."

"That feels nice, Ian. Did the married men advise rubbing your wife's back?" Not waiting for him to answer, she went on. "I think every matron in the room had advice for my wifely duty."

Laughter rumbled in his chest. "And will you be taking their advice, wife?"

Absently playing with the silky strands of his hair, she thought about her answer. Would she? Some of it, maybe.

"Is it such a hard question, then?" Annabelle heard his amusement and smiled.

"No, it's just that I'm not sure."

"You sound serious, wife. What advice has you wondering?"

"It's about the marriage bed."

"Out with it, wife."

Annabelle smiled in spite of herself at her husband's demanding tone. So it was a subject that interested him as well. Somehow, she thought it might be.

"I am supposed to lie perfectly still and not cry out, or you will get a disgust of me."

She was unprepared for Ian's bold laughter. Pulling on his hair she said, "It's not funny, Ian. I already know I cannot stay still when you kiss me and touch me intimately. How am I to stay still when you do more?"

Ian lifted her chin with his finger. His eyes mesmerized her. "I dinna want you to lie still, Belle. The fire of your passion is a very good thing and I dinna want you to dampen it. Do you understand?"

She nodded her head. "I understand." She had expected this response, but a tiny part of her had been afraid that her uninhibited reaction to his touch was wrong. "Thank you."

"Dinna thank me. Your response to my touch is a gift you give me, lass."

"What a nice thing to say." She yawned.

He did not respond, but kissed her softly before tucking her head under his chin. Her eyes grew heavy as his caresses lulled her into a

239

peaceful state of lethargy. It was evening when Ian gently shook her awake. "Come, wife, we have arrived at the inn."

Annabelle rubbed her eyes and stared, blinking up at her husband. He waited patiently for her to come fully awake. Rumbling came from the vicinity of her stomach.

"I believe I am hungry."

"Aye, you are hungry." Ian lifted her from the carriage and carried her into the inn.

"I can walk, Ian. Let me down." Annabelle struggled vainly for Ian to release her.

"I like holding you." The tender warmth in his voice transfixed her.

"I feel like a child still in leading strings."

Ian pulled her close to his hard frame. Lightly brushing the side of her breast with his fingers, he whispered in her ear, "You dinna feel like a small child to me."

Annabelle laughed breathlessly. He refused to set her down until they had entered the inn and the proprietor had given them directions to their private parlor. Relief flowed through her that Ian did not intend to go straight to their bedchamber.

Sparse but elegant furnishings gave the parlor a welcoming aspect. An elegant table covered with an embroidered linen tablecloth sat between two chairs in front of the fireplace. A cozy fire burned in the grate, warding off the evening chill. Moving closer to the table, Annabelle saw that it was set with china and crystal more in keeping with the home of a wealthy peer than a small inn.

A box, the size of a book, that matched the one Ian had given her with her betrothal ring, rested next to one of the china plates. She put her hand out and caressed the delicate rose carved into its top. She noticed, then, that the china had been painted with Ian's crest. How? Overwhelmed, she turned to face her husband.

"Everything is perfect."

"I am glad it pleases you, Belle."

"How did you manage all of this?" She swept her arms out to include the table and everything on it.

He shrugged. "'Twas no hard. I had the china painted when I first got to London."

"Why?" She could not take it in. "Surely you were not concerned about household matters so much as finding a wife and gaining your inheritance."

"There is no china at Graenfrae." He ran his finger along the outer edge of a plate. "'Twas something my grandfather sold to finance his cause. After I chose you to wed, I dinna wish you to be too disappointed in my home. So, I commissioned a few household items. Lady Beauford was a great help."

"My aunt?"

He nodded. "Aye." He met her eyes, his intent. "I dinna want you to be deceived. Graenfrae is a simple home. 'Tis naught by the standards of London. Even with the new dishes and linens, 'tis no like the home you are used to. 'Tis a deep cavernous castle."

He did not sound apologetic, just pragmatic. His tone of voice and stance told her that he found his home acceptable, but was not sure of her reaction. He wanted her to like his home, or he would not have gone to the trouble of buying the lovely china and new linens.

She smiled at him. "I am sure I will love Graenfrae."

He relaxed and nodded. "Aye. You will. 'Tis the loveliest place on earth with the heather blooming purple in the meadows and the grass lush and green."

"It does indeed sound lovely. Robert's favorite country estate is near the border. He believes its beauties more than make up for the lack of social amenities."

"And Lady Hamilton? Does she like it as well?"

"Yes, I believe so. She teases Robert about moldering away on his estate, but she readily agreed to coming late to the Season this year."

The landlord came bustling into the room, followed by a serving wench, her arms laden with choice delicacies. "Everything arrived as Your Lordship said it would. We've set the table with your things just as Your Lordship instructed."

As the girl set the food on the table the landlord happily proclaimed that his wife had cooked all day to provide the delicacies

Ian had requested. Ian seated Annabelle at the table and the landlord served them himself.

After the man left, Annabelle could not take her eyes off of her husband. She had been starving, but now all she could think of was the effort Ian had made on her behalf.

She waited until the landlord left to speak. "Thank you. Your thoughtfulness has made the end of my wedding day as perfect as I could ever imagine."

Suddenly his eyes darkened. He smiled, but did not look amused. "Nay, lass, your wedding day is not over, but when it is you will indeed think it has been perfect."

At the rich promise in her husband's voice, her heart beat a wild rhythm. Not daring to answer, Annabelle set to eating the feast Ian had provided. Biting into a succulent pork cutlet, she felt the juices dribble down her chin. Before she could wipe it away, Ian reached across the table and softly tended to her with his napkin. The tender touch felt like a caress. Annabelle's breath became shorter and she looked at Ian with all of the love that she felt in her heart.

"Dinna look at me that way, wife. Ye'll be missing your dinner if you do."

Aware that Ian's more pronounced burr confirmed his emotionally charged state, Annabelle's heart hammered in her chest. The promise in Ian's words was both thrilling and frightening. She enjoyed his touch, but could not get the image of his aroused manhood from her mind. Surely he was too big to join with her intimately.

If that was not enough of a worry, he had yet to see her completely unclothed. What if he found her lacking? What if she could not please him making love as she had with their pleasurable touching? It was a worry. Lowering her eyes to the tablecloth, Annabelle tried to concentrate on her dinner.

"Coward." Ian's softly spoken taunt could not go unchallenged.

Quickly raising her head to meet his gaze she was momentarily stunned into silence by the warmth she found in his eyes. "I am not a coward." Rather than sounding certain as she intended, her voice came out a breathless whisper.

"Aye, you are. I'll wait though. You'll need your dinner to keep your strength tonight."

"Is that a threat?"

"Nay, wife, 'tis only a blessed promise."

"Ah, so this night I will feel blessed, but tired. Is that it?" Annabelle could not help but bait him.

"Aye." He sounded so arrogant.

"How can you be so sure I'll like it?"

"You will." The man was too confident by half.

"Maybe I won't. What do you think of that?" After all, he had been the one to say that making love was different than their pleasurable touching. What if it was too different?

"I think you are finished eating."

Her mouth felt dry and Annabelle took a large swallow of her champagne. "I'm not quite finished yet." She prevaricated, hoping he wouldn't notice that she was simply pushing the food from one side of her plate to the other.

He noticed.

Standing up, he put his hand out to her. "Come, bride, it is time you became a wife."

Searching for something to delay the inevitable, she caught up the box. "I have not yet thanked you for the gift, Ian. It is lovely."

The box was heavy. She opened the lid and stared in amazement. A golden choker of rose blooms nestled on the black velvet. She lifted it out and tears sprang to her eyes. "It's beautiful."

Her words came out in a whisper, but he heard them. "'Tis your wedding gift."

His statement triggered her memory. "I have a gift for you as well. It is in my valise." His eyes were so intent she almost lost her train of thought. "In our room."

He smiled. "Come, then, Belle. I have an overwhelming desire to see my gift in our room."

He did not mean the books. His eyes spoke of a much more personal gift he wanted. Desire and trepidation shuddered through

243

her. Annabelle placed her hand in his and felt his warmth invade her. It was going to be fine. Other brides had made it through this ordeal as well.

"'Tis not an ordeal. Trust me, you will like it even better than what we have done before."

Mortified, Annabelle realized she had spoken aloud. At least Ian wasn't angry. He hadn't taken kindly to her calling the wedding an ordeal, but he seemed to understand her nerves regarding the marriage bed. Gentlemen were funny.

Chapter Nineteen

There was nothing amusing about it, but Ian was laughing all the same. The daft man expected her to change into her night things while he was in the room.

"You cannot be serious. Ian, I am not going to allow you to help me change and you might as well understand that right now."

Her voice was rising. Soon she'd be yelling like a fishwife. Why had she agreed to leave Purdy behind to pack the remainder of her belongings? Someone else could do it and then she would have another woman to speak to, someone to help her undress and ready herself for the night ahead.

Ian didn't budge. "I would leave you to dress yourself, but in your current state you'd probably lock the door the minute I was on the other side."

Annabelle couldn't very well scoff at his words, as the idea had some merit. How did other ladies overcome this horrible fear?

As if he could read her mind, Ian said, "Dinna be afraid. We will not do anything you dinna want to do."

"I do not want to get undressed."

He shocked her by agreeing. "Fine."

"It is?" She sounded like a mouse. Clearing her throat she spoke again. "You don't mind?" That was much better.

"Nay."

She sighed with relief.

"Come here."

"Why?" She asked the question even as she started toward Ian. If he could be accommodating, then so could she.

"I want to kiss you."

"You do?"

Laughing, Ian answered. "Aye, I do. Are you going to question everything I say tonight? You like kissing me."

Annabelle considered this. "I don't think I'll question everything you say." She moved closer to her husband. "I do like kissing you."

She liked the other things he did as well. It was only the marriage act that had her so frightened. That and completely exposing her unremarkable body. What would she do if he took one look and the lambent desire in his eyes turned to boredom?

"Good."

She nodded. What was good?

He put his hands on her arms and drew her slowly toward him. For a moment he just held her, letting her settle against him. She loved the feel of his hard muscles against her cheek and hands. A strong desire to caress those muscles through his shirt assailed her.

"All right now?"

She was trying. "Yes."

Taking her chin gently in his fingers, he lifted her face toward his. His kiss was like wind gently caressing her lips, lasting only a moment. Sighing, she cuddled against him and he kissed her again. His hands strayed to her back and caressed her through the silk of her gown. His touch was so light, so gentle, so very warm.

Annabelle gave in to the urge to touch him and rubbed her fingers over his broad chest. He groaned. His response made her smile until his hand moved around to cup one of her breasts. Air came whooshing out of her lungs in a gust. He softly kneaded her flesh. Sensations shot through her. Her nipples hardened, straining against the fabric of her bodice. Small jolts of pleasure traveled down her body and concentrated at her feminine center.

She wanted his lips. "I thought you wanted to kiss me."

He lowered his head and took possession of her lips. His mouth moved over hers, overpowering her thoughts with raw sensation. He licked at the seam of her lips.

"Open your mouth for me, wife."

She obeyed with a sigh of surrender. It felt so good. His tongue played a sensual dance in her mouth. She held him more tightly, sure that if she let go, she would fall. His hand that was not kneading her breast worked its way around to her buttocks. He squeezed her soft flesh, pushing the juncture of her thighs against his.

Sensation tore through her. The intimacy of his touch marked her as his. She could feel his hardness, but it did not worry her. She was still fully clothed.

Coherent thought scattered as he rocked his hips against hers. Pleasure arced through her most feminine place and she groaned against his lips. Eager to feel more of him, she untied his neckcloth and pulled it off. She wanted to unbutton his shirt, but her trembling fingers fumbled against the task. Finally she had his shirt open and her hands slipped in to touch his chest and move around to explore the plains of his back.

"Aye, Belle, that's right."

His approval made her bolder. She slipped her hands down his back and caressed the spot just above the waistband of his breeches. "You are so strong and hard, Ian." She pressed her fingers into the muscles of his lower back. "I love the way your body feels."

Ian stopped her words with his mouth. His movements took on a desperate quality. He thrust his hardness against the apex of her thighs again and again. Helpless to resist his onslaught of passion, she met his thrusts with those of her own. Insatiable need built up inside of her.

In her passionate frenzy, she slipped her hands down and pressed his backside. She wanted him closer. The awesome knowledge that he was her husband and she had leave to touch him like this sent Annabelle's heart spinning. His groans and short breath told her that he liked what she was doing.

"Dinna do that, lass."

The harsh words were like being dunked in an icy brook. She

immediately stilled. She looked up at him. It took a moment for her passion-hazed eyes to focus. A fine sheen of perspiration stood out across his brow. His eyes were so dark with emotion that they were almost black.

"Do you not like it?" she asked.

"I like it too much," he replied.

He looked like a man in agony. He looked like a man on the verge of losing his control. He did not look like a man who did not like what she had been doing.

She wanted more of his mouth. Putting her hands in his hair she pulled his mouth down to hers. She pressed her lips against his so forcefully that their teeth touched.

He groaned and opened his mouth for her questing tongue. She played her tongue against his. Ian shuddered and swept her up in his arms. He carried her to the bed.

Annabelle wondered if they could make love with her clothes on and then could not think at all as Ian pulled down the bodice of her dress and chemise to expose her breasts. She felt overwhelming sensations as her nipples reacted to the air. Ian's hand closed around one breast. He took her nipple between his thumb and forefinger and rolled it back and forth.

She arched against him. She would have come off the bed, but for the weight of his body against hers. "*Ian.*"

He continued his ministrations to her breast with his hand while his mouth trailed hot, wet kisses down her neck across her collarbone and to her other breast.

"I love what you do to me. I love you, *Ian.*"

He stilled for a moment and looked into her eyes.

"You are mine."

She nodded frantically. She would agree to anything to get him to go back to his sweet torture. She never wanted to belong to anyone else. He took her nipple into his mouth. She screamed and he growled with male satisfaction. She could not stand the torment. Her lower body bucked against his, seeking the release she had found in the carriage and at the inn the day Ian had proposed.

His mouth and hands abandoned her and Annabelle's eyes flew open. She wanted to protest, but could not make herself speak. He tore his shirt off and the rest of his clothes followed quickly. The sight of his vibrantly erect manhood sent shards of desire shooting through her.

Before she could comment, he had lifted her skirts to her waist and settled back on top of her. The feel of his naked hardness against her skin thrilled her. It felt so right.

"Ian, please, do something."

He kissed her. Within seconds she was writhing under him again, this time her bare legs twining with his. She felt his male hardness at the juncture of her thighs and cried out. She wanted him. All of him.

"Aye, Belle, 'tis time."

His words came to her through a haze of passion. She barely registered them. He spread her thighs until she was completely open to him. He caressed her inner thighs and she grew feverish with desire for him to move his hand where she was longing for it to be.

Desperate, she grabbed his wrist and placed his hand on the juncture between her thighs.

"Aye, you're as hot for me as I am for you, Belle."

His fingers slid in and out of her moist passage, spreading the wetness to the rest of her feminine flesh. Soon she was slick with her own excitement. He rubbed against the small nub above her most secret place. Her hands gripped the blankets under her.

Somehow, it was more than before and she did not think she could stand it. "Ian, I cannot bear this."

He moved until his hardness was at her entrance. Slowly, he began to slip inside. It was the most amazing experience Annabelle had ever known. She gasped as he filled her, joining his body with hers.

He had been right. This was different. This was a miracle. Her body resisted him. She felt a small amount of pain. She almost cried in frustration. It wasn't going to work.

"You are too big. Ian, we do not fit."

"You must trust me."

She tensed under him. "But it hurts, Ian."

He continued to press forward. "I know, Belle, but it will only hurt for a little while."

Her pleasure receded as the pain in her body took control. She pulled on his hair. "I don't like this."

He leaned down and kissed her with a hot open-mouthed kiss. She remembered the times in the past he had told her to trust him. He had not disappointed her. He must know something she did not. She began to relax again under him. He continued to kiss her until she was once again roaming her hands over his body. She shifted under him, trying to get more comfortable at the invasion.

"Nay, Belle, dinna move, lass, or I will be lost."

Pleasure warred with the pain at their joining. "But I want to."

Groaning, he slid his hand between their bodies and caressed her. Her body tensed, but this time with pleasurable anticipation. She pushed against him, wanting more of his fullness. It still hurt, but her pleasure overrode the pain.

"Aye, lass, that's right."

With one final thrust he was inside her. She shouted a protest against the tearing sensation. It hurt! His lips muffled her yell, so she pounded on his back and twisted her mouth away from his. "Stop, Ian, *this is not working.*"

He stopped, his body completely rigid above hers. He looked into her eyes. He leaned down and tenderly licked away her tears. "Do ye trust me, Belle?"

How could she not? "Yes, but—"

He would not let her finish. "Then trust me to give you pleasure past the pain. 'Tis only this time that will be this way for you. Do ye believe me?"

She nodded. She truly did believe him. Ian would never lie to her.

"Can I move now?" he asked.

The sharp pain had started to recede already. She nodded again, hoping it would be over soon. He moved slightly and she felt another spurt of discomfort and an equal measure of pleasure.

Sweat stood out on his forehead and his face was a mask of

tightly held control. It occurred to her that he held himself back with a great deal of effort. Somehow the knowledge dispelled the last of her fears. She moved slightly under him and felt pleasure cascade through her body.

He began to move again, slowly. She did not want him to go slow. She lifted her hips against him demanding that he move faster. He complied. It was not fast enough. She wanted more. She needed more.

"Ian." She yelled his name.

He thrust against her. Her entire body felt on the verge of a great precipice. Ian gave a shout and climaxed inside her. She went over the precipice. Her body convulsed around him. The sensations went on and on.

"Now you belong to me."

She would have smiled at his possessive tone, but she was too languid. After the final tremor had shaken her body, she went limp under Ian.

He leaned down and kissed her softly. "Ye can always trust me, Belle."

She smiled. "Yes."

The weight of his body made it difficult to breathe, but she did not want him to move. Now he belonged to her as well. He lifted himself off her. He walked away and she could not summon the strength to see what he was doing. She nearly jumped off the bed when she felt him wiping her legs with a wet linen.

He finished and threw the linen aside. "Now, can I help you undress?"

She laughed. A small amount of concern remained about his reaction to her body. She was not built like a Cyprian. However, she had to admit that he had seen most of her already. Besides, a man could not fake the kind of passion he had just exhibited.

She stood up. "Very well."

His eyes filled with tender warmth. He teased her, "Your gown is well and truly crushed now."

She looked at the white silk ruefully. He was right. It was also ruined. She sighed. "Do not tell my aunt or Diana. They spent a great deal of the last three days making sure that this dress was just perfect."

"I'll no tell. 'Tis a fact that the woman wearing it is more my concern."

She realized that Ian wanted to see her body just as she could see his. She liked his hard masculinity, but found herself unable to take more than sparing glimpses at his nakedness. Perhaps when they had been married longer, she would not be embarrassed to look at his body.

She offered him her back. He reached out and began to untie the ribbons that held her gown together. When he finished, he gently slid the silk over her hips. He did not stop there. Without pausing, he untied her chemise and slipped it off of her. Gooseflesh broke out on her heated skin as her body became completely exposed to Ian's gaze.

She was afraid to see his reaction and equally afraid not to. Giving herself a short mental lecture on being a goose, she lifted her eyes to meet his. What she saw there made her suck in her breath.

"Ye are beautiful, Belle."

Her eyes filled with tears and she launched herself at him. He wrapped his arms around her. She felt so perfect. She fit him like the heather fit the meadows around Graenfrae.

She was his.

She sighed against his chest. "This is nice."

It was more than nice, but he wouldn't frighten her by saying so. Her unexpected timidity about making love had shocked him. She hadn't shown any of that fear when they had kissed and touched intimately before. There had been more than one point at which he wasn't sure he would be able to continue to master his body's reaction to his wife.

In fact, if she didn't stop wiggling her naked body against him, his self-control would vanish now. She had no concept of her appeal. When he started to grow hard, he thrust her from him.

"What is the matter?" Her gaze dropped to his rapidly swelling manhood and she sucked in her breath. "Oh."

"Aye. Where is your sleeping robe? I dinna ken how much good it will do, but I'll not maul you when you are tender."

She walked toward him and stopped. She grimaced. "I am a little tender."

"I ken."

Her grimace turned to a smile. "You really should do something about your arrogance, you know."

He shrugged.

She laughed softly. Her small pink and white breasts shivered with her mirth. Where was her bloody nightrobe? He was going to toss her on the bed and ravish her in another moment. Why had he insisted on seeing her perfect body after they had made love? He knew the answer before he asked the question.

Because he needed to.

He stormed over to the wardrobe. Someone had unpacked their clothes and hung them. He grabbed what looked like a sleeping robe and thrust it at Belle. "Put this on."

She obeyed him, chuckling all the while. "Would you have me believe that mere sight of my unremarkable body is enough to throw you into a passionate frenzy?"

She thought this amusing? Was not his throbbing manhood testimony enough to his predicament? He growled and she laughed harder. "'Tis the truth, I would put play to your amusement, lass, if I dinna ken how tender you are."

She tied the belt on her robe. Her smile was warm and accepting. "You are a true gentleman, my love."

Her words poured over him like a healing balm. The discomfort was worth that look of approval in her eyes. He pulled on his breeches, forcing his unruly self into confinement.

She came toward him with a package wrapped in brown paper. "Here."

He took the present and stared at her.

"Open it," she instructed.

He ripped the paper off and smiled in wonder at the books on his favorite subjects. He did not know what to say. No one had ever made an effort to give him such a perfect gift before. His family generally rolled their eyes at his interests. Belle understood.

He swept her into a crushing embrace. "Thank you."

She reached up and kissed the underside of his chin. "You are welcome. I bought them at Hatchard's the day Mr. Thorn found us."

She had risked her life and his wrath to buy him a wedding gift. A feeling he did not understand welled up inside. "They are perfect."

She sighed. "I am glad. I wanted so much to please you."

The truth of her words was in her voice. A heady feeling of contentment settled over him. His happiness was important to his new wife. He vowed he would do anything to keep her safe and protect her happiness as well.

She yawned.

"Come, Belle, 'tis time for bed."

She nodded.

He wanted nothing more than to curl her sweet naked body next to his, but knew he could not stand the temptation. "'Tis best if you wear a sleeping gown."

She gave him a slow, sweet smile. "All right, Ian."

He tortured himself watching her slip off her robe and don the sleeping gown. By the time she was finished, he was panting like he had been chasing footpads.

She climbed into the bed. He blew out the candles in the sconces by the door. He took off his breeches and slid into bed beside her. She lay on the other side, her arms on top of the blankets, stiff as a fire poker.

Ignoring the voice of reason, he hauled her into his arms. She immediately snuggled against him, laying her head against his chest. He blew out the candle by the bed and then resettled her on his chest. Her soft curves were doing things to his noble intentions. "Stop your squirming."

She stilled. "Is that better?"

Not by much. He still wanted to make love to her more than he wanted to take his next breath. "Aye."

"Ian?"

He thought she was tired. "What?"

"When will I meet your family?"

His muscles contracted. The thought of introducing Belle to his faithless brother and family who all believed that he had tarnished his honor when he broke his betrothal made him uneasy. It had to be done. He made a decision then. "We will stop by Lansing Hall on our way home."

"Do they live very close to us?"

Too close. "Aye."

She played with the hair on his chest. He sucked in his breath. She did not seem to notice. "Do you think Squire Renton killed Mr. Thorn?"

He sighed. He dinna want to discuss that foul man on his wedding night. "Aye."

"Why?"

"He no longer had use for him."

She shivered. "That is so cold."

"The man is a bas—blackguard."

"Yes."

She was silent for a long while. He hoped she was going to sleep. "Will he come after us?"

He nearly swore at the fear he heard in her voice. "What would be the use? You are now married to me. He canna touch your fortune."

She sighed. "I know." She let her fingers trail down his chest to his stomach. "He seems unbalanced though, as if he is motivated more than just by greed."

He had a hard time concentrating on her words when her hand was touching him. "I will protect you."

He thought he heard her say, "Who will protect you?" but his mind was fully occupied with her roving fingers. She was tracing the line of his hair down below his waist. Her hands trailed down to his aching manhood.

"It would appear your problem is not resolved yet, husband."

"You are too tender." 'Twas all he could think to say. He wanted desperately for her to disagree.

She curled her fingers around him. He nearly came undone. "Then you will have to be very gentle, won't you?"

He was gentle. She was demanding and finally they were both satisfied.

When they had found their completion and she lay completely limp beneath him, she sighed. "You were right."

He could not summon the energy to lift his head and ask what she meant.

She told him anyway. "Making love is more than just touching. I felt my soul linked with yours."

He smiled in the curve of her shoulder, satisfied.

C3

Ian woke early the next morning. Belle's body cuddled close to his. Her sleeping gown rode up around her hips. Her naked legs rubbed against his as she squirmed in her sleep. He felt passion stir, but something else as well. Something far more rare and precious.

Contentment.

He could never remember feeling this content. Memories of life at Graenfrae as a child and his father were fleeting. He could only remember snatched images of a giant man carrying Ian as a small boy on his shoulders and the lectures.

His father had drilled Ian's responsibility to the people of Graenfrae into him. It was that burden of responsibility that had served to make Ian the outsider at Lansing Hall. No matter how kind his stepfather, Ian would never forget his own people. Graenfrae needed him.

As soon as Ian had finished school he had moved to Graenfrae, determined to continue undoing the damage his grandfather's rebellion had done. His stepfather had insisted that Ian attend local gatherings. The earl had impressed upon Ian that he would need good relationships with his neighbors to make Graenfrae prosper.

It was at one of these gatherings that Ian had met Jenna. Jenna's Scottish blood and concern for the needs of others had led Ian to ask for her hand in marriage. Besides, she had been beautiful.

Looking at his sleeping wife, Ian wondered how he could ever have been deceived by the charms of faithless Jenna. Belle's beauty shone through her sparkling eyes and lips quick to speak her mind. His gaze shifted to the books resting on the table beside the bed. She wanted to please him.

She loved him.

His hold on her tightened. Her eyes fluttered open and he watched as her expression warmed. She smiled. "Good morning, husband."

"Good morning, wife." He lazily caressed her hip.

She nuzzled closer and touched his chest. "This is a very nice way to wake up."

"Aye."

"Will we wake up this way every morning, do you think?"

He grinned. "God willing."

She blushed. "I did not mean that."

"What?"

"Making love. I was not discussing making love, although that is indeed a very pleasant pasttime. I mean to ask, will we share a bedchamber at Graenfrae? Or will I have my own bed and you have yours?" She kept her gaze focused on his neck as she asked the questions.

His reaction to her question took him by surprise. The very idea of her sleeping anywhere but with him left him furious. "We'll share the master bedroom like my parents." He took her chin and forced her head up so that he could see into her eyes. "Do you object?"

She shook her head as vigorously as his grip would allow. "No.

None. I like waking up in your arms." She blushed at the admission and he couldn't resist kissing her.

He spoke against her lips. "Aye, I like waking up with you as well, Belle."

Her hands slid up and clasped behind his neck. She moved her face forward the small space that separated them and kissed him. Her lips were soft and pliant on his. He wanted more. The erotic noises coming from her said she did too. He slipped his tongue into her mouth. Within moments they were lost again in the maelstrom of passion that erupted each time they touched.

Ian's next coherent thought was that waking up every morning with his passionate wife was going to be exhausting. When he said so, he was surprised that she did not erupt in feminine indignity. The cause was apparent at once. Belle had fallen back asleep. She curled trustingly against him, her body still damp from their lovemaking.

He would have to tease his wife about her stamina. It was his final thought before drifting into oblivion.

The sound of Belle talking to someone woke Ian. His hands instinctively went out to find his wife and met nothing. Belle was not in the bed. The bed curtains, which had been open earlier that morning, were now closed. They cast a shadow of darkness and Ian could not tell how late he had slept.

He parted the curtains slightly and spied his wife speaking to a chambermaid. It appeared that she was supervising the filling of a tub near the fire. He smelled bacon. His stomach rumbled. He waited until the maid left and Belle had bolted the door before throwing back the curtain and rising from the bed.

"I take it the bath is for me." She had already dressed in a fashionable carriage dress of Bishop's Blue.

She spun around. "You are awake."

He did not think she needed an answer.

She didn't. "I have already had my bath."

He felt keen disappointment that he had not been able to watch his wife bathe. Ah well, they had a lifetime of such pleasures.

"I do not know which you would prefer first, your breakfast or

258

your bath. I fear your breakfast will grow cold if you bathe first and the bath if you eat first." She chewed on her lower lip as if the problem were insurmountable.

"Perhaps you could feed me while I bathe."

Her eyes lit up. "That is just the thing."

He laughed. "'Twas merely a jest, Belle. I dinna expect you to feed me."

"I think, yes, I think I would like to feed my naked husband in the bath. It would be a novel experience." She looked like she was contemplating some new delicacy.

He wanted to laugh again, but could not. The idea was too tempting. He shrugged. "If you like."

She smiled radiantly at him. "I think I shall like it very much." She tapped her chin, as if in thought. "I believe I should like a promise that you will do the same for me in the future."

The picture of his wife's luscious body in the bath caused a stirring below his waist. "Aye, you have my word."

She clasped her hands. "Well?"

He quirked his brow. "What?"

"Shouldn't you get in the tub?"

His wife had little inhibition about his naked body. He amended that thought as it struck him that although she conversed freely with him, she had kept her eyes firmly fixed on his face. She was full of contradictions.

God willing, he would have a lifetime to figure her out. He walked over to the tub and stepped into the steaming water. He sank down and groaned with pleasure at the feel of the hot water on his lower limbs.

Belle moved a chair next to the tub and sat with a plate of breakfast. They said a quick blessing and then Ian began to wash. She fed him a strip of bacon, sharing it with him. He took a bite and then she took one. Every time he bit down on the bacon, he remembered that Belle's lips had just touched the same spot. It was one of the most erotic experiences he had ever had. By the time she had shared three strips of bacon and a piece of toast with him, he was hard and throbbing.

"I dinna think I can take any more, lass." He almost strangled on the words as his wife licked some butter from her lips.

"Are you full? I must admit that I am ravenous this morning."

"I am hungry, wife, but not for food."

Her eyes finally traveled his body and he felt pure male satisfaction at the look of wonder on her face. "Oh. I believe we will have to forego the rest of your breakfast until after your bath."

She jumped up and scurried over to look out the window. His laughter followed her. He finished bathing in quick time. Without the temptation of his wife, his body settled down. She kept her face averted while he dressed.

It made him want to laugh again. "'Tis all right to look at your husband, Belle."

She nodded, but did not turn around. "Yes, of course, Ian."

He finished tying his cravat. "You can turn around now."

She did so and the look of warmth in her eyes as they met his almost sent him to his knees. He had gone to London to find a woman to meet the requirements of his stepfather's will. He had found far more. He had found a treasure.

"Shall we go? I have already instructed the innkeeper to prepare our carriage."

She certainly was not shy about taking charge. "You have?"

"Yes. I am eager to reach home. There are still several days left in our journey. I did not wish to waste this one hanging about the inn."

He liked the fact that she already saw Graenfrae as her home. "Then let us be off."

She asked, "How long until we get to Lansing Hall, Ian?"

His gut clenched. He would have to tell Belle about Jenna and his brother, the current Earl of Lansing. "We should reach there in three days time."

Three days to unlock the silence that had lasted for two years. He hoped it would be enough.

Chapter Twenty

Annabelle worried her lip.

Ian's posture on the seat opposite resembled the Elgin Marbles. He behaved nothing like the man who had spent the three previous days teasing her, talking to her and kissing her in the carriage as they traveled north.

She had tried several times to draw him into conversation, but he would not be drawn. Even her attempts at flirting had fallen flat. True, she had little experience in the matter, but it should not be so difficult to get the attention of a man who had been unable to keep his hands off of her for three solid days.

Should it?

Feelings of insecurity plagued her. Could he be bored with her already? She sighed. "Are we near Lansing Hall?"

His eyes narrowed with irritation. "'Tis the third time you have asked that, lass."

She lifted her shoulders and let them fall in a delicate shrug. "I will probably ask several more times until we get there. It appears to be the only question you deign to answer and I grow weary of the silence."

"I dinna ken you expected to be entertained every moment."

He crossed his legs, his calf brushing hers. Despite her annoyance with him, her body reacted immediately. Gooseflesh rushed up her legs. She had to stop herself from rubbing her calf against his. He appeared oblivious to the touch.

"I do not expect to be ignored."

"I told ye before, Belle, I dinna want to spend my time catering to a woman's whims. Surely ye can stand a few hours of silence in a carriage."

Stung by his words, the insecurity she felt intensified.

He had said *that,* but for the last three days he had treated her with nothing but consideration. It made her angry. Marriage to Ian had been a risk. She had taken it willingly.

She loved him.

How dare he tire of her after only three days of married life? She was his wife, not a nuisance. She gave him a fulminating stare.

"I can tolerate any amount of silence necessary." She spoke with dignity and then whispered under her breath. "It is a great improvement over conversing with a faithless and stubborn husband who treats me as a nuisance."

She had not whispered quietly enough.

"*Faithless?*" His roar deafened her. "In what way am I faithless, wife?"

He made the term "wife" sound like an insult and right now she felt like it was. "Fickle, then."

He glared at her. "What the bloody hell is that supposed to mean?"

She glared right back. "Do not curse at me." She would not be intimidated when her heart was busy breaking. "I mean exactly what I say. You cannot keep your affections fixed on one woman for more than three days of married life."

His body tensed as like a coil, ready to spring.

She ignored his anger and pressed on. "Had I known you were so easily bored, I would never have married you."

His first reaction had been mild compared to the look of fury that suffused his features now. "Ye regret marrying me?"

Without any warning, he lunged across the carriage seat and pulled her into his arms. "That is too bloody bad. We are married and 'tis for life."

He then settled his mouth on hers in a punishing kiss. She

struggled against him, but he held her too tightly to break away. His mouth demanded a response and she was helpless to withhold it.

She berated herself even as she softened against him. Sliding her arms around his neck, she kissed him back. The moment her hands touched him, he gentled the kiss. He moved his lips over her cheek and down her neck. Shivers of sensation shot through her.

"Ye belong to me, Belle, now and forever."

He was back to being possessive. She would have made him aware of his inconsistency, but she could not speak. His mouth covered hers again. He coaxed her lips apart and slipped his tongue inside. Flicking his tongue against hers and withdrawing it over and over again, he teased her.

Somewhere in the last few moments his fury had given way to passion. Her own senses were already ignited. She moved against him, restless for more of his touch. He did not disappoint her. Sliding his hands around her back, he undid the tapes on her traveling gown. The fabric slipped down and exposed her breasts. His hands took full advantage, touching her intimately. As her nipple peaked against his palm, he gave a pleasure-filled sound.

Breaking away from her mouth, he trailed hot kisses down to her breast and took her already taut nipple into his mouth. Annabelle came apart. He had barely begun touching her and she felt on the verge of release. She did not understand it.

"Ian, I need you."

He gave a harsh laugh. "So, in this ye do not regret marrying me."

She wanted to yell at him. She wanted to explain that she did not regret marrying him at all. She wanted him to tell her why he had been so cold. She tore at his breeches instead. He helped her and soon his ready manhood sprang free. He was not cold now. His heat made her burn.

She tried to lie down on the seat and pull him on top of her. He would not let her. Frantic to feel him inside of her, she gripped his hard manhood and squeezed.

He groaned, but he still did not allow her to lie down.

She did not know what to do. This was different than anything they had done previously. He had teased her and touched her in the carriage, but she knew that right now she had to have him inside of her. "I only regret the time you are taking to fill me."

He looked into her eyes and smiled. "Then I must take care of your needs, lass."

With two lithe movements, he lifted her leg to straddle him and slid inside of her damp heat. She cried out his name at their joining. Her last coherent thought was that he was definitely not bored with her. She rocked back and forth against him, seeking release from the torrent of sensation in her body.

She began to tighten and Ian fastened his lips over hers. His mouth swallowed her scream as she convulsed against him. Ian continued thrusting and she did not think she could stand it. Then he exploded inside of her and she went limp.

Her head rested against his snowy white shirt. She took deep shuddering breaths.

"Did I hurt you? Belle, I dinna mean to hurt you." Ian's voice was laced with concern.

She did not know what he was talking about and then she tasted the salt of tears. She was crying. "You did hurt me, but not just now. That is not why I am crying."

He gently caressed her cheek, wiping away the tears. "Then why are you crying?"

She took a gulp of air and let it out slowly. "I don't know."

"Then how do you ken 'tis no because I hurt you?"

She did not wish to discuss the logic of her tears. She snuggled against him and felt his manhood jolt in response. He was still embedded in her heat and she reveled in the sensation of oneness they shared. "This is very strange, is it not?"

"What?"

"We are both clothed and yet you are inside of me. Although my breasts are naked, your cravat is still tied in a perfect knot. I am on top of you and you are sitting up. I did not realize that lovemaking could be so flexible."

His laughter held none of the harshness it had moments before. "Aye, 'tis flexible. There are many more ways to make love, Belle."

She smiled against his shirtfront. "Will we try them all, do you think?"

"Aye. We have a lifetime." He spoke with fervency and then waited, tense, for her to reply.

"Yes, we do."

He relaxed. She rubbed her fingers across the lapel of his traveling coat. "Ian, I did not mean that I did not want to be married to you."

He rubbed her back. "I ken."

The carriage went over a rut and she bounced against Ian. He groaned and pulled out of her. She did not move from her intimate position, however. "Ian?"

"Hmm?"

"Do you think I am wanton? I do not believe that Diana has ever done this sort of thing with Robert."

"'Tis no matter. I like this sort of thing and you are my wife."

She couldn't help smiling at the arrogance in his voice. "Then you do not think I am wanton?"

He pushed her back until their gazes met. His eyes were dark with some mysterious emotion. "If you are wanton, you are that way only with me. 'Tis a blessing to me, Belle. You make my life more than duty. You give me pleasure."

More than duty. It was a nice start in her campaign. She smiled ruefully. Clearly kissing would not be enough in her battle to prove to Ian that he could love her. She did not mind. The extra strategy was very pleasurable. She determined then and there that if it took wanton behavior, she would be as wanton as they came to show her husband that he needed her and no other.

She squirmed against him. Her legs were growing cramped. He understood and lifted her until she sat next to him, tucked into the curve of his arm. The exhaustion from their lovemaking and the sway of the carriage lulled her to a drowsy state.

"Belle, there is something I need to tell you."

"Hmm?"

"Remember, I was engaged once before?"

"Yes." She covered her mouth as a yawn escaped. "You told me that she betrayed you."

"Her name is Jenna and she is married to my brother, the Earl of Lansing."

Every bit of stupor vanished. Annabelle shot up next to Ian. "She betrayed you with your own brother? Ian, that is terrible. No wonder you did not want them to come to the wedding." She thought for a minute. "You are taking me to meet them. Why? Have you forgiven them their betrayal?"

"I dinna ken. All I do ken is that if I had married Jenna I would not have found you."

Annabelle felt her throat constrict. "Ian." She threw her arms around him and kissed him soundly. He responded by locking his arms behind her back and returning her kiss with overwhelming intensity.

Somehow she would help this proud and loyal man find peace with his family.

She pulled back, breathless from the kiss. Her self-assurance restored by their lovemaking and his confidences, she sought to tease him. "I may require you catering to my whims and providing entertainment on long carriage rides."

He gave her a wicked grin. "I'll entertain you this way any time you like, lass."

She felt a blush start up her neck and burn in her cheeks. So much for being utterly wanton. "What happened?"

Ian did not appear disconcerted by her rapid jumping of topics. "Jenna was the daughter of one of my neighbors. She showed compassion for her father's tenants. I thought she would make a good wife."

Jenna was also beautiful. She dreaded the answer, but could not stop herself from asking the question. "Did you love her very much,

Ian?"

He shook his head. "Nay. I dinna love her at all. I told you that before."

He had, but she needed to hear him say it again. "You loved your brother."

"Aye."

"You trusted them both and they betrayed you."

His eyes darkened with some painful memory. "I caught them kissing in the garden."

She felt an icy sense of unreality. For a man with Ian's fierce loyalties this would have been a devastating blow. "What did you do?"

"I wished them happy, announced to my family that we wouldna suit and went home to Graenfrae."

"Your brother married Jenna."

"Aye. My family believed that he was nobly stepping in to cover my lack of honor in breaking the engagement."

She could not believe it. "Did you never tell anyone the truth?" She already knew the answer. A man like Ian would not sully his beloved brother's name.

"Nay."

She wrapped her arms around his waist and hugged him tightly. "Ian, you are incredible. Is it any wonder I love you so much?"

He shuddered under her touch. Bending his head to kiss her, he demanded, "Say it again. Your pledge means so much."

She smiled against his lips. "I love you, Ian, now and forever."

Only a tiny part of her heart sighed when he did not return her pledge. One skirmish at a time.

慓

Ian did not protest when Belle insisted on stopping at an inn and refreshing herself. Her crushed gown and the tendrils of hair escaping from her chignon attested to their recent occupation in the carriage. He did not want her to be shamed by her appearance in front of his family.

They left the inn after Belle had changed into a Capucine traveling dress trimmed in deep brown braid. The dark orange tone startled him at first, but he could not deny that it highlighted the gold flecks in her hazel eyes. Neat curls framed her face under her poke bonnet.

He found it almost impossible to believe that this was the same woman who had come apart so passionately in his arms as the coach rocked northward. Her gloved hands were folded demurely in her lap. 'Twas as if she would no more lift her skirts in a moving carriage for her husband than she would walk down St. James street for the dandies and beaus to ogle.

She showed no sign of unhappiness at his earlier conduct. He still found it unbelievable that he had taken such complete leave of his senses. His only excuse was the terrible rage that swept through him when she said she regretted marrying him.

He had submitted to the desperate need to prove her false. In the process, the terrible numbness that characterized a visit with his family was gone.

She had done that for him. His generous and loving wife had dispelled the demons that plagued him at the prospect of seeing his brother. The betrayal no longer lay like a stone in his gut. There was no room with the new feelings his sweet wife inspired.

The carriage stopped in front of Lansing Hall. As he stepped out, he thought how little the huge house had changed. Its stone façade was still covered with ivy and the imposing steps leading to the front door were as always swept and pristine.

He lifted Belle down and turned with her toward the house. His mother stood on the top of the stairs, the front door open behind her. Her black gown set off her fragile beauty and lovely blonde hair, sprinkled with gray.

"Hello, Mother, I have brought my wife to meet my family."

He did not know what he had expected, but his mother giving a choked cry and rushing down the stone steps was not it. She threw her arms around him and hugged him tightly.

"What is the matter?" He pulled away from her and looked closely at her face for fresh signs of new grief. All he could see were the soft lines of laughter that had always characterized his mother's eyes and the same muted sadness she had worn at the funeral for his stepfather. "Has something happened?"

She shook her head, but when she tried to speak, tears choked her. He waited, unwilling to enter the hall until she explained her bizarre behavior.

Belle came to both their rescue. "I believe, Ian, that your mother is pleased to see you."

When his mother nodded in agreement, but continued to blink back tears, he wanted to shout.

"'Tis no a cause for tears then."

Belle asked, "Have you been back to Lansing Hall since you ended your first betrothal?"

Understanding dawned. It mattered to his mother. His separation from their family had hurt her. Why had he not seen this before? "Nay, lass. I have not been back." He spoke to his wife, but did not take his gaze off of his mother.

From the corner of his eye, he saw Belle nod. "Then there is your explanation. Your mother has come to the conclusion that there will finally be peace again in your family." Turning to her new mother-in-law, Belle smiled. "I do believe that you are right. Now that Ian is married, he will no longer have time to brood over past altercations. He will be too busy keeping me out of trouble, you see."

As so often happened around his wife, laughter replaced his mother's tears. "I imagine he will." She smiled at her son. "Come, we must get your wife inside. The evening is coming and with it a chilly wind."

Ian had not noticed, but Belle shivered beside him. He immediately set his mother away from him and drew his wife's arm through his to lead her inside. His mother wrapped her fingers around his other arm and they proceeded into the hall.

"Where is Lansing?" He had not called his brother by his given name, Edward, since the betrayal.

"I am right here."

Ian swung around at the sound of his younger brother's voice. He inclined his head in greeting. "Lansing."

Edward was a younger, blond version of himself. Right down to the proudly arrogant stance he took. "MacKay."

Ian felt his mother stiffen next to him. She stepped away and gave him and Edward equally disgusted looks. He was not surprised. What did surprise him was that his wife did the exact same thing. She, however, did not content herself with a good glare.

"Lansing? MacKay?" She crossed her arms over her breast and tapped her little booted foot in a staccato tattoo against the marble tile of the hall. "Senility is generally reserved for the aged. I did not realize that gentlemen of your years could actually forget one another's first names."

Ian wanted to laugh, but held back as his wife continued her tirade. "Let me help you. Lord Lansing, may I present to you, your brother, Ian?" Belle turned toward his mother. "Mother, you don't mind me calling you mother?"

His mother shook her head. Her dazed eyes fixed on her whirlwind daughter-in-law.

Belle nodded her approval. "Good. Mother, would you please reintroduce Ian to his brother?"

With a barely concealed smile, Lady Lansing complied. "Ian, may I present your brother, Edward?"

Edward glared at Belle. Ian assumed his brother did not find her little comedy amusing. "I know my brother's name."

Belle sighed. "I am so relieved. The idea that I had married into a family with a disposition for weak minds quite frightened me."

Edward's face turned nearly purple with fury. Before he could vent it and give Ian a good excuse to plant him a facer, his mother interrupted. "Let us go in to the drawing room. It would be unkind to force Jenna into the hallway to meet her new sister, in her condition."

So, Jenna was with child. Ian felt no jealousy. He could only think how much he would like to see Belle big with child. She moved back to his side and took his arm. Edward led their mother into the room ahead of them.

Ian felt a twinge of concern when they entered the opulent surroundings. Lady Beauford's drawing room paled in comparison to the opulence of Lansing Hall. What would Belle think of Graenfrae with its interior stone walls and sparse furniture? He looked down to see her reaction to his brother's home.

She was oblivious to her surroundings. Her eyes were fixed on the woman sitting with her feet propped up by the fire.

Jenna's fiery red hair was piled on top of her head in a cascade of curls. Her mourning black set off the milky white smoothness of her skin. At one time Ian had found her beautiful. Now her demurely set lips and perfectly composed features appeared anemic next to his own spirited wife.

Edward immediately went to Jenna's side, as if to protect her from some unseen enemy. Edward glared at Ian. With a shock, Ian realized that he was that perceived enemy. "I am not going to eat your wife for dinner. Relax."

Jenna's eyes widened.

Belle tugged on his arm. "Behave yourself. Can you not see that your sister is in a delicate condition? You must not upset her with your lamentable sense of humor."

At the look of shock on the three other faces in the room, Ian decided it was time to introduce his wife. "Mother, Lan-" He looked down at his wife, who gave him a severe frown. "Edward, Jenna, let me introduce my wife, Annabelle."

Edward leaned against the wall near the fireplace. "So, Father's will was enough impetus to actually see you married. I did not believe I would live to see the day." His voice dripped with sarcasm.

Ian considered pushing Edward's teeth down his throat with a fist. Belle's fingers lightly rubbing his tensed forearm forestalled him.

"Aye. I have married and fulfilled the requirements of the will. I will now inherit the money that should have been mine regardless."

As he said the words, Ian realized how much he minded the fact that his stepfather had put conditions on keeping his agreement with Ian's mother before their wedding. She had married the earl with the understanding that he would settle a portion on Ian for his estates.

Edward was not the only member of his family who had betrayed Ian.

"Do you really believe that some paper marriage to an aging spinster fulfills his wishes?"

Belle gasped next to him. Her grip on his arm tightened.

Ian felt dangerously close to violence. "Paper marriage?"

"*Aging spinster?*" Belle's bellow was a fair imitation of his own.

She saved his brother's life. Ian laughed at his brother's ignorance and glanced at Belle. She dinna look like a chit fresh from the schoolroom, but she was far from aged. It was in that moment that Ian realized how angry his brother must be to have insulted his wife with such a ludicrous slur.

Jenna yanked on her husband's arm. "That was very rude. You must apologize to our new sister."

Ian was stunned that Jenna would take Belle's part.

Edward looked as if he would refuse to apologize. Jenna rubbed her protruding middle. Edward sighed like a beaten man. He faced Belle.

"I apologize. My comment was out of line."

Far from being mollified, Ian could see that Belle was just gearing up for an argument. "I should say so. I—"

Ian did not let her finish. "Edward has apologized. You will leave it at that."

She challenged him with her eyes. "I will?"

He smiled. "Aye."

She melted under his smile and gave him one of her own. "Very well."

Jenna stood up with her husband's help. "I believe I will take Annabelle to her room. Mother, would you like to join us?"

Lady Lansing agreed quickly. Ian could have insisted on joining them, spoiling their obvious ploy to leave him and Edward alone to talk. He didn't. He wanted to talk to his brother. He no longer had the desire or the energy to sustain his feud with Edward. Belle was right. He needed all of his wits to keep her out of trouble.

He watched Belle leave the room, his mother on one side and his sister-in-law on the other.

Ian moved over to stand by the window. He looked into the fading twilight at the park he had not seen in two years. It had been too long. He should have forgiven earlier.

Until he met Belle, he had not known how.

She had shown him how to accept the flaws in others. She loved her brother even though Hamilton criticized her involvement in women's rights. She loved her aunt although Lady Beauford criticized Belle's dress and her unmarried state regularly, not to mention having a strange idiosyncrasy about not using coal. She loved Ian in spite of all of his flaws.

It was that knowledge, more than anything else that made Ian turn to his brother and smile.

"'Tis no a paper marriage, you ken."

Edward actually smiled back. "That is obvious. The sparks fly between you like tinder and wood. I spoke out of anger. If it is any consolation, I am certain to pay for it later with Jenna. She had to be quite angry to chastise me before witnesses."

Ian understood. He dinna look forward to being on the receiving end of Belle's temper either. "You did me a favor."

"What?" Edward looked wary.

"If I had married Jenna, I wouldna have found Belle."

Edward nodded. "You love her."

How could his brother be so foolish? He did not love Belle. That would open him up to betrayal, wouldn't it? The question was too disturbing to deal with right now. "I dinna ken about love, but I need her."

Edward gave him a knowing smile, but did not argue. He was silent for a long time. Finally, he spoke. "We did not betray you. The kiss you saw was me saying good-bye."

"Why?"

"I knew I loved her. I guessed that she shared my feelings and I determined to leave Lansing Hall until you were back at Graenfrae and we were both safe from temptation."

"Should I believe you?" He asked the question almost musing to himself.

Edward took it to heart. "Yes." He cursed. "You are not the only member of this family with honor. You should have let me explain then."

Ian felt chains loosen and fall away from his heart. "If you loved each other, why not tell me? Did you believe it would be better for me to marry a woman who loved my brother?"

Edward frowned. "I thought her feelings would change after you wed. I hoped they would."

Ian shook his head.

His brother was a fool. The best thing that could have happened was for Ian to have caught him and Jenna in the garden. All an ugly misunderstanding and he had lost two years of his life with his brother because of it. And gained Belle. From evil came good.

He sighed. "Are you happy?"

Edward nodded. "Yes. It really hurt her, you know. You just taking off. Even if I had not loved her, I would have married her."

Ian believed him. Another misunderstanding. He had felt that Edward had been given a hero's role when in fact he had been betrayer. Now, he knew his brother had truly acted the hero, at least in part. Ian did not know if he would ever share the same closeness he once had with Edward, but he no longer carried the deep burden of pain and betrayal that had weighted his heart for so long. "She is blessed to have you for her husband."

Edward looked startled. "I am blessed to have her for my wife."

"Aye." Ian surprised himself by smiling again. "Soon you will have a child."

Edward grinned. "Yes, but if anyone told me how difficult pregnant women could be, I would have stayed celibate."

Ian laughed at his brother's lie. "Not bloody likely."

Edward joined in his laughter. "No. I guess not. But just you wait. When Annabelle starts increasing, you will find all manner of excuses to keep you about the estate."

Ian doubted it and he doubted his brother did either. If the look of concern on his face could be believed, Edward kept a very close eye on his pregnant wife.

Edward's next words confirmed it. "I had better check on Jenna. She should not be climbing the stairs so often, but she will not listen."

Ian followed Edward up the stairs to find Belle. He wanted to see if she would be interested in giving his future niece or nephew a cousin.

He found her pacing their bedroom. She stopped and faced him, her stance challenging.

"Lady Lansing wanted to give us separate chambers, but I explained that you prefer to share one."

She frowned at him as if she expected him to deny it. She was still angry about the aged spinster remark. He almost smiled, but did not want to bring out the wrath simmering below the surface. "Aye."

She relaxed somewhat. "Yes. Well then." She peered into his face. "How did your talk with your brother go?"

He wanted to pull her into his arms. The wary look in her eyes stopped him. "We discussed what occurred two years ago."

She nodded, but did not speak.

"They weren't going to betray me. Edward planned to leave until after the marriage."

"Why did he kiss her?"

"He was saying good-bye."

She snorted. "Most people say good-bye with a word or a handshake."

Belle did not think much of his brother. "He loved her."

"Did she love him?"

Ian nodded. He hoped they were about done with this conversation. He needed to feel his wife's body against his.

Her eyes glistened. "I'm sorry."

He could not hold back any longer. He pulled her close. "Why are you sorry, lass?"

"Because your fiancée loved your brother. She should have loved you." She sounded so sincere. He did not dare laugh.

"They are happy."

She sniffed against him. "She is very beautiful."

He shrugged. "Her beauty holds no appeal for me now."

"Did it before? Did you want her, Ian?" He could tell the question was difficult for her to ask.

He swung her up in his arms. She gasped. He leaned down and placed a hard, possessive kiss on Belle's soft lips. "I dinna want her, not the way I want you every waking moment."

She locked her hands around his neck. "Are you happy, Ian? As happy as your brother?"

"Nay."

She went stiff in his arms.

"I am happier than my brother could ever hope to be. He only has Jenna. I have you."

He fell on the bed with his wife under him.

She smiled, a smile full of mystery and promise. "Let me show you how happy I can make you."

"Ah, lass, 'tis my only wish right now."

"We haven't a lot of time. Your mother said they keep country hours. We have to dress for dinner soon."

"So, stop talking and kiss me."

He muffled her laughter with his lips.

Chapter Twenty-one

Ian lay curled around Belle in their bed at Graenfrae. He smiled when he thought of his worries about how she would fit in among his people and what she would think of her new home. The people adored her. He and Belle had been there less than a month and she had already started a school for the tenants' children, a group for men and women interested in the plight of women in Great Britain and had charmed his housekeeper into keeping fresh flowers in all the public rooms of the castle.

Belle took personal care of his library and their bedroom. He had discovered the source of a beckoning scent of roses in his library only that morning. She had placed bowls of dried rose petals and heather on several shelves in his library. He should mind that his private retreat now smelled like flowers. He didn't. It reminded him of his wife and he liked it. He wondered if that had been her plan all along.

She seemed to be on a campaign of keeping herself at the edges of his consciousness when they were not together. She would walk into his library when he was going over the estate books, brush a light kiss on his cheek and float out again. When he was out checking on the estate, he would spy her across a field conversing with a tenant. She would give him a jaunty wave and blow him a kiss.

She immersed herself in the improvements he wanted to make to Graenfrae. None of his projects was without her influence. She talked to farmers' wives, found out their needs and reported back to him. She continued making subtle and not so subtle changes to their home as well. The linens he had bought in London covered their tables and were draped over furnishings throughout the house. She made sure that surfaces were polished and threadbare upholstery was repaired.

Yet, she insisted on keeping the natural décor to their home. She had told him in no uncertain terms that she loved it and did not want to live in a replica of her aunt's more formal house. She liked her Scottish castle just fine.

She loved her husband.

Ian still felt amazement at the passion and approval she showed him daily. She exhausted him nightly, forcing him to teach her the flexible intricacies of making love. He almost laughed out loud. Forcing indeed. He hungered for her company and the silky smoothness of her body constantly. Far from making excuses to be out on the estate, he sought ways to do his business from the castle. He wanted to be with his wife.

His favorite time of the day had become evening when Belle joined him in his library. She curled up in a chair near the fire and read while he studied new farming and sheep breeding methods. She wanted his mother to come for a visit. He wanted his wife all to himself.

His mother would be arriving within the week for a prolonged stay.

She wanted to invite Hamilton and his wife to stay before Lady Hamilton could no longer travel. He told her to wait until after the baby was born.

The Hamiltons would be arriving in a few weeks and a bloody entourage of servants to care for the increasing marchioness.

Ian could not deny his sweet wife anything, except three little words. She told him she loved him every night after they made love and several times throughout the day. He knew she was waiting for him to respond with his own pledge. He hated the uncertainty he felt at those times.

He wanted to love her. She deserved it. Maybe he did love her, he just dinna ken. Tonight, tears had slipped out of her eyes after her declaration and she had turned away from him. He had pulled her body flush with his and whispered words to soothe her. Words about her beauty, words about her honor and loyalty until finally she had shushed him and bid him sleep.

He could not sleep.

Although his wife's breaths had grown even ages ago, he laid awake wondering if he would ever be able to give her the words she longed to hear.

If he did not, would her love shrivel and die?

Unable to stand his own musings any longer, he quietly slid from the bed. Perhaps a walk would clear the muddle from his mind. He went out through the kitchen. The air was cold and he took several deep breaths. Movement near the stable caught his eye. A lone rider led three other horses away from the stable.

Someone was trying to steal his horses.

Astonishment kept Ian immobile. The cloud that had covered the moon shifted and suddenly moonlight illuminated the rider.

Renton.

The blackguard had Nightsong and two of Ian's other horses. He would not bloody well get away with it. Ian let out a piercing whistle. The effect was startling. Renton shot up in his saddle and whipped his head around to see where the sound had come from.

Nightsong stopped immediately and when he did, so did Ian's other horses. The squire tried yanking on the lead, but the horses would not move.

Ian stepped out of the shadows. He whistled twice more, short, piercing sounds only seconds apart.

"Who's there?" The squire was still trying to pull the horses and came flying off his own when Nightsong reared back, pulling his lead from the squire's fingers.

The tall black stallion came galloping toward Ian. Ian praised his horse and commanded him to stop as he ran around the animal, looking for the fallen squire.

Renton was already standing, his face set in a snarl. "I should have known. You have foiled my plans for the last time."

The moonlight glinted off a pistol in the squire's hand. The sound of it cocking was not nearly as terrifying to Ian as the sound he heard from behind him. Belle's voice confirmed Ian's tormented suspicion.

"You will not shoot my husband."

The squire looked over Ian's shoulder. Ian didn't dare turn around to see his wife. The demented man had a gun cocked and ready.

Renton said, "Lady Annabelle. How kind of you to join us."

"Belle, leave. Now." Desperate to get his wife out of danger, he spoke his demand with arrogant authority.

The squire shook his head. "No. I do not think that would be wise. She would only call for help to save your sorry hide." He waved the gun so that it pointed at something behind Ian. Ian had no doubt that something was his wife. "Lady Annabelle, I will have to insist that you stay."

The squire appeared to believe that he had the advantage. Ian let him continue in his foolish assumption. The bloody gun still pointed at Belle.

"You know, I thought I would just steal your horses. An eye for an eye, you see." Renton's gaze took on a wild expression. "They came and took my hunters. All of my prime cattle sold on the auction block to settle tradesmen's bills." The squire's voice rose shrilly. "They paid my worthless tailor with the blood money they got from selling my animals."

"Surely, you did not think you could continue to spend without paying your debts."

Ian wanted to cup his hand over his wife's mouth and stop any more words from coming out. He wanted the squire's attention on him. The gun pointed at him. "Be quiet, Belle."

He felt her glare through the thin fabric of his shirt.

"I see domestic discord. How very sad. Had you married me, my dear, you would not have subjected to such brutish behavior."

The squire was back to sounding like a gentleman at a society function.

"Had I married you, I would undoubtedly be dead like poor Mr. Thorn."

Ian edged backward toward the sound of his wife's voice.

"You know about Thorn? That explains how this barbarian has

succeeded in besting me. He had information I was not aware he possessed." Renton shrugged. "You may be right about your death. I assure you that I would not have killed you before I got my heir off of you."

Belle's gasp of outrage came from somewhere to Ian's left. He shifted that direction and kept inching backward. He could only hope that his wife would not take a notion to obey him at this late date and stop talking. Her conversation was keeping Renton distracted.

She did not disappoint him. "I would sooner die than let you touch me, you foul murderer."

The evil parody of a smile was back. "I believe, my dear, that I will accommodate you."

The calm certainty in Renton's voice terrified Ian. The man's madness was beyond help. The squire tensed to shoot and in that second Ian turned and leaped. The shot rang out and Ian landed on Belle knocking her to the ground. He whistled for Nightsong and commanded the horse to stand between Belle and the madman. In his madness, Renton would not shoot a horse.

Ian made a running leap at Renton. He caught the fleeing man by the ankles and pulled. Renton went crashing to the ground. Ian took advantage of his opponent's fall. He dove at the squire, landing a punch on the man's jaw.

"No. Damn you." Renton swung wildly, but in his fury he missed Ian completely. "You cannot win."

Ian swung back and then drove his fist into the face of his opponent, cold-cocking him. Ian leapt to his feet and raced back to Belle. She was standing, holding on to Nightsong's bridle. He breathed a sigh of relief.

"I told you to leave." He had not meant to shout.

She smiled, or was that a grimace of pain? "I did tell you that I would not be any good at obedience."

He moved closer, inspecting her for the source of weakness he heard in her voice. "Aye, you did, lass." Then he saw her left shoulder. Blood soaked her wrapper.

She looked at him, her eyes glazed with pain. "I believe... I have been shot."

She pitched forward and fainted. Ian caught her and swung her into his arms. The stable master came staggering up, rubbing his head. "The bluidy bastard got me."

"Are you all right?"

"Aye, just a sore head and me temper is right riled."

Ian nodded toward the fallen squire. "Take care of him and the horses, then. I've got to rouse the house and get a doctor."

"What happened to our lady?"

"The whoreson shot her."

The stable master cursed. "Bluidy thief. I'll take care of him all right." He squeezed Ian's arm. "She is a strong lady, laird. She'll no give in to a wee gunshot wound."

Ian prayed the man was right.

He walked into the kitchen bellowing for his housekeeper. Mrs. MacTavish came running, her mobcap flying.

"Call for a doctor and bring hot water and cloths to our bedroom."

"Aye, laird. I'll bring the spirits as well. Me old aunt said they stopped the wound from catching fever."

Ian nodded. He carried Belle upstairs, taking the steps two at a time. He laid her gently on the bed. She must not die. He could no live without his opinionated and strong-willed wife.

ℭℨ

Annabelle opened her eyes and tried to make sense of the scene around her. She was naked except for the bedclothes covering her. Her shoulder burned like it had been set afire. Memory returned quickly. The squire had shot her.

"Lass, ye are awake," Ian said.

The relief and tender concern she heard in his voice soothed her. He stood near her head, an expression of anxiety in his brown eyes. His hand rested on her shoulder that had not been wounded. Another small, wiry man stood to her husband's right. He must be a doctor. Ian would not allow another gentleman into their bedchamber.

The doctor prodded her shoulder.

She grimaced. "That hurts."

Ian glared at the other man.

"I need to see how serious your injury is, Lady Graenfrae."

She nodded slightly. He dabbed at her shoulder. She winced when he touched her, but stopped herself from crying out. Her husband looked close to the end of his tether as it was.

"'Tis no serious."

She frowned. "It certainly feels serious to me."

The doctor shook his head and smiled. "'Tis merely a flesh wound. The bullet only grazed your shoulder."

Ian's hand on her good arm tightened. "Ye'll be fine, wife."

She frowned at his pronouncement. Of course she would be fine. Her frown turned into a scream when the doctor poured fiery liquid over her wound. Ian's hold on her good arm was the only thing that kept her from coming off the bed. The doctor finished bandaging her and gave some instructions to Ian before leaving.

"'Tis a blessing that."

She looked up at her husband's words. "What?"

"That you dinna have more than a small scrape."

"*A small scrape?* It feels like my shoulder is on fire. It hurts, Ian," she wailed. She wanted to be comforted.

He touched her cheek. "I am sorry it hurts, lass."

"You saved my life." It would take a very long time to forget the crazed look in the squire's eyes when he had pointed his pistol at her and pulled the trigger.

"I love you."

She stared at him. Irrational anger surged through her. "*I had to get shot and almost killed before you could tell me?*"

He laughed. "You werena near killed. You heard the doctor. 'Twas a scrape."

His words and laughter made her even angrier. "Don't you dare laugh at me, Ian MacKay. I have waited for weeks to hear you say the words."

His expression turned serious. "Lass, I would have given you the words, but I dinna ken if I could love you as you wanted me to. My father taught me about duty. My stepfather taught me about honor. It took a fiery tempered spinster to teach me about love."

Her anger drained away as quickly as it had come. She smiled mistily at her husband. "I am not a spinster, Ian. I am a wife."

He returned her smile and leaned down to kiss her softly on her lips. "Aye. My wife. I love you, Belle."

∽

Annabelle handed Diana her tea.

"I should be doing this. You have barely recovered from your injury," Diana said.

Annabelle frowned. Her recovery had been more unpleasant than the gunshot wound. Both Ian and his mother had a terrible tendency to hover. When Jenna sent word that her time was near, Annabelle had said good-bye to her mother-in-law with a mixture of sadness and relief.

Annabelle had been healed for weeks, but Ian still refused to let her roam the estate without an escort, balked when she wanted to go riding and in general fussed like the loving husband he was.

"My injury has not pained me for several weeks." Annabelle patted Diana's arm. "You on the other hand would do well to leave the tea pouring to me."

Diana responded with a rueful grin. "I suppose my ungainly middle would put the tea tray in jeopardy."

Annabelle laughed. "Only if you got too close."

"I had no idea that pregnancy was going to be so difficult."

Annabelle ignored her friend's complaint. She knew that Diana could not wait to become a mother. Although, she had to admit that the other woman was more unwieldy than she had expected. "Are you sure twins don't run in your family?"

"Do not even jest that way."

Annabelle's gaze flew to her brother standing in the doorway. His face had an ashen cast to it.

"I was merely teasing, Robert. Do not take it so much to heart."

Robert glared at her and moved to sit next to his wife. "It is not an amusing jest."

"Aye. You shouldna worry a man about the woman he loves. He's bound to lose his composure." Ian had followed Robert into the room and was in the process of squeezing Annabelle next to him on the small settee.

Annabelle turned to meet her husband's eyes. "I will endeavor to remember that."

He brushed her face with his fingers. "See that you do."

Squire Renton was a madman and Annabelle had been relieved when he was sentenced to transport to the colonies. Ian did not believe he would survive long in Botany Bay. She could not grieve the possibility of the madman's demise. However, she did not hate him. After all, he had been the one to finally force the lock open on Ian's heart so that her husband could acknowledge his love for her. He had no problem saying the words now and told her several times a day.

She smiled happily at him. "You know, some perils are worth the risk."

Ian's eyes grew dark with emotion. "Aye. From evil comes good."

Out of the corner of her eye, Annabelle saw Diana turn to her husband and beam at him. "Yes, from evil can come good. I have never been so happy and so secure in your love as since you discovered Mr. Thorn's scheme."

Ian regained Annabelle's full attention when he whispered a question in her ear. "Are ye secure in my love, lass?"

She turned until her lips were a mere breath from his. "Can you doubt it?"

Then she kissed him. It was a soft, chaste kiss, sealing her words.

Robert choked. "Annabelle, I think you forget that there are others present in the room."

Annabelle did not look at her brother when she answered him. She was busy watching Ian's lips. "I'm perfectly wanton. Ask Ian. He likes it."

She kissed her husband again.

Ian winked at her.

Diana said, "I think it is time we took our leave, Robert. As you know, wanton behavior requires privacy."

Annabelle found Robert's blush hilarious.

Robert looked down at his wife. "Are you sure you are up to the journey home?"

Diana gave an exasperated sigh. "Robert, I have no intention of delivering our baby in anyone's home but my own." Diana softened at the look of pallor that came over her husband's face. "I am more than fit for the journey."

"Then I guess we had best be on our way. The carriage has already been brought round."

Annabelle and Ian followed Robert and Diana outside to see them off. Annabelle stood secure in her husband's arms as they watched the retreating coach carrying the Hamiltons toward home. She sighed. It had been a wonderful visit, but she was glad for the privacy. There was something she wanted to tell Ian.

"Well, lass, are you well pleased now that you have had your visitors?"

Belle smiled at Ian's surly tone. "Yes. Although, I admit I wish that Ceddy and Vivian had been able to come before going on their wedding trip."

He rubbed her arms. "They promised to come for a wee visit when they return."

He stressed the word "wee" and Annabelle bit her lip to keep from laughing. "That will be nice... Ian?"

"Aye?"

"Do you think it is very wanton to make love to your husband in the middle of the day with the dust from your guests' departing carriage barely settled on the drive?"

His answer was to sweep her in his arms and run up the stone steps. He did not stop until they had reached their room. He lowered her to the floor and she immediately set to the task of removing his cravat and shirt.

He shuddered under her roving fingers. "You make me so hot, I burn."

They made love and afterward she lay in his arms, their naked limbs entwined. Golden light cascaded through the window as the sun set. Annabelle snuggled into her husband's side. "About visitors."

His growl made her want to giggle. "There will be no more visitors for a while. I want my wife to myself."

She ran her fingers over his chest. "In about six months I believe we are going to have a visitor who will be making a very long stay. I hope you do not mind."

"My mother can stay with us, but surely she'll want to return to Lansing Hall occasionally."

"I am not talking about your mother."

Annabelle found herself flat on her back with her husband looming above her. "What are you saying?"

"This baby fever seems to be contagious."

"Are ye saying ye've caught it, lass?"

"Yes."

He went completely still and then he swooped down and buried her mouth in a joyous kiss. "I can only hope that if we have a daughter she is as beautiful and strong as her mother."

She could not help the tears that welled up in her eyes. She was so very happy. She had far more in Ian than she could ever have hoped for.

He loved her.

He cherished her.

He wanted her.

She blessed his stepfather and the man's unconventional will.

287

"Ye'll have to be very careful now that ye are increasing."

Annabelle groaned, but she couldn't work up any real chagrin. After all, Ian loved her enough to cosset her. She had done well for a woman labeled *The Ordinary* her first Season.

About the Author

To learn more about Lucy Monroe visit www.lucymonroe.com. Send an email to her at lucymonroe@lucymonroe.com. She loves to hear from her readers. You can also join her mailing list by visiting her website.

What if you're in love–but you can't make love?

Last Chance, My Love
© *2007 Lynne Connolly*
Book One of the Triple Countess series.

Miranda and Daniel, Earl and Countess of Rosington, are in love, but for the past five years their love has been purely platonic. Because if Miranda has another child, she will die.

Daniel resolves to take a mistress, one who will understand the purely physical business arrangement, but when Miranda discovers his plan, she can't bear it. So Daniel's brothers scheme, and Daniel finds himself on the losing end of a wager.

Daniel and Miranda must pose as a simple innkeeper and his wife, forced to work together to save a failing business. Their masquerade brings them into temptation, their searing desire for each other threatening to ruin their good intentions, but it also brings danger, in the presence of the brutal father of a young girl who turns to them for help.

Can Daniel and Miranda save themselves, their protégée and their marriage?

Available now in ebook and print from Samhain Publishing.

Enjoy the following excerpt from Last Chance, My Love...

Daniel closed his eyes, and then opened them again to see Miranda, calm now, watching him. "I have needs. I thought I could do it, but I could never have gone through with it. I couldn't hurt you any more than I had already. I thought you would understand. I didn't know you hadn't realised just how serious your illness was. There is no doubt, Miranda. I spoke to another doctor, and he said the same. With your history, another child would be your death."

"What did you tell him?"

"That you had two boys, and the second birth was worse than the first. About the bleeding, and the fever."

They stared at each other, remembering the horror of that time. Then she said the bravest thing he'd ever heard. "I'd do it again, go through the birth and the illness. If it meant you would love me again, I'd go through it all without a qualm."

Now it was his turn to weep. Tears sprang to his eyes, and he blinked them away. "I couldn't let you." His voice came out hoarse and thin. "I don't want to lose you."

Miranda studied him, her head tilted slightly to one side. "You *should* want to lose me. You could marry again, and continue your family." When he would have responded, she laid a gentle finger across his lips. "No, there's no need. I know you would not, but there are many that would. Is that why you won't touch me? The whole reason? Please, Daniel, the truth. If you can't want me, I'd like to know. You did seek out a mistress, after all, and she did look most unlike me."

Lifting a hand, he moved her finger from his lips and tugged on her hand, forcing her to lie down once more. He pulled her close, so she lay with her head pillowed on his shoulder, looking up at him. "No. If I took a mistress it would be someone like her, someone who didn't remind me of you in the least. She is dark where you are fair, dainty and small where you are tall and elegant. I want only one Miranda." He kissed her temple. "And in any case, I didn't choose her. She came looking for me."

"She did?"

"She had her own reasons. She isn't a hardened courtesan, although her mother is. She wants Blyth, and thought she could make him jealous."

"Did she succeed?"

"She must have. After all, it's Blyth's doing that we're here, isn't it?"

He wondered at her frown, but thought no more of it until she sighed and said; "I confess, it was partly me." He stared down at her, unsure of her meaning. "I saw you with the girl, and I was jealous. Jealous, Daniel. I thought I was over such things, I was convinced you didn't want me any more, not in bed at any rate, and so it didn't come as a surprise to hear the rumours and then see you with her. Blyth was with me that day, and he saw my distress. He promised to do something about it."

A chuckle rumbled through his chest. "Properly gulled I've been. You and Blyth made hay with me, didn't you?"

"I'm sorry."

His free hand slid over her waist. "Don't be. I think it's done us good. At least we both know now." She moved closer, snuggling in. The movement made him gasp. "Miranda, be careful. You know I won't make love to you, don't tempt me anymore. It's not fair."

She lifted her hand to his chest, covered with fine lawn, but he felt her fingers gently tracing patterns on it. "I know you've taken the entire responsibility on yourself. I know you want to preserve me. What if I don't want to?"

He caught her hand with his own, and curled it inside the warmth of his. "Miranda, if you get with child again, you will die. I can't do that to you. If I think of it, it fills me with terror. How could I face the boys?" He paused. "How could I live without you?"

She stared at him, her mouth slightly open, moist and inviting, even though he didn't think she meant it that way. With a groan of submission, he bent his head and kissed her, dragging her close with both arms, holding her as though he would never let her go.

Since that day he escorted her to the house, after their visit to the farmer, Daniel had longed to kiss her again, but known he couldn't trust himself not to go further. Now he couldn't help himself. Her body, so warm, nestled against his, her lips opening softly for him, inviting him to slide his tongue inside. It was more than a man could stand.

Daniel caressed her mouth, warm and sweet, and felt her response with joy, a slow burn starting somewhere deep inside. He leaned over her, revelling in the feel of her body under his.

An impulse he had learned how to control. While enjoying the kiss Daniel drew part of himself back, tucked it away again. The wild part, the part that urged him to take her now and never mind the consequences. That part must stay hidden inside.

Finally he drew back. He reached up to smooth her hair, soft caresses replacing the abandon he longed to release. She smiled. "That felt good. It won't come all at once, Daniel."

"What won't?"

"Restraint. What you don't want us to do. I still want to, I don't care, but the risk isn't all mine, is it?" He shook his head. "I have to think of the children, and of what it would do to you. But I'm not giving up. There must be a way, Daniel, there must. There are times every month—"

"I've thought of that. It won't do, Miranda. There are ways to make conception less likely, but none to stop it completely. If there was a way, believe me, I wouldn't let you leave this bed for a fortnight."

"You want me?"

This was no time for half truths. "I never stopped wanting you. When I withdrew from your bedroom, I persuaded myself it was for your own good. Perhaps, if you thought desire had left me, you might find it easier to bear. I know your nature, you see. You hate to see anyone suffer."

She lifted a hand and caressed his cheek in the age-old caress of lovers. "But you did, and so did I. I mean it, Daniel. We'll find a way, I'm determined on it."

"I've thought about it for years. Years, sweetheart."

"Have you ever asked anyone else about the problem other than the doctors?"

His eyes widened. "No, of course not. It's no one else's business."

"Just for advice? Blyth is very experienced—"

He couldn't suppress a slight shudder. "How could I ask my brother something like that? And Blyth is so volatile still, there's no saying what he might do."

Her hand still rested on his cheek, as though it belonged there. Which, in a way, it did. "He's not as volatile as you think. Oh, I'm sure he was as a boy, but he's turned the fortunes of his estate around. You don't do that without clear thinking and planning."

He touched his lips to her palm, lapping it gently with his tongue before turning back to her. "You might be right. But I don't think I want to ask him."

"I shall find something out," she said firmly, then smiled. "But not tonight. Enough, I think, to know we both want the same thing. You've brought me joy with the sadness tonight, Daniel. It was agony thinking you didn't want me anymore. How could you think anything else?"

He closed his eyes against the loving understanding in hers Understanding he didn't deserve. He'd thought he was acting for the best, and it seemed to be the other way about. "I don't know. I thought you wouldn't want to any more, when the result cost you so much pain. I didn't want you to see I suffered, so I didn't let you see."

"It doesn't matter. I have you back, and that's enough for now." She leaned up and touched her mouth to his. He responded to the tender caress in the gentle spell she wove around him. He could trust her not to push him over the edge. The only danger now was if they both succumbed at the same time. He relaxed his hold on her and leaned back. "I'm very tired suddenly."

She snuggled close and lifted her leg over him, but only as far as the knee. "Revelations can make you tired. We should sleep. We have another busy day in the morning, running the inn."

He smiled. "So we do."

hot stuff

Discover Samhain!

Romance, fantasy, mystery, thriller, mainstream and more—Samhain has more selection, hotter authors, and everything's available in both ebook and print.

Pick your favorite, sit back, and enjoy the ride!
Hot stuff indeed.

Samhain
Publishing
Ltd

WWW.SAMHAINPUBLISHING.COM

GREAT
CHEAP
FUN

Discover eBooks!

THE FASTEST WAY TO GET THE HOTTEST NAMES

Get your favorite authors on your favorite reader, long before they're
out in print! Ebooks from Samhain go wherever you go, and work with
whatever you carry—Palm, PDF, Mobi, and more.

SAMhAIN
PUBLISHING
Ltd

LaVergne, TN USA
15 April 2010
179418LV00002B/18/P